The Salt Covenants

A Novel By

Sylvia Bambola

Heritage Publishing House

"Bambola's gift for storytelling in this work of historical fiction is nothing short of remarkable. The reader is skillfully and masterfully drawn into this time in history in 1493 Seville during the Spanish Inquisition and The New World. A riveting tale that all comes "alive" while captivating the reader with passion and intrigue. *The Salt Covenants* is a novel you won't soon forget . . . it has left an indelible imprint upon my heart. I highly recommend it. Truly delightful!"

Sallie Yusko

Pastor, founder of Women of Worth and Destiny, conference speaker and writer

"In her historical novel, *The Salt Covenants*, Sylvia Bambola paints a masterpiece with words. Rich in character, language, and emotion, this novel is a powerful story of love, friendship, and forgiveness. I marvel at her ability to place her characters in my heart to stay."

Micki Sorbello

Artist and free lance writer

"Bambola masterfully weaves historical gleanings into this epic tale of romance and adventure set against the backdrop of the Spanish Inquisition. You won't want to put it down."

Cristaña Carlton

Musician, composer, teacher and author

"An enthralling page-turner! Sylvia Bambola's historical novel is full of heart-felt emotion as she weaves a tale of one woman's courage, hope and love."

Gina White

Mixed media artist

Also by Sylvia Bambola

Rebekah's Treasure
Return to Appleton
Waters of Marah
Tears in a Bottle
Refiner's Fire
A Vessel of Honor

The story and main characters in this novel are fictitious. Any resemblance to actual persons or events is strictly coincidental. However, all historical novels must, of necessity, be based on fact. Set in 1493 Seville where the Spanish Inquisition rages, as well as in the New World where life is alien and difficult, I have tried to portray the novel's backdrop as accurately as possible. Some useful information has been inserted in the back matter to aid the reader in clarifying some unfamiliar words (see glossary) as well as a list of "bells" and the Jewish months and feasts.

Dedicated to

Gina and Cord
my delights

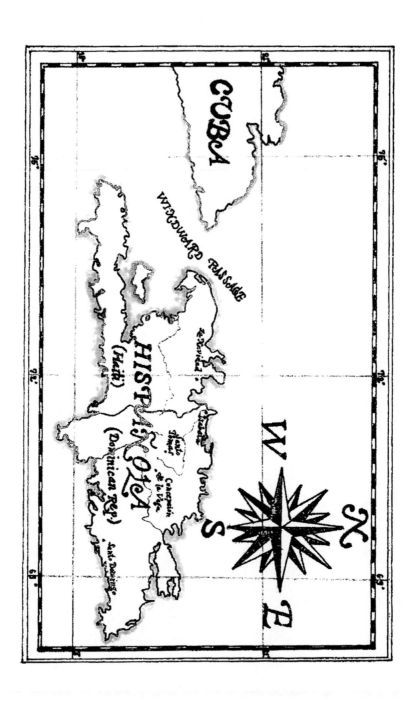

Chapter 1

Seville, Spain 1493

I have broken Mama's heart.

That thought has festered a fortnight. Our physician, Hernando Diaz, would call it a lingering agitation, the kind that upsets the bodily humors. He is full of such vague assertions. I am not as vague. I picture sores, like the ones on Catalina's legs, marring the fabric of my brain and robbing it of peace.

The soft shuffle of Mama's feet pulls me from my thoughts, and I turn from the cupboard. *Please . . . look at me.* But she does not. Her eyes have not met mine in weeks. And the silence between us is as thick as the Pillars of Hercules. It is strange, this silence, so foreign to us who once discussed the writings of Maimonides and Rashi for endless hours. I have the power to repair this breach but I will not. Even now that knowledge overwhelms me, and I wonder at the wisdom of my confession. I have learned too late that confessions are not always the satisfying exercise one anticipates, unless they are made to God.

"I have checked the larder for mold, and bunched the sage." I wait for Mama's response, but she just raises her knife in the air. The metal glints as it catches the light coming through the small overhead windows. In one swift motion she drags the blade across the edge of her thumb nail. A sliver, like an almond chip, flies across the room and disappears. My heart flies with it, for I know she is testing to see that the knife conforms to *halakah*, to Jewish law.

Oh Mama.

1

A rivulet of sweat works its way down her cheek, then her chin, then follows along the hollow of her neck, and ends at the large emerald hanging below her throat. Grandpapa's gift. She has not worn it in months. Many claim emeralds bring success. Does she wear it now hoping to successfully turn me from my course, from the course I have foolishly revealed to her?

My stomach churns as I remove the ring of keys pinned to my bodice. The keys are a trust, an honor bestowed, for they secure all that is valuable in our home. It is a privilege reserved for the woman of the house or a trusted steward. I am neither, though Papa says I am better than any steward he has known. And Mama says my skills and good sense have earned me the honor.

But that was before Eastertide.

I unlock the spice cabinet; then take out a cone of sugar, all the while keeping Mama in my line of vision. She is busy stoking the embers beneath a large clay pot. Already the aroma of galingale and grains of paradise fills the room. Because she uses the large pot and not the one hanging from the tooth iron rack, I know there will be guests at our table tomorrow, and I am encouraged. Perhaps they will bring laughter into our sad home.

But my feelings of hope plummet when I notice the large leg of lamb sitting on the woodblock. Mama will certainly purge it to make it ritually clean. I watch her slice the lamb lengthwise, remove the vein, then begin to remove the fat. The back of my neck is a tangle of nerves as I glance around to see if anyone is watching. A foolish gesture. It is, after all, Friday, and as usual all our servants have been sent to the groves.

I squeeze the sugar tighter as Mama works. I must not speak. But even before the thought becomes vapor, I blurt, "Inesita Garcia was burned at the stake for purging her meat like that. You *must* stop this. Eventually someone will see. Eventually someone will tell."

Mama looks up and finally meets my gaze. Her eyes are as blue as the rivers of Galicia, testifying that Ashkenazi blood intermingles with the Sephardic. Surprisingly, there is no anger in them, only shame for what I know she considers a cowardly remark. But I cannot stop now. I have opened this wound, and that took as much courage as Mama opening the lamb, though I doubt she would see it that way.

"We must be careful, now that Catalina has been discharged."

Mama blows the tendril of hair that has escaped her netted halo-like headdress, and I notice, with surprise, how gray she has become. "Am I a child that you need to caution me? Do I not always send the servants away and prepare the Sabbath meal myself?"

"More than one person has been called to the Holy House because of the testimony of a vindictive servant."

"She had to be discharged. This is a respectable home. The scabs alone condemn her."

I carry the sugar to the table where the mortar and pestle sit. A month ago I overheard our physician call Catalina's scabs, *las buas*. These days *las buas* is as common as cankers, and I am old enough to understand how they are passed between a man and a woman when the oil lamps go out.

I also understand Mama's objection. Catalina is not married.

"I do not question your action. I only remind you of its danger."

"Danger?" Mama stops working the meat. Her long linen apron, newly made from the quarterly allocation of household fabric, is still unstained. In it she looks like a large sail blowing out over the deck of her kitchen. "Danger?" she repeats. "When you have been through as many pogroms as I, then speak to me of danger. Besides, what has changed? Why are you so worried now?"

I am amazed she is actually speaking to me. Oh, how I long to throw my arms around her! To feel her kisses on my cheek! But I stand my ground. "This time it *is* different, Mama. This time they come not as a howling mob carrying clubs and torches, but with satin robes and soft voices and ringed fingers, and call us to the Holy House. And soon we could all end up like Inesita Garcia, burning at the stake."

Mama's shoulders roll forward as she returns to the lamb.

"They have confiscated all of Inestia's property." The sugar makes a dull noise as it slips from my sweating palms onto the wooden table. "Even her three houses, which her children occupied, now belong to the Crown. We must be more cautious. Surely you understand the added danger that discharging Catalina has produced?"

Mama's knife again catches the light. The kitchen, though larger than most, and with a flooring of urnel stone to cool the feet, feels as stifling as a tomb. Mama's face glistens with perspiration as she cuts the lamb into small cubes then tosses them into the steaming clay pot.

When it is clear Mama has nothing more to say, I begin scraping small clumps of sugar into the mortar. *If only Mama and I could be as we once were.* That thought swirls as I grind the sugar and mix it with cinnamon. *If only I could find the right words.* I chop almonds, then cilantro which I add to the cinnamon-sugar, and which will, along with lemon slices, form the garnish over the stew. *If only I could make her understand this new love I have for the Nazarene, the man-God who now consumes my heart like a bonfire.*

Absently, I prepare the sugar cakes that will end our Sabbath meal and balance the bodily humors by aiding digestion. *If only Mama would look at me, with forgiveness and love and understanding in her eyes. If only . . . .*

And just when I think she might, the bells chime None, destroying the moment by reminding her that she is surrounded by the enemy; for to the north lies the convent of Saint Leandro; to the East, the Church of Saint Esteban; to the west, the Church of Saint Isidoro; and to the southwest, the great Cathedral.

Anger mars her face as she abruptly walks over to me. A cloud of flour swirls upward when she pats her apron. Then one hand finds its way to my neck, and I feel her warm, soft fingers tug at the strip of leather that hangs there . . . leather that holds a crucifix hidden beneath my bodice. And by her action I know she desires, at long last, to speak to me about my grievous transgression.

Her fingers shake as she draws out the crude carving of oak I made myself. She holds it a moment before sliding her thumb across the leather strap. I know what she is thinking. Her revulsion is clear.

The strap is not unlike the leather tied around Inesita Garcia's neck while being lead to the *auto-de-fe'*.

"What will you tell your husband?" Mama's voice is tight, and I am startled by its severity.

I shrug. The truth is I have thought little of him. He is a stranger, someone I have seen only once, and who is now a vague memory of curly black hair and long spindly legs.

"What will you tell him?" Mama repeats through lips pinched as thin as her knife blade, and with her thumb remaining on my leather strap.

Suddenly I am offended, though I tell myself I have no right. Nine years ago I was married, but it will be another year before my husband and I consummate. More than sufficient time to formulate a plan. "I will tell him nothing," I finally say.

"Your wedding followed Jewish law. The presence of the rabbi and two Jewish witnesses made it so. Would you dishonor that with your treachery?"

"Would the Holy One expect me to violate my conscience? To give up the truth of what I know? To reject the Savior?"

"The marriage contracts are signed! You took a holy oath!"

"I was *seven*, Mama."

"A little young, perhaps, but it was needful. Papa knew that soon there would be no Jews left in all Seville. Where would we have gotten our witnesses with the Expulsion Edict already yellowing on the nail post in the public square? He was right in rushing the marriage. But rushed or not, it is lawful, and young or not, you made a vow."

It was no easy task to dissolve such a marriage. Only death or divorce could do it. And neither would come by my hand. "I will honor my vow."

"But will he? If he finds out what you have done, he can divorce you. He would have every right. He married a follower of the Law of Moses and now has an *Edomite*, instead. Have you thought of what that will mean to the family?"

I had not, but obviously Mama has, and it takes only a minute to understand she is concerned about losing the valuable trade alliance my marriage has secured. I feel resentment. *Am I wrong to be angry?* I know my character is lacking. I have confessed my pride and bad temper to the Holy One so often I am sure He is weary of hearing my voice. But still I suffer from these defects.

"My husband and his family became *conversos* when we did. Many forced converts have become sincere Christians. Perhaps they have, too." *Besides, were daughters only good for furthering trade?*

Mama's face turns as red as the rose petals my sister, Beatriz, keeps in a jar. "*Never* say such a thing. The Evil One might hear and bring it to pass. Your husband is still a devout Jew. I only pray he fails to discover that you are not. All *must* go as planned. Before *Tisa B'Av* your sister will consummate her marriage, and next year, you. Preparations are already being made. Suitable gifts for both grooms have been commissioned." Mama lowers her voice to a near whisper in embarrassment. "And the silk has been purchased for your gowns."

The gowns Mama speaks of will be worn for the Cathedral ceremony. She has told Beatriz and me time and again that we must, each in turn, endure the humiliation of being married by a priest, then sitting with our husbands under a veil-covering during the nuptial mass that follows.

"I will honor my vow," I repeat.

"Yes, but if your husband finds out . . . . ." Mama looks inconsolable, and with the ever increasing number of gray ringlets escaping her net, she also looks old. I feel pity, but there can be no relenting for I have made an irrevocable covenant with the Nazarene.

"Over and over I ask myself, 'Why have you done this?' On the day of the Great Pardon do I not walk barefoot and fast and ask forgiveness of all those I have wronged? What sin still lurks in me? There must be a remaining transgression, otherwise you could not have done this to the Holy One. Or to Papa and me. Or the rest of the family."

"I only follow my heart."

"Your brothers have not followed theirs! They wanted to remain in Seville, but instead married Ashkenazi to secure our access to the ports in Kiev and Hamburg. Without complaint, they left those they loved, moved to faraway lands, married wives they had never seen, learned new languages, and with Papa's and my connections in the Ottoman ports, increased the family fortunes."

"But you needed Genoa and Antwerp, is that it? Ports Beatriz and I secured through our marriages."

"You need not sound so smug. You are old enough to understand what is at stake. If we lose those ports now, can Papa send money to the scattered Jewish communities? Or to our relatives? Or help the *conversos* right here in Seville? And how will he ever become powerful enough to secure our position with the Catholic Kings? I speak of survival, Isabel." Mama returns to the hearth and rests her hands on plump hips. "We have worked hard to ensure our future. Will you throw it away now by this . . . this *folly*?"

I have been preparing for this quarrel since the beginning of Eastertide when I first confessed to Mama that I had made a covenant with Jesus; that I had given Him my heart. But now that it is here, I have difficulty remembering the words I have spent so many hours rehearsing in my mind. "This is about more than trade, Mama," is all I manage to stammer.

"Yes, so much more, Isabel, so much more. Just tell me how you can turn your back on the Holy One and the Law of Moses and align yourself with these . . . these *idolaters*, these . . . these worshipers of the one from Nazareth?" A wrinkled handkerchief flutters in Mama's hand. She has pulled it from the large pouch in her apron. When I was younger she kept her pouches filled with sweets and little wooden puzzles and colored ribbons and combs for Beatriz and me. Now I think it is filled only with handkerchiefs. She dabs the perspiration on her neck, and when she thinks I am not looking, she dabs her eyes.

"Oh, Isabel! Isabel! Think. You will never be happy. They will never accept you as one of them. They call all Jewish converts, *marranos*. Pigs! We convert and still they call us pigs, these followers of this Nazarene of yours. What can be done with such people? How can there ever be peace between us?"

Mama absently stirs the stew with a long wooden spoon. "And even your own people will despise you. You will forever be in the middle, neither Jew nor Gentile. Belonging to no one. Consider how difficult it has been for Papa and me, even with all our connections and good works to our people, and even with most understanding that ours was not a sincere conversion. Attitudes are changing, Isabel. Many of our people no longer trust those of us who have converted yet still remain true to the Law of Moses."

She puts down her spoon and picks up the whetstone to strop her knife. "Many rabbis criticize us for not leaving with the others. They call us 'renegades from Judaism.' They say the 'leprosy of heresy' is upon our foreheads. And now, you have proven them right."

The repetitious sound of metal against stone is almost hypnotic, and builds steadily as Mama's hand moves faster and faster. How does she keep the pace? The quick jerking of her wrist, the way one shoulder twists and untwists, the way her head tilts forward then back all remind me of the movements of the madman I have seen tied to the rood screen at the Cathedral.

Then she stops, and the handkerchief once again appears in her hand. An unexpected breeze floats through the small windows and I smell lavender, the scent Mama uses to perfume her clothes.

"I know this is difficult for you, Mama. But the rabbis have been arguing this matter for years. They understand how our people have been forced to bow to the Roman Church and convert in order to survive. How many *Responsas* have we read together? Each contradicting the other; some saying conversion, if not sincere, means nothing and does not separate the *converso* from Judaism, while others say the opposite, and still others claim the truth is somewhere in the middle. Can you follow a law if you do not even know what it is?"

"Now you speak ill of our rabbis?"

"I am only saying you have done nothing to disqualify yourself as a true daughter of Israel."

The handkerchief is stuffed back into its pouch, then Mama opens the sack of freshly ground flour and begins preparing the collar of dough she will use to seal the juices in the pot. I suspect that in addition to giving her something to do, she is more comfortable with her back to me.

"If I live as long as Abraham, I will never understand why you have done this terrible thing, Isabel. I repent of ever educating you." Mama drops her rolling pin and turns to me. "But how could I not? All the women of my family have been educated in the languages, in Torah and Tenakh and Jewish law. But the *Responsas* . . . perhaps those I should have left out."

I walk over and take her hand—which is pudgy and soft and well-tended—and hold it like a precious gem. I am grateful for Mama's tutoring. Unlike Ashkenazi Jews who leave education to the fathers or rabbis, and whose girls are rarely educated, Sephardic Jews leave education largely to the mothers who generously teach their daughters.

"Education is a gift I wanted to give you and your sister," Mama says, squeezing my hand before drawing away. "It was so you would be jewels on the crowns of your husbands. You are the child of my body. You are my heart. All I ever wanted for you was good. But I no longer know who you are."

Absently, I finger my crucifix, and seeing Mama's displeasure, quickly tuck it beneath my bodice. Can I blame her for saying she does not know me when I hardly know myself? I have become like shapeless water lapping the shores of an unknown land. Before my first conversion, the one forced on me years ago, my name was Deborah, after the prophetess and judge of Israel, the valiant Jewess who accompanied the army of Barak to battle. That first conversion brought me the name, Isabel, after our queen, a name I did not want. And now my second conversion, this conversion of free will and devout yearning, has yet again brought me a name I do not want—*Idolater*.

My first conversion caused me to be despised by both Jews and Christians, "People of the Book" who should not despise at all. And now my second conversion has caused me to become a stench in my own family's nostrils. I know the Holy One can do all things, that He can bring me through. But I am weak of character, and all I can think of is: *How am I to survive this?*

Chapter 2

How wondrous is the sound of laughter! Truly, "a merry heart doeth good like a medicine." Already my heart is hopeful as laughter rises, like musical notes, from the throats of our guests, and fills our house. To me, Beatriz's laughter is the most beautiful, being the perfect blend of lute and lark, and is the chief reason my heart soars. That, and her calming presence. She sits beside me, holding my hand, but it is Don Sebastian who holds her attention. And, not surprisingly, she holds his.

Our merry party has already gathered around the table, having washed hands in large basins with scented olive oil soap from Florence. We have said the blessing, and the linen wick of the seven-strand Sabbath candle still burns in the clay pot, although hidden from view.

The trestles and boards are covered with Mama's prized table linen of Aylsham, a fact that is sure to impress since everyone knows the best tablecloths come from England. Our cloth is still as white as bolted flour, and benefits from passage of a slick stone. A napkin of lesser quality—of Avignon—is provided for everyone because Mama hopes to keep the guests from wiping their soiled fingers on her precious Aylsham cloth. To the side of each napkin is one of Mama's prized silver knives. No one has to share a knife or bring his own at Mama's table; another fact of which she is supremely proud. And next to each knife are a lead-glazed wine goblet and one or more trenchers—those stale pieces of bread we use as plates—with the pile of trenchers highest in front of Don Sebastian's father, Señor Villarreal, thus according him the respect his exalted rank deserves.

Also sitting in front of Señor Villarreal is Papa's prized saltcellar, shaped like a whelk shell and made of gold. It is filled with salt from the Bay of Bourgneuf which, according to Papa, is the best salt money can buy. The saltcellar usually stands near the master's place but Papa has relinquished that honor to his guest. I think to better show it off.

My stomach growls, and I am pleased to see the servants bustle in and place small bowls of warm Sabbath stew between the guests; one bowl for every two people. Happily, I share a bowl with Beatriz, for she never dips her sop twice and always leaves the best pieces of meat for me. She is generous to a fault. Not like me. Far too often I accept the meat without protest.

Beatriz wears a dress of green velvet and brocade, with a pearl encrusted neckline. Her voluminous black hair is pulled tightly back and held by a gold pearl-studded hairnet, revealing the delicate lines of her face. She has never looked more beautiful.

Papa complimented me today on my appearance, calling me radiant in my new golden velvet dress with lace-sleeves. He said I reminded him of a glorious moon. But if I am the moon, Beatriz is the sun. And when the sun shines, who ever sees the moon?

"How nice to have our city back. Or nearly. Too long our streets have been clogged with visitors." Don Sebastian's voice is merry. "Seville has proven she cannot endure the excitement of both a Fair and Christopher Columbus."

We all nod. People came from miles around to see the great Admiral, and when he left, many remained to attend our yearly Fair.

"Three weeks! That is how long it took the silk merchant to deliver my order," Don Sebastian continues. "Such tardiness would be inexcusable during lesser times." He addresses us all, but his eyes are focused on Beatriz. "Now we have only the Fair to contend with. And not for much longer."

The sound of Sebastian's voice has caused a deep flush to creep over Beatriz's face, a flush which only enhances her loveliness. Her altered countenance causes me to smile, for she is normally poised and self-controlled, unlike me who could easily show this sort of emotion if I had a husband who visited me daily. If I had a husband I dearly loved.

"Admiral Columbus marched all the way from Seville to Barcelona with his entourage of Indians and parrots and leashed dogs and chests of treasure." Señor Villarreal plucks a piece of bread from one of the many breadbaskets then uses it to remove a large chunk of lamb from his bowl. "The popinjay!"

"He has garnered a great victory in both sailing the uncharted waters of the Ocean Sea and discovering a new route to the Indies," Papa responds, taking salt from the saltcellar with the point of his knife, and placing it on one of the trenchers in front of him. "And as any man with ego enough to embark on such an adventure, he requires the appropriate admiration."

Señor Villarreal nods. "Crowds swarm him wherever he goes. And outside the great Cathedral in Barcelona they packed the plaza where the King and Queen awaited him under a gold canopy. They say the king was in good spirits even though he was still weak from his injuries received at the hand of that assassin." You could always count on Señor Villarreal to be full of court gossip. "The Queen even had a chair placed next to her throne, and invited Columbus to sit beside young Prince Juan while her choir sang '*Te Deum Laudamus.*'"

"An appropriate honor." Papa was ever kind.

"And I suppose that ridiculous rumor of Queen Isabel selling her jewels to finance the Admiral's voyage still circulates?" Mama's face betrays her contempt. Talk of Christopher Columbus always provoked her wrath because the day before the Admiral set sail on his Ocean Sea voyage all the remaining Jews of Spain, those who refused to convert, were expelled, and somehow she has come to connect the two events in her mind. "I suppose the Crown fears it will become known that *Jews* gave the Queen the money for the adventure."

It was true. Gabriel Rodriguez Sanchez, a courtier, and Luis de Santangel, the Queen's financial advisor, both Jews, supplied most of the money. The rest was secured privately by Abraham Senior, a Jew, and Admiral Columbus himself.

"And I suppose the Queen does not want it known that the Admiral is also a Jew. A *converso.*"

This was less certain. Though Admiral Columbus has been accused of being a crypto Jew—one who still secretly followed Judaism even after becoming a *coverso*—it has not been proven.

"Such hypocrisy! Everyone knows King Fernando's own great grandmother was a Henriquez Jew." Mama wipes the perspiration off her forehead with her napkin.

And I pull a white handkerchief from my bodice and dab my perspiration as well. It is not the heat that makes me perspire—though it makes us all look like wilted lettuce—but this unfortunate conversation. The servants, who bustle back and forth, are surely listening. Though our servants are all *conversos*—with the exception of Gonzalo Vivar, an Old Christian and our master gardener at the groves—it is not safe to speak in front of them. Even *conversos* have been known to report inappropriate conversations to the Holy Office.

I dip my bread, though my appetite is lost, and desperately hope the conversation will change as more servants bustle in and pile a salad of lavender, rue, and parsnips on the trenchers before us.

"Yes, they try to deceive us." Mama is like Don Sebastian's new wild Andalusian stallion, in great need of a bit. "But what can you expect from people who believe Jews caused the Black Death, torture children, and poison wells?"

"It is rumored that Admiral Columbus already plans a second voyage." I rest my sop on my trencher. If Mama is not stopped, she will spoil more than my appetite. "I cannot imagine planning a second voyage so near the heels of the first."

"The Sovereigns have already granted him a new patent for the voyage," Señor Villarreal says.

"And right here in Seville, Bishop Juan de Fonseca is already organizing an army, and equipping seventeen vessels for the expedition," Papa adds.

"Oh, how I would love to be in that company!" Don Sebastian blurts. "What sights! What adventures to be had! How I envy the lucky lot."

Beatriz drops my hand. There is a stricken look on her face, and on Don Sebastian's, too, when he realizes what he has said.

"Of course . . . I would *never* leave Seville." He focuses only on Beatriz. "I talk as a fool. Had I wanted to leave I would have taken my place at court long ago." His eyes plead forgiveness, and when my sister smiles—that smile of sweetness and malleability which seems so pleasing to men—he brightens.

"And speaking of court, how is your son, Antonio?" Papa asks Señor Villarreal.

"He has recently returned from Queen Isabel's castle in Segovia. You recall I mentioned that her gracious majesty sent him there for a rest, for she feared he was greatly overworked at court."

We all nod.

"His last letter was full of court news. Oh, the intrigues! Such intrigues. You would think it could keep a young man entertained. But, no, Antonio longs for Seville, though it is hard to imagine why. I am only grateful he knows his duty. Not like Sebastian here. I fear Sebastian only follows his own inclination for pleasure." The look on Señor Villarreal's face is stern, but his voice is laced with indulgence, and even pride, over his son's willfulness. "Our family has served our rulers since Sancho the Great. As long as there is a Castile, we will serve her at court. So Antonio will remain for he surely knows his duty."

Mama's eyes sweep over me as though accusing me of not knowing mine.

"But in these troubled times, even powerful *converso* families like ours must take every precaution," Señor Villarreal says, lowering his voice. "I am comforted that Antonio's position is secured by his marriage to Doña Maria de Murcia. It pays to be connected to a venerated family of Old Christians. That alliance has silenced many of Antonio's enemies, to be sure."

"We hear Doña Maria will be presenting Antonio with an heir before year's end," Papa says.

When I see Mama lean over the table and open her mouth, I quickly add, "Will you attend the happy event, Señor?" for I fear she will once again speak foolishly. In the background I hear Don Sebastian ask a servant to remove his salad of lavender and rue, and bring him lettuce instead. Lately, the only salads he eats are those of lettuce. I pretend not to hear. Everyone knows that lettuce subdues feelings of lust. I am sympathetic. Surely my own nature would be as carnal if ever I loved someone as much as he loved Beatriz. "Will you visit them?" I repeat.

Señor Villarreal sprinkles a generous amount of salt over his stew. "I fear my health will not permit such an arduous journey. My gout is relentless and shows no signs of improving."

"It is rumored Tomas de Torquemade also suffers from gout. May it be so!" Mama has once again injected herself into the conversation. And nothing good can come of it, for Tomas de Torquemade is Grand Inquisitor and head of the *Suprema* which governs all twenty-three Inquisitional Tribunals scattered across Castile and Aragon. My stomach has soured completely.

"Perhaps it will be the gout that kills him and not an assassin, as he fears."

Now even Papa looks disturbed. "And his fear is great, for why else would he have his food tasted for poison? Or have fifty men on horseback accompany him wherever he goes, and another two hundred on foot? Should a man so close to the Almighty, as he claims to be, have such a fear of death?"

"This will interest you, Isabel," Señor Villarreal says, clearing his throat. It is clear that Papa and I are not the only ones disturbed by Mama's conversation. "Since you love books and learning, this will surely interest you. Our Queen employs a *woman* Latin teacher for her children. And since she has made known her great desire for Castilian women to participate in all the new studies coming out of Italy, women even lecture at our Universities."

"There is such a thing as too much education." Mama again. "I believe our Isabel is proof of that."

I pick up my sop, which now looks soggy and unappetizing, and take a bite. Though the stew is delicious, my appetite does not revive. "I do not believe one can have too much education." My voice is calm but my stomach lurches when I see the disapproval on Papa's face.

Papa loves me, of that I have no doubt. And he thinks me as beautiful as Beatriz, for he has often told me so. He has also said beauty can be marred by a contrary nature. And since he has said this many times in my presence, I have come to understand that he refers to *my* nature. And to further prove him right and that my character is blemished, I repeat, "Truly, it is impossible to be too educated."

"Everyone knows that women who study excessively get wandering wombs." Mama is persistent.

"The Holy One has given Isabel a fine mind." Beatriz speaks for the first time. "And it must please Him when such a mind is trained."

Now it is I who take her hand under the table and squeeze it in gratitude. In only a few words, Beatriz has settled the matter, and amidst the bustle of servants pouring wine and refilling stew bowls, the conversation drifts to the unseasonably hot weather.

And once again I see the power of an unblemished character.

Chapter 3

The sweltering weather has driven us downstairs a full two months early. I prefer my upstairs bedroom where I spend the cooler seasons. It is larger and has a marvelous window that catches the sweet east winds coming from the Sierra Morena. Downstairs, my bedroom faces west. An unfortunate position, for when conditions are right, the west wind carries a foul odor from the Guadalquivir River banks where tanners clean their hides, then stretch them over large open wood-frames to dry.

My inward grumbling spoils the triumph of generosity I experienced when I traded rooms with Beatriz years ago. Both of Beatriz's rooms face east and are larger than mine. And her upstairs has a balcony which means it also has a large double door that admits rivers of light, and overlooks our tranquil courtyard.

The size and brightness make Beatriz's rooms ideal for studios where she paints tiles for the Carthusian Convent. The Abbess claims no one's tiles are more prized than my sister's. It is no exaggeration to say Beatriz's birds and flowers are exquisite, and her geometric shapes, flawless. There is no end to the work she can have if she wants it, though to her it is not work at all but a labor of love.

Papa says it is fortunate the Abbess is so fastidious with payment, for Beatriz never keeps records nor does she ask for her wages. And Papa claims it is a great comfort to him to know Beatriz has a husband wealthy enough to hire any number of servants to care for her needs as well as run their household when they unite, for we all understand that Beatriz is incapable of caring for herself.

Though it is a failing, we hardly notice, so enamored are we of her other attributes. My sister excels in four things: in her beauty, in painting, in playing the lute—which is so masterful I have seen grown men cry—and in her excellent character.

So it is understandable why I am not sorry I relinquished my rooms. I am only sorry that my own character is so flawed that sometimes I feel the need to complain inwardly over the small inconveniences it has produced.

I have been dressed since the bells chimed Prime, spending the time in prayer and meditation, and waiting for the rest of the house to awake. I can hardly wait to tell Beatriz what has happened. Last night, just before bed and away from the servants, Mama did something she has not done since Eastertide. She offered me her hand to kiss, and after I did, she placed it, in the Jewish manner, upon my head and drew it down over my face in the form of a blessing.

Now, the first sounds of life send me racing down the hall. Mama and Papa's door is ajar, and through the opening I see Papa lay *tefillin*. I know I should not watch but I pause to observe his simple act of devotion. Carefully, he ties one of the small black leather boxes, filled with four paragraphs of Torah, to his forehead. The other box he binds to his hand in obedience to Deuteronomy's command to place God's word "as a sign upon your hand and as frontlets between your eyes."

Next he covers his eyes with his hands, then sways back and forth. In a sing-song voice he begins the *Shema*. As I watch, my heart fills with anger, and I tiptoe away. Why should someone who loves the Creator be forced to conceal his devotion and do all in secret? The injustice burns me to the marrow.

I still feel its sting when I knock on my sister's door, then enter without invitation. Beatriz is sitting on her bed in a new brown undergown reading from a small book of Psalms. At once, her presence calms me.

She smiles, then closes her book. Like Papa, her hair is black as ink and hangs in thick shiny waves around her shoulders. On her face is the expression of an untroubled conscience.

"You will be happy to hear my news," I say, embracing her. And then, without giving Beatriz a chance to utter a word, I tell her about Mama's blessing.

"Oh, Isabel, I have been praying for this! My heart has been heavy of late with you and Mama at odds." She kisses my cheek. "I knew the Holy One would repair the matter."

Then suddenly she jumps. "Oh, I must hurry and dress! Best not to keep Mama waiting after all my pleading to take us to the Fair."

Beatriz has been working on Mama for days. Mama believes, as do I, that this being the last week of the Fair there will be nothing left worth buying. Even so, I have kept silent not wishing to spoil Beatriz's pleasure. But I find it strange that she is so anxious to go. Unlike I, who love the marketplace, shopping seldom excites her. She has refused to tell me the reason for her interest but I suspect it has something to do with Don Sebastian.

I watch Beatriz slip a farthingale of willow twigs around her slender waist. Over that she pulls a gold and cream gown with a V-shaped waistline and lightly embroidered stomacher. When she is dressed, she skips across the room to where her hairnets and combs sit on a small table. "Such a happy beginning to the day. Surely the rest will prove to be as wonderful."

Her words make me uneasy, perhaps because I remember Aunt Leonora, may her memory be for blessing, telling us how we should never allow the Evil One to see our happiness, lest he spoil it. But looking at Beatriz now, at her bright shining eyes that dance like candle flames, at the bounce in her step, at her breathless anticipation of I know not what, it is difficult to imagine anything spoiling her happiness today, and I quickly send up a silent prayer to God, *let it be so.*

෴

Mama, Beatriz and I walk down Abbots Street with one eye on where we place our feet. The street is littered with discarded contents of chamber pots as well as rotten food thrown for the pigs to eat. We all wear shoes of slashed velvet and *pantofles*—wooden platforms lashed to our shoes by fabric straps. They keep the dark sludge that runs through the street from spoiling our shoes or the hems of our gowns. But they make walking difficult, and we move slowly. This suits me since I want to see everything and can do so leisurely without worrying that I hold up the others.

The air crackles with excitement. Noisy crowds push and shove and elbow their way past us. And I love it. We saunter merrily down the street, smiling and pointing at whatever catches our eye. Our arms are locked.

"I am so excited," Beatriz whispers, leaning closer. But when I ask why, she only shakes her head.

I am still thinking of ways to extract Beatriz's secret when we find ourselves on Mateos Gago Street. Here the street is even more crowded, and we are pulled southward like small boats caught in a current. It is a direction I do not want to go, for southward lies the walls that enclose the forty-acres of buildings comprising the old Jewish Quarter. Once, its narrow streets bustled with activity; its courtyards bloomed with flowers and potted fruit trees; and the air was pungent with the smell of eggplant stew and Almazan sausage. Moors live there now, and some Old Christians, though hardly enough to call it a thriving community for there are many other vacant houses to choose from throughout the city. In addition to Jews leaving Seville during the Expulsion, four thousand *converso* families have fled their homes in fear of the Inquisition.

Mama is sure to say something inappropriate when she sees the old Jewish walls, so I grab her hand and my sister's, and forcibly head in the opposite direction. When Beatriz appears disappointed and begins to lag behind, I realize she was the one who drew us southward, and despite her pleading stare, I lead us away.

"Why are we walking in circles?" Mama asks, a bit winded. "Please decide where you wish to go."

"To the Church of the Savior," I quickly say.

Mama nods. It is a reasonable answer for many small shops line its walls; shops where one can purchase anything from hawks and bells, to chestnuts, and herbs fried in batter.

"But first we must visit the Plaza Mayor," I add.

Again Mama nods. Many of the booths belonging to merchants who have come to Seville for the Fair are set up in the Plaza Mayor— the city's main plaza.

I lace my arm through Beatriz's, thinking how fortunate we are that every year the world drops the best of its treasures into the center of our lovely city: sable and ermine from Russia; Moorish rugs, saddle blankets, brass lanterns and screens; gems, cloves and cinnamon from the Orient; wool from England; and silks, satins and brocades from North Africa.

With each step, my excitement grows. We walk past streets named after the trade practiced there: *Boteros*, makers of wineskins; Rosary Slope; Silk Street. Wherever we go there is noise and confusion. Minstrels thread the crowd, playing flutes and lyres, and pulling along a string of noisy merrymakers. Then comes a man on stilts. We watch until they all pass, fanning ourselves with limp handkerchiefs as the sun climbs higher. All around us, vendors shout their wares amid the rattle of donkey carts and pack-mules. Adding to the noise are heralds on horseback shouting out their own announcements and news.

Mama bustles ahead to the arched opening in the church wall where the large cloth-hall sits in the Plaza Mayor. I purposely lag behind with Beatriz then pull her to a stop. "Just what are you up to?"

Beatriz grins and pulls out a handful of gold *florins*. "I have been saving my wages." She looks almost childlike, and as eager as a graylag.

Instantly, I grab her hand and thrust it into her pocket, for every Fair brings out prostitutes and thieves and sundry unsavory characters who will pluck your treasures if given a chance.

"A gift for Don Sebastian?" I say, guessing the obvious, for what else would cause her such excitement?

She nods. "Sebastian has a new stallion and talks of getting a mare to breed with it. I want to buy him one at the Horse Fair."

"*The Horse Fair!* Are you mad? Mama will never let you go to that vulgar place." When I see her downcast expression I quickly add, "Well . . . perhaps . . . if we ask, Mama may agree. Come." I take Beatriz's arm knowing we embark on folly. What do we know of buying horses? Papa keeps five at our house by the groves but aside from watering and feeding the beasts, we know nothing. We lack the discernment of a well-disguised blemish, or a partially healed injury, or even general infirmities . . . conditions that unscrupulous merchants often try to conceal. But the fact that Beatriz has not considered these things proves her simplicity, her trusting nature that all will turn out well.

We catch up to Mama who is already at the tent's opening, and follow her inside where dozens of tables hold bolts of cloth from all over the world. The ecru bolts of cheaper cloth—those which are unbleached and undyed—are on tables off to one side. Mama heads in the opposite direction, to the most expensive cloth— the scarlets and reds of Florence.

In my haste to follow, I bump into the Keeper of the Fair—a tall, burly man with enormous eyebrows, and dressed in a fine padded doublet of pale green silk and matching hose. He carries an iron ruler, the standard by which all material, cut and sold, is measured.

I apologize, then head toward Mama, pulling Beatriz behind me, but not before I see the unpleasant glint in his eye. He has the eyes of a condor, and they follow Beatriz. Her eyes are on a shimmering bolt of green silk. While she and Mama examine it, I stand guard, trying to put myself between those eyes and her. But when the Keeper of the Fair turns his attention elsewhere, shouting and waving his ruler in the air, I giggle out of pure relief.

It might seem foolish to be so protective of my sister. She is, after all, the eldest. But she is as innocent and guileless as the birds and flowers she paints. And though we both know the world is full of evil, for you cannot be a Jewess and be ignorant, Beatriz is still trusting. She sees no danger in pulling out a handful of coins in the middle of a Fair, nor would she see danger in the glint of a man's eyes. And since her beauty and sweetness of character draw men, both good and bad, like the red crest of a widgeon draws its mate, it falls on me to be discerning for both of us.

"What will you buy today?" Mama says to Beatriz over my shoulder, obviously referring to the bolts of cloth in front of them.

There is a long pause. "A mare for Sebastian," she finally answers.

Mama laughs, for it is plain she thinks Beatriz is teasing.

"No, Mama, truly. I have long desired to buy Sebastian a wedding gift."

And that right there is further proof of her naivety, because Beatriz actually expects Mama to see nothing wrong with her plan to purchase a horse.

Mama's face is one of bewilderment. "But why, daughter? You know Papa and I have already commissioned a gift for Sebastian, a special leather saddle from Cordova."

"Yes, and a perfect gift too. Sebastian will love it." Beatriz hugs Mama's thick waist. "But would it not be even *more* perfect on the back of a new mare?"

And to my utter surprise—though I should not be surprised for it is impossible to deny Beatriz anything—Mama entwines Beatriz's arm in hers and says, "Perhaps it would. And if we wish our business to be concluded before the bells chime Sext and it is time for our noon meal, we must be off."

So away we go to the Horse Fair.

༄

The crowd—mostly men, all shouting and waving and wet with sweat—is rougher here along the sprawling grounds of the Guadalquivir River bank. And everywhere mules and donkeys and horses are traded or sold, or shown off in hopes of being so. Everyone speaks at once, though how they can speak at all amid the odor of sweating bodies and dung rising like steam beneath the hot, baking sun is a mystery. I cover my nose with a handkerchief.

Already I am sorry we came, and see, by Mama's face, that only Beatriz is happy to be here. The Horse Fair is as old as Seville herself, for here Romans bought horses for their generals. Now Castilian nobles come to buy theirs.

The Moors have the best ones, certainly the best Andalusians. Already Beatriz is gently pushing her way toward a merchant who holds one by the reins—a beautiful spotted gray.

As soon as the merchant sees Beatriz's interest, he hops upon the mare's back as easily as if it were the back of a goat, and without benefit of a saddle, breaks into a trot. The merchant settles his hand high on the horse's crest, tightens his legs slightly against its flank while easing the pressure on the bit. Then horse and rider become one. I remove the handkerchief from my face, no longer aware of the smell or dust or heat. I am thrilled beyond measure for here is a contradiction in a world where domination is all. Horse and rider move in perfect submission to one another, but in that submission I see freedom. At that moment I would have bought the horse myself, if it were not for Beatriz.

When Beatriz claps her hands with pleasure, the rider pulls the horse to a stop and dismounts. A small crowd has gathered. It is plain to all that Beatriz is determined to have the mare. And just when Mama steps forward to haggle its price, for she well knows Beatriz will pay whatever is asked, a man steps forward too, and when he does, a hush falls over the crowd. Then one by one everyone steps aside, leaving the man and Beatriz quite alone in the circle.

She has not noticed him at all. Rather she whispers to the horse and strokes its neck. It is a strange picture, this man—round and stern-looking in his spotless white cassock and lace trimmed surplice, and my sister—with her face nuzzling the Andalusian, and dust swirling around them both.

And then he looks at her.

The throng has pushed me back, and now people, three deep, stand between me and the circle. Even so, I see it, the glint in his eyes, though it scarcely resembles the Keeper of the Fair's glint. These eyes are hungry and fierce, like the eyes of a lynx. Because all is still quiet, I am able to hear him say, "You wish to purchase this horse, my child?"

For the first time Beatriz looks up, is startled, then shaken when she sees the friar. But to her credit she remains composed, and smiles and inclines her head in a gesture of respect, and finally answers, "Yes."

"Then I shall not contend for it," Fray Alonso de Montemayor says.

Two inquisitors oversee the Tribunal in the archbishopric of Seville, and Fray Alonso de Montemayor is the worst of them. It is he who has taken the old Andalusian proverb, "Every pig has its Saint Martin's Day," and applied it to the Tribunal. His meaning is clear since on Saint Martin's Day Christians slaughter their pigs to make sausages, and *conversos* are often called *marranos* or swine.

Mama grips my arm in terror while the sound of my own heart rages like the Guadalquivir River in my ears. But we fear two different things. She fears Fray Alonso, the Inquisitor, while I fear Fray Alonso, the man. I hear my sister say, "You are most kind, your Excellency, but I would not think of depriving you of your pleasure. The horse is yours."

He stares at her with dark smoldering eyes that raise the hairs on my arm. The ugliness of his stare is plain. If possible I would have flung my body into the air and landed as an impenetrable pillar between them. Instead, I try to force a path into the circle, but I am pressed on all sides. Even Mama has a firm grip on my arm. And just when I can bear it no longer and am about to shout my sister's name, Fray Alonso abruptly turns and walks away, taking with him the dozen armed men who had been waiting patiently nearby.

～♡

Beatriz seems to have forgotten her encounter with Fray Alonso, and talks only about her new mare, which she has named "Blessing", and is now safely in our stables by the groves.

But I have not forgotten.

For days I have thought of little else. And though my mind cannot produce a single reason to worry, I am greatly shaken. I am still thinking about it when I hear voices coming from Papa's study. Against my better judgment, I tiptoe closer.

"I tell you it is true," Don Sebastian's voice sputters through the slight opening.

"Surely, no. Not our Beatriz. There must be some mistake."

"My spy is loyal and . . . well paid. His information is never wrong. He says that Fray Alonso *himself*, and not the public prosecutor, drew up the arrest papers and gave it to the police."

"This must be the work of that vile Catalina! If revenge is her goal, then no revenge could be crueler."

"My spy does not know whose hand has brought this about, but I promise you this, if anyone comes for Beatriz they will taste the edge of my sword!"

"Lower your voice! Do you want someone to hear? Such talk will only cause more trouble. We must keep our heads."

My moist, trembling fingers tug along the heavy door's edge, opening it enough to see Papa struggle to raise his portly frame from the worn desk chair, then head toward Sebastian. He pats Sebastian's shoulder, then hands him a goblet of sherry—a manly diversion of nerves—and I feel guilty for observing it. But things are happening here, awful and dangerous things involving my sister. Like a stubborn fly, I remain glued to the door until someone tugs at my sleeve. My heart jumps when I see Beatriz.

"Come away," she whispers sweetly, but her eyes tell me how improper she thinks my behavior is, and her untroubled countenance tells me she has not overheard the conversation. For her sake alone

I leave the door, but not before seeing her scan the opening for a glimpse of Sebastian.

"He is so handsome." Beatriz says in her soft, lilting voice, a voice that has, more than once, coaxed me back to sleep after a nightmare.

Was this a nightmare? Or had my ears heard true? Was Beatriz in danger? And if so, *why*? Had Catalina really made accusations against Beatriz as Papa believes? It did not make sense. If Catalina sought revenge she would accuse Mama, the one who discharged her, not Beatriz.

"Do you not think he is handsome?" Beatriz presses.

"Yes," I say, pulling her down the hall toward the wrought-iron grille that opens into the courtyard where there will be no danger of Beatriz overhearing Don Sebastian or Papa.

We pass the large marble fountain and head to a bench beneath an orange tree where we sit. Around us are pots of lavender, and to one side, a well-tended herb garden. It is peaceful here, and because of our wealth and the way our house is situated, it is a courtyard not shared by other homes. Still, peace eludes me.

"He is much admired." Beatriz's voice is glum. "Women look at him in ways that are shameful. And I confess, Isabel, more than once it has caused me to blush." Her fingers entwine mine. "He could have his pick of any woman."

"But he is married to *you*." I try to keep my face from showing any fear for I am still thinking about Papa's and Sebastian's words.

"We have been married so long, and yet not married, not truly. Perhaps someone else has caught his eye, and he wishes to be free. It has happened. It *could* happen. My heart would surely break. For me there is no other man."

"And for him there is no other woman." I kiss her fingertips. I believe what I say, though I worry over other matters concerning Sebastian's character—rumors of his many tavern fights, his gambling debts, his propensity to seek out worthless companions. But these I keep to myself. "It is not uncommon to be nervous before one's wedding. Do not distress yourself. Before long, you and Sebastian will be together, and no two people will ever be happier."

The wrought-iron gate creaks, and suddenly Sebastian stands before us, harried and breathless, and appearing greatly distressed. "I have come to take my leave." He looks past me to Beatriz. "Your father . . . wishes to resume working on his ledgers. But he has said I may come tomorrow. Perhaps then you will allow me to escort you to . . . to . . . wherever you like."

Beatriz is delighted, and rewards him with a smile.

"Tomorrow, then." And as quickly as he appeared, Don Sebastian is gone.

The next day Beatriz is unable to go with her husband when he arrives, for that morning, before the bells chimed Prime, a police officer appeared at the door with a writ of arrest and took her to the Holy House.

Chapter 4

For three days we have huddled like rabbits in a hole, not leaving our house or receiving visitors except for Don Sebastian and his father, Señor Villarreal. The Villarreals have hired an army of spies, may the Holy One heap blessings on their heads. But as yet, these spies have gleaned nothing of value.

We are still greatly stunned by what has happened, and confused. The police have not impounded Beatriz's goods, the normal procedure when one is imprisoned by order of the Inquisition. We tell ourselves it is a good sign; that things are not as bad as originally feared.

For my part, I just want everything to be as it was. And this yearning has made my mind a grinding wheel that turns over and over the same two thoughts: *surely*, this is a mistake; s*urely*, Beatriz will be home soon. And early on, when I told Papa this, he gently reminded me that only three outcomes are possible, and a mistake is not one of them. Either Beatriz will be found not guilty of charges yet to be stated, and a charter issued, then read in all the churches proclaiming her innocence. Or Beatriz will be found guilty and reconciled back to the Church, and ordered to do penance ranging from attending daily Mass to imprisonment. Or finally, she will be found guilty, relaxed to the secular arm, and burned at the stake.

Even after Papa's patient instruction, my mind continues to grind out the same two things: *surely*, this is a mistake; *surely*, Beatriz will be home soon. I suppose it is a way of keeping my sanity.

How does Papa keep his? I look at him now. Dark, plum-like pouches cup his eyes, proof he has slept little; or eaten, for that matter, though I had the cook make Papa's favorite chicken soup with rose water. These days, his broth is anxiety, of which he has drunk deeply and which has aged him years. But he insists that all will end well, and tries to appear confident.

Mama, on the other hand, hides in her room and cries. We have all done our share of crying. But for Papa's sake, I try to be strong. It would not do to have both Mama and me weeping in our rooms.

"What more can be done?" Don Sebastian is like a wild stallion, clomping back and forth in front of Papa's desk. Any minute I expect him to rear up and lay waste the furniture.

Papa frowns and pinches his thumb between his fingers. "All has been done that can be."

But Papa's words seem to have no effect, for Don Sebastian continues to seethe like a vat of mutton soap. Nothing seems to comfort him. Yesterday, Papa confided in me, I suppose because Mama was not around, that he fears Don Sebastian will do something rash, though Papa failed to explain why he thought so. My mind sees Don Sebastian on his new Andalusian, charging up to the Holy House and freeing Beatriz with his sword, killing dozens and dozens in the process.

And to my shame, the thought delights me.

"There must be *something* we can do." Sebastian voice is as thin as air. "Surely, some action is required?"

His need for action mimics mine, for doing something, anything, is preferable to this endless waiting. But Papa has already done all he can. He has sent Beatriz two beds and a small table, along with two chairs. Also with these came food, a brazier and cooking utensils, plus clothes and the numerous personal items I bundled. And since he fears, as do I, that Beatriz will fair poorly in captivity—neither cooking nor caring for herself properly—Papa has hired the scrawny young daughter of our cook to attend her. This was no small task since any servant who accompanies one accused must stay imprisoned during the entire inquisitional procedure. Considering that some accused Judaizers have been jailed for years, only a loyal servant or one well paid would consent to such a thing.

And Papa has paid well.

"*Why* have no charges been made?" Don Sebastian stops in the middle of the room, searching our faces. It is a proper question. Before the setting up of any inquisitional court, two books are compiled: The *Book of Testimonies* and the *Book of Confessions*. The first book, containing the statements of all accusers, is assessed by a theological consultant. Only if two or more accusers are believed credible does the prosecutor formulate his charges, have the defendant arrested, his goods sequestered, and an inventory made of all property. None of which has been done in Beatriz's case.

"If there are no charges and Fray Alonso only *suspects* Beatriz of Judaizing, why has he arrested her instead of ordering her to report daily to the court for questioning?" Don Sebastian presses.

Eyes reveal too much. I lower mine to keep him from seeing my fear; a fear which I have, since Beatriz's arrest, been pushing into a small deep place within me. I glance at Papa to gage his feelings but his face is as blank as vellum, though surely he must have this same fear. We have all heard stories of beautiful young women summoned to the Holy House on charges concocted in order to satisfy the wanton desires of a prosecutor or a *nuncio* and sometimes even an inquisitor.

"We must write *tachas* for Beatriz," Sebastian blurts, looking like a madman, and like a madman, has jumped from thought to thought. In one leap he has landed on the idea of preparing a defense for which there are no charges. Even under the best circumstances, preparing a defense is difficult since the identities of the accusers are kept secret, and even their accusations.

But writing *tachas* is one of only two recourses available to the accused, and consists of compiling a list of those who might have reason to submit a false testimony. If the names on the *tachas* match the names in the *Book of Testimonies*, and if the reason for their ill-will can be proven by two witnesses, the prosecutor must discount the testimony.

The second recourse is to prove the defendant was a devout Christian.

"Come. Let us all write *tachas*," Sebastian repeats. And in two strides he is beside Papa's desk, frantically scanning the tabletop for paper and quill.

But Papa is already holding several sheets of rag-paper and quickly dispenses them. Then he hands us each a quill.

I am seated in a small cushioned chair near the table, and bend at once to my task by penning the name: CATALINA. But aside from this I cannot think of another word to write. Perhaps I am too distracted. The room is hot and stale. There are no windows, and the door is closed against prying servants. When I breathe I feel as though I am dragging air through gauze.

Don Sebastian, on the other hand, is in his chair, writing furiously. *But writing what?* Perspiration runs along his cheeks, his breathing is labored, but he is so absorbed by his task he appears to notice neither, and I feel pity.

What far reaching consequences this has for him.

If Beatriz is reconciled and released, their children will forever be prohibited from certain benefits and honors and even offices. They will be restricted in their clothing, not allowed to wear camlet, silk or gold, or the color red. Nor can they ride a horse, bear arms or become a surgeon, landlord or apothecary. Their names will forever be linked with scandal and shame. And if the worst happens, if Beatriz is burned at the stake, she will take both her and Sebastian's hopes with her.

And what of Beatriz? Even if she is exonerated and issued a charter, will there not be changes etched into her character? Qualities removed or damaged? Qualities such as trust and love? How can she possibly be the same Beatriz?

And what of Papa and Mama? They are old, and age makes hardship more difficult to bear.

And me? If something happens to Beatriz, if she is altered in any way, can I still align myself with those who destroy my own people in the name of the Savior I love?

I ponder these things, and for the first time understand that nothing will ever be the same.

❀

Your sin has brought this on our house.

Mama's words burn deep. I have carried them around, like swallowed coals, for days. I know she is remorseful. She has told me so every day for the past five days. But words said cannot be unsaid. And that delicate fabric of renewed fellowship we have so carefully reconstructed has come undone. For though I have forgiven her, I know Mama still believes her words are true.

What makes it bearable is that I know they are not. I have not abandoned the Law of Moses as Mama charges. It still fills my heart, as does the Savior. Neither am I responsible for Beatriz being in the Holy House, though I sometimes worry Papa and Don Sebastian will take Mama's words to heart.

Mama is finally out of her room, and she and Papa and Don Sebastian whisper for hours on end in Papa's study, but stop when I enter as though I am a spy for Fray Alonso himself. Even so, I have overheard Mama say that once an inquisitor questions one family member, he is not content until he has questioned them all. I have also heard her tell Papa that in order to protect their own families, our husbands will surely divorce Beatriz and me.

All this secrecy has made me feel excluded. Am I being childish? Beatriz is, after all, my sister. Have Mama and Papa forgotten that? I worry greatly over what is happening in that strange, frightening place. I have written *tachas* until my fingers hurt, naming every person who has ever said a cross word to Beatriz. And though that number is few, I have inflated the list by adding every person I even suspect of jealousy or ill-well, and embellished their every look and word and gesture to prove my point. But now, even those names have run out and I can write no more, and must turn to that which is left me.

And so I pray.

~⊙

"But I do not wish to go!" My voice sounds childish even to my ears, and petulant, too.

Mama dismisses me with a click of her tongue, just like she used to when I was small. "It is Papa's wish that you go to the groves. This is no place for you now, Isabel."

"How can I leave? I *must* be here when Beatriz comes home." My voice wails, for by the firm set of Mama's chin and by the fact that this is Papa's idea, I already know I have lost.

"There is no telling when Beatriz will return. When she does, we will send for you."

And as quickly as Mama can pluck a chicken, I find myself packed up, trunks and all, and sent off to our estate by the groves, banished from my parents, and left alone to imagine all manner of horrors occurring at home.

And I wonder why.

~⊙

From the window in my room I see the stables and one of the gray Andalusians Papa keeps for herding our cattle. The horse has gotten into one of the stone chests containing grain and whose top has been left open. I watch to make certain that the servant who has come to retrieve the animal does not mistreat it. When I see that the servant plans no violence, and that he gently leads the horse away, I lose interest and turn my attention elsewhere.

36

Off to the side are the orange groves. Our bitter oranges are prized throughout Castile for the tang they give to foods. So too the blossoms, for their oils make orange blossom water used to perfume our stews.

Papa says the money made from our groves alone is able to sustain the entire estate. In turn, our estate provides meat and vegetables for us, our servants, and many local peasants, for we stock a variety of animals as well as cultivate several large vegetable gardens. Since the distance from the groves to our house in the city can be covered twice before the bells chime from Prime to Tierce, it is convenient for Mama to send our servants here every Sabbath eve.

Our house is large and beautiful, and the groves and vast tracks of land go far beyond what my eyes can see. My family has owned this estate since the time of the Moors. After the reconquest of Spain and Portugal, many Jews lost their lands to Castilian nobles seeking to enlarge their own holdings. But not our family because, as Papa says, "they wisely befriended the nobility."

Not far from the stables is our vineyard, where a band of peasants now work the vines, pulling leaves off old branches to increase the plant's vigor. We do not sell our wine. It is only for our use. And since our vineyard produces more grapes than we need, Papa has made an agreement with the local peasants. They work the vines and share the bounty. Sometimes the peasants take more than they should, but Papa never complains. The vineyards are hard work. Not like the orange groves.

As I watch them labor, I think about my friend, Blanca Nuñez. Mama has asked me to invite her to the groves while I am here. I do not believe it is out of concern for any loneliness I might feel, but because Blanca's father, Señor Alberto Nuñez, is Papa's new partner. Though Papa is a successful spice merchant, he is always looking for new investments and has recently purchased a herd of black-faced merino sheep from North Africa. The merino produce high quality wool which Señor Nuñez, a wool merchant, will market.

Perhaps I am unkind to accuse Mama of selfish motives but what else am I to think when she has acted so cruelly; keeping secrets and sending me away?

Out of spite, I have not extended the invitation. Instead, I have spent the last two days in solitude, praying and meditating on the Psalms. And now shame fills me. What a child I am! Pouting and exhibiting such a deficiency of grace. My flawed character continues to be exposed like a tapestry on a wall.

My penitent mood drives me to the trunk for paper and pen, and I begin composing an invitation to Blanca. Only three words are written before I crumple the page, for I suddenly realize I have no desire to see her. And it has nothing to do with spite. It is for reasons of my own, and they are these: Blanca and her family are *conversos*, and like many *conversos*, they have come to believe in neither the Law of Moses nor the Nazarene. I know this from being at Blanca's house on the Sabbath. Neither she nor her family observes the Sabbath by cleaning their house or lighting candles or wearing fresh clothes. In addition, she speaks ill of the Mass and the Pope, and even the Savior.

I do not judge Blanca. But being with her now would be difficult. She would find it hard to understand my current troubles. And while I am worrying about Beatriz, she will want to sit outside for hours bleaching her hair in the sun and sharing servants' gossip. And what if Beatriz comes home and I, because of duty to my guest, am unable to attend her immediately?

And so, I resign myself to being alone.

It is a glorious morning, and I have decided to spend it out in the groves with Gonzolo Vivar, our master gardener. I have dressed in light homespun for the occasion, and covered my braided hair with a coarse veil.

Gonzolo is already working the groves when I find him. I smile and wave and rush to where he and his two sons hoe weeds from around the trunks of several orange trees. I am pleased when I notice his eldest son, Enrique, is nowhere to be seen.

I pick up a hoe, which must belong to the missing Enrique, and join the group. "I wish to help," I say, feeling more excitement than I have felt in days over the prospect of hard work; over the prospect of subjugating my mind to my body, and of ceasing my endless brooding.

Gonzolo appears embarrassed, and wipes his sweaty brow with the back of one hand. "Your parents . . . would disapprove, Doña Isabel."

"Then let it be our secret," I say, hacking at a clump of weeds. His two sons smile, but Gonzolo appears deeply disturbed.

"You know what little care the orange trees require. A little weeding, a little pruning, a little mulching . . . do not trouble yourself."

I am about to answer when a large hand pulls the hoe from mine. It is Enrique, tall and broad, his crop of wild black hair swirling in the wind. It has been years since he left the groves, and though this is the first time I have seen him since his departure, I still recognize him by his eyes; those hard, angry eyes.

"I heard you were back." I force a smile.

"This is no work for you, Doña Isabel." His voice is polite, but holds menacing undertones. And seeing there is nothing left for me to do but leave the grove, I walk away.

For seven days those eyes watch me, follow my every move, and make me remember that even as a child Enrique behaved in this manner, and that his behavior always frightened me. It frightens me now. And puzzles me, too, for surely his many travels should have produced greater interests than observing one simple Jewess.

Since I have had my fill of him and his eyes, I have decided to go home. I am using it as a subterfuge, an excuse to return to the city and be closer to Beatriz. Even now, Gonzalo is preparing a mule for me. Later, he will send my trunks on a donkey cart.

My only worry is that Mama will send me back.

I stand knocking at the door, feeling like a stranger in front of my own house. *"Please let Papa answer,"* I whisper under my breath even though I know Mama carries the keys. The door opens slowly, and there is Mama, sunlight streaming across her face, revealing web-like lines around her eyes and forehead, and exposing the tired sag of her cheeks. I feel pity, and ask the Holy One to forgive the unkind thoughts I have had of her. And when Mama sees me her face is not angry . . . no . . . there are tears in her eyes, and she enfolds me in pudgy arms then kisses my head and whispers in my ear, "Oh, Isabel, how I missed you!"

I make my way down Abbots Street as fast as one can who wears *pantofles*, and worry I will be late for Mass. Mama and Papa disapprove of my going to daily service, a habit cultivated since returning from the groves and discovering I am still without allies. Though Mama missed me, and despite her warm greeting at the door, she has kept me at a distance. And attending daily Mass has only made matters worse.

She was especially unhappy this morning, giving me unpleasant looks as I readied myself, but it would take more than unpleasant looks to stop me today. It is the feast of Saint Elmo—the patron saint of sailors—who died a martyr when his intestines were pulled from his body by a windlass. Perhaps God will be especially kind and hear my prayers today, for ever since Beatriz's arrest, I too feel as though I have been disemboweled.

I rush along, not mindful of where I step. The Cathedral will be crowded. Many livelihoods are tied to Seville's inland port, to its ships and commerce. People will be anxious to light candles.

A beggar up ahead, threadbare and teetering on dirty crutches, catches my eye. My fingers fumble for the few *blancas* lodged deep within my pocket. The *blancas* clink when I drop them into his hand making his eyes shimmer with gratitude. Such a small gift can only satisfy when one has nothing. I use the illustration to raise my spirits. After all, Papa has abundant resources that can be used on Beatriz's behalf. Surely, *surely*, it will buy us justice in the end.

But it has been so long—over a month now since Beatriz was arrested. And though Don Sebastian's spies most certainly have gathered some scraps of information, the news cannot be good, otherwise Mama, or at least Papa, would have told me.

I quicken my pace. Ahead looms the Giralda Tower. Once the minaret of a Moorish mosque, the Tower has been refitted by Christians and is part of the Great Cathedral. Christians are still refitting it. Already, masons gather for the day's work and the master mason, with gloves and walking stick, is issuing orders.

The Plaza in front of the Giralda swarms with people. As I wait to file through the massive wooden doors, the masons and stone dressers lay out their tools. I love watching them. Their work is tangible and ongoing. Once scaffolding of lashed-together poles covered all the walls of the great church. Now only one wall is covered. It appears it is easier to refit a temple of stone than a human temple, as, according to the priest, we are. I have changed little despite all the cutting and honing that has been going on in my life. And this saddens me as I enter and take my place in back.

We are packed like reeds. From my position I see little, but content myself with the thought that though I cannot see, I am seen by God. Within minutes the bell—which signals the beginning of service—rings out over the vaulted ceiling, a ceiling that soars, like the sky itself, over my head.

Benches are clustered along the side and front, but none throughout the main area where I stand. Many have brought cushions or small stools for sitting, a common practice since the church no longer provides straw for the floor. A melodious Gregorian chant fills the air, and the procession of priest, choir and clerks begins. Everyone who is not already standing, rises. An organ plays. More chanting follows. Finally, the priest mounts his pulpit, makes the sign of the cross and begins his *thema*, a short Gospel text in Latin which he will later translate.

I am distracted by the woman next to me. Her bodily humors are clearly unbalanced. As I listen to her wheeze, my mind wanders. I am thinking of the Feast of Corpus Christi which is barely two weeks away. It is the feast honoring the Eucharist. It was just a year ago—while six altar boys, all grandly dressed in red jackets and plumed hats, were dancing *Los seises* with their castanets—that I first began to ponder the sacrifice of the Nazarene. While the boys danced and their voices soared in sweet song past the unfinished choir loft and then to the top of the vaulted ceiling, I suddenly felt a deep longing to know more of the one who stretched out his arms and bled for me . . . me, Isabel of bad temper and contrary nature. And even afterward, when monks and priests and Castilian nobles on horseback all escorted the gold jewel-encrusted chest containing the Host throughout the streets of Seville, I pondered it.

Now, I think only of Beatriz. *Will she be home to see the dance of* Los seises *this year?*

Something the priest says draws me back. His *thema* over, he is deep into his sermon. The unpleasant quality of his voice makes me strain to hear.

". . . and the mere presence of Jewish blood suggests a proclivity in that person to undermine Holy Mother Church and its dogma. Thus, it is our duty to carefully scrutinize all New Christians, for every *converso* is a potential Judaizer."

My insides tremble as I squeeze past the dozens of people who surround me. Through a partial opening I see the madman who is tied every day to the ornate rood screen that separates the choir from the nave. He is tied there in hopes he will benefit from attending Mass. The figure of a cross has been shaved into his hair. Spittle trickles from the corners of his mouth as he thrashes back and forth. I watch for a moment, then quietly slip out the door.

༄

It is the month of *Av*, and customary for Jews to read the Book of Deuteronomy. The Feast of Corpus Christi has come and gone, along with the pomp and ceremony of *Los seises* and the street procession that followed, neither of which I attended. In fact, I have not attended Mass since the Feast of Saint Elmo.

Shavuot, the day of first fruits, has also come and gone without Mama or Papa staying up all night to study Torah. Nor did they read the Book of Ruth in the morning.

The day of Beatriz's wedding has come and gone, with everyone pretending they did not know what day it was, though Mama spent much time smoothing out Beatriz's wedding dress as if expecting her to come through the door at the last minute and put it on.

And now it is the eve of *Tisha B'Av*. Tomorrow we commemorate the destruction of the two Jewish Temples, but tonight Papa and Mama fail to eat bread dipped in ashes as is the custom. I am stunned they have not observed *Shavuot*, and now *Tisha B'Av* eve. Has Mama finally understood the danger of doing such things? I do not ask, but perhaps like me, she and Papa are too busy waiting.
Waiting for Beatriz to come home.

༄

One noteworthy thing did happen late *Tisha B'Av* eve. It was the arrival of the writ of divorce from my husband. Mama said she had been expecting it. I did not ask how she knew. Let her keep her secrets. The truth is, I care not that at sixteen I am already a divorced woman.

I only care about Beatriz.

⟳

It is pouring. I have been listening to rain hit the tiles of our roof, and watching it from my bed as the water cascades past my window. The customary fresh smell that accompanies rain fills my room, and the oppressive heat which we have endured for so long has finally lifted, at least for a time.

It is a soothing activity, this listening and watching. I have not felt so calm in weeks. Mama and Papa, though glad for the rain, said it is appropriate that it rains today, on *Tisha B'Av*, for it shows that all of heaven weeps. It is a day of great mourning for Jews, and they are called to fast and pray.

But Mama and Papa do not fast. Rather, they ate a large breakfast of eggs and meat this morning, and more than one plateful, too. And they made no effort to honor the day in other ways, though to be fair, Papa did read the Book of Job as is the custom.

Even so, I am scandalized. I know I have cautioned Mama time and again to be mindful of what she does around the servants, but this flagrant disregard for our traditions is shocking. It is foolish to feel this way, considering Beatriz is imprisoned in the Holy House, but I do. To add to my foolishness, I have decided to fast and pray, and abstain from bathing or washing and wearing shoes, as is the custom. In order to do this, I have feigned illness, and taken to my bed where I have lain all morning. Mama thinks I am downcast about the divorce. She has told Papa so. But nothing could be further from the truth.

Now, after so many hours in bed, restlessness makes me rise and walk barefoot into the hall. And that is when I hear it, a small noise at the front door, like that of a kitten scratching to be let in. Who could be out in this downpour? Surely not the baker peddling stale bread for trenchers?

I unpin the keys from my bodice. Since Beatriz's imprisonment we have been locking the door, day as well as night. I pause to listen. The noise has stopped. Out of the corner of my eye I see Mama speaking to one of the servants. Papa, visible through the partially opened door of his study, is bent over a ledger. No one has noticed the sound, and just as I decide it was my imagination and turn to go, I hear it again. This time I race to the door, unlock it, then fling it open. And there, standing in the pouring rain with her hair loose and wet and clinging to her face, and her soggy clothes hugging her body so tightly it reveals how thin she has become, is *Beatriz!* I let out a cry that sends shoes slapping the tiles of the hall, and then I throw my arms around my sister and lift her into the house.

We are all a tangle . . . Beatriz, Mama, Papa and I . . . as we hug and kiss and cry. The front door is still open, and against the splatter of rain and tears my heart beats out a steady rhythm: *Beatriz is home, Beatriz is home, Beatriz is home.*

Chapter 5

The morning bells chime Tierce as I finish plaiting Beatriz's hair. Fourteen braids in all, woven together at the back of her head, mimic the style of multiple plaiting that is all the rage in Florence. Her reflection in the mirror tells me she looks beautiful. Mine is drab, for I wear a plain brown linen skirt with a lighter brown bodice that is frayed around the neck. Also, my straight auburn hair lacks adornment and is pulled back and held by simple brown netting. My attire is deliberate, the better to make Beatriz shine.

One by one, I slip pearl-studded hair pins among Beatriz's braids. It is an excessive decoration on a day we neither plan to go out nor entertain. I do it in hopes of lifting my sister's spirits. Her brow sags across a pale forehead. Her lips are pinched. Since her return, I have not been able to get two words out of her, though I have employed all my skill. My impatience bubbles like a vat of Mama's stew. Only love restrains me. It is obvious that Beatriz has been deeply wounded, a wound requiring time to heal and much patience on my part. But it is oh, so difficult. I want her to tell me everything because maybe the telling of the thing will bring her back from that dark place wherein she now resides.

Maybe it will help her be Beatriz again.

"There!" I slip in the last pearl. "Now you *must* come out of your room so Mama and Papa can see how beautiful you look."

Beatriz shakes her head. She has been in her room for three days, refusing to join us in the great room, or even sharing her meals. Mama has indulged her, making the servants bring food to her, but the piled trenchers they carry back after each meal reveal how little she eats. Nor has Beatriz employed herself in any industry, for her tiles remain just as she left them. And this troubles me, because too much solitary brooding is sure to produce more ill-health.

I bend and kiss Beatriz's cheek while glancing at her reflection. Staring back are those eyes that have haunted me, even in my dreams, ever since her return, for they are not Beatriz's eyes.

"This will not do," I say, trying to sound jovial. "We have been far too lenient. Spoiling and coddling you, and allowing you to languish all alone, when what you need is your family to talk to, and kiss you, and love you back to health. I am determined to see you leave your room today!"

"Oh, Isabel, I cannot. I have no strength."

"You must muster it, for we will not be able to keep Don Sebastian from storming your room much longer." I say this in jest, and am astonished when Beatriz pales, and seizes my hand.

"No . . . I cannot see him!" Her nails dig into my flesh. "*Please*, Isabel. Do not let him come."

I grab Beatriz's thin shoulders and pull her off the stool, then drag her stumbling to the bed, where I make her sit down. Then I sit beside her.

"He *will* come, Beatriz, and why should he not? He wants to speak with you and Papa about the new wedding plans. If there is some reason to prevent his coming, you must tell me now. You cannot keep silent. Help me understand."

We sit so close our shoulders touch. Then I feel her body slump. "I am with child." Her voice is calm, but she trembles against me like a wounded sparrow. And when I look into her eyes, so shadowed and troubled, I see the awful truth, and know what has been happening at the Holy House all these months.

"There were never any charges, Isabel. I was never suspected of any crime. Fray Alonso released me when he learned of my condition, no doubt in hopes of expunging himself from any wrongdoing. It will be easier for him to claim I am with child by another if I am released before I show."

"Then . . . Fray Alonso is the . . . *father?*"

Beatriz rests her head against my shoulder, I think because she cannot bear to see the look on my face, and whispers, "Yes."

My arms pull her close. It is horrible to hear, and yet it is what I feared. The clergy have long been noted for their immorality. Many priests keep mistresses who bear them illegitimate children. And even priests who refrain from flaunting their mistresses often have housekeepers who share their beds. And now, Rodrigo de Borgia—the new Pope of Rome who has taken the name, Alexander VI—insults Christendom further by openly flaunting his own Roman mistress and numerous children. And who is there to stop it? Even important men, like Cardinal Cisneros who is much favored by the Queen, have been unable to bring reform.

I am shaken to the marrow, and cling desperately to my sister. And for the rest of the morning we sit and cry, and hold each other tightly while Beatriz tells me all that was done to her in the name of Christ.

⌒つ

The house is in an uproar. I have, with Beatriz's permission, told Mama and Papa all that has happened, leaving nothing out. *Oh how difficult!* After uttering the cruel truth, I had to endure watching Mama and Papa weep with grief.

Doctor Hernando Diaz has been called, and while we await him, I try to coax Beatriz to eat. She is as thin as an oleander leaf, and I tell her she must now eat for two—a grave mistake, for afterward she curled up on her bed and refused everything. She has not spoken a word since telling me all. Not even to Mama. Instead, she keeps to her bed, and stares at the wall with a dreadful blank look.

I have been silently praying that the Holy One sends us a remedy for our troubles. What is to become of Beatriz? What kind of future can she possibly have now? Surely Papa will propose a divorce. Can there be any other solution for Beatriz and Sebastian? I push these thoughts from my mind. The only thing that matters now is Beatriz and the baby. Hopefully, Dr. Diaz will provide the proper medicines; though I wish the midwife was coming instead. But as we wait, Beatriz seems to slip further and further away.

And I am greatly afraid.

Doctor Hernando Diaz sniffs the urine in the clay bowl, examines it for sediment, then takes a sip, tasting for sugar. He places the bowl on the floor, and glances at where Mama and I watch from the foot of the bed. His look tells us that all is well. I hear Papa pacing outside, and long to relieve him of his worry, but fear of missing anything keeps me in place.

"It seems all the humors—the bile, black bile, blood and phlegm—are in balance." Doctor Diaz picks up the small sandglass he used when taking Beatriz's pulse and slips it into his costly Cordovan-leather bag. He has already inquired about Beatriz's stool and diet, and I know what he will say next.

"But I recommend bleeding her as a precaution."

"If we had wanted to bleed her we would have called the barber!" I blurt, still disappointed it was not the midwife who was here to examine Beatriz's injury to her secret parts, parts which a doctor, out of propriety, does not examine. But Mama and Papa felt it best that a general inspection by Doctor Diaz be done first.

Mama is obviously displeased by my outburst, but the thought of someone cutting my sister when she has already endured so much in body, and is so fragile in mind, makes me bold, or perhaps contrary, I know not which. "There is no need to bleed her." My voice is laced with an authority I do not feel.

Doctor Diaz looks from me to Mama, and when Mama does not contradict me, and when the bells chime Vespers, he shrugs. "Ah, well, perhaps a sleeping dram, then?" Mama nods, and he quickly pulls a small pouch from his bag, measures out a spoonful of white powder, and empties it into the goblet that stands on the table where Beatriz keeps her combs and hairnets.

Mama summons one of the servants and asks her to bring water. And when she returns, Papa creeps in and hovers nearby. Water and powder are mixed and given to Beatriz, then Doctor Diaz closes his bag. "The hour is late. If you need me, I can return tomorrow."

Mama thanks him, then from her pocket pulls several coins which she deposits into his hand.

"Perhaps you can give her milk of pulverized almonds, or a bit of barley water laced with licorice and figs." His fingers close around the coins. "She does look rather fatigued and thin."

Despite my efforts to be generous in thought, I am convinced this last morsel of advice is the result of a bad conscience for having given us so little for our money. Though I should not be angry, I am. Doctor Diaz always charges two *reales* for purges and unguents that the corner apothecary sells for one, and in that respect exemplifies our Castilian proverb regarding physicians, "Take while the patient is in pain."

But when I look at Beatriz lying so quiet and still on the bed, and turned from us to face the wall, I realize it is not the money that angers me. Everyone, including Doctor Diaz, knew Beatriz had been imprisoned in the Holy House. Because Doctor Diaz is an Old Christian, and because it would be folly to accuse Fray Alonso of any wrongdoing in his presence, we did not tell him of Beatriz's true condition. But oh, how certain we were that once he examined her, he would discover the truth for himself. But if he did, he has not said.

And that is why I am angry. Because in matters like this it is always easier, even for decent people, to pretend nothing is wrong.

∽◯

Doctor Diaz's potion has given Beatriz a peaceful night's sleep. I know, because I stayed in the room with her; watching her for hours, listening to her gentle, rhythmic breathing. And this morning she even had a bowl of chicken broth before the midwife came.

The midwife, who is a *converso* and knows much about the healing arts, understands right away what has happened to my sister. "There are still signs of the violence done her." She speaks only to Mama. "But your daughter is healing well . . . in body." There is a frown on the midwife's face as she applies a salve of alkanet to Beatriz's wounds. "Do you wish me to administer a broth of iris flowers, dittany root and pennyroyal leaves? To cleanse the womb?"

Beatriz, who has been silent until now, wails so loudly Mama is forced to sit on the bed and cradle her like an infant in order to quiet her. Finally Mama shakes her head "no" in response to the midwife's question.

Even before the midwife came, this matter was settled. "The baby will be part of our family," Mama and Papa decreed. Their courage makes me proud, but a little frightened too, for I am not sure I can love any child of Fray Alonso's.

The midwife does not press the matter. Instead, she busies herself by straightening the covers then scatters fennel on the floor to sweeten the air and discourage the presence of evil spirits.

Gradually, Beatriz calms. And after Mama eases her onto the pillow and tucks the sheet beneath Beatriz's chin, she is able to extract from her a promise to see Don Sebastian tomorrow.

The meeting will be difficult, and more than likely have a sad ending for them both. But I am greatly encouraged, for this is the first time Beatriz has shown any interest in resuming her life.

May the Merciful One make it so.

Before the bells finish chiming Prime, I am out of bed, throw on an old chemise and race to Beatriz's room to tell her that shortly I will help with her hair. Today, she must look her best. Not only for Don Sebastian, but because it is important she begin feeling like herself. I know it will take more than pretty dresses and braided hair to make Beatriz forget the injustice she has suffered, but I am certain these small victories can, over time, garner the larger victory of having our Beatriz whole again.

I tiptoe past Mama and Papa's room, not wanting to disturb, for I know Papa is laying *tefillin* about now. At Beatriz's door I knock softly, then enter before she can answer. "Come, sleepy head. Up and about!"

No response. Perhaps Doctor Diaz's sleeping potion of two nights ago has sufficiently broken Beatriz's anxiety and enabled her to sleep like she used to, for Beatriz was always the last out of bed in the morning. I decide to let her sleep while I dress, so I turn to go. That is when I see it, the large red spot on her bedding. I tiptoe closer. *No, it cannot be.* I stretch out a shaking hand to touch the spot, and feel it is wet. *Oh Merciful God!* With one jerk, I pull back the linens. Blood covers Beatriz's body. It saturates the bedding beneath her. One of Mama's kitchen knives lies beside her. It, too, is streaked with blood.

Beatriz's face is as white as a shrike's breast. I scan her body and stop at the slash lines across her wrists. I hear myself scream. Then I shake my sister, calling out her name again and again. But she does not stir. And when I put my hand to her nostrils, I feel no air. I moan like a wounded animal as I pull her thin limp body up into my arms, and hold her. We are cheek to cheek; my round, warm cheek pressed against her cold, sunken one. Her blood runs down my arms, and the blood on the mattress soaks my chemise as I rock back and forth. Then the door flies open, and Mama and Papa enter.

I know not what happened after that, or how they were able to pry my arms from Beatriz's body, but suddenly I find myself in a chair by the large table full of Beatriz's tiles, listening to Mama's anguished cries and to Papa saying between sobs, "*Kadosh, Kadosh, Kadosh,* Holy, Holy, Holy. May His great name be blessed forever and to all eternity." It is part of the prayer of mourning.

And then he covers my beautiful, gentle Beatriz with a sheet.

꩜

Someone has taken Beatriz's tiles off the long table in her studio and pulled the table into the center of the room where Beatriz now lies beneath a fresh coverlet. Another fresh sheet drapes her bed, and I am grateful I cannot see the blood-soaked mattress. Mama stands by Beatriz's head while I stand by her side. We must prepare her for burial.

Mama begins by gathering Beatriz's long loose hair into her hands. She will wash it with hot water, then brush it out while I wash Beatriz's body. It will be just us two attending my sister. Before the Expulsion, Mama and Papa would have hired professional keeners to wash Beatriz while they sang dirges and lamentations. But I am pleased it is only Mama and I, for our hands will be more loving in our work.

I slip my cloth beneath the sheet and begin by washing my sister's arms, then her chest, and am startled by the sharp protrusions of her ribs which I feel even through the wet cloth. She is thinner than I imagined. Next, my cloth moves across the bones of her hips. They too are protruding and hard, like the knobs of a stew bowl. But between the bones, there is a barely perceptible rise, and I think of the baby who has died, a baby Beatriz could not let the midwife destroy even while she herself lacked the strength of soul to bring it into this world.

Babies who die in their first year are not greatly mourned for it is all too common. But I mourn Beatriz's baby now, and wonder how I ever questioned loving it. It is, after all, Beatriz's. I indulge my grief over the baby because it keeps me from the larger grief, that grief which is so great and dark and deep it makes me feel as though I have fallen into a pit, and I know not how I will ever climb out.

Mama is feeling her own anguish. Her face is as tight as the hide on a tanner's frame. Neither of us speaks, and in the quiet I wonder what the next days and weeks will bring. Will Mama cover the mirrors and place a bowl of water on Beatriz's bed along with a towel, a saddler's needle and lit candle so Beatriz's soul can come to bathe? Will she ban meat for a week and set a place for Beatriz at table, or keep food around Beatriz's bed? I fear she will, thus giving our servants more fodder for the Inquisition. And alongside my fear sits shame for being such a coward.

Mama finishes washing Beatriz's face then takes a coin from somewhere inside her bodice and places it into my sister's mouth. And while she winds a long strip of cloth under Beatriz's chin and around her head to keep the mouth from opening, I finish my job. Then we carefully wrap Beatriz in a white muslin shroud. After the men bring the coffin, and put her in, we will place a small pillow filled with virgin earth beneath her head.

Then Beatriz will be ready for burial.

Our large procession makes its way to the Jewish cemetery. Because my sister has taken her own life she cannot be buried with the Christians. This does not grieve Mama since it saves her the trouble and danger of secretly burying Beatriz with her own people, then sending a weighted coffin to the church. The procession is made up of me, Mama, Papa, all our servants—including the young scrawny daughter of our cook who wails uncontrollably—all our *converso* neighbors, and even some Old Christians, including Gonzalo Vivar, his wife and three sons. Doctor Diaz also walks with us.

We follow the plain wooden coffin that is carried by Don Sebastian, his father Señor Villarreal, Señor Nuñez, and one of Señor Nuñez's sons, and wind through streets full of causal onlookers and noisy vendors and merchants too busy to stop and look at all. Down Abbots Street we move, passing houses and shops, loaded donkey carts, and lame beggars squatting on corners. Then we pass the walls of the Jewish Quarter until at last we enter the cemetery where a sad picture of neglect and desecration greets us.

The cemetery has not been used since the Expulsion, except secretly by crypto-Jews brave enough to do so. The once well-tended field is now overrun with weeds and refuse. Many of the gravestones have been broken by vandals; some completely destroyed. Off to one side is a freshly cleared patch of ground, the work of Don Sebastian—who refused to allow the servants to do it.

The men lower the coffin into the open hole, while one of the *conversos*, a former rabbi and himself a crypto-Jew, begins to recite the Ninety-First Psalm. People moan and cry and throw dirt over their shoulders. And when it is over I am the only one who has not shed a single tear.

After the burial everyone comes to our house to eat the burial meal. According to tradition, this meal of mostly round foods such as olives and hard boiled eggs, is "symbolic of the roundness of the world and the mourning which comes to us all." Mama even paid the baker to deliver a basketful of round bread. To this we added red bream and herring.

It pleases me that we do not sit on the floor, as is the custom. Mama has had benches and stools and every available chair brought out for our guests and placed near the tables laden with food and wine. With Old Christians present, it is dangerous to follow our customs too closely.

It is fortunate that Mama understands this, especially since Enrique Vivar follows me everywhere with those dark brooding eyes of his. Does he hope to entrap me or my family in some way? Even now, as he pushes chunks of herring into his mouth, his eyes are on me. And I cannot escape for I am speaking with Doctor Diaz who has sought me out and positioned himself in such a way that my back presses against the table's edge while he himself blocks me in front.

". . . and naturally I understood your sister's physical condition, but one cannot always know the condition of the soul for it is not available for scrutiny as are the bodily humors. But I never expected . . . ." Doctor Diaz's voice breaks.

I know he is telling me he is sorry that Beatriz has died, and perhaps even sorry he did not do more. I smile and say, "I understand," but not out of a heart of forgiveness but because I am weary of Enrique's gaze and see that a space has opened up through which I can make my escape. I use the excuse of wanting to find my friend, Blanca Nuñez, and dart through the opening, only to be stopped seconds later when a hand, rough and calloused, touches mine. I am surprised to see that the hand belongs to Maria Vivar, Gonzalo's wife. I do not know Maria well. I have only spoken to her a few times since whenever I am at the groves she is always scrubbing clothes or cooking or working the vegetable gardens.

"I am so grieved, Doña Isabel." Her brown eyes, set amid a worn leathery face, are full of kindness.

I nod and smile, for her kindness sake, and because she seems sincere.

"You do not understand." When she puts her face closer I see something true and loving and wonderful in her eyes. "I *am* grieved that your sister was called to the Holy House. Grieved about the prosecutor, the police, the *nuncio,* the . . . inquisitor. It makes me *ashamed.* So ashamed I feel I must ask your forgiveness. Please forgive me. Please forgive all of Spain's Christians."

My heart jumps. Never have I heard such words. Many good Christians have spoke out against the Inquisition and the treatment of Jews; venerated men such as Hernando de Talavera, confessor to the Queen; Alonso de Oropesa, General of the Spanish Hieronymite Order; and Cardinal Juan de Torquemada, uncle of the hated Tomas de Torquemada. But never have I heard a Christian ask *my* forgiveness.

Before I can say a word, Maria squeezes my hand and disappears.

↶᷁

It is late but I do not sleep even though a pleasant breeze sweetens the air in my room, and even though I am exhausted from the day's sad events. I have lain in my bed for hours trying to gather courage. The bells chime Martins, telling me I can delay no longer. I force myself up, quickly dress, then pull a white linen handkerchief from beneath my pillow. Tied in it are hundreds of lavender seeds which I have been saving to make a garden by our home in the groves. Now, I have a new home in mind.

I tiptoe down the hall, past Mama and Papa's room, relieved to see the door closed and that all is quiet. But before exiting the house I head for Beatriz's room; I think to bolster my sagging courage by reminding myself why I am about to do this mad thing.

Suddenly, Mama's soft trilling voice sputters through Beatriz's door. *What is she doing here?* I hesitate. Discovery will end my plans. Even so, I open the door slightly. Mama's back is to me. She sits on the floor facing Beatriz's bed, singing *guayas*—dirges of sorrow and affliction. The sound is utterly mournful.

To my surprise I see Papa, too, just a sliver of his back because he is in the part that Beatriz used as a studio. When I open the door wider, more surprise. He has fired a brazier. But on such a hot night what need was there to warm himself? It is difficult to see what he is doing, so I open the door as far as I dare, and stick in my head just as he pulls his *tefillin* from his tunic. It is long past the time for prayers. Even so, I expect to see him strap one leather box to his forehead, the other to his hand. Instead, he places them on the brazier. No . . . *impossible* . . . he would never burn his *tefillin*. But yes, that is exactly what he *is* doing. The leather smolders, and a small flame ignites one of the thin straps. Unable to watch any longer, I close the door, then dart from the house into the street.

A half moon hangs in the sky, providing enough light to see large objects, but not enough to see the sludge that runs through the streets. I keep close to the buildings. Already my shoes—an old pair of leather ox-mouths—are damp. The nearer to the Guadalquivir River I get, the windier it becomes. My hair, which is not bound or netted, swirls around my face. It is madness to be out at such an hour. If someone sees, surely I will be mistaken for a prostitute or some unfortunate beggar. I pray to the Merciful One and ask His protection, then quicken my pace. And God is merciful, for I encounter no one.

It is a long walk, and I keep to the shadows until at last I stand in front of the cemetery. Many consider it bad luck to visit a grave twice in the same day, but I care not. I think only of Beatriz. Even so, it will be difficult getting to her grave. Between us is a littered field of headstones, pottery shards and refuse. I move slowly, taking teetering child-like steps. Before I reach Beatriz's grave I fall twice, tear the hem of my skirt, bloody my hands, and rip my shoes.

But I forget all this when I see the mound under which my sister lies. I kneel beside the freshly turned earth then pull the handkerchief from my pocket and lift it, asking God's blessing before scattering the seeds over the mound. Now, instead of a tangle of weeds, my gentle Beatriz will lie beneath a blanket of lavender.

After tucking the empty handkerchief in my skirt, I place my hands on the frayed neckline of my bodice and rip it. Then a sound—a mix of words and sobs both strange and terrible—fills my mouth as I begin the *Kaddish* of mourning.

Chapter 6

Mama said we must go to the *auto de fe*. The thought of leaving our house today, especially to see that vulgar display, is unbearable, but I did not argue. By the fearful look on Mama's face, I am beginning to understand why Papa burned his *tefillin*. Now, instead of looking forward to the prospect of staying in my room behind closed doors, I must dress in finery; I, who am as shattered as the pottery that pierced my feet last night. And amid the velvet and brocade swirls my fear that in addition to destroying his *tefillin*, Papa has also destroyed his prayer book and *Tanakh*.

The bells have just chimed Tierce, and my hair is braided and hidden beneath a netted halo-headdress. But I resist putting on my farthingale and red undergown and grey velvet dress with dagged sleeves, the longer to keep my pained feet soaking in a basin of hot water.

"Come, Isabel, do not tarry," Mama's voice sputters through my partially open bedroom door. I dry my feet, then wrap them in strips of cloth to protect the torn and tender skin. Then I put on my red hose and red velvet shoes, and finally my dress. And before Mama can call me again, I am in the hall.

It is plain, by the look on Mama's face as well as Papa's, that they take little pleasure in this outing. But like yoked oxen to a plow, we are driven by the hand of the Inquisition, and there is little to be done except walk the rut.

༄

Mama, Papa and I stand in the Plaza Mayor beneath the vaulted walls of The Church of the Savior. There is little room to maneuver, for we are a sea of people all here to witness what our priests call "a necessary tool." Even the window seats in the buildings surrounding the Plaza are filled. Many have been sold at a good price to others who desire a comfortable view. For the enterprising, money can be made even from an *auto de fe*.

The Tribunal likes its *auto de fes* to fall on holidays in order to ensure large crowds. Today is not a holiday. Still, the people have come, and some, like us, wear fine clothes as though attending a grand festival. I despise the hypocrisy. It would be better if we were in sackcloth and ashes.

We all form a large semi-circle around two wooden platforms that stand in the center of the Plaza. On one platform is the cloth standard of the Inquisition, picturing a green cross, an olive branch and a sword. The standard is veiled now by a black cloth, and was carried to its place of honor yesterday while we were burying Beatriz. All night, monks and soldiers have guarded it. On the second platform stands the civil executioner. Since the Church has no authority to execute anyone, condemned heretics must be handed over to the secular arm. It is on this platform that the prisoners will stand.

Papa has secured us a place in front, the better to be seen by the Inquisition's spies. Perhaps one will report what good Christians we are. And though it is easy to understand why Papa has forced us to come, it makes me burn with shame. My feelings are irrational. But how can you control emotions that are as raw as the entrails of the dead pig Mama ordered from the butcher this morning?

We have never had pork in our house, though many crypto-Jews make a practice of keeping a few pigs for show. But I am deeply offended and sickened by the thought, and do not understand the extreme turn my parents have made. What good can come of all this?

The sun climbs higher, striking the whitewashed walls of the church, and I think of how Seville, this gleaming whitewashed city, has soiled herself by erecting platforms of shame.

As the bells chime Sext I see the White Cross—pieces of which will be used on the pyres—being carried at the head of a long procession that winds slowly towards us. Behind the cross are the clergy; behind them, the prisoners who walk barefoot and carry extinguished candles.

The crowd becomes restless. Obscenities are hurled, like spears, as the prisoners pass. A woman spits at one of the barefooted figures, but her spittle falls short and lands on a little boy instead. Two rotten eggs hit the first prisoner in the face. Several more land on the others.

There are three prisoners today, and I know each one, though not well. They wear tall pointed caps, and over their clothes, *sanbenitos*—large tunics resembling a scapula which covers most of their bodies, and bears their name.

Two—both women—wear black *sanbenitos* with pictures of red flames licking upward; a reminder to all heretics of hell's awaiting agonies. Their red caps and *sanbenitos* tell us the women will be "relaxed" to the secular arm.

The third prisoner, a man who has been "reconciled," wears a yellow *sanbenito* with a picture of two red crosses and upside down flames, indicating he has been spared burning at the stake. The man will wear his *sanbenito* until his sentence is served, removing it only in his house. And when his sentence is finally completed his *sanbenito* will hang in the church, next to the other *sanbenitos* of those "relaxed" and "reconciled" so that all can remember his sins.

Now, Fray Alonso takes his place on the platform near the veiled Green Cross. He is followed by the second inquisitor. Then come the canons, municipal authorities, nobility—of which Don Sebastian and his father are numbered—and last of all, the clergy—robed and looking like a flock of blackbirds.

As the priest delivers his sermon extolling the faith and denouncing heresy, both Señor Villarreal and Don Sebastian appear greatly agitated. From this distance it is difficult to discern the reason, though it is clear Señor Villarreal clutches his son by the arm. More than one head has turned to stare.

The priest exhorts the two condemned prisoners to repent and receive the Eucharist before it is too late. If confession and repentance come, they will not be burned alive, but garroted first by a metal collar.

Suddenly, one of the women screams "I want to confess! I want to confess!" She is Constanza Gomez, a seamstress. She once made Beatriz a gold velvet gown for Purim. "I repent!" she cries. "I desire only to be a true daughter of Holy Mother Church." She is at once removed and taken beneath the platform where her confession will be recorded.

This takes some time, and while we wait I notice that Mama, who is next to me, has suddenly whitened. "May the Merciful One seal his mouth!"

I look and see Don Sebastian, more agitated than ever, pointing to Fray Alonso. Whatever his words, they cause a stir because Señor Villarreal tries to pull his son off the platform. The other nobles and some of the clergy put their heads together and whisper. And Fray Alonso suddenly looks fierce.

My heart lurches, for I finally understand. Yesterday, after the burial meal, Papa took Don Sebastian and Señor Villarreal into his study, and told all. Don Sebastian is rash, even more so than I, and wild. I fear for his safety, for if he loses control of his mouth and accuses Fray Alonso in public, even his exalted status may not be enough to save him.

Constanza Gomez finally returns to the platform, and a momentary calm descends as her statement is read. She has confessed to Judaizing. Her sins are eating unleavened bread and observing the Sabbath by cleaning her house, lighting Sabbath candles, eating Sabbath stews and wearing clean clothes. In her statement she repents and announces her desire to become a sincere Christian. Then Constanza's candle is lit, and the monks chant the *Veni Creator* while a priest removes the black veil in order to expose the glory and triumph of the Green Cross. All around us people clap and cheer.

When it is finally quiet, each prisoner is made to step forward while his sentence is read. The woman who has refused to confess is old, with a small stooped body that seems to list, like a leaking ship, to one side. Her charges of Judaizing consist of possessing a Jewish prayer book, never making the sign of the cross as other good Christians do, burying her husband in one day as is the Jewish manner, sitting on the floor during the burial meal, purging her meat, and finally, when baking bread, pinching off a piece of dough to throw into the fire as a tithe.

She straightens, as much as she seems able, while the charges are read. There is a defiant tilt of her head as she stands silent, neither recanting nor begging for mercy, and I think of all the prophets of Israel who stood up to kings and tyrants through the ages. And I am proud. But I am also sad, for she will go to her death not knowing her loving Messiah and Savior. And for the first time I wonder at the Catholic Kings. I have long viewed the Inquisition as evil but was it . . . could it be possible that true zeal, and not a quest for more power and wealth, as many have charged, is what stirred the hearts of our Kings to create this terrible tribunal? Could it be, at least in part, that they, too, were saddened when faced with the prospect that some of their people would die without knowing Jesus? And could their stated fear that Judaizers, if not stopped, would lead many down the path to hell, be actually sincere?

I hear Fray Alonso's voice declare the old woman a heretic, and to have incurred the sentence of anathema, that all her goods would be confiscated dating to the time her heresies began, and that her descendants, now and ever more, would be excluded from public honors and office, and I find the declaration a pale substitute for true zealousness for God.

Next, the man steps forward and is charged with Judaizing for refusing to eat pork which he claimed, in a previous declaration, upset his bodily humors. He is also charged with swaying back and forth in the Jewish manner while praying. He loudly recants his heresy, then ends with an oath to never repeat his sins. Everyone bursts into the

Miserere Mei, then prayers are said, followed by more singing. And finally, Fray Alonso grants the "reconciled" man absolution, and hands the two women over to the civil executioner.

The plaza empties as most of the crowd follows the prisoners and police. Fray Alonso, as befitting his rank, has left his platform first, followed by the second inquisitor who is of equal rank though never appears so. And now the remaining assortment of dignitaries begins to thin. Mama indicates her desire to leave by tugging at my arm, but I do not move. I am watching Señor Villarreal and another nobleman half drag, half pull Don Sebastian off the platform as he points to Fray Alonso's back and, in a loud voice, shouts, "Murderer! Murderer!"

For two days I have been allowed my solitude, staying mostly in my room while Mama runs the house and I stitch myself together. And since my fragile emotions appear no better for my solitude, I have decided to show Mama the same kindness. I will see to the house for the next several days and allow her to keep to her bed. I am on my way to tell Mama this when I hear her and Papa and Señor Villarreal talking in Papa's study. It would be the most natural thing for me to join them. But nothing seems natural now. And of late I have not been welcome in their circle or confidant to their secrets. So I tiptoe rather than walk to the door.

"And you have placed him under guard, your own son?" Mama's voice indicates she is horrified.

"What was I to do? He behaves like a madman, drinking all day and shouting Fray Alonso's name. I had to lock him away when I discovered he was conspiring, along with some of our knights, to *assassinate* Fray Alonso."

"He cannot be serious." Again Mama sounds horrified.

"He babbles about how twenty years ago the *conversos* of Seville secretly recruited a militia when they thought the Old Christians were plotting to attack them. He says the *conversos* were feared then, and he will make them feared again. He wants to raise an army not only to kill the inquisitors but to destroy the Inquisition."

"If this gets out it will be disastrous," Papa says.

"It may already be too late. He spoke rashly at the *auto de fe,* and some of our enemies heard."

"What can be done?" Papa again.

"I have ordered my son be given no more wine in hopes of restoring his wits. He is sick with grief over the loss of Beatriz, and that, coupled with the wine has made him foolish. Also, I have sent spies to see what damage has been done, and if it is repairable."

I tiptoe away, burdened by the news. Was Don Sebastian so anxious to join Beatriz he would actually try to assassinate Fray Alonso? It was unthinkable. Even if he succeeded he would be no better off than a wild boar, hunted down without mercy. I return to the solitude and safety of my room. Aunt Leonora, may her memory be for blessing, always said trouble was like a grape. It came in clusters. If that was so, *what else would happen?*

It is not long before the answer comes. Just as the bells chime Sext and we—Mama, Papa, Señor Villarreal and I—sit down to our noon meal, there is a knock on the door. Since I have the keys, I rise to open it. My mouth goes dry when I see the policeman holding a summons. And without reading it I know I have been called to the Holy House.

I sit on a small bench facing a long wooden table that is several feet away. My bench is in the center of the room. It has no backrest. Already, I grow weary from sitting erect but try not to show it. Instead, I calmly rest my hands on my lap. On the wall behind the large table hangs a crucifix as tall as a ship's mast. It gives me comfort. Not like the rest of the room with its walls covered in dark heavy wood, overlaid by large wooden archways and columns. The size of the room and the great vaulted ceiling makes me feel small and insignificant. The effect, no doubt, is calculated.

Fray Alonso sits in a tufted high-back chair at the end of the long table. He does not face me directly. His fingers, which look like fat spider-legs, crawl over the open parchment before him. His other hand, looking soft as lard, lies idly next to a well-seasoned quill. He is wide of girth and flabby of face. Mama always said Seville's inquisitors grew fat on *conversos*. After all, did not inquisitors receive seventy-five pounds of sugar every major festival? And who paid for that if not the *conversos* whose property was confiscated by the Inquisition? And what of those appetites too shameful to mention? Did not the daughters of *conversos* satisfy those as well?

For some reason, Fray Alonso's fingers absorb my interest. They are ink stained beneath the nails and around the cuticles, and I cannot stop thinking that these dirty, insect-like fingers have touched my beautiful Beatriz. The thought gnaws me until, God forgive me, I envision myself cutting them off, one by one. And at once I understand two things: Don Sebastian's need to do physical harm, and the low estate to which revenge can bring a person.

"Your sister claimed that both she and you were schooled in the classics. That you know how to read and write not only our language, but Latin and Hebrew as well."

The question puzzles me, for I cannot see its reason. And my answer, "Yes," does not please him, but makes his brow turn down and his double chin quiver.

"And your mother is so educated?" His voice is harsher now.

I nod, feeling increasingly uncomfortable, for I begin to see where he is headed. Jewish women were more learned than the average Castilian woman. And this has been the cause of much jealousy in the past.

"History proves your race to be an arrogant one." Fray Alonso taps his fingers on the table. "After the great riots years ago, Queen Catherine wanted to confine your people to ghettos and force them to wear a red circle on their clothing." He chuckles. "A good way to mark all defectives. Pity she did not follow through. It would have kept your people in their place. Kept you from thinking too highly of yourselves."

I sit quietly, not knowing what to say, and not wishing to antagonize him by saying something rash, all the while hoping I look small and frail in his eyes. And for once, my contrary nature shrivels like a beaten dog and slinks somewhere deep inside me.

Fray Alonso folds his filthy fingers beneath his chin and looks at me so brazenly that if the secretary—who sits at the other end of the table taking notes on his writing board—were not in the room, I would be exceedingly afraid.

"So . . . with all this ability, I assume you have studied and read many Jewish writings. Perhaps even studied the rabbis?"

"I read the Psalms, Your Excellency."

"And?"

"And Cardinal Juan de Torquemada's book, *Meditation.*"

Fray Alonso squints at me so long I fear he does not believe me, or worse, that he thinks I mock him. "It would be better if you read nothing at all," he finally says.

"God has given me a brain. Is it sinful to use it?"

"*Yes* . . . if that brain is used for the destruction of the gospel. If it is used to Judaize and lead others astray. If it is used to destroy Holy Mother Church."

I am stunned by his vehemence. "I have no such intent. I am a sincere Christian. Besides, how can a mere woman like me destroy the Church? How can one person destroy what God has built?"

My questions seem to please him, for he settles back in his chair. Fingering his parchment, he stares at me for what seems an eternity, and when I finally blush, he reaches over to a nearby trencher on which sit two plump poached quinces, and plucks off the fattest.

Quinces from Toledo are the most prized, and though I cannot be sure the quince—which is now between Fray Alonso's teeth—is from that locale, I suspect it is, for Fray Alonso does not appear to be a man who denies himself anything or settles for less than what he can have.

"Do you believe Jews should be punished for killing Christ?" he finally says, after bolting down the fruit.

The question is a pit into which he hopes I fall. But gathering my courage like a gleaner gathers scattered grain, I answer, "Christ said no man takes his life from him. He said he lays it down himself." Never before have I seen such hatred. It smolders and boils and flames his eyes.

"You are a handsome woman, though not as beautiful as your sister." The eyes have become slits through which pulsates a heat I can almost feel. "It would be a pity if you, with your soft, lovely flesh, would have to be burned at the stake." And then he signals his secretary—who is calmly dipping a quill into an ox-horn inkwell—that the interrogation is over.

I leave the Castle of Triana, now called the Holy House, the headquarters of Seville's Inquisitional Tribunal, and exit the gate. No charges have been made. I need only to appear again for questioning next week. Though I well know the danger ahead, I feel strangely calm and hurry home to share the news.

When Mama opens the door, she enfolds me in her arms without saying a word, and holds me fast as she weeps at my neck. Afterward, she pulls me down the hall, telling me with her eyes, and by pressing a finger to her lips, to remain silent until we reach Papa's study, where he sits, looking shorter than usual, behind his table.

She makes me take the best chair, then asks what happened. I relay the events of the morning, leaving out my feelings of fear and revenge. They listen, without saying a word, until I finish.

"May the Lord smite that evil man!" Mama presses her palms together as though praying.

Papa's face is ashen as he rests his elbows on his table. "Mama said it was cruel to keep you at a distance and not let you know what was going on. But it was needful, Isabel. We have learned much from our spies, and it is not good news. We have kept it, and our plans, from you because you cannot confess what you do not know. Fray Alonso appears bent on harming you. Perhaps he wishes to harm us all. Whatever his intent, we must keep you in the dark a while longer for your safety. But trust us, Isabel, we think only of your good."

Mama's red, puffy eyes tell me she has been crying far longer than when she greeted me at the door, and Papa's strained appearance makes him look like an old man. How could I have misunderstood? How could I have been so childish that all I saw was my own pain? Their silence, their sending me away to the house by the groves, their not observing *Shavuot* or *Tisha B'Av*, Papa burning his *tefillin*, the butchered pig, our going to the *auto de fe*, were all for my benefit, so that I might be kept safe. How could I have been so resentful? Whatever they know, whatever their spies have told them, frightens them, and they have born it alone and without my help or even my gratitude.

And I feel so ashamed.

Fray Alonso looks especially sour today, and his acid appearance makes me squirm on the small bench. At one end of the long table the secretary busily scrapes his vellum parchment with a razor, and I wonder why he does not use the new, cheaper rag paper for his notes. But the secretary is quickly forgotten when Fray Alonso snaps, "Tell me about your great grandparents."

Of what interest can this be to him? "They died in Tunisia, at least my great-grandparents on Mama's side."

"Ah, Tunisia. And why were they there?"

My heart beats faster as I begin to see what he is after. "Because they left Castile, Your Excellency."

The Fray leans over the table. "You mean they left rather than *convert* during the riot and great conversion?"

"Yes," I say softly. Mama has often told me that many of her relatives perished during those pogroms and how others, including her great-grandparents, left Spain rather than convert. But what did that have to do with me?

"So your family spurned the Church when they were given the opportunity to come into its fold?"

"They were beaten and robbed and told they would be killed if they did not submit to baptism. Because of this, they chose to leave Spain. I would call it a tragedy rather than an opportunity." I know I have answered foolishly, but revulsion, not fear, overwhelms me.

Fray Alonso's eyes narrow. "If that is your view, why did you and your parents not leave during the last riot or during the more recent Expulsion?"

I swallow what feels like a rock in my throat. I know why Mama and Papa stayed; it was because they wished to keep their vast fortune intact. A portion of Papa's money went to support relatives who had fallen on hard times since the Expulsion, and another portion went to the scattered Jewish communities at large. Jews in Seville and Cordoba were expelled nine years before the other Jews of Spain. Vineyards were sold for cloth, a home for a mule. Those who had wealth were forbidden to take it out of the country in the form of gold or silver. Only bills of exchange, negotiated with bankers, were permissible. And on the way to Portugal, Turkey, or other lands, many Jews were killed along highways, and gutted by thieves who believed they had swallowed gems or gold. Oh, yes, I understand why they stayed. But can I tell Fray Alonso? No. Not if I wanted my family to remain alive.

"*Well?* Why did you not leave during the Expulsion?"

"It is as I said. I am a sincere Christian. Why would I want to leave Castile?"

Fray Alonso leans back, probing me with his eyes. "It is obvious you are not your sister. She was . . . soft, delicate, like the petal of a flower. While you are more like an almond." He smiles as though pleased with his imagery. "Yes, you are like an almond, an *unshelled* almond. Perhaps next visit I will take you to the dungeon and let you see how we deal with the vain and the uncooperative. Perhaps next visit, we can begin peeling that shell."

Beatriz told me of her trip to the dungeon, where Fray Alonso took her just before her release so she could see what would happen "if she spread false rumors." It was there that Fray Alonso told her any attack on him would be considered an attack on the Inquisition itself. And she described to me the woman she saw tied to a scaffold, her head lower than her body, her face covered with a cloth; then of the pitcher of water poured into her mouth, forcing the cloth into her throat and creating a sensation of drowning. But it was Doctor Hernando Diaz who told me long ago, after a young boy drowned in the Guadalquivir River, how sometimes the inquisitors try to extract a confession by making a person feel like he was drowning. Doctor Diaz ended by assuring me that before anyone could be tortured at the Holy House unanimous consent of the Inquisitorial Committee was required. It is only this knowledge that now keeps me from retching with fear.

When I return home, Mama is as gray as the ashes in a brazier. And this time she does not enfold me in her arms, but pulls me, with trembling hand, to Papa's study. And Papa does not sit behind his desk, but sits in a small cushioned chair. Two empty chairs surround his, and Mama points to one. I sit down while she closes the door. Then she takes her seat. Our chairs are so close we can talk in whispers, and surely that is the purpose, for plainly Mama and Papa do not wish to be overheard.

Mama asks what happened at the Holy House, and when I tell her she seems distracted. I race through my story, and when finished, Papa is the first to speak. "It has been decided you must be sent away to safety."

I nod, for there is soundness in this. "I will pack and leave for the groves at once." When Mama begins to cry, my heart jumps. "Where then? Where would you have me go?"

"Fray Alonso will *never* stop." Mama wipes her face with a handkerchief then covers my hand with hers. Blue worm-like veins bulge beneath her wrinkled skin. It is a large hand that has wiped tears, braided hair, and tended wounds. But it was not large enough to save Beatriz from Fray Alonso and the power of the Inquisition. Nor is it large enough to save me. "No, Fray Alonso will not rest until he gets what he wants. And he has the full power of the Inquisition to do it. Must I bury another daughter?"

My heart beats like the wings of a tern as I think of where I will be sent. To my brothers in Hamburg? Or Kiev?

"Señor Villarreal has learned Fray Alonso plans to arrest his son." Papa wrings his hands. His head droops downward as though wishing to avoid my eyes. "Don Sebastian is in grave danger. Will two families be destroyed? Shall we be led like lambs to the slaughter and do nothing?" When he lifts his head, there are tears in his eyes. "I cannot allow it, Isabel. I cannot allow you to be shattered like your sister. Arrangements have been made. You will marry Don Sebastian, and the two of you will leave Spain."

Marry Don Sebastian? How can I marry him? It would be indecent to marry anyone before the full year of mourning Beatriz's death was over. But Papa's face is set, telling me he considers this tradition inconsequential in the face of our larger problems. "Is . . . there no other way, nothing else to be done?"

Papa shakes his head, and Mama weeps softly into her hands.

"Then, where will we go?"

"You will go to the new Spanish settlement in the Indies, to La Navidad with Christopher Columbus. Señor Villarreal has learned from his son, Antonio, that though La Navidad is not large—since only thirty-nine men were left to build a fortress out of the wreckage of the *Santa Maria*—Columbus's plans are much grander. It is said that the Admiral will pattern the Indies after the Spanish enterprises in the Canaries with large land grants going to influential families. There he will create trading houses to control all commerce between Spain and the Indies. And you and Don Sebastian, as Villarreals, will eventually have your share in it.

"Even now, Columbus's seventeen ships are nearly ready, and wait in the harbor at Cadiz. Everyday, volunteers are turned away, so eager are men of consequence and vision to go on this voyage. Señor Villarreal and I have paid a small fortune to secure both your passage and Sebastian's. And you will be well protected. Antonio assures his father that hundreds of soldiers will accompany the ships, *hidalgos* among them, and at least twenty *Lanzas* from Granada. And it will not be as uncivilized as you might imagine. At least two physicians will go, as well as carpenters, potters, stonemasons, blacksmiths, and others necessary to build a fine settlement."

"But it is still Spanish territory, Papa."

"Yes, but with a vast Ocean Sea to separate it from the Inquisition, a vast Ocean Sea to separate Fray Alonso from *you*. And should he ever find out where you are, he will be powerless to hurt you, not without formal charges, and those he cannot issue unless two credible witnesses testify against you. There will be no time to erect Holy Houses and Tribunals in this new land. Everyone will be too busy building trade routes and plucking fistfuls of gold from the ground. You will be safe there. It will be a good place for you and Don Sebastian to begin a new life, free from the sorrows of this one."

"Would it not be easier for me to go to my brothers?"

"You cannot travel alone. You must have the protection of a husband. You must marry. And as long as Don Sebastian can make his way back to Seville, neither one of you will be safe."

Mama dabs her eyes with a handkerchief. "Señor Villarreal believes if his son stays on the continent he will, sooner or later, return to Seville and make good his threat to kill Fray Alonso. You know how rash he is! Only the space of an Ocean Sea can prevent him from doing this. Only an Ocean Sea can keep him from his foolish notions of revenge."

"Then I must leave for Don Sebastian's sake?"

Papa sighs. "It is the plan Señor Villarreal and I think best, for both of you. Would I send you so far, otherwise?" He rises to his feet as though unable to sit any longer. Beads of perspiration dot his forehead. "These are difficult times. Trouble spreads everywhere. Jews are no longer welcome in many countries. And even *conversos* are treated badly. Who knows about Kiev or Hamburg, which way they will go? Already there are many in Hamburg who dislike our people. I do not want to pull you from one brazier only to put you into another. Your future lies in the Indies, Isabel. And so does Don Sebastian's."

"You did not mention women, Papa." My voice sounds small in my ears. "Will there be other women?"

Papa wrings his hands. "I . . . believe not for the Sovereigns have failed to encourage women to go on this voyage."

My mouth drops, and in spite of myself my lip quivers.

"It is not as bad as you imagine," Mama adds. "Gonzalo Vivar and his entire household, including his wife, will go with you to help you build a new life. Maria will be a great comfort. Solicit her aid at every opportunity. I am sure . . . yes, quite sure that . . . all will be well with you."

But Mama's face betrays her, for her eyes tear, and worry lines crease her forehead. I make no effort to hide my feelings, either. I am stunned and angry over these odious plans. I have seen the Indians Columbus paraded through the streets of Seville, their painted, half-naked bodies, the wood carvings and parrots and masks of gold—heathen, all. I take no comfort in knowing the Vivars will accompany me. And though Papa relies heavily on Gonzalo and will sorely miss him, and though this kindness to me has and will continue to cost him a great deal, I take no pity on my father.

"How is that possible? How were you able to convince Gonzalo to go?" I finally ask.

"I convinced him by promising to pay him more than he could make in three lifetimes." Papa's breath comes out as a sigh, as if seeing, for the first time, his household and those he loves slowly disappearing like the southern marshes in summer.

I sit in my chair, unable to say another word. And what is there to say, anyway? Deep down I know Mama and Papa are right. I must leave Seville. But these plans they have laid out for me like an embroidered rug, showing me where my feet must travel, is to me an awful penance for sins I did not commit.

For now I must marry a man I do not love and move to a faraway land I have no wish to see. As I sit defeated, my head hanging, Mama rises and presses a sizable leather sack into my palms.

"You must take this with you—a gift from Papa and me. It is not a wedding gift, or a gift for Sebastian, but only for you. You must keep it safely hidden."

Not bothering to glance at the sack, I let it fall to my lap, and feel it is heavy.

"Look inside," Mama says, her mouth pinched as though holding back a sob.

I have no interest in looking, but out of a habit of obedience I comply and untie the string, then pull open the sack's mouth. I expect to see it full of *reales* but see gold *florins* instead, and know that here sits a great fortune. When I try to protest, Mama puts a finger to my lips. "A woman must have some security."

Chapter 7

The last wedding I attended was well before Eastertide when Blanca Nuñez's older sister married a *converso*, a merchant of costly Cordovan leather. It was a most agreeable wedding, and I envisioned my own would be similar, perhaps because we are social equals, though Papa is wealthier.

For the wedding, Señor Nuñez hired an army of servants, including a laundress to wash the linens, several turnspits—to tend the mutton, venison, beef, and chickens on spits—a small company of minstrels who played both the pear-shaped lute and five-stringed viol, and a man to cart away the refuse. An array of fruit—including the costly quince—cheeses, confections, wafers from the wafer maker, and an assortment of spices were paraded out by a regiment of servers, while acrobats and musicians and wine by the barrelful kept the guests cheerful.

The bride, who rode into the courtyard on horseback with her maids trailing on foot, was showered with rose petals and then crowned with a wreath of olive branches—a gentile tradition. Beneath the wreath was a lace cap.

She was dressed in gold brocade trimmed with ermine, and over that she wore a velvet surcoat. On her feet were velvet shoes embroidered with gold thread. She looked nothing short of regal.

My white silk gown pulls tightly across my chest and strains along the shoulders. Mama had to sew an inch of lace to the fabric around my wrists to conceal the fact that the sleeves are too short. She has also added another inch of lace around the hem for the same reason.

79

She has done all she can on such little notice, but the dress still looks ill-fitting, and bears witness to what everyone knows—I wear Beatriz's gown. A short silk veil, held on my head by a thin gold chain, also belongs to Beatriz.

We have assembled not in the great hall but in a small, dimly lit room tucked deep within the bowels of the keep—the most protected part of the Villarreal castle—in consequence of the danger that surrounds us all. Outside, two hundred armed men fortify the grounds.

Though the stone walls of our room are whitewashed and draped with fine tapestries, it is an unpleasant, somber looking chamber. The one consolation is that in the dim light it is difficult to see Don Sebastian's face, thus sparing me from viewing the sorrow and anger that is surely etched there. But even the dim light cannot hide the fact that Sebastian reels to and fro from too much wine. Obviously, he has not followed the custom of a groom fasting before his wedding. I am not offended. I can only imagine how difficult this is for him. Perhaps this explains why Señor Villarreal has allowed him wine, for he must imagine it too. As the bride, I have fasted, but more to please Mama and Papa than anything else.

We are a small group. Only Sebastian and I, Mama and Papa, Señor Villarreal, a *converso* rabbi—the one who read the ninety-first Psalm at Beatriz's grave—and two crypto-Jews unknown to me but who, Mama informed me earlier, will serve as witnesses.

With a heart as heavy as the cannon protruding from Señor Villarreal's redan, I put one velvet-covered foot in front of the other and begin the traditional walk around the groom. While the rabbi recites his blessings, I encircle Sebastian seven times, all the while trying to ignore that he smells like a wine barrel. And when I stop and give him my hand, he staggers and sways so much I consider pulling it away. But too late. He slips the ring on my finger and seals my fate.

For better or worse, I am now Señora Villarreal.

Earlier, Mama explained that after the ceremony we would depart from custom. Instead of my husband and me retiring briefly to our room and then joining everyone in a celebratory meal, we will eat a simple veal and venison stew with our family, the rabbi, and two witnesses, then retire early. The reason is that we must depart well before sunrise to avoid detection.

So we sit at a small table, our solemn band of eight. The table is set with two large baskets of bread, and with a knife and spoon for everyone. A plain silver saltcellar, instead of an elaborate one of gold, sits in front of Señor Villarreal, revealing the low esteem in which he holds this proceeding.

Bowls of stew have already been set out but only the rabbi and two witnesses appear to be eating. No one else seems hungry. Our bowl, Sebastian's and mine, is still full, and sits between us. Carefully, I dip bread and take a bite. Sebastian takes no notice of it or me, but holds his goblet up for the wine steward to see. Within seconds, the steward sends a young servant girl to fill it.

Though I have no appetite, I force myself to eat. Tomorrow, we will leave without breakfast and walk many hours before taking a meal. Perhaps it is a failing, this tendency to always look ahead, for it can create an excessively practical nature. Clearly, Sebastian does not look ahead. He guzzles wine and exhibits not the slightest inclination to eat, which means tomorrow he will be weak and hungry and sick, leaving others to shoulder the burden of his care. But I cannot fault him. This is not the wedding he envisioned, the wedding he has awaited for nine years.

And I am not Beatriz.

Up to now, there has been little conversation. But Papa breaks the silence by lifting his goblet and praying a blessing. The wine steward quickly sends another servant to refill Sebastian's cup, and we all raise our voices in response as though we are the merriest of celebrants. But I catch Mama dabbing her eyes, and see Papa sag, ever so slightly. And even Señor Villarreal looks as though he sits on brass nails, with that pained expression lurking just beneath his smile.

When it suddenly occurs to me that this may be the last meal I will ever have with Mama and Papa, I am overcome with the desire to fly into their arms and weep at their necks and beg them, in a loud voice, to let me stay in Seville. But the sight of Sebastian—slumped over the table barely able to hold his head—stops me. I am married now, and such behavior would be unseemly and bring shame on both my parents and me.

With great effort, I rein myself in and sit quietly, taking small bites of stew with my sop. But from that moment on, my eyes and ears serve as nets to catch Mama and Papa's every move, their every word. Just as Mama stores up vegetables and fruits in pickling jars after harvest, to be tucked away in the larder, so I put things into my memory jars: the sight of Mama's sweet plump face; the way her forehead sinks low over the bridge of her nose when she worries; her generous laughter; her soft warm fingers; her arms that are ever ready to help carry a load or dispense hugs. And Papa: the way he pinches his thumb when he worries; the way he compresses his lips when he is proud of something I have done; the way his smile is crooked on his face but so pleasant it makes you smile too; the way his eyes tell me he loves me even when I have disappointed him.

I watch Mama's hand disappear beneath the table and know she has discreetly taken Papa's, perhaps because the same thought has just occurred to her. She straightens, as if drawing strength from the stout, loving man beside her. The muscles of both their faces tighten as they force a smile, all for my benefit, just as all their actions over the past month have been for my benefit. They sit straight and dignified in their chairs, trying hard to give me, as a gift, this last picture of themselves, a picture of love and courage and strength. I use all my senses to take it in until Papa rises, walks to my place, covers my hand with his, and says in an unsteady voice, "'May the Lord make you like Sarah and Rebecca, like Rachel and Leah. May you be fruitful, favored by your husband, and be blessed with children.'"

And when he is done, I know it is time to say good-bye. And while we— Papa, Mama and I, hug and kiss, Mama slips something around my neck. I look and see it is the emerald necklace that Grandpapa gave her. Before I can protest, she presses her finger to my lips. "The green stone of Zebulun. For success and goodwill." Then I feel Sebastian's unsteady hand tugging on my arm. Though everything within me longs to stay in the tender embrace of my parents, I pull away and reluctantly follow my husband into the gloom of the corridor.

Mama has prepared our room, for it is well lit and clean, and smells of lavender. Sebastian enters first, and I closely behind. We have not spoken a word the entire walk down the corridor, though prayers filled my heart, for I feel in great need of the Holy One's comfort. I can only guess how Sebastian feels.

The bed has been carefully arranged with clean linen and half a dozen pillows. Again, Mama's work. And I wonder if someone will ritually examine the sheets tomorrow for the show of virginal blood. My heart flutters like a breeze-blown leaf. Will my husband find me pleasing? *Husband.* The word makes me tremble. Quietly, I slip out of my gown.

Sebastian has sunk down onto the bed, and tries removing his shoes. He belches once, then twice, then slides, like a child's rag doll, off the bed and onto the floor. He mumbles something before pulling himself up, and when he does he actually looks at me and seems startled to find me standing nearby. He nods as though remembering I am now his wife, but his face remains expressionless.

Out of modesty I do not remove my undergarments until I have gotten into bed and covered myself with sheets, just as Mama instructed. And then I wait. And while I wait I find myself hoping that Sebastian is too drunk to consummate. It is a wicked thought, a selfish thought. Even so, my heart sinks when I see Sebastian, without a stitch of clothing, snuffing out the lamps. When he slips beneath the sheets and lunges for me, I smell anew the odor of wine. I close my eyes as clumsy, wine-stained hands grope and tug. And in the dark I hear only two sounds: the pounding of my own heart and Sebastian's voice whispering over and over and over again, "Beatriz. Beatriz. Beatriz."

Chapter 8

Seville to Cadiz, Spain

The bells chime Lauds as I try to rouse my husband.

"Sebastian," I whisper into the ear of the sleeping man next to me. "You must awake." I shake him gently, then more vigorously, but he remains as motionless as one dead.

Finally, I arise, light a lamp, and wash. Next, I braid my hair; secure it in a hairnet, then dress in my traveling clothes.

Mama thought wool or linen or cotton was best for travel, for they are the cloth of everyday, and would make us less conspicuous. But Sebastian has ordered I wear clothing befitting the wife of a nobleman. So I dress in a skirt and bodice of brown brocade, which Mama has lined with taffeta to protect me against fleas and lice. Over that goes a brown hooded traveling cloak, also lined with taffeta. When I finish dressing, I return to the bed.

"Sebastian, you must get up. Sebastian!" Neither my words nor my vigorous shaking stir him. Without another word, I leave the room.

It is difficult to see in the semi-dark corridor. Only a single lantern, affixed to the wall, guides my steps. But presently I hear voices and see a light streaming from one of the rooms, and head that way. There, two servants struggle to fasten Sebastian's trunks. I am about to ask for assistance, when out of nowhere a man appears, a gentleman knight, by the look of him, for his chest is covered in Brigandine plate armor and a sword is belted to his waist. Though there is a swagger to his walk and a smugness that is displeasing, I decide to enlist his aid.

"Pardon," I say, blocking his way. "Perhaps you can assist me."

The man bows, somewhat irreverently, I think, then introduces himself. "Arias Diaz, Señora Villarreal, at your service."

It is indelicate to ask a stranger for this type of aid, but I know not what else to do so I point down the corridor. "My husband . . . is in need of a kindness."

Arias nods as he studies my traveling clothes, then smiles. Everyone in the castle knows Sebastian drank heavily yesterday. It takes little effort to understand that the bridegroom now lies on his bed in a stupor. "Of course, Señora. Do not distress yourself. I will see to it. Señor Villarreal has anticipated your need." And with that, Arias saunters down the hall.

Four men are needed to lift Sebastian's trunks into the donkey cart. My trunks are managed by two. When the cart is loaded, Arias helps Sebastian into the space left for him, for it is plain to all that Sebastian is unable to make the journey on foot. Señor Villarreal has come to supervise the loading and to see us off. When he gives the order to exchange the donkey for an ox, I am relieved, for no mere donkey could pull such a load. And then Señor Villarreal's hand-picked soldiers, fifty in all, gather in the courtyard, ready to accompany us as far as the old Roman amphitheatre outside Seville.

Out of the corner of my eye, I see Señor Villarreal deposit, what I know to be a sack of coins—for they jingle—into Arias' hands.

"Watch over Sebastian," I hear him say.

And when Señor Villarreal gives the order to strike the ox, my emotions get the better of me and I fly, weeping, into my father-in-law's arms.

Please tell me I do not have to go.

His cheeks are wet, too. He is, after all, losing a son, for when will he see Sebastian again, in this earthly realm, at least? Though the servants all carry lanterns, his expression is obscured, but by his generous hug I sense he feels my compassion, and in turn gives me his. I am the unloved bride of his son. And he has no remedy except to keep me in his prayers, which he whispers quickly in my ear that he will do. Then he pries me from him with the words, "Go with God."

~⊙

Our destination is Cadiz. It would have been easier to sail south, down the Guadalquivir River past San Lucar and the Guadalquivir estuary to Cadiz, but with Fray Alonso's spies everywhere, it is too risky. So we are forced to go on foot, stopping first at the ruins of the Roman amphitheater in Italica where we will be joined by the Vivar family.

Though Mama dislikes anything pagan, Beartiz and I did manage just once, after much pleading, to get Papa to take us to the amphitheater. It was the year my sister and I learned that the Roman Emperor, Hadrian, was born in Italica; the same Hadrian who tried to build the pagan city of Aelia Capitolina over the ruins of Holy Jerusalem.

I think of that visit now as I trudge silently behind the ox-cart, barely able to see where my foot falls. And after some time, the sound of the cart wheels becomes louder as dirt gives way to the remnants of smooth paving-stones, telling me we are on the tree-lined road that Hadrian built.

Somewhere alongside this road is a milestone with the inscription *Hadrianus Augustus fecit*. I threw pebbles at it when I was here last—a childish gesture, but I did it because this awful place made Beatriz cry. She cried when she saw the arena where gladiators fought and died, and where animals were hoisted by an underground elevator to be slaughtered in sport. But I did not cry. I had seen too many *auto de fes*. And who ever wept over an animal? Did not all Seville love the bullfights where the sons of nobles went to prove their courage and prowess? The fine animals destroyed there are hardly given a thought.

But later that day I felt anger when Papa took us to the ruined houses of the people who frequented the amphitheater—ruins that were covered in beautiful mosaics of fish, palm trees and birds. And there it was, the contrast: beauty and ugliness, cruelty and gentleness, side by side, just as it has existed for centuries, and just as it exists even now. And as I listen to the rattling of the cart, I marvel that *this* is the world God so loved. *This* is the world to which He sent His only Son.

I am still marveling when Arias Diaz gives the order to stop. As the cart slows, I see moving shadows, and realize Gonzalo Vivar and his family have stepped out from behind the ruins. Though it is difficult to see, I know that it is Maria Vivar who takes her place beside me.

What a comfort to have a woman so near! My hand reaches for hers, and finding it, I give it a squeeze. Proper etiquette has been violated. It is unseemly to show such affection to a servant, especially a servant one hardly knows. She responds by a squeeze of her own, making me understand that though she is more than twice my age, she is as frightened as I.

The clanking of pots breaks the silence as the Vivar men quickly redistribute their possessions, possessions which they carry in large sacks, and sling over their shoulders. Then Arias gives the order to move out, and I release Maria's hand but not before feeling that a bond has been forged between us.

We have walked for hours, and my traveling clothes have begun to feel as heavy as mail. The sun beats relentlessly. Perspiration wets my face, my neck, my under arms, and we have yet to encounter the full heat of the day.

Sebastian snores loudly in the rattling ox-cart and I feel ashamed. The fifty soldiers who accompanied us to the amphitheater have long departed. And it is daylight. We are now easy targets for the many bandits known to pillage along this road, and it is unseemly for an able-bodied man to avoid his responsibility of providing protection. I only pray we encounter pilgrims for there is safety in numbers.

"You must be hungry, Doña Isabel." Maria touches my shoulder. "And tired. Perhaps we should stop." She points to the small sack on her back. "I have made *empanadas*."

I look at the sack and know that Maria, being an Old Christian, has not purged her meat like Mama. And surely her pastry contains pork fat. But I am a sincere convert now and such things as laws of ritual purity should not concern me.

Still . . . it pricks.

I smile and nod, even though when we arrived at Dos Hermanas I had planned to distribute the *empanadas* Señor Villarreal has provided. But how can I disappoint Maria? Her face is so full of sweetness and a desire to please. And I *am* hungry. So I signal Arias Diaz and instantly he is by my side.

"How may I serve you, Doña Isabel?" His words hang in midair like droplets of oil; his small black eyes, like those of a hawk, search my face to determine my pleasure.

"This is a good place to stop." I gesture with my hand. Several trees stand nearby, trees large enough to provide shade from the fierce sun. And trees in this area are scarce. For miles we have passed nothing but marshes and flat planes full of grazing sheep and horses, though in the distance date and pomegranate orchards could be seen. "It is a good place to eat and rest."

"Indeed! An excellent place, Señora." Arias Diaz bows slightly. "I will see to it at once."

And within minutes, we are all sitting on blankets shaded by a large spreading pine and eating Maria's tasty *empanadas*—folded pastries filled with all manner of good things. Mine is stuffed with lamb and raisins, and seasoned with cardamom and fenugreek. I have already taken an *empanada* of eggs and almonds with saffron, cinnamon and sugar to my husband, for I remembered Beatriz telling me of his fondness for sugar and eggs. But I was unable to rouse him, and so I left it, wrapped in coarse homespun, by his side.

Happily, Enrique sits off by himself. It is curious, but since joining us at the amphitheater he has kept his distance and seems uninterested in my activities. It is a relief. I can only attribute this to my married state, or more accurately, my marriage to a *Villarreal*. Surely, now, Enrique will cease to be an irritation.

"The *empanada* is delicious," I say.

Maria smiles. "You are most gracious, Doña Isabel."

When I lean closer and whisper, "Please call me Isabel," I see a horrified look on her face.

Old Christians never use the respectful term "Don" or "Doña" when addressing a Jew. These terms were reserved for Old Christians of nobility or those of great distinction such as Admiral Columbus who was granted the honor of being called "Don" by Queen Isabel herself. The term might be used to venerate an already exalted *converso* such as Señor Villarreal, but hardly for an ordinary one, even one who is a wealthy merchant. I cannot say why Maria and her entire family feel the need to violate this tradition. Perhaps it is years of working for my father. Or perhaps it is because they are simple peasants unused to the etiquette of noble society, but we are embarking on a different life now where I foresee few allies, and even fewer friends.

"Please call me Isabel," I repeat. "It would please me greatly." And when the look of horror disappears, and Maria covers her mouth and giggles, I know it pleases her, too.

"But only when we are alone," she hastily adds.

❧

The first person to greet us as we enter Dos Hermanas is an elderly man, neatly dressed in patched clothing, carrying a leather flagon and cup. The ox-cart rattles to a halt, and we all watch and wait as the man pulls the hemp stopper from the flagon, pours a bit of its contents into the cup, and offers it to Arias, who has, without being asked, made himself appear as the head of our expedition.

Arias gladly sips from the cup for we all know the man is a wine crier, hired by the local tavern to cry the wine to passersby, offering them samples as inducement to further partake at his master's table.

Arias drains the cup, then wipes his lips with the back of one hand. "By Saint Peter's beard, this is good! A Pierrefitte I wager." The wine crier smiles. "Come take us to your tavern that we may wash the dust from our throats." And with that, Arias slaps the wine crier on the shoulder then allows him to lead us all, like sheep, to the end of a narrow side street. The ox-cart pulls to a stop in front of a structure whose partially fallen bricks reveal that the walls beneath are made of rammed earth, so common in this area. Over the door, tacked to several bricks whose days also seemed numbered, is a sign, *Posada*, indicating that behind the tavern is an inn for sleeping.

Arias roughly prods Sebastian before half-lifting, half-dragging him from the ox-cart. Then he deposits my husband on the ground, draping his upper body over the side of the cart to keep him from falling.

"Come, Don Sebastian, you must fortify yourself," Arias says.

When I lean over the cart and pick up the uneaten sugar and egg *empanada* and try to hand it to Sebastian, Arias shakes his head. "The condition of his stomach is much too delicate, Señora. Better a cup or two of Pierrefitte."

My fingers curl around Sebastian's arm in stubborn resistance, holding him in place. In the other hand I show him the wrapped *empanada*. "Is it wise, my husband, to drink on an empty stomach? Perhaps just a little of this will do you good."

When Sebastian looks at me through swollen eyes, it is as though he is seeing a stranger. I could be anyone, Maria Vivar even. But he is polite. "You are kind, but Arias is right. A little wine would be better, I think." And with that Sebastian, aided by Arias, stumbles into the tavern.

The two cart drivers scramble behind them, followed by Gonzolo and his sons, all eager to take their place at one of the rough-hewed tables and wash their throats. But I remain outside. Papa's business associates always complained about the filthy conditions of our taverns and inns, calling them worse than pigsties. And they talked of the ever present prostitutes, many of whom were just laundresses or servant girls looking for extra money. And on more than one occasion, they have filled my head with stories of robbers and cutthroats who, they claim, roam these establishments as freely as the lice. And now my husband has entered such a place.

"Will you not go in, Isabel?" Maria asks.

I shake my head.

"A wise wife aids her husband. Even if that aid is unwelcome."

"I . . . know not how to help him."

"Then you must pray for wisdom." Maria pulls me gently by the arm into the tavern.

The large room is poorly lit. The corners and one wall are completely obscured by shadows where men sit whispering and drinking from clay goblets. Sebastian, with Arias at his side, is already lounging at a long table in the center of the room. Sounds, like dry bones rattling across a tabletop, fill the stale air. When my eyes grow accustomed to the poor lighting I see dice being flung about, first by Arias, then Sebastian, then by three roguish-looking men who sit with them. Papa's business associates have often spoken of sharpers, those who frequent taverns using crooked dice, and how even the dice makers' guild, with all its laws, has been unable to stop them.

Maria grabs my arm when I head for Sebastian, and pulls me to a small table nestled against the shadowed wall. Reluctantly, I sit, then watch in horror as Sebastian takes his bag of coins and plops it on the tabletop. Arias waves to the tavern keeper to refill the goblets that already sit by their elbows. A slender servant girl appears from nowhere and pours wine, though I doubt it is the expensive Pierrefitte Arias praised so highly on the road. The girl lingers beside Sebastian, or rather his large leather pouch. Her bodice is loosely secured, making me wonder if she is not looking to ply another trade. But all eyes are riveted on the dice as they bounce across the table, and finally realizing she has little chance of gaining anyone's attention, she saunters over to us.

"Wine, Señoras?"

Maria looks hesitant, and since I suspect she is worried about spending money unnecessarily, I decide to pay for us both. "Two Marlys, please."

"We do not carry Marly."

"You carry Pierrefitte, but not Marly?"

"Who said we carry Pierrefitte?" She puts one hand on her hip as she rests her pitcher on the table. "We carry no French wines here." There is derision on her face. "We serve only local ones, and some sherry from Jerez."

"Then we will each take a cup of your local wine."

The tavern maid leaves laughing, as though enjoying a secret joke, and returns moments later with two goblets filled with, I am soon to discover, one of the most delicious wines I have ever tasted.

It feels good to sit, and I stretch my legs beneath the table. But this attitude of rest is short lived, for Arias continues to encourage Sebastian to increase his wager at every throw of the dice. And in response, Sebastian tosses out gold *florins* as if they were copper *blancas*.

I realize then and there that I will never make Sebastian a proper wife, for I possess neither Beatriz's sweet indulgent nature nor her detachment from worldly things. I am far too practical, and my business head screams silently at the careless squandering I see before me. Only great effort keeps me from rushing to the table and pleading with Sebastian to leave. Though such behavior would be unseemly and would surely embarrass my husband, these considerations are not what stop me. Rather, it is my love for Beatriz. I have married her beloved. And she would not wish me to be a cold and disrespectful wife, or heap abuse upon Sebastian's head, no matter what his failings.

My own bag of gold *florins* is safely hidden on my person. Did Mama know of Sebastian's carelessness with money? Is that why she gave me this great sum, as means of protecting myself? And for the first time I am truly grateful for her gift.

"The world is not always kind to women," Maria says, as though reading my thoughts. "And men do not always understand our need for security."

I watch Sebastian guzzle wine and fling more gold coins across the table.

"A woman . . . I know, of low birth and no skills, was forced, after the sudden death of her husband, to work as a prostitute in order to care for her young children." Maria's face is tight; her eyes study me. "People say unkind things about her, but what could she do? There was no one to help her. Though I tried . . . I did try but could do little . . . not enough . . . no not enough."

My forehead knots. "A relative?"

"My sister."

When I suddenly think of Beatriz and see her as she was after returning from the Holy House, my heart aches. And by the look on Maria's face, I know that is how she feels about her sister, too.

"Many times I worry that this could be my fate. If God is not merciful I could . . . ." Maria stops in mid sentence when I shake my head.

"No, never," I say, covering her hand with mine. "For we must . . . we *will* look out for one another."

We are on the road again. Had we not been tossed out onto the street like the contents of a chamber pot, we would still be in the tavern, with Arias and Sebastian drinking and gambling. But a fight ensued when Arias accused one of the men, surely a sharper, of using crooked dice. Sebastian, too, joined the fracas and cut one of the men's ears with his sword, removing half the lobe, while Arias kept the other two sharpers at bay. Arias would certainly have run them through had not the tavern keeper and five other men intervened. Amid shouting and scuffling and drawn swords the tavern keeper was able to put an end to it all by promising he and his men would lower their blades if Arias and his party left immediately. And so we did. Otherwise, I am certain that more than an ear lobe would have been lost.

We head for Lebrija, a two day's journey. From there we will go to Jerez, another day's march, then on to Cadiz, which is an additional day. Five full days in all if you count today, which is almost over, for soon the sun will set.

There is little between Dos Hermanas and Lebrija except open country. I dread having to sleep on the road tonight with just our small party, for I know the highwaymen are everywhere. And just as I send up prayers to the Merciful One for protection, I spot a large group of pilgrims resting by the roadside, and I can barely contain my joy.

The pilgrims greet us warmly. There is only one woman among all the men, and she travels with her husband. She is perhaps Mama's age, and as wide of girth. But I suspect, by the way she walks and the manner in which she carries her large bundle, that she is as strong as any of the others. She looks pleased to see us, and at once, as though desperate for female chatter, falls in beside Maria and me. And soon we are off; Arias in front with the pilgrims, Sebastian asleep in the ox-cart, and the women behind.

I learn the woman's name is Teresa, that she and her husband are returning from their pilgrimage to Roc Amadour, and that her home is in Jerez. She babbles endlessly but I find both her manner and voice pleasant.

". . . naturally I was grieved," Teresa drones, hardly taking time to draw breath while removing the bundle from her right shoulder to her left as easily as if it were a shawl, "grieved that I could not climb the hundred and twenty-six steps on my knees as my husband and all the other men did, but how could I strip to my waist then bind my bare chest with chains? What do the friars care that they break an old woman's heart by creating pilgrimages only men can make?"

She finally takes a breath, then sighs. "I had to content myself to mount the steps of the Chapel of Our Lady on foot—hardly a feat of consequence since I could not bloody my knees. But later, when my husband arrived and stood beside me, and the priest uttered the prayers of purification before unfastening my husband's chains, what joy I felt! What holy joy! For I, silly as it may seem, envisioned he was praying these prayers over me as well.

"My husband has not removed the medallion of the Virgin from his person since the priest gave it to him." She laughs gaily. "Nor has he been slow to show his official certificate to anyone who cares to see it. I tell him this is prideful, and that he is sorely in need of another pilgrimage."

Maria bobs her head in admiration. But I see nothing admirable in any of it. This desire to strip and be chained, and to rip open one's knees on rough stone chapel steps baffles me. How can this please God when the Savior Himself said, "*It is finished*"? What sacrifice can compare with His? Or what more needs to be done in order for one to be acceptable? But I say nothing. Instead, I listen to Teresa talk endlessly about other pilgrimages where she and her husband saw dozens of holy relics including a piece of the True Cross, the skull of St. Philip and the arm of St. James encased in silver, and all the while I wonder if Mama was right in saying that I will never really be one of them.

This is the fourth day of our journey. Last night we stayed in Lebrija at an inn that was full of bedbugs, making everyone scratch till dawn, though I was hardly bothered due to my taffeta lining. I have not stopped blessing Mama for her kindness in sewing it.

We all slept in one room—the Vivars, the two servants, Arias Diaz, all the pilgrims, Sebastian and I, as is the custom in most inns. The straw was so filthy it reeked, and more than one rat scurried by. And so many in our company snored it sounded as if a herd of animals had been trapped inside with us.

My consolation is that Sebastian and I could not "use the bed"— Mama's expression for when a husband and wife join flesh. And oh, how great is my guilt for feeling this way! Is it not the Creator's wish that we be "fruitful and multiply"? Still, I cannot bear the thought of Sebastian touching me again or whispering Beatriz's name in my ear. Worse still, I am certain it will be some time before Sebastian and I can come together in this way since it will take many weeks to reach the Indies and build our home, and this fills me with joy. I have confessed my sin over and over to the Merciful One, but nothing changes. My desire remains the same: *If only I can stay in Spain while Sebastian sails to the Indies.*

⌒◌

The sun bakes my head as I trudge along the dusty road to Jerez. It has been baking my head for hours, and I pull off my hood to allow the air to dry my damp neck, leaving bare my braided hair. A Jewess, once betrothed, never uncovers her hair in public. I glance anxiously to where Sebastian sits bouncing up and down in the ox-cart, but he has not noticed my actions. I should not be so concerned about following tradition and ritual law, but it is still difficult for me to leave the old ways behind. Also, I have no wish to upset Sebastian. Unlike me, he is a crypto-Jew, and uncovering my hair will offend him; though these days nothing seems to arouse any feelings in Sebastian, neither good nor bad, unless it is a game of dice or a goblet of wine.

Maria walks ahead with her husband and sons, while Teresa strolls quietly beside me, surely a miracle from heaven since she has not been silent for three days. Perhaps she has just come to the end of her pilgrimage stories. Even so, I like this kind, talkative woman, and will miss her when, at Jerez, we will part ways.

I have never been to Jerez, but Papa has told me of its high Moorish walls opening to four gates and overlooked by fifty towers, and of the ancient palace in the southwest corner of the city with its imposing "tower of homage." I am about to ask Teresa to tell me about it—for I doubt we will have time to see the tower for ourselves—when all of a sudden I hear piercing shrieks, and see a large cloud of dust. In seconds, we are surrounded by a dozen men, who, judging by their fierce cries and raised weapons, have come to rob us.

Immediately, Arias unsheathes his sword, and to Sebastian's credit, he, too, pulls a weapon and jumps from the cart. Meanwhile, the pilgrims have drawn their own swords. When the bandits see they are outnumbered, they scatter. And as they do, one of them notices me and Teresa. Seeing we are not protected by any of the men, he runs toward us in obvious hopes of obtaining some booty before making his escape.

"Surrender your valuables or I will run you through," he says, reaching us and placing his blade against my throat.

I do not move so much as an eyelash for I am paralyzed with fear. And suddenly everything looks as though it is suspended in honey, slow moving and opaque: Sebastian and Arias scrambling past the other highwaymen trying to reach me; the robber's eyes flashing and his chest heaving as he readies to thrust his blade into my throat; Teresa pulling the bag from her shoulder and swinging it at the highwayman's head, hitting him so hard the dagger flies from his hand onto the dirt and he with it; Teresa's foot appearing from under her cassock-like garment and kicking the bandit in his chest, making him unable to rise; the other thieves scurrying away without so much as a backward glance at their companion. And all the while I am thinking how it really is a miracle of heaven that Teresa was by my side, and how she is so fearless. And then I think of my new life and the possible dangers that await. Oh, how I wish I was more like Teresa. But even as I think it I know it will take another miracle to make me that brave.

❧

The Bay of Cadiz sparkles like Mama's stone of Zebulun, and forces me to shield my eyes. Maria Vivar stands beside me. All morning we have been on this rocky promontory watching boats row to and fro between shore and the anchored fleet that bobs in the distance. We have been coming here for days, and know this is the fleet that will take us to the Indies.

"The innkeeper's wife claims that all the ships will be overcrowded with goods and passengers," Maria says, "that not one more person could fit on the decks."

"Not surprising for we know how men love adventure. And surely there are aristocrats and knights enough to fill all the ships of Spain. Each seeking his fortune."

"And leaving his woman to bear the burden of it."

I glance at Maria. "Most of the women will bear it at home, for I fear there will be few of us on this journey."

"I know . . . but it pleases me that I am here with my husband and sons. At least they will have someone to care for them." Maria opens her small homespun bag which is filled with *empanadas* purchased from the vendor outside our inn. She offers me one. And when I take it, I think not of Jewish law, even though I know the *empanada* is full of pork.

We find a smooth spot, and sit. Below us, fishermen spread their nets over large boulders near the sandbank to dry. They and their families have been fishing these waters for centuries. Oh how I wish I could join them in their simple obscure lives, to be hidden among their nets and boats, hidden from Fray Alonso, Columbus's fleet, the Indies, and . . . Sebastian. Surely there is room for one more in their humble dwellings, for one more to live safely and peacefully there in the shadows?

My eyes drift to the sailors who congregate along the bank. Columbus's men, to be sure. They are everywhere. Just as talk of his new voyage is everywhere. No escaping it. Unless you were a gull and could fly up to the clouds and . . . *where?* I turn to look behind me. To the left an earth-and-stone wall runs parallel to the shoreline, and behind that, the clearly visible naves and Tuscan columns of the Church of Santa Cruz. How well it reflects the realities of my life. Behind me lies the Inquisition and possible imprisonment, and that has propelled me to this vast empty space of which nothing is certain. Yet here I am, with nowhere to go but forward. There can be no more thoughts of running away. No more thoughts of another life. This is the life I have been given. This is the life I must live.

I shove the last bite of greasy *empanada* into my mouth, then rise. "Come, Maria. We must be off. Tomorrow we sail, and we still have much to learn from the innkeeper's wife."

Chapter 9

Cadiz to Canary Islands

The long wooden oars slap the water like hands striking the soft cheeks of a child, and my stomach lurches. Another slap, and it lurches again. Perspiration dampens my hair and runs in rivulets down my forehead and neck. The hood of my traveling cloak has become a suffocating barrier to the plentiful breeze, and I consider removing it until I remember Papa's warning. "Be discreet. Avoid attracting attention when boarding the ship." For according to Papa, "the sight of a beautiful woman might arouse suspicion." Papa was always kind and tended to exaggerate my virtues. Even so, I leave the hood in place.

The slapping oars bring me ever closer to a large *nao* anchored between another *nao* and a smaller *caravel*. The innkeeper's wife, who was once married to a sailor, has told me there are three *naos* in Admiral Columbus's fleet, all with deep drafts of six feet, and that *naos*, according to her deceased husband, lumber like oxen. Also, there are fourteen *caravels* which are more maneuverable and better in the shallows. But aside from the size, my eyes discern little difference.

As is the custom, there is no name on the vessel toward which we row, but sailors on shore have nicknamed her *Tortoise*, for they say she is the slowest ship in the fleet. To me, the looming round–bellied vessel with furled sails is both beautiful and terrifying. And though I have spent the last four days learning all I can from the innkeeper's wife, I feel ill-prepared for what lies ahead. And so desolate.

If only Maria were sitting next to me. But she and her husband and sons trail in the boat behind. Sebastian's presence gives me no comfort, or even Arias'—with all his fierce abilities as a knight—for they barely look at me, and talk only amongst themselves. The sudden sight of a white flag fluttering atop the mizzen mast, with its green cross, prompts me to pray for courage.

But the Merciful One has little time to answer, for presently we— our two oarsmen, Sebastian, Arias and I— and all our trunks, tie up alongside the *Tortoise*.

"You will have to climb Jacob's Ladder," says an oarsmen pointing to a long ladder hanging off the side of the ship. He leers at me much like the Keeper of the Fair leered at Beatriz, and it is plain he expects some reward in watching my assent.

The ladder is rope with wooden plank rungs, and appears frail and oh, so high. I have on fresh traveling clothes, and the skirt, which is voluminous, will be difficult to control if the wind grabs it.

Sebastian offers me his hand, which I take to steady myself in the rocking boat. Then I lunge for the thick ropes of the ladder, and clutch them firmly while I make my climb. My palms sweat as I move slowly from one rung to the next. And a wind does come, but fearing to release the ropes, I ignore it and let it take hold of my skirt. Finally, at the top, two ship's boys help me board.

I can only imagine the perverse pleasure I have given the oarsmen. Not surprisingly, I see them grinning when I peer over the gunwale. But I am surprised to see Arias grinning, as well. And when I realize he does so without fear of offending Sebastian, I feel shame. I have been told sailors are superstitious and dislike both women and priests aboard their vessels, for they believe nothing summons the devil faster against a ship. Still, were women not respected at sea? And what of Arias Diaz? What was his excuse? Or Sebastian's?

I wait by the gunwale as Sebastian boards, followed by Arias, and then our trunks, which are hoisted up in nets with block and tackle. And as soon as all our trunks lay piled near the waist hatchway, a man with thinning gray hair and ears the size of oranges, appears. In his hand he holds the passengers' list. A ship's boy, barefoot and wearing only a pair of wide-bottom pants that comes to his knees, whispers to me that this man is the ship's master. I know from the innkeeper's wife that it is the ship's master, second in command to the captain, who manages the everyday administration of the ship, including the stowing of cargo. I am relieved, for this is the man whom Papa has bribed.

"Only two trunks each." His face is firmly set.

Instantly, Sebastian pulls out a bag of coins, unties the string and produces a *florin*. "I believe there is some error. I have three trunks, and they all must go."

"Your name, Señor?"

I am stunned when Sebastian replies, "Don Sebastian Villarreal." *Were we not supposed to be discreet? And not use our names?*

The ship's master appears flustered as he fumbles through his papers.

"Perhaps it is under the name of Vivar," I quickly add, and see instant displeasure on Sebastian's face. But Papa has told me we would be listed under the Vivar name and why. Though the corrupt Bishop Fonseca took bribes from eager adventurers desiring passage, and though he ended up listing two hundred souls on his registry as unnamed "gentlemen volunteers" Papa did not approach him with a bribe. "Better to ply my money at the port of Cadiz," he told me, "far from Fray Alonso and his spies." So he paid the ship's master on the *Tortoise* to write on the passengers' list the following: Vivar, Gonzalo—native of Seville, with his wife, Maria Heredia, native of Seville, and their sons, Enrique, Juan and Luis, and three servants; we—Sebastian, Arias and I—being the servants.

"Please check under Vivar," I say again, ignoring Sebastian's glare. Though Señor Villarreal, too, has instructed Sebastian on these particulars, he seems determined to pretend otherwise.

The ship's master clears his throat, "Yes, here you are, but still there is a limit, two trunks only. And yours, Señor, are so large I could rightly count each one as two."

Without a word, Sebastian takes the ship's master's hand and shakes it. I suspect he is palming the coin. I am sure of it when the ship's master quickly slips something into his pocket.

"Ah, what is this?" he says, pointing to his papers. "You are most fortunate, Señor. Most fortunate. It appears I carry less baggage than originally thought. You may take one more trunk, but only one."

Six trunks lay at our feet: Sebastian's three and my three. Sebastian frowns, then looks at me with distant eyes, and shrugs. "It will not be my codpieces or doublets or jerkins that are dumped into the sea."

It is interesting that codpieces, those triangular protective fabrics used to emphasize a man's groin, should be mentioned first as though in Sebastian's mind this is a matter of manly honor. Without a word, I open my trunks and hastily consolidate what is most needful. Then my extra trunk is netted once again, and sent back down to the oarsmen who will take it to shore where they will, no doubt, divide its contents. And this vexes me greatly since I cannot bear the thought of those leering men handling my clothes as if they belonged to a common strumpet.

And when I once again notice the fluttering white flag with the green cross it reminds me that in addition to praying to the Merciful One about my fears, I must also pray to Him about one of the seven deadly sins . . . my pride.

There are so many of us; almost one hundred twenty passengers plus crew, aboard the *Tortoise*. We, and all the nobles and gentleman knights, huddle like Papa's merino sheep beneath the forecastle. And like his sheep, we each butt this way and that trying to secure our place.

The peasants—who have been brought to work the gold mines and farms and whatever else the nobles want—crowd below the quarterdeck. But there are others too: a notary, one of seventeen notaries who are on other ships, and a royal scribe, with a second scribe sailing on the flagship. And at least thirteen members of the clergy are said to be on the passengers' list—no doubt giving the sailors much cause for concern.

Not surprisingly, nearly half the clergy are Franciscans for they are eager missionaries and certainly have great aspirations of converting all the Indies. But only one sails on the *Tortoise*—a Catalan friar from the Montserrat monastery, Bernaldo Buil. He is a man of great influence for he has authority over the other twelve. And this disturbs me, for Franciscans are known for their zeal in persecuting both Jews and *conversos*, a zeal second only to the Dominican's—which is legendary. But I am grateful that no *Lanzas* are aboard. For these members of the Holy Brotherhood, the Crown's police, are ruthless, cruel, and have authority to strike down a life with impunity.

Sadly, Maria and I are the only women on our vessel, and though the passengers have separated themselves by rank, it is decided Maria and I will sleep together, surrounded by our men. It pains me that Gonzalo and not Sebastian conceived this plan, though to be fair it was a great concession on Sebastian's part to allow peasants to share his space.

For me, it means protection and privacy both, since Maria and I cannot swing over the bulwarks nor hang amongst the rigging on the leeward side of the ship every time we have need of a chamber pot as we have seen the men do. Though even with each of us shielding the other with a blanket, using a chamber pot on this forever rolling ship will not be easy.

We stake our claim with bundles and blankets before leaving the men. Gonzalo instructs Maria to "be careful" when we say we are going for air. Sebastian only nods. He is busy playing dice with Arias and two others.

Maria and I walk closely together. It is a strange feeling to be surrounded by so many men. We especially avoid the sailors, since we know their resentful attitude toward us. Our traveling cloaks are tightly wrapped around us. Our heads are hooded. We talk in whispers and avoid looking anyone in the eye.

When we reach the gunwale we rest against it, allowing our forearms to dangle over the side. I have left the men not only to take air but to say "goodbye" to the land I love. When I see Maria's face as she gazes on Cadiz, I know she is saying "goodbye" as well.

"Will we ever see Spain again?" Maria's voice breaks.

"If God wills." I sound braver than I feel.

"You still love her even though she has been so unkind to your people?"

Her frankness startles me, but pleases me too, since it suggests a budding friendship. "It is the only home I have ever known."

"Then perhaps God, in His mercy, is sending you to a better one."

I think on it a moment and wonder if indeed this is all part of the Holy One's plan. But when I remember my wedding night, the weary journey on foot to Cadiz, the attack by bandits, the dirty inns, Sebastian's drinking and gambling, and his great neglect of me, it is hard to imagine such a thing. And when I do not answer, Maria thoughtfully drops the matter.

As we lean against the gunwale, I smell whale oil and see one of the younger ship's boys oiling the planks.

"Hope they tarred and tallowed the hull better than last time," he says to another boy watching him. "Nothing sinks a vessel faster than shipworm."

I am busy worrying how quickly shipworms can ruin a vessel when one of the boys shouts, "Admiral Columbus! It is the Admiral."

I glance at the *nao* next to us, and see a tall, broad man walking the deck of the forecastle. And indeed it is the same man who filled the streets of Seville with his entourage of soldiers, seamen and Indians. I am told on this voyage his entourage consists of thirty household members and personal retainers, as well as five of the six Indians from his previous trip.

The *nao* is obviously the *Mariagalante*, for the innkeeper's wife told me the *Mariagalante* is the flagship, though it still puzzles me how ships can have names yet bear no marking of these names on their hulls.

The Admiral gives orders to the man next to him, a ship's officer by the look of his clothing, for he wears a laced doublet of dressed leather, white hose, and a bright red cloak.

At once, colorful flags of stunning beauty are hoisted on both the mizzen and main mast: first the expedition standard of a green cross on white with the Sovereigns' green initials; next the flag of Castile and Leon; and then a flowing red and white pennant. Then elsewhere two other flags are raised, one of which, I hear someone say, is Columbus's coat of arms.

A shout is given to "hoist sail" and the deck crew of the *Mariagalante* swarm the rigging, some to the spars and ratlines, while others haul and tally sail. And all work in time to a chant-like song.

Within minutes, three large sails, each displaying a sizeable red cross, unfurl, followed by two smaller sails, and an upper bonnet.

I watch the *Mariagalante* raise anchor, watch the wind fill her canvas, watch her glide past us and go deeper into the Bay of Cadiz to take her rightful place at the head of the fleet and I am filled with a sense of wonder and awe.

But as our own sails unfurl my awe and wonder disappear, and my stomach lurches. All around us sailors tug and groan against the ropes. Others scramble to lace together the upper bonnet and mainsail. When a shout is given to "weigh anchor," I clutch Maria's arm.

"Courage, Isabel," Maria whispers. "Perhaps we should join the men."

I shake my head and bite the inside of my mouth to keep from crying. "No. I will stay as long as I can see Cadiz." And that is what I do. I stay, pressed against the gunwale, listening to the water lap the sides of the hull as the wind lifts the sails and takes us further out into the bay where we maneuver behind the *Mariagalante*. One by one the ships weigh anchor and fall into formation. People on shore shout and wave. Then comes the blasting of horns and trumpets and lombard cannon, all to wish us God speed.

How long I remain pressed against the side of the ship I cannot say. I only know that when I finally release both Maria's arm and the gunwale, my heart and Cadiz have shriveled to specks.

∽ↄ

A group of nobles, all minor aristocrats, surround Sebastian, talking and laughing and drinking the wine from one of the many barrels Sebastian's father, Señor Villarreal, bribed the ship's master to store in the hold well before our boarding.

"One would have to travel far to find finer wine than that coming from Señor Villarreal's vineyard." It is the voice of Arias Diaz. "It is even finer than a Vernaccia."

It takes all my willpower not to laugh. Vernaccia, the highly prized wine from Genoa, is so expensive only the very wealthy can afford it. Hardly the drink of a minor knight like Arias.

"I have not had the privilege of tasting the Genoese brew," another noble says, "but certainly Don Sebastian's wine is far superior to that of our ship's." He lowers his voice. "Everyone knows how the corrupt hands of Bishop Fonseca have watered down the fleet's stores."

"And that is why Providence has brought us Don Sebastian and his excellent barrels," says another.

The men take turns extolling the virtues of Sebastian's wine, seemingly eager to ingratiate themselves, for who in Spanish aristocracy does not know the name of Villarreal?

It troubles me that Sebastian has revealed his identity before we are well out to sea. I am fearful of Fray Buil who always seems to be nearby. And I still worry that somehow Fray Alonso will learn of our departure and overtake us. But Sebastian seems unmindful of these dangers, and even now delights the nobles, who crowd his elbows, with stories of his older brother, Antonio, and his many intrigues at court.

I hardly remember Antonio, for he has been at court for years. And though I suspect Sebastian's stories are great exaggerations, intended to illustrate the high esteem in which Antonio is held by the ladies at court, and indeed by the Crown itself, I find myself thrilled by them, too. When Sebastian has exhausted his treasure-trove of tales, the nobles begin talking about Don Antonio's wife.

". . . and I swear by the true cross that I made three pilgrimages to Our Lady of Guadalupe begging her to allow me just one encounter with the fair Doña Maria de Murcia. That is, before she was wedded to your brother. Her beauty is legendary. I hear no man can resist her. And I hear that even while great with child, her beauty continues to be extolled at court."

"I have only seen Doña Maria once, but she is all they claim."

"And I, too, can swear it is true, for two years ago, just months before she married Don Antonio, I had the privilege of escorting her entire party to the Church of Santa Clara de Moguer, for she and her cousins were making a vigil. What beauties! Though to be sure none was fairer than Doña Maria."

Several others add their praise, and then I stop listening for I am remembering that today is the twenty-fifth of September. The month of *Tishrei*. The stress of travel has made it impossible to observe *Rosh Hashanah*—when the story of Abraham is read and sweet foods are eaten to ensure a sweet new year. It is a most holy time of prayer and contrition, and ushers in the High Holy Days— the ten days of repentance that end with *Yom Kippur*, the Day of Atonement.

Now seated on a blanket next to Maria, I lower my head to silently offer prayers of repentance to God, but before long I feel Maria nudge me.

"You are being paid a compliment, Doña Isabel."

I look up and see Arias Diaz smiling at me. "I was saying, Doña Isabel, that while I too have seen Doña Maria de Murcia and admire her beauty, Don Sebastian need not envy his brother, for his wife is equally as fair. Perhaps you will kindly remove your hood and attest to the validity of my words."

I am shocked by his boldness, and even more shocked when Sebastian smiles approvingly. But what can I do? Can I humiliate my husband by refusing? So, instead, I humiliate myself and pull back the hood of my cloak, exposing my long dark hair which hangs in one thick braid down my back. Heads nod, and admiration marks the faces of the nobles, even Sebastian's. Then I cover myself, but not before noticing that Fray Buil is watching me from across the deck.

One of the ships is taking on water, and after only six days of sailing southwest by south we are forced to put into port at Grand Canary to repair the vessel. Since Admiral Columbus believes it will take all day to caulk the leaking seams with oakum, the passengers have been given permission to disembark.

As soon as our feet touch sand, Sebastian and Arias and an entourage of raucous nobles go in search of a tavern, and no doubt, a game of chance. We have been warned against wandering the streets of the "lower city". It is hardly a city at all, but an area nearest the waterfront and laced with filthy alleyways where rogues and drunks and disreputable street peddlers are purported to inhabit. So Maria and I quietly walk the beach. For my part I am grateful to be off the *Tortoise* and on ground that does not pitch and roll. I drink in the sweet air and watch a large blue chaffinch fly overhead.

Not all have gone, like Sebastian, in search of pleasure, for the sand is littered with men, and as we walk my heart sinks. Maria and I are on a mission. We are determined to search for all the females that have come on this voyage but so far have found none.

We walk with our hoods up and our cloaks gathered around us, but still the men stare. They are mostly from Andalusia, but some from Galicia, Santander and Catalonia, and even a few from as far away as Portugal and Florence. And all have come to seek their fortunes and gain new titles—the nobles and knights, anyway. The peasants and tradesmen outnumber them greatly, and why they have come, I cannot say. It seems unlikely they will ever gain wealth or titles, and I cannot imagine how a mere salary from the Crown would be sufficient inducement to leave home and family.

Suddenly, Maria yanks my arm. "Do my eyes deceive me, Isabel? Is it possible . . . is it possible that up ahead stands another *woman*?"

I look and see a portly man sitting on the beached remains of a ship's mast. His simple clothing tells me he is neither noble nor knight. But next to him stands a woman, hooded and cloaked as we are. My heart pounds, and I caution myself against rashness, for I would like nothing better than to rush upon her and administer the type of hugs and kisses given a sister. Instead, I allow myself the luxury of squeezing Maria's hand then feel her squeeze mine in return. And by the time we reach the spot where both man and woman now sit, I have reined in my excitement to a tolerable level.

The woman rises first, and appears as elated as we. "By the arm of St. Lawrence!" she says, then blushes. "Pardon . . . I . . . I have forgotten my manners." When she bows slightly I realize my cloak has opened, revealing my traveling clothes and disclosing my wealth.

Quickly, Maria introduces me, and soon we are all talking as if old friends; a spectacle that would surely cause Sebastian untold vexation. The couple is husband and wife—a Señor and Señora Lopez. He is an assayer, skilled in determining the properties of precious metals, and she, a seamstress. And from the discoloration under her nails, I know she is also schooled in the art of dying fabric with madder and wood ash.

Señor Lopez talks first, mostly about gold and how rich everyone will be. He is certain that nuggets, the size of biscuits, will be found lying about, though what makes him believe this is a puzzlement.

Next, Pasculina Lopez talks about fashions and fabrics, describing in great detail some of the gowns she has made for the wives of nobles. After a time, Señor Lopez yawns, excuses himself, and sits back down on the water-logged mast. And though he is obviously bored by our conversation, I judge him to be a kindly man for I see the pleasure in his eyes over his wife finally having some female companionship.

After we have exhausted our conversation on clothing we then talk about the voyage and the weather, and finally I say "goodbye" for I am determined to see if there are any more women to be recruited into our sisterhood. Maria quietly follows. We walk the sandbank stepping over shells and ocean debris, and around men and more men, and when at last we have walked it all we understand that only three women will be going to the new Spanish settlement in the Indies.

Owing to calm winds it has taken us five days to reach the island of Gomera, though it is not that far from Grand Canary. The one blessing is that during this time Maria and I have been able to wash our hair and bodies. When there is little wind, sailors often haul buckets of seawater for bathing, and one of the ship's boys was kind enough to haul water for us.

Now we are anchored in order to take on additional provisions of wood and fresh water and salted meat, as well as breeding stock of pigs, goats, cattle, sheep, and chickens. We have been told it will take several days to load everything, leaving the passengers free to roam the island.

Sebastian and his band of nobles have disappeared long ago for parts unknown. So have the Vivar men. But the three of us, Maria, Pasculina and I, stay near the shore. For most of the day we have watched boatload after boatload of supplies being rowed to the fleet. Where will they put it all? Before sailing from Cadiz the ships were loaded with provisions of fresh fruit, olive oil, sardines, raisins, salted flour, vinegar, biscuits, and the like—enough for the trip to the Indies and back.

The ships were also loaded with a mountain of supplies for La Navidad which included dried beans and wine, plantings of sugar cane, orange and lemon trees, and bags of seeds for crops. Also for Navidad were tools and household items and weaponry, not to mention mules and the twenty *Lanzas* horses as well as their war dogs. And on top of all this, the holds contain the luggage of nobles and knights. Can any more room exist? It is hard to imagine.

"I wish to return to the ship," I say to Maria and Pasculina. "But there is no need for you to come." I do not tell them that today is *Yom Kippur*, the Day of Atonement, and I want to spend time, before the ship fills for the night, in honoring it. I was unable to perform *mikvah* yesterday, the customary ritual bath which the women of my family take before *Yom Kippur*, but I did use some of my allotted drinking water to wash my face and hands, much to everyone's dismay. Nor was I able to eat our customary meal of olives and unleavened bread followed by meat. I had a biscuit dissolved in saltfish stew. And though there will be no *Neilah* service tonight, I will stand by the gunwale for at least an hour as is the custom of standing in the *Neilah*, and will think of the Nazarene, who is *my* atonement. And there I will quietly sing praises to Him for what He has done for me. And my heart will swell with overflowing love for the Bearer of my sins.

But when I turn to go, Maria restrains me. "Doña Isabel, please do not venture away from us."

I smile, grateful for her concern, then gently remove her hand, and head for the longboat. "Pardon," I say to one of the oarsmen as I pull my hood further down over my forehead, "what are you carrying?"

The oarsman thrusts the paddle end of his long wooden oar into the sand as though erecting a barrier. "Gomera cheese." His voice is sharp.

"Well, please leave room for me, for I wish to be taken to the *Tortoise*."

He glares as though I've just said I carry the plague. "Find another boat!"

I turn to go then stop as the two oarsmen prepare to push their boat off the sand. *This will not do.* Must I always curb my natural inclinations? I will never be Beatriz. Why continue to try? Besides, how suitable would her soft, gentle nature be to this life I now find myself living? If my character is flawed, then let the Holy One purge it. And if not, if He has given me this sometimes untamed, sometimes obstinate character that I might survive a harder life, who will have pity if I do not submit to it and life treats me ill? Without a word, I return to the boat and jump in.

"What? *You again?*" the oarsman snarls. "Did I not tell you to take another boat?"

"To the *Tortoise!*" I reply, fighting to keep my voice calm. And after the briefest hesitation, I allow my robe to open, revealing my traveling clothes. And just as I hoped but not entirely expected, the oarsman dips his oars and says, "Yes, Señora."

It is the thirteenth of October. We are just leaving Hierro, one more small island in the Canary chain, and finally heading to open sea. Maria and I sit on a blanket beneath the forecastle. Opposite us, Sebastian and the nobles congregate and drink wine. Shipboard rumor says it will take another twenty days before we sight land, then perhaps another week before we reach the settlement of La Navidad, but already there is much grumbling.

Sailors complain that the wine barrels leak and that wine spills into the hold and spoils some of the dry provisions. Even now, the ship's cooper is in the hold tightening casks and caulking leaks. Everyone blames Bishop Fonseca, and accuses him of purchasing poor quality barrels out of his ample allowance, then pocketing the difference. They do it in low tones out of fear of Fray Buil. But with the barrels leaking wine, the weevils infesting biscuits, and mold covering raisins, complaints of how Fonseca lined his pockets with gold at their expense can be heard everywhere.

Maria and I try not to listen, and engage in our own conversation.

"What else will we plant in our garden?" Maria says.

We have spent most of the morning planning what we will plant when we reach the Indies, and so far neither of us has tired of the subject. "Certainly chickpeas and lettuce, and of course melons. We must have melons."

Maria laughs. "And oranges?"

"Yes, oranges, too."

"And cane sugar, perhaps? Admiral Columbus must believe the Indies can support such a crop since he carries so many plantings."

I shake my head. Papa has told me about the sugar fields of Valencia, and how they require at least thirty workers to not only tend the fields but work the mills. Such an enterprise was beyond the ability of two women. "Let the Admiral plant his cane. We will concentrate on other crops." Without consulting our husbands, Maria and I have formed a partnership in the manner of the partnership Papa formed with the peasants who tend his vineyards. "We need to cultivate crops we can sell. And you, with your knowledge, must guide me."

"Do you really believe there is profit to be made in this . . . this selling of vegetables?"

"Look around." I lean closer. "What do you see? Men in search of wealth and glory. What else do they talk about except gold? Or the Indian women. But mostly gold and how they will find it. And while they look, who will plant their gardens? Or pickle their harvest? The peasants? No. They will be forced to dig this gold for them."

Maria nods thoughtfully. "But the nobles claim there are plenty of Indian women to be had. Surely, they will force them to plant and harvest their crops."

"Does it seem reasonable so many women will be available? Surely they will have men and crops of their own to care for. I think it a foolish assumption. And, in the end, Maria, they cannot eat gold."

Maria's face tightens. "Yes . . . gold. There is much talk of it. The Admiral has boasted it will be found everywhere. Even the miners and assayers who ship with us say so. And gold, even the promise of it, can make men mad." She shakes her head. "Will it ensnare *our* men? Make them mad, too?"

I glance at Sebastian who is already mad with wine, and is laughing and talking loudly. And then I look at the Vivars. They are on the main deck with the other peasants. Gonzalo hangs over the gunwale, heaving the contents of his stomach, something he does every time we set sail. Juan and Luis smile and talk, while Enrique stands by, scowling.

"Who knows what will happen to our men," I finally say. "But whatever does, we will still have each other."

Chapter 10

Ocean Sea to La Navidad

On this vast glistening waterway that stretches as far as the eye can see, the days blend together like sifted wheat. The single consolation is that by weeks end we will sight land, or so we are told. There has been no lack of wind to fill our sails—praise be to God. Though we are still the slow tortoise we have always been, for some reason the *Mariagalante* has become as slow, and neither of us can keep up with the other vessels. More than once they have shortened sail in order to close the distance between us.

This pacing the *Mariagalante* has afforded me an opportunity to observe the Admiral, for almost always he can be seen on the quarter deck or forecastle. I observe him now. He is taller than those around him, and stands erect while studying his charts. His white hair, which some say was once as red as cane-apples, protrudes beneath a dark velvet cap.

I am standing by the gunwale, wondering if the Lord will allow the Admiral to finally find the great Khan and the fabled city of Quinsay with its silks and spices and roofs of gold, when all of a sudden drops of water, the size of starling eggs, begin to fall. They fall so hard and thick it is as if the sky has opened and released some great river upon our heads. The boatswain blows his whistle alerting everyone to the danger, and sailors rush about donning "rough gown," their foul-weather gear.

The wind has picked up, and the once pleasant breeze now howls like a beast. As canvas rips in the wind men scramble to lower sail.

The waters, too, have changed, for waves as high as towers wash over the sides, and someone yells "we're letting water!" Four sailors work the pumps, bringing up foaming bilge. And though they work with all haste, the water coming over the sides from the sea is greater than the water being pumped back into it.

The officer on the quarter deck shouts down an order to "rig the tiller" as it bumps and thrashes the helmsman. It takes several tries before the helmsman can secure it with the relieving tackle. And as I watch him struggle, it suddenly occurs to me that we may all perish.

I pray for God's mercy, and when I look up I see that the very sky is at war. Lightning slashes the air like *Lanzas* swords, and the thunder is louder than a dozen cannons firing at once. I cling to the gunwale for fear of being washed overboard. Maria, and even Sebastian, are shouting for me to come to the shelter where they huddle below the forecastle. And though the distance is short, I cannot, because the ship pitches so violently.

Another wave crashes over me, leaving me gasping for air. I barely recover when over comes another. If I stay on deck much longer I will surely die. I try inching my way toward safety.

All the sails are down now, and the *Tortoise* runs before the wind with bare masts. We are like a toy in the heaving water. And just when my grip on the gunwale weakens and I am certain the sea will have me, a strong arm pulls me across the deck and lashes me to the mainmast. I cannot see who performs this kindness for my eyes burn from the salt, leaving me nearly blind.

"Thank you," I murmur, but hear no response. I sense, rather than see, that sailors around me are roping themselves, too, as they cry out to God in terror. Many swear vows. Others promise to make pilgrimages to Our Lady of Guadalupe or Loreto. Someone says it is St. Simon's Eve and that we must pray to him. So everyone shouts prayers into the wind while I pray silently to the God of Abraham, Isaac and Jacob.

Suddenly, amidst the thunder and lightning, the captain appears. He shouts that we need more ballast or we will capsize. Then he rips at the roping, and roughly pulls seamen to their feet with orders to fill all empty provision barrels with seawater.

I remain lashed to the mast, pitching back and forth, wet to the bone, with eyes stinging and my mind full of Mama and Papa and Beatriz. I am remembering the smell of Mama's lavender, the feel of Papa's leather bound ledgers, the shine of Beatriz's beautiful black hair. I remember these and a thousand other things, and all are followed by this one thought . . . soon I will be with the Nazarene.

"Señora? Señora Villarreal, are you injured?"

I open my eyes and though I can barely see, I am able to make out the round face of the young ship's boy who first helped me with my trunks.

"Are you hurt?" he repeats.

I run my hands over the front of my dripping cloak. "No . . . I think not." Then I notice that the deck has stopped rolling and that the sun is coming out from behind the clouds.

"I thought for sure you were done for. You would have been, too, if you had not been lashed."

"Then you are the one who saved me?"

"No. Not I." He unties my ropes.

"Who then? I must thank him."

"I saw no one, Señora. Only you by the gunwale just as a great wave was about to take you." He helps me to my feet.

"Fray Buil," Maria says, suddenly appearing beside me. "It was Fray Buil."

"*Fray Buil?*"

Maria drags a wet palm across her dripping face and nods. "He grabbed you before you could be washed overboard."

At once I look for Fray Buil but he is on his knees, fingering his beads. All around me sailors are praying, too. The *Salve Regina* and *Gloria* fill the air. I drop to the deck and kneel among them. And bowing my head I recite, beneath my breath, the eighth Psalm in adoration and praise for the One who spared my life, all the while wishing He had done so by any other hand than that Franciscan's.

⁓

"Our provisions are dwindling," Maria says, taking a small bite of her soaked biscuit.

The smell is sickening, for the mixture in which she dunks it is stale, foul-smelling water mixed with ship's wine—which has soured. In addition, the recent storm has stove-in some of the water and wine casks, creating a great shortage. For this reason, the captain has a standing order to raise a corner of the main sail each time it looks like rain. But it has rained so little that so far the bellied-canvas has caught only enough water to fill three small buckets.

"Soon our food will be gone." Maria continues nibbling her biscuit like a rodent.

I look away so she cannot see my worried face. We sit together under the forecastle amid Maria's family and a few nobles. A large rat scurries by, then disappears into a wood pile. And in one corner a handful of roaches swarm a fallen fragment of hardtack.

It is barely daylight.

"I find if I take only a few bites now and then, I feel no hunger at all."

I know Maria says this because she is trying to be brave. The ship's stores are only for those salaried by the Crown. The others, like us and the "gentlemen volunteers," must provide for themselves, though wine and water are made available to all. In addition, the ship's boy cooks only for the crew while everyone else must cook for themselves.

"I plan to make a fish stew today," I say. "Please share it with me."

"You know I cannot."

The voice of a young ship's boy drowns out my objection as he begins his song announcing daybreak and time for morning prayers.

"Blessed be the light of day and he who sends the night away." Then he leads the sailors in the *Pater Noster* and *Ave Maria*.

Soon there is a flurry of activity. The pilot throws a large wood-chip off the bow to plot the ship's speed; four sailors work the pumps, emptying the bilge, while others haul sea water for washing the decking. Still others scrub the main shrouds, the lower rigging, and the deadeyes of urine and human waste deposited during the night by passengers and sailors who failed to hang far enough over the ship's side. The more experienced seamen check the running gear for slack in the lines, and others tar stays.

Four ship's boys haul the iron firebox from the hold to the main deck and set it up on the lee side of the ship, away from the prevailing wind just as they do everyday, weather permitting.

I watch one of them fill the floor of the box with sand before adding logs and kindling the fire. Then he begins cooking the crew's one hot meal of the day. When he has finished, the passengers will each take their turn, though these days fewer and fewer prepare hot food. Most, like Maria, eat hardtack soaked in water and wine. After twenty days at sea, everyone's provisions are dwindling, and this has caused many to sicken. Even the sailors are failing, for they eat little food and still must work hard. But I do not fear for them as I do for Maria.

"You have eaten nothing but one biscuit a day for the past three days," I say, noting her sunken eyes. "You cannot continue this."

"I must conserve."

"You look poorly. Perhaps if you ate some of my . . . ."

"Oh, Isabel, you must trust God for we are all in His hands."

My mouth hardens. I *know* God carries us all. But what Maria doesn't understand is that my grief and worry have allowed an ugly thought to take root. One I cannot shake, and one that causes me great shame. *If I must lose someone let it be Sebastian and not Maria.*

"I have enough biscuits for ten days, and honey and saltfish, too," I press. "And there are the sacks of dried beans and wheat in my trunk if we become desperate. Señor Villarreal was most liberal in his preparations. We can share. It is my allotment, not Sebastian's, so you need not worry."

"Isabel, I have already told you I cannot. My family and I would deplete your stores too quickly, leaving you with nothing. And you must not eat your beans and wheat, and neither can I eat mine, for we must save them for when we land or we will have no provisions while our crops grow. They are all that stand between us and starvation."

I look away, defeated. I can barely stomach the smell of Maria's foul brew, and wonder how I can eat another stew made of this same mix of vile water and wine. Everything on this ship is vile. Even me. I have not bathed hands or face in days. Fresh water is scarce, and there have been no calms for sailors to haul seawater. My clothes, soaked with perspiration and saltwater, smell like rotten fish. We all reek. Even Sebastian, who is normally foppish, gives little attention to his matted hair or scraggly beard, or the large stains on his jerkin. And while I watch Maria carefully wrap her half-eaten biscuit in homespun, then carefully tuck it beneath her bodice as if it were a prize *florin*, I cannot help wondering what is going to become of us.

Maria and I stand by the gunwale. I have forced her here hoping the sun, which is just beginning to show itself, and the gentle breeze, which is steadily blowing us westward, will improve her health. We still pace the *Mariagalante*, though I barely notice her, for I have lost interest.

"Shall I begin?" I say. It is Sunday, and in honor of the day, we have agreed I should read from my book of Psalms until Fray Buil is ready for Mass.

Maria nods, and before I can pull the book from my bodice someone from the *Mariagalante* shouts, "Land in sight!"

The words are as sweet as the notes Beatrice once played on her lute, yet I hardly believe them until the sailor repeats, "Portside! Portside! Land in sight!"

At once, Maria and I move with the others across the deck and see an island. It is lush and mountainous, with vegetation growing right down to the water line. And the vegetation is so dense it is impossible to glimpse the interior. Oh, how majestic and beautiful it is! I have not seen its like in all of Andalusia.

Someone begins the *Gloria*. Others join in. Maria crosses herself and mumbles the *Pater Noster*. I remain silent, for my senses are too full of perfumed air, the cry of gulls, the warm caressing breeze, the taste of salt spray. And as our ship slowly passes this glistening jewel, all I keep thinking is that this is what the Lord's garden must have been like when Adam first saw it—beautiful, unsullied, full of promise. And to my surprise, I find myself weeping, but I know not if for joy or sorrow.

❧

"The women, I am told, are most obliging and so agreeable that many of the men had three or four of them."

"I, for one, refuse to believe it."

"Oh, it is true, I swear! A ship's boys who sailed on the *Pinta's* last voyage told me. He said he saw it with his own eyes. Women walk around as bare as babies. So do the men. Now what could be more pleasant than an agreeable woman without clothing?"

My cheeks burn as I listen to the nobles behind me. Sebastian is there, too. They all sit around the main mast. Maria and I stand by the gunwale. We are amid a chain of islands and have anchored while a *caravel*, on Admiral Columbus's orders, searches for a suitable harbor. We have passed six islands in all, and each one named by the Admiral himself. Still, no order has been given to disembark, and I grow restless for land.

The nobles are loud, their conversation tiresome, surely due to their own restlessness. I ignore them by watching Admiral Columbus board a boat loaded with a cross, a standard, the flag of Castile and Leon, and some men from the *Mariagalante*. One nearby sailor tells another that Columbus goes to take possession of the island in the name of the Catholic Kings. And it must be so, for when they land, they plant the cross, then the standard and flag—all things I have seen before. Still I watch to keep my attention from the odious conversation behind me, but it is no use.

"If the women are really as you say, it will indeed be compensation for having to live in a crude, untamed land. For what else can Navidad be but a backward outpost if only thirty-nine men were left to build it? Hardly a Madrid or Barcelona or Seville."

The men laugh, and Sebastian's laughter is heard above the others.

"Yes. A small price to pay. With all the women we want for pleasure and for cooking our food, we can go about the business of plucking gold from the ground. Soon enough we will all return to Spain rich as kings."

"And with more titles added to our names, for what else do our sovereigns love more than gold? You will see how they shower us with honors when we bring it to them. For who is not in want of more honors? Unless, of course, you are Don Sebastian, who has title and honors enough."

"Not to mention, gold enough."

"And a most beautiful wife."

"It makes you wonder why Don Sebastian ever consented to come on such a tedious journey. Tell us, Señor, what do you hope to gain from this adventure?"

My husband laughs. "Indeed, what is there for me to gain? As you say, I already have everything. But perhaps, just perhaps, I will forget."

"Forget? Forget what?"

"Perhaps I will forget that I am still alive."

There is an uncomfortable silence before a voice breaks it. "Do not distress yourself, Don Sebastian. Men like us do not live long enough to see our grandchildren." The voice belongs to Arias Diaz.

"Then here is to wine, women, dice, and a short life," Sebastian bellows.

"I will add my goblet if you include in that toast—gold and titles."

"As will I, for who cares if life is long or short when you have all these things."

Over my shoulder I hear the sound of laughter and cups clinking. I am still looking at the island where Admiral Columbus and his men have gathered, and my heart is heavy. The land is beautiful and fresh and new, but it appears that to this new land we have brought all our old sorrows.

The next morning we set sail, and go only about eight leagues before spotting a large island with mountains that remind me of the Sierra Morena. From the highest peak flows a waterfall that glistens like a string of diamonds as it tumbles downward. It is breathtaking. But more importantly, it is *fresh* water.

At once a party of sailors and soldiers are sent ashore. As soon as the island is declared safe, Maria and I will go, too. Oh, what a thought! We will take fresh clothes, a bar of good Italian soap, and scrub ourselves until we are red! It is this thought alone that makes staying on board one more day, bearable.

Maria and I are devastated. For three days we have waited for permission to go ashore, and finally we received word. We cannot and this is why: the captain of one of the *caravels*, sent to explore the island, has found an Indian village. The Indians, whom everyone calls "Caribs," fled, leaving their village deserted. And in the huts, human skulls were found suspended upside down in slings and filled with all manner of dry goods! One soldier even found a human arm in a cooking pot! What kind of land is this where men eat other men? I am sickened to the core, and wonder how the Holy One could have sent me to such a place.

The one good thing is that the captain rescued nearly half a dozen Taino women—women not from the barbaric Carib tribe and victims of "bride capture," according to one of Columbus's Indian interpreters. And some boys were rescued, too, and all taken aboard one of the ships. Maria and I are anxious to see what the Indians look like, especially the women, but their ship is too far away. But I, for one would not care if they had two heads and three arms. Any woman, no matter how strange, will be a welcome sight.

⤸

"We need volunteers."

My stomach lurches when I look from the captain's troubled face to Sebastian's, and see my husband's eyes glow. Next to Sebastian stands Arias Diaz, eagerly fingering the hilt of his sword; and nearby, a young, handsome nobleman, Juan Ponce de Leon, one of Bishop Fonseca's two hundred "gentlemen volunteers."

"Who will step up and be counted?" the captain asks.

"Look no further, Sir." It is Juan Ponce. "Before you stand three able men, all keen eyed and quick with a blade."

The captain clasps Juan's shoulder. "You understand the island is full of man eaters, foul creatures, lower than beasts, for what man would use human skulls as containers?"

"Indeed," Juan Ponce says.

"Do not restrain yourselves, or fear to deal harshly. The lives of good men depend upon it."

"I have no such fear," Arias Diaz says stepping forward. "They will taste my steel—and without mercy—to be sure."

The captain nods. "Yes, and justly deserved, too, but do not forget the purpose of your mission. You are to find the lost men."

Three days ago a captain from another ship took six of his men and went ashore to explore, and no one has seen them since. One rescue party has already been sent, but has yet to return.

"Only God knows what dangers await you," the captain says, frowning.

"We are equal to the task." Sebastian's eyes are blazing now. "If the men still live, we will find them."

Other nobles add their voices, vowing to rescue the missing men and to wreak vengeance if any harm has befallen them.

I want to rush to Sebastian's side and beg him not to go, but by his face I know he is determined. And then I feel shame, for it is not love that prompts me, but fear of being left alone without a protector and having to manage for myself.

The captain orders the marshal of the fleet to pass out weaponry to those who have volunteered. When the marshal hands Sebastian a *cuirasse*, I see Sebastian frown. He has fine chain mail in one of his trunks and is obviously disdainful of wearing what he believes to be an inferior leather breastplate. Arias Diaz, who wears his Brigandine plate, smiles slyly at Sebastian as though taunting him that he wears the better armor.

Then the marshal passes out swords to those without, and even hands out three long, slender arquebuses, though the nobles handle them so poorly I wonder if they even know how to fire them.

The rescue party gathers by the gunwale, ready to descend Jacob's Ladder. Juan Ponce is the first over the side, and when Sebastian is about to take his turn, the thought of his hollowed-out skull filled with dried herbs and hanging in some hut is more than I can bear. And since I have ceased trying to be like Beatriz, I quickly squeeze through the throng of noblemen and reach my husband just as his leg straddles the gunwale.

"God be with you," I say in a low voice. And surprisingly, Sebastian is not angry; rather he is touched by my childish display for he actually looks at me and smiles.

"Fear not, Doña Isabel. Our cause is just." And then he disappears over the side.

༼ ༽

Two days later, the search party, sweaty and tired but intact, returns to our ship not having sighted the missing captain and his men, and I find myself giving thanks to God.

Three days after that, just as the sun is burning off the morning mist, cheers go up all around when the missing captain and his six men appear on shore. With them are several Indian women and a few boys. Already, a boat is on its way to collect them all.

While the boat rows to shore, I watch the women. They are beautiful, the color of copper, and their bodies so firm and shapely their nudity hardly seems a sin but rather a testimony to God's marvelous creation. I suppose they are Tainos like the other women who were rescued, and not Caribs. I have learned that Taino means "good or noble" which is what these Indians call themselves, and it must be true since Admiral Columbus himself has described how gentle and kind they are.

The women wear colorful loin clothes, and their long, coal-black hair hangs loosely down their backs though it is cut short across their foreheads, just above the eyebrows. One woman wears a shiny object in her nose, and by the way it glints in the sun I fear it may be gold. Everyone aboard ship is already crazed with thoughts of gold. Surely, this will only add to the madness.

And my fears are realized when one of the nobles, who is also watching intently by the gunwale, says to those around him, "What need have we of mining gold when we can pluck it off the Indians! Look, there, how gold hangs from the very nostrils of that beauty."

Others crowd around, and quickly the talk of gold and the pleasures of having such women as the one on shore, abound. When I can bear it no longer, I leave my spot and return to the crowded space below the forecastle, but not before seeing Sebastian point toward shore and hearing him say, "I wager I will be the first to have my way with that one."

꙳

For seven days we sail in a westerly direction, passing numerous islands and anchoring here and there just for a few hours at a time. The only thing worth noting throughout it all is the encounter with a canoe of Indians, which I witnessed since it occurred not ten cubits from where I stood on the *Tortoise*.

The Indians appeared from nowhere, stumbling upon us by chance, I think, judging by the startled look on their faces. One of them, a man, was painted completely black, and had a tattooed face. The others had painted noses or eyes. They all looked as foolish as jesters. But perhaps we appeared foolish to them too, us women in long skirts; the nobles with their tight hose and codpieces and braid-trimmed doublets. We watched each other for some time, the Indians from their canoe, we from our ship. Then a battle ensued when a boatful of seamen tried to capture them. Shots were fired, and answered by a hail of arrows. Two of the arrows struck a sailor in his chest; another pierced a seaman's side. The Indians, too, received wounds. Blood was everywhere, and I had to turn away.

Was there no place on earth where men did not war with each other?

꙳

I am weary of all this sailing, and of this ship. *Oh, how I hate this ship!* Today we sailed into a harbor which Admiral Columbus calls Monte Christi, and there we have anchored. The Admiral claims the large island in front of us is Española, the very island where he left the thirty-nine sailors to build La Navidad, though the settlement is still further along the coast. Further, always further.

Will we ever reach it?

The only good news is that there are no shortages of fresh water or fruit, and both keep our hunger at bay, for our food supply is completely gone, that is Maria's and her family's and mine. Sebastian still has a little hardtack and saltfish left. And of course we have the stores in our trunks which we refuse to touch.

Maria and I have used several bucketsful of fresh water bathing our hair and bodies, but it was necessary. My nails were as black as the wings of a swift and I could not endure them, or my smell, any longer. We have also changed our clothes, though we had to do it on deck with only a thin blanket to give us privacy. We are still not allowed ashore. Ever since the bloody encounter with the Indians, all the ship's captains have been wary of letting their passengers disembark. Consequently, Maria and I have not seen Pasculina for some time. I pray for her continually and often wonder how she is faring. I feel pity, for she is all alone among a sea of men. At least I have Maria for comfort.

Dear Maria. What would I do without her?

To pass the time, she and I walk the deck or stand by the gunwale listening to the idle chatter of the crew or nobles. And several days ago I heard a story I wish I had not for it troubles me still because it reminds me of Sebastian's boast as he pointed to the Taino woman on the beach. The story concerns Michele de Cuneo, one of Admiral Columbus's lieutenants, who captured a beautiful Carib woman. And after taking her back to the *Mariagalante*, he proceeded to try to have his way with her. But when she resisted, he beat her with a rope until he broke her resolve, and thereafter treated her as a whore. I am still outraged that any man should mistreat a woman so, but I have not even spoken about this to Maria, perhaps because de Cuneo is a high ranking officer. It would be unseemly to speak ill of such a person with a peasant. Though I want our friendship to be genuine, custom and etiquette continue to hang heavy between us.

I am still pondering this when a boat loaded with nobles—including Sebastian, Arias Diaz and Juan Ponce, all wearing breastplates and carrying weapons—tie up alongside the *Tortoise.* They have been scouting the island along with sailors and soldiers from other ships. By their faces, which are furled and strained, I know something is wrong. I wait quietly by the gunwale watching the men ascend Jacob's Ladder. Maria stands beside me. When all are on board, our captain, who had remained with the ship, approaches the boarding party.

"Bad tidings mar your faces." He turns to the first mate, who was part of the expedition. "What has happened?"

The first mate gives no reply, but stands looking troubled. He is lean and muscular. And the scar running the length of his right cheek suggests he is not a man to shrink from danger.

"*Well* . . . what has happened? Speak up man!" the captain snaps.

"We buried two men." The first mate shows no emotion, but there is a catch in his throat. "They have been dead for some time. One had his feet bound, the other, a noose around his neck. They were Spaniards from . . . La Navidad."

The next day another scouting party finds two more dead bodies floating in the stream. We are all worried, though no one will say it out loud. But our faces reveal the truth. And certainly the same two questions that spin around in my mind also spin around in everyone else's. *Will there be any left alive at Navidad?* And . . . *since we are in Taino territory, was this the work of the Tainos, those good and noble people?*

All night I am restless with my thoughts, and sleep little. When I do, I am plagued with unpleasant dreams of which I remember only one. In it I am walking through a barren land. League after league I walk, seeing not so much as a bird or rabbit or flower or tree, and I ache with loneliness.

⌒⃝

"You cried out in your sleep last night," Maria says.

We are standing in our customary place by the gunwale, and both the high position of the sun and the rumbling in my stomach tell me it must be noon. At first light the entire fleet weighed anchor and began sailing along the coast of Española. The captain has told us Admiral Columbus expects to be at La Navidad by nightfall, and since his telling I have felt an inexplicable dread.

"You must have had a nightmare," Maria says, pressing the point.

"Why? What did I say?"

"You said the same thing over and over: 'Where are you? Where are you?'"

I laugh to cloak the truth, for I have come to understand that my troubling dream reveals my growing fear that I will end up all alone in this strange, frightening land.

⌒⃝

We have been sailing westward for hours. I know this for the bell telling the ship's boy to turn the sandglass has sounded so many times I have lost count. But the sun is setting, and Columbus has finally signaled the fleet to drop anchor.

From my place at the gunwale, I gaze at the distant land. Somewhere in the shadows is La Navidad, and tomorrow we will sail into her harbor and go ashore. It is difficult to believe that after so long at sea we have finally arrived. Curiosity, and eagerness too, consume me. Oh, to be on dry land again! The ship's boy who sailed the *Pinta* claims this is a land of great beauty, with large mountains, sparkling rivers and loam valleys. But in the fading light I see a high mountain range and little else.

Suddenly Maria appears beside me. "I am sure it is a fine land, Isabel, and you are young and strong. You will make a good life here."

"I will try, for my children's sake, should it please God to bless me with any."

"Oh, fear not. You will have many children."

For some reason I do not share Maria's confidence. I glance at Sebastian who sits on the waist hatch, talking. The sun is nearly gone, and though I can barely make him out, his voice rises above the others. "I wager I will find *two* women even more beautiful than our good friend Michele de Cuneo has found, and I will need no rope to tame them."

"And what need do you have for such women when you already have the beautiful Doña Isabel?" It is Juan Ponce.

Before Sebastian can answer, a ship's boy appears, carrying the binnacle lamp signaling the beginning of evening prayers, and everyone kneels as the boy chants the *Pater Noster*.

This same ritual is being observed on all seventeen ships, and when it is over, I hear Admiral Columbus on the *Mariagalante*, for we are anchored nearby, shout an order to fire two lombard shots to alert our brethren on land.

Then we wait for the responding cannon fire. And wait. Until at long last we understand that only silence answers. And in the growing darkness we see no campfires or oil lamps. Nor do we hear voices or the clanking of pottery or tools.

All we hear is our own breathing.

Chapter 11

Española

"A good omen!" shouts a seaman on the ratlines, pointing to the gulls circling overhead.

I pray he is right as we navigate the harbor of La Navidad and head closer to shore. It is barely an hour into the forenoon watch but already the sun warms my head. I wipe perspiration from my brow, then remove my hood, revealing my hair, which is bound in plain netting. I have made peace with myself about this covering and uncovering of my hair, for in this strange land where air is hot and heavy with moisture, there will be many challenges. Therefore, I am determined to adapt myself by setting aside those minor traditions of my former faith—to which I am still attached. Besides, where in Scripture does it say Sarah or Rebecca or Ruth always covered their hair?

Since I have been so free with my hood, I decide to open my traveling cloak as well. Beneath the cloak, my clean skirt and bodice are plain undyed linen. Will Sebastian be angry? He has always insisted I dress according to my rank. But surely much labor awaits us at the settlement. And my practical nature shrinks from the prospect of ruining my silks or brocades.

I stand alone at the gunwale, for Maria is packing her possessions in anticipation of leaving the ship. I have been packed since dawn. The ship is strangely quiet, and through the stillness the first-mate can be heard ordering a sailor to the "chains," and my heart jumps. *Soon we will anchor.* The sailor climbs the overhanging platform and takes soundings by heaving lead.

"Twain! Twain!" he shouts, pulling up his rope.

Soon we will land. I am sick with excitement and dread, both, but I think the silence on board unnerves me more than anything else. No one has forgotten last night and how our cannon shots went unanswered. And in this eerie stillness I hear my name.

"Doña Isabel."

I jerk backward when I see Fray Buil at my elbow. He wears a coarse monk's cloak with the cowl down at the back of his neck. Wrinkles, as fine as silk threads, crease the sides of his eyes. He is shorter than I; a great surprise since his presence has always been so commanding. With pounding heart I gaze at his face and see a further surprise—kindness in his eyes, and laughter, too, when he sees me hastily gather my cloak.

"You need not hide your clothing. I do not despise simplicity." His voice is more youthful than his face. "Rather, I delight in it, as you can see." He lightly taps his unadorned frock.

"I . . . I just wanted to be prepared for the work ahead which . . . ."

He puts up his hand to stop my speech, for it is vain and silly, as we both know. "I came only to say you have been in my constant prayers. I fear life here will be hard. But you must remember this, Doña Isabel, God's hand is on you."

"Yes . . . thank you," I manage to say, for I am stunned. "And I want to thank you for saving me during the storm. Many times I have wanted to seek you out in order to extend my gratitude." It is a lie; for though I sought Fray Buil immediately after the storm, since then I have done all to avoid him. And when he smiles, almost the way Papa smiled when he caught me in some misdeed, I know Fray Buil has caught me in mine. And then, without another word, he walks away.

Maria and I stand anxiously by the gunwale. The sandglass has twice been turned since the boatload of sailors and soldiers from the *Mariagalante*

have rowed to shore and disappeared into the interior. Admiral Columbus has given the order that none should head to the beaches until the scouting party determines that it is safe.

My eyes hurt from staring so long at the island, for the sun is strong and its glare on the water is enough to blind. Still I cannot avert my eyes. Neither Maria nor I speak. A heavy silence hangs over the ship. All on board quietly await some sign from shore.

Then suddenly the small band of sailors and soldiers appear on the sand and climb into their waiting boat. All around us men from other vessels shout to the boat that now rows back to the *Mariagalante*.

"What is the word?"

"How find you our comrades?"

"Does La Navidad still stand?"

Maria hastily crosses herself, then takes my hand and clutches it fiercely, for no one on the boat answers. "What is to become of us?" she whispers.

"Perhaps the news is not so bad." I try to sound calm. Surely the Merciful One would have pity on so great a number, for many hundreds of souls sail with this fleet. "We must await word before losing heart."

And before the sandglass is turned yet again, word does come: Navidad, both its huts and fenced blockhouse, has been burned to the ground, and all the inhabitants slain.

We have been anchored in the harbor of La Navidad for eight days, and as usual Maria and I have been confined to the ship. Sebastian and several nobles, including Arias and Juan Ponce, have been to shore many times, and from listening to their guarded whispers, as well as to the guarded whispers of the crew, I have gleaned what has happened. Some of the thirty-nine men at La Navidad died fighting amongst themselves over gold and women, but most were killed by Tainos for

what Admiral Columbus calls their "licentious conduct" in taking multiple Indian women for their pleasure without regard to the feelings of
their husbands or families. The Admiral has been told this by the local
Tainos through our Indian interpreters.

All this increases my concern for Sebastian. He has made foolish
boasts regarding the Taino women, boasts I pray he will not try to carry
out for if he does, I fear he could end up like the men of Navidad.

                                                                                  *

The thin, pale nobleman, who looks about Sebastian's age, moans as
I press a damp cloth to his burning forehead. Sweat runs down his
temples, matting the hair around his ears, and his body shakes with
fever as I hold him in the crook of my arm.

"You must say the *Ego Pecator*, my son," Fray Buil whispers as he
kneels on the other side of the stricken man. "Ramon. Ramon Gomez,
pray the *Ego Pecator*. I will help you."

Ramon rolls his eyes.

"Release him," Fray Buil says, looking at me. I obey by gently laying Ramon's head on a soiled blanket smelling of vomit. I think it
smells of vomit. I am not sure, for there is such a collection of foul
odors all around us that it is impossible to discern from what direction
they come. As I smooth the young nobleman's blanket, Fray Buil dismisses me impatiently with a wave of his hand. Then with solemn face
and solemn voice, he administers the last rites of Extreme Unction. If
the nobleman recovers, he will forever be obliged to fast, abstain from
relations with his wife, and walk barefoot.

I watch the friar apply anointing oil, and listen to him whisper
Latin prayers. More and more he reminds me of Papa: the way he
so seriously tends to his duties; his stern manner when wanting to
convey authority; and those eyes that are always kind. And because
of these things I am beginning to lose my fear of him. I tell myself
to beware, for he is a Franciscan still. And I tell myself how quickly

those kind eyes would change if he discovered I was a *converso*. But it is no use, because in my heart I believe him to be a sincere man of God.

"Rest now," Fray Buil says, and a moment passes before I realize he is speaking to me.

"Is he . . . ?"

Fray Buil shakes his head. "No, not dead. Perhaps God will yet perform a miracle."

I hear the rattle in Ramon's throat, the same rattle I heard when Aunt Leonora died, may her memory be for blessing, and I know God's miracle must come soon or not at all.

"Rest," Fray Buil repeats. There is concern in his eyes.

I rise obediently. *I am so weary.* So very weary of this ship, of the stench, of the close quarters and lack of privacy, of the rats and lice and roaches, of the constant pitching and rolling. We have beaten against the wind for twelve days. Admiral Columbus, finding Navidad unsuitable for resettlement, has been leading us eastward along the coast where the prevailing wind is a constant adversary. Days go by when we sail no further than a few leagues. And though we have dropped anchor several times and Columbus has gone forth with his party to scout the land to determine its suitability for settlement, he is never satisfied, and we are obliged to go farther.

Always farther.

"Doña Isabel, can you assist me?" Maria sits on the floor squeezing water from a cloth onto the dry, cracked lips of another noble. "He will not drink."

I step over a sick ship's boy, and cringe when I see Doctor Spinoza bleeding him. The boy looks paler today. Two others, both soldiers, lie nearby. Ten, in all, have fallen sick and are packed together under the quarterdeck, brought here to keep them away from the healthy and to make it easier for the doctor to render treatment.

I lower myself to the floor beside Maria. The stench is overwhelming. Most of the sick have lost control of their bowels, and these vapors of human waste along with the smell of vomit—for many have heaved the contents of their stomach, as well—float all around us. Though two ship's boys daily wash the planking, and another the blankets when time permits, the stricken men and their clothing remain unwashed, for who is there to do it? I cannot. Modesty forbids it. It is most unseemly for a woman to bathe any man, especially one not her husband.

"Try a cup," I say, taking hold of the sick nobleman's head and raising it slightly, the better to bring the cup to his lips. Maria struggles to her feet, takes his empty cup and dips it into one of the three water buckets cradled in a wooden rack. When she returns, she puts it to his lips. He takes a sip and turns away. We try twice more, but it is no use. I fear Fray Buil will again be administering last rites. We put a clean folded blanked under his head, arrange his covers, then leave him in peace and head for the gunwale.

Here the stench is not as bad, for with the strong easterly wind comes a clove-like scent from the mountains of Española. I fill my lungs with it as I watch Maria, barely breathing at all, slump over the gunwale. She looks so worn.

"You are not eating enough fruit," I say.

"I eat more than my share."

"Your cheeks are as pasty as dough. With weather like this you should look like a Taino." I gesture toward the sky where the sun blazes brightly.

"Can anyone feel as he should? With so much sickness all around? With this disease of the bowels that infects more daily and makes men lose their desire for food? Can a man have strength without food? Even my husband, Gonzalo, has begun to complain that his appetite has lessened. And last night, he barely climbed the ropes in time before his bowels betrayed him. I prepared fennel water, and made him drink. But if the Admiral does not let us land soon, I fear we may all die."

I look away, for what can I say? I know she is right. Every day someone else falls ill. "Tomorrow you must rest under the forecastle with your husband and not help me with the sick."

"Oh, that will please him, Isabel. You know how he detests me going beneath the quarterdeck." She pats my hand. "It displeases Sebastian, too."

I just nod, for I have no wish to tell her the reason it displeases Sebastian is not fear for my safety, but because his friends worry I might bring back the sickness to where we all sleep. And though Sebastian has told me about all the noblemen's complaints, he has not forbidden me to tend the sick. Both the ship's doctor and Fray Buil have asked that Maria and I assist them. One can refuse a physician, but can anyone refuse a man of the cloth?

No. Not even Sebastian.

"How curious," Maria says, pointing to the sudden flurry of activity on the *Mariagalante* that sails beside us.

I look and see their leadsman heaving lead and presently our leadsman does the same. And then to my amazement, orders go out from the *Mariagalante* to all the ships to drop anchor. And while seamen unlash the two anchors from the catheads, our captain, without emotion, tells us Admiral Columbus has signaled him with news that he has chosen this area to settle.

After three long months at sea, we have arrived.

Chapter 12

La Isabela, Española

S team moistens my face and arms as I pour hot water into the wooden trough Gonzalo made me. Though the bank of the Isabela River, as Columbus has named it, is nearby, it has taken much of the morning to carry enough water from there to our temporary camp site, and then to heat it for doing laundry. The water of the Isabela River is so clean and clear one can see right down to the pebbled bottom. And the taste! It makes your mouth dance. But I suppose after drinking the swill on board ship for so long even the waters of the Donana marshes would be pleasing.

I separate the bundle of soiled clothing at my feet into piles of inner and outer garments, and listen to the bleating of sheep in the distance. South of us, pens have been constructed for the livestock, including the prized horses of the *Lanzas*. The cows, pigs, and even the chickens thrive, but the horses struggle to adjust to the hot moist air, as do the sheep. The sheep, especially, fare poorly, and some have already died.

Our temporary settlement, called Marta, is most pleasing. The location is faultless. It is as if God has formed this parcel of land in anticipation of our arrival. The great Isabela River empties into the Bay giving our ships access to its mouth where all manner of provisions and supplies, and of course livestock, have been unloaded onto its banks.

And those who have examined the soil say it is rich. Not only farms will thrive, but in certain sections near the river there are wondrous stores of alluvial clays for making bricks and pottery. Even now, a large kiln is being built for the firing of roof tiles. It is said Admiral Columbus's house and the storehouse, which will also serve as an armory and meeting hall, will be the first to have a tile roof.

The Admiral—I still call him that though Columbus now carries many new titles, including Viceroy and Governor of the Indies—has named the actual town *La Isabela*, after our Queen. La Isabela is a lombard shot from the river, and after hauling water for much of the morning at Marta, where the river is only a few feet away, I know this will be a problem. The Admiral has promised canals will be dug. But with so many sick, and with most of the healthy men busy building the church and hospital and their own homes, I am sure the canals will not be built for a very long time.

I back away from the rising steam, and bend to where a box sits near my feet. It is brightly decorated with flowers and birds, painted by Beatriz long ago as a gift. I open it and pick through dozens of sheepskin pouches. Under my breath, I bless Mama for packing it so generously. Every household has such a box full of herbs, spices, and curatives. But few have one as beautiful or robust as mine, and I fear I am overly proud of it.

The scent of cinnamon and saffron, pepper and mace, spices so needful in cooking, fill the air as I poke amid the pouches. And along with these rise the vapors of chamomile which calms the stomach, and basil used to subdue fever. I find the proper pouch, open it, make certain it is caustic soda, then pour a bit into the scalding water. Then I add wood ash before plunging in ten of my linen chemises and an equal number of Sebastian's codpieces.

"I have no chicken feathers to remove the grease from Sebastian's jerkins," I say to Maria and Pasculina who stand before their own troughs. "I have asked our ship's boy to gather some gull feathers. Do you think they will work?"

"Gull feathers! Bah! What can they do? I would rather have a ball of that lovely Italian soap of yours," Pasculina says, her bodice drenched with perspiration.

"You would waste such a treasure on scrubbing clothes? When mutton fat soap would do?" There is scorn in Maria's voice. "Was not Doña Isabel generous enough when she allowed us to use her olive oil soap for bathing?"

Two days ago after landing, we—Pasculina, Maria and I—bathed in the Isabela River with my scented soap.

"I am not ungrateful." Pasculina looks offended. "And I do not expect Doña Isabel to give me her soap for doing laundry. I was only dreaming out loud."

I swish the clothes around in the water with the large wooden paddle Gonzalo also made, and laugh. It feels good to laugh, and I throw back my head to allow the last ounce of laughter to tumble out. Surely I look like a madwoman, but I care not. There has been precious little laughter these many months, with the long trek to Cadiz, the sea voyage, the hard work of setting up camp at Marta, the scores of people who have fallen ill, and the many who have died.

"You know what I dream?" I say, when I have stopped laughing. "I dream of sitting under the shade of my own orange tree sipping scented water and gazing at my beautiful stone house."

"And I dream of my vegetables being plumper than everyone else's, and people coming from miles to inquire about the secrets of my garden," Maria says.

"And I dream that all the nobles wear my . . . ."

"Only one dream," Maria interrupts Pasculina in a scolding voice, "and you have already dreamed of washing your clothes in good Italian soap."

We giggle like children until an angry voice breaks in. "*What are you doing?*"

I turn and see Sebastian, his face white with rage.

"Is my wife no better than a peasant? Have I not wealth enough to hire someone to wash our clothes? Have I not continually asked you to remember your position? And mine?"

I stare, dumfounded.

"I *forbid* you to do such work! Do you hear? I *forbid* it!" The veins in Sebastian's neck look like fat worms.

Despite my best efforts, I frown. It is plain Sebastian fails to understand our situation. There is no one to do this labor. Many able-bodied men have been ordered by Columbus to Marta to fell trees and clear land for planting crops. The rest—those not laid low by sickness—have been ordered to La Isabela for the building of the new settlement. And the ship's boy I keep supplied with copper coins to run errands and bring me news says even noblemen have been ordered to clear land and build, though they complain bitterly that nobles, even petty nobles, were not born to labor with their hands. They claim such labor is a repugnant curse and beneath contempt, as are those who labor.

But I am not nobility. I am a merchant's daughter. Mama and Papa have taught me to work. And instead of repugnant, I find it satisfying, and at times, purifying. Surely, such toil can chasten or cleanse a character of pride, and thus be a means of learning the humility of the Nazarene.

"There is none to do this work, Señor," I finally say. "For Maria and Pasculina cannot. It is difficult for one woman to haul enough water for washing. But it is impossible for one woman to do it for two."

"Then you refuse to obey my command?"

"No, Señor," I say, bending over and picking up one of his greatly soiled jerkins, all the while trying to ignore the offensive odor it exudes, "as long as you are content to wear this as it is."

Rage colors Sebastian's ears, then his cheeks, and finally his forehead. I fear he will say something harsh, and humiliate himself. But he simply turns on his heels and walks away.

I know he heads for La Isabela's large rocky promontory on the other side of the Bay. Everyone says it is a good place to build a town, for it rises nearly ten cubits above the sea on one side, and is bordered by a great mountain on another. Soldiers, especially, are pleased for they say these things make the town easier to defend. In addition, a great quantity of limestone lies between Marta and La Isabela where masons are, even now, cutting blocks for the church. And if these were not blessings enough, it is so beautiful many call it *Isla bella*-beautiful island—instead of Isabela.

And though these are all hopeful signs that life here will be good, I somehow cannot believe that it will apply to *my* life, for my husband is ashamed of me, of the way I dress and the way I work. And today, because of the manner in which I spoke to him, I believe I have made him loathe me as well.

༄༅

"Pack your things. You are moving," Sebastian says, coming from nowhere and with such bluster he looks more like a soldier storming an enemy's rampart than a husband approaching his wife.

His voice tells me he is still angry even though we have not seen each other for two weeks. Perhaps I have added to his anger by wearing a plain linen skirt and bodice, and by binding my hair with plain cotton netting, and this in sharp contrast to the fine clothing he wears. Had I known he was coming, I would have dressed more appropriately, even though it would be a hardship in this heat.

"Well, Señora? Must I wait all day?"

Without a word, I enter the canvas shelter that our young ship's boy erected for Maria, Pasculina and I, and which has been our home in Marta since landing. Though our men have not been with us, for they have been busy building our houses, we have not been without protection. All twenty of the *Lanzas* have stayed with us on Marta. They have stayed to protect their war dogs and corralled horses— horses they will not even allow Admiral Columbus to use for the clearing of land or the hauling of heavy materials. They have also stayed on Marta to avoid work, for they say skilled horsemen should not be forced to labor with their hands. This has been a constant source of strife for Columbus. Twice he has come to Marta and argued with the *Lanzas*. And this refusal by the *Lanzas* has emboldened the nobles to

147

complain against Columbus. And many have begun openly defying him by refusing to work as well.

For my part—though it is selfish and reveals a poor faith in God's protection—I have been happy to have the *Lanzas* here. Since learning the fate of the thirty-nine settlers at Navidad, I have been uneasy about the Indians. When we first entered the harbor, many came to the shore to watch, but none have come to Marta. And I attribute that to the presence of the fierce *Lanzas* and their dogs and horses.

At La Isabela, it is different, for there is a large Taino settlement nearby, and I have been told Indians come and go all day to barter. But that does not concern me, for in Isabela there are hundreds of men to protect us.

"Doña Isabel, the boat cannot wait all day!"

Sebastian's impatient voice makes me quickly stuff my trunks with hair brushes, shawls, some clothing and bedding. Outside are my cooking pots and spoons, a few bowls and . . . the trough. My trunks are too full to hold the trough, so I quickly grab a woolen blanket and walk outside. Without looking at Sebastian, I spread it on the ground and place my pots and spoons and bowls in the center, then the trough on top. I tie the four corners, and tell Sebastian I am ready. Then he, by some silent signal, sends four peasants into the tent. Minutes later they return carrying my trunks while two others pick up the bundled blanket. Another signal from Sebastian sends them to the riverbank.

Maria and Pasculina have discreetly removed themselves, and are sitting beneath a tree grinding wheat. I know they will not come to me for fear of Sebastian, so I walk to where they sit, feeling strangely disquieted.

"I will see you in La Isabela." My voice breaks.

The women nod and smile, but say nothing, for my husband stands close by. But just as I am about to join Sebastian, Maria takes my hand, squeezes it, then as a mother hen shooing her chick, waves me away. With a heavy heart, I walk with Sebastian to the river. A longboat will take us around the bend to our home just north of here. There, I will begin a new life with my husband. Already my trunks and bundled blanket are aboard. But with all my heart I wish I could stay at Marta with my friends.

⁓᷈

I walk silently down the wide dusty street. If Isabela had a bell surely it would be ringing None, for the sun is westerly. Sebastian, who walks beside me, wears a cream silk doublet with a collar lined in lace. His beard is trimmed. The light brown curls protruding from his velvet cap appear shiny and clean. Though it might be reasonable to believe he has done this for my sake or for the sake of the occasion—that of entering our new home together for the first time—I cannot believe it is, for surely he would be more congenial. But his face is as sour as one of our Seville oranges.

Behind us, the six peasants carry my trunks and blanket. "Is our house near? Our bearers tire."

Sebastian remains silent. All around us carpenters and masons send up such a cacophony of noise I wonder if Sebastian has heard me. "Are we nearly there, my husband?" I ask again.

If I had not been watching him intently, I would have missed the slight shake of his head, for that is all the answer I receive. Since Sebastian has given me such little response, and since we have walked a good distance, I slow when we reach the Plaza and the church that anchors it. Surrounding the church are scores of sweaty men wielding hammers and saws. Others set stone. To one side, more men prepare thatch for the roof. I am surprised when I hear one of the bearers say, "Tomorrow, Fray Buil dedicates La Isabela at Mass," for it seems impossible to me that the church will be ready in time.

"We must allow our bearers to rest," I say, seeking shade beneath a tall pine and wiping the dampness from my forehead with one of Mama's lavender-scented handkerchiefs. She has hidden many such handkerchiefs in my trunks, along with sprigs of dried lavender and pouches of lavender seeds. And though it pleases me, it also makes me homesick.

The bearers gratefully set down my trunks, then talk in low voices amongst themselves. But Sebastian paces like the chained lynx I once saw at a Seville Fair, and makes me so agitated that after only a few minutes I signal the bearers that we are to continue.

"Which way?" I ask, and Sebastian points toward the right, to a narrow street. On the corner is a large hut of wood and thatch, surely the hospital, for sick men lay all over the grounds. My stomach lurches when I see that some have sores on their faces and hands. *Pox?* Oh merciful God! Pox has killed one of three in many Castilian towns.

"No, it is not plague," Sebastian says, seeing my fear. But the deadness in his voice makes me shudder, for it is as one saying, "No, it is not Sunday" or "No, it is not raining."

We pass the hospital where Dr. Chanca, physician to the fleet, stands in the doorway talking to two men. One I recognize as Dr. Spinoza from the *Tortoise*. I hear them discussing bodily humors. They look weary. Surely their burden has been great. My ship's boy tells me nearly one hundred souls have died since landing, including all ten who were ill on the *Tortoise*, as well as three of the five Tainos who came from Cadiz as translators for Columbus. Even our Admiral is sick.

Already La Isabela has a good size cemetery.

"I understand Admiral Columbus himself gave out the land plots for the building of homes," I say, as we turn down yet another street, this one lined with small huts of wood and thatch.

"He did. According to *rank*."

"Then the nobles and knights all have their homes together?" When Sebastian nods, my heart drops for this means I will be separated from Maria and Pasculina. "And the peasants and artisans? Where are they?"

Sebastian's face tightens. "The wide street by the Plaza divides the settlement in half. It also divides it by rank. Peasants live further east of the road. You will have no trouble finding your way there."

The derision in his voice causes my anger to rise. "It is easy to be proud when you can choose your company from among hundreds of nobles. What if you only had two peasants from which to choose it?"

"Then I would choose solitude," Sebastian says curtly, as he points to a house larger than the others on the street. "Your new home, Doña Isabel." The deadness in his voice is chilling.

The house is perhaps two hundred cubits square while the neighboring houses are nearer a hundred. The thatched roof is tall, and rises upward in the center like a cone, I suppose the better to assist the movement of air. The doorway is uncovered and a small window is visible in the back through which flows a delightful breeze.

The house is well constructed, more so than most others I have seen. In fact, some are so poorly made I fear it will take little more than a good wind to knock them down. But what can be expected from men on short rations or who have been brought low by sickness? All the more our house is a wonderment. Surely it has cost Sebastian much, far more than he will ever admit, for skilled hands have fashioned it. And few hands in Isabela, especially skilled ones, are available.

I gaze silently at the structure. In light of the other huts, it is a palace. In light of what most Castilian peasants are accustomed to, it is more than adequate. In light of what Sebastian is used to, it is akin to a barn for housing animals. Even I have never lived so poorly. But I am determined to be grateful to God and my husband for the blessing of this good, sturdy abode.

"It is very fine," I say, smiling at Sebastian who seems embarrassed by my good humor.

He gruffly orders the peasants to take my trunks and bundle into the house. I follow, and stand quietly to one side while the peasants deposit their burdens, then leave. I feel Sebastian's eyes watch me as I examine the interior. The floor is dirt. A large bedroll leans against a side wall. A wooden rectangular table sits near the opposite wall, and on it is a single glass oil lamp, unlit. Against both sides of the table are long wooden benches. I find it odd that Sebastian's trunks are nowhere to be seen. My two flank the window wall.

"You have done well," I say, afraid to praise Sebastian too highly for fear of upsetting him. I know he views his surroundings as intolerable.

He stands before me stiff and awkward, and I feel pity. I have married a boy but live in a land requiring a man. I glance at the bedroll. It is said a Jewish husband rarely tires of his wife since he cannot "use the bed" whenever he pleases. For during his wife's monthly flow, when she is *niddah*—unclean, he may not touch her. And though Sebastian and I have only lain together as man and wife once, I believe he is already tired of me. I will not lie and say it disappoints. Still, we must somehow find a way to make a life together. And I quickly send up a silent prayer to the Holy One to make it so.

"I think you will be comfortable here," Sebastian says, turning to the door.

"You . . . are not staying the night?" My mind returns to his missing trunks.

"Arias waits." His face reddens, then becomes hard, as though I have criticized him in some way. "A man must have his diversions. What does a woman know of the pleasures of dice?"

"It is our first night in our home," I say softly. "Do you not want me to cook for you before you go?"

Sebastian's eyes narrow. "Sometimes, Isabel . . . sometimes when your hair is arranged in a certain way or when you tilt your head just so . . . I see . . . Beatriz. And I cannot bear it. Do you not understand that?"

And before I am able to answer, he is gone.

It is the Feast of the Three Kings, and those of us who still have our health have gathered in the church to commemorate the dedication of La Isabela. Surprisingly, a roof covers our heads, due only to the diligence of the men whose tools sounded well into yesterday's sunset. But all are not happy with our church. Some complain we lack a reliquary chest holding the bones of some martyr. They fear their prayers will be hindered because of it. I have yet to understand this need to have fragments of dead saints encased in gold or silver, or the need to "swear by the relics," as so many Old Christians do. But being a *converso* and not born into this tradition I suppose I never will.

We press together, for the church is not spacious. I am pleased to discern little body odor. It is plain most have washed for the occasion. Their hair shines, their beards are trimmed, their clothing clean. I too have bathed, and wear a fresh green velvet skirt. My bodice, which is also green velvet, contains several inlays of green silk. Around my neck is a thick gold chain, and my braided hair is covered by a silk headdress.

I have not seen my husband since yesterday when he escorted me to our house, nor can I find him now among the sea of heads, for most face Fray Buil who stands in front by a stone altar saying Mass. Surely Sebastian is here, numbered among the faithful, for though he is a crypto-Jew he would not dare miss this commemoration service. I glance around again, this time looking for Maria or Pasculina. It is useless. A large man wearing a tunic of coarse homespun and a *venera*—a silver medal of the Virgin around his neck—has just stepped in front of me. I say nothing for we are all crowded together like sheep in a pen. And since I cannot see Fray Buil or his many attendants, my mind wanders.

It is January, according to the Christian calendar, though I am still accustomed to calling it *Tevet*. And last month, the month of *Kislev*, I failed to honor yet another of our holy days. It would have been nice remembering *Hanukkah* and how the brave Maccabees recaptured the Temple. And though I have no *menorah*, perhaps I would have lit a candle and recited the three *berakhots*, or even had fried food, as is the custom.

What would Mama say if she knew how little I have followed our Jewish laws or traditions, or that I have missed so many feasts? Perhaps she would say it was prudent. Certainly, she would be surprised by my disappointment over it; especially after being so insistent we stop these very observances.

Fray Buil's voice rises, capturing my attention once more. He is in the middle of his sermon, and I lean forward, straining to hear.

"The *Patronato Real*, the papal degree giving our Sovereigns ecclesiastical control over the Indies comes with the corresponding responsibility of our Sovereigns to convert the Tainos and to uphold church precepts. It is our Queen's fondest wish that we bring our Indian neighbors to Christ. Therefore, we must remember her command in all our dealings with the natives, and treat them accordingly. And finally, it is the duty of the Crown's agent in the Indies to respect church edict and see that it is carried out. It would be great *folly* to ignore the council of the duly appointed shepherd of this church."

Everyone is so quiet you can hear the west wind rustling thatch overhead. Fray Buil has just issued a rebuke to those who have dealt unkindly with the Indians, for it is well known how men, coveting both the Tainos's belongings and their women, have taken unfair advantage. He has also rebuked our Admiral; for it is no secret Columbus and Fray Buil have had numerous disagreements.

Someone coughs, another clears his throat, then men shuffle their feet, until finally Mass continues with one of the many priests leading the Creed.

Suddenly, the large man in front of me weaves, then slumps forward, and I fear he will faint. There is little air, and we are tightly packed. I step aside as much as I am able, and gesture for those around me to do likewise. When there is enough room, the man lowers himself onto the lime-mortar floor. His face is deathly white. Heads have turned because of the commotion, among them Sebastian's. I smile warmly when I see him, for I am determined to be a cheerful wife. Surprise marks Sebastian's face, then the corners of his mouth curve upward. It is evident he is pleased by my good appearance. And just when Sebastian takes a step toward me, the man on the floor heaves the contents of his stomach. I pull Mama's lavender scented handkerchief from my bodice, and bending over, wipe his face. Then more commotion follows as men lift the barely conscious man and carry him toward the door. When at last my gaze returns to Sebastian I see the familiar disdain, and after dispensing a slight nod, he turns away.

The next day on the way to early Mass, I see Sebastian in the Plaza. He stands among a group of soldiers wearing his chain mail and a sword belted to his waist. Next to him are Arias Diaz and Juan Ponce de Leon. When he sees me he lifts his hand as though to gain my attention. I wait in stunned silence as he walks over. *What can account for this unexpected congeniality?*

"Admiral Columbus has ordered two platoons into the interior," he blurts as soon as he is near. "We go to explore, and search for gold. We have also been ordered to find the Taino chief who killed our men at La Navidad."

"You volunteered?"

"Yes," his breath catches with excitement. "I and Arias and Juan Ponce. But fear not. We go well armed."

I look at the men behind him. Some carry crossbows, others swords or pikes. Two carry new muskets that shoot small lead balls. All, like Sebastian, wear protective breastplates, though only Sebastian and five others have fine chain mail.

"There will be hardship," Sebastian continues. "Our food will be rationed. A pint of wine and a pound of rotten biscuit a day is about all we can expect." He seems proud of his impending privation. "Twenty of us will go under the command of Alonso de Hojeda. Another twenty will be lead by Gorvalan."

The names mean nothing to me, but by Sebastian's excited manner I know he feels honored to be among their number. "How long will you be gone?"

"Who can say? But the job must be done and when it is, I shall return."

His face is boyish and handsome, so bright with excitement, and I feel pity that only a quest for danger and gold was able to stir his heart. "I will keep you in my prayers," I say, as I turn and walk toward the church.

⤴

"Look how they have mildewed!"

I follow Maria along the furrow of wheat we planted well before The Feast of the Three Kings, and see blight everywhere.

"And look how they wilt beneath the hot sun." She runs her fingers up a stem. "Even if this were not so, even if the wheat stood as straight and unblemished as the staff of the Good Shepherd Himself, it would be all stalk and no head. And look there." She points to another patch where chickpeas are planted. The entire field is wilted.

"What can we do?"

"You should see the olive trees!" Maria says, ignoring my question as she tows me through her gardens. "Not one has taken root. And the vines! They do not like the soil. They barely grow, and are sure to produce grapes as small as rat droppings. And the lettuce? Shriveled. All shriveled."

I dig my heels into the dirt, bringing myself and Maria to a stop. "Surely we can do something. You must know a way of bringing life back into our crops."

She shakes her head. "It is beyond my skill, Isabel."

"But Marta is good, fertile land!"

"Not for our Castilian crops."

"Has anything survived?" I feel desperate, for though we find exotic fruits here and there, and eat them, and though our ship's boy catches fish for us, the wheat we brought from Cadiz is nearly gone, and we have no reserves of food. And if Maria, with all her skill, cannot grow our crops, how will we survive? "Are there no crops left?"

"Some. The orange and lemon trees grow faster than weeds. And our melons are as big as the wheels of an ox cart. And the cauliflower and cabbage! They are the size of a man's head! Cucumbers and radishes also grow well, better even than in Seville. Of these, we will have a bountiful crop."

I sigh with relief, for starvation is not as near as originally feared. "God is merciful. We will have enough vegetables and fruit. And if we learn to fish, it can be our meat. But bread, Maria. How will we ever survive without bread?"

I bend and scoop up a handful of dirt, then rub it between my palms. It is rich and dark, as good as any soil I have seen. Surely the thick vegetation around us testifies to this as well. But if Maria cannot discover the secret of making our wheat and chickpeas grow in it, we must find someone who can.

"Come, Maria." I slap my hands together to remove the loose dirt. "Time we became acquainted with our Indian neighbors."

Her name is Bata, or so I believe, for that is what it sounded like when she said it. She smiles, showing perfectly even white teeth. Her forehead is flat, following the Taino custom of purposely reshaping the foreheads of their infants by binding flat stones or other hard flat objects to them. For some reason, they consider a flat forehead beautiful. Her ears are pierced, and in each opening she wears a colorful parrot's feather. Her black hair is thick and straight, and more beautiful even that Beatriz's. She is unmarried for she does not wear the customary short skirt of a wife, but is completely bare. Also, she wears the headband of a single woman on which is attached a small, grotesque face made of tightly braided cotton. It is her *zemi* or god, or at least one of them. Around her neck is another *zemi*, this one of carved stone. And I wonder if she wears them for protection from us.

She looks so wild and pagan, so utterly different from anyone I have ever known, it actually astonishes me that I have sought her out. It is true that since our coming to Isabela the Tainos have shown us nothing but kindness. And they have displayed a great willingness to share all they have. But there is a dark side too. Father Ramon Pane has spent much time trying to convert them to Christ, and has seen how their houses are filled with *zemis*; how they purify themselves by inserting bone spatulas down their throats to induce vomiting; and how they use bone snuffing tubes to inhale some demonic potpourri.

Would Mama approve of me doing business with Bata? Would Papa tell me that anything this heathen touches would be unclean and therefore should not be allowed in my house?

I struggle with these questions as I gaze at her sweet face, a face that looks younger than mine. She holds a basket of cassava bread, which is unleavened and reminds me of the bread Mama used to make for Passover. I put up three fingers to show how many I want, then hold up a ribbon of red silk, which to my mind is a fair trade considering that both bread and this quantity and quality of ribbon is worth the same amount of copper coins. She takes it with her free hand and as she rubs it between her fingers her eyes widen with pleasure.

We stand in the dense woods outside Isabela, obscured from view, and I feel like a thief. We are violating the rule of barter. Only Admiral Columbus's accountant is authorized to trade with the Indians, though no one enforces this decree any more. Too many of the food supplies have spoiled, making men hungry and more than willing to break the rules by bartering privately.

Bata gestures for me to take my loaves, which I do. Then it is Maria's turn. She holds up a small leather pouch and indicates she wants to trade it for ten loaves. As the women gesture back and forth, I notice Bata's woven basket. It is skillfully made, as good as any I have seen woven by Moors. The weave is simple and tight, perfect for a floor mat. It is impossible to keep myself or my house clean with a dirt floor. But a mat, or several mats joined together, would remedy the problem.

When Maria concludes her business, I point to Bata's basket. "Teach me to weave." When she looks puzzled, I pull a large leaf off a vine then rip it into strips. Quickly, I weave the strips together, and again point to her basket. She smiles and nods.

"No, no. Not for a basket. For a mat." I bend over and lay the loosely woven leaves at my feet. "To cover the ground."

Again Bata smiles and nods, and this time I know she understands. And as she gestures for us to follow her, I cannot help but wonder what Sebastian would think of all this.

I sit just beyond the doorway of my house on the wooden stool Gonzalo Vivar made me. The light is better out here for weaving. My fingers move swiftly as they work the shredded roots, over-under, over-under, pulling, tightening. My fingers have become skilled in this employ. Already, dozens of mats cover the dirt flooring of my home, each with the edges bound and all woven together, making the covering solid and continuous.

My fingers comb the surface of this, my last mat, searching for loose loops or unsecured ends. Finding none, I bind the edges. How will I explain this to Sebastian? My labor will displease him. So will consorting with a Taino. To my shame, I would not hesitate to tell him I paid Bata to make the mats if so many people had not seen me on my stool.

As I secure the last loop, I consider the problem. Then consider it further as I weave this new mat to the ones on the floor. Finally, the answer comes. I will tell Sebastian the truth. All of it. For while he has been off these past many weeks in search of gold and revenge, I have learned a new way to keep our house clean . . . and a new way to grow crops.

❦

"Gold! Gold! They have found gold!" a noble shouts, running down the street, waving his arms. I watch him disappear around the corner, then watch others scurry after him. By the commotion coming from the Plaza, I know Sebastian and the others have returned.

I go into the house, remove my linen skirt and bodice, wash my face and hands, then slip on clean clothing of brown and blue brocade. Then I pull off my plain net as I gaze into the mirror that has traveled with me all the way from Seville, and which now hangs on one of the wooden posts. My fingers move swiftly, braiding hair and inserting pearl studded pins. And as I do, I realize I feel no excitement at the prospect of my husband's return. Will he notice my hands? They are rough from making mats and from working with Maria on the mounds at Marta. I picture his scowling face and disapproving eyes. It makes me dread our meeting. And as I head for the Plaza I issue silent prayers to the Holy One.

Please let there be peace between Sebastian and me.

❦

"I tell you the Cibao goldfields will make us all rich!"

"It is true! I have seen them. Nuggets the size of chicken eggs!"

"Have you forgotten the Crown must get its share? And Columbus, too. What does that leave for the rest of us?"

This talk is everywhere as dirty, tired soldiers gather with townspeople. Everyone seems eager to tell a story or hear one, but I have yet to see my husband. Finally, I stop in the center of the Plaza, shield my eyes from the harsh overhead sun, and scan the faces up ahead. Arias Diaz stands near the church with a cluster of soldiers that I recognize as being part of Alonso de Hojeda's group. They talk and laugh, and gesture with their hands.

I head for them. Surely Sebastian is nearby. When Arias sees me he breaks from the others. "Señora Villarreal." He dips his head in a bow. "I was about to come to your house."

The smile that covered his face moments ago has turned into a thin tight line. My heart jumps. "What has happened?"

"An accident. A most serious accident, Señora. Your husband has been taken to the hospital."

"He is wounded?"

Arias studies his boots. One hand fingers the hilt of his sword.

"Is he wounded, Señor?" I repeat. "Or is he *dead?*" There, I have said it.

"It is a head wound, Señora. We have carried him unconscious for two days."

My stomach lurches as I picture Sebastian's skull pierced by a Taino arrow. Perhaps I was wrong to befriend Bata. Perhaps these Tainos are not the kind, gentle people Columbus once thought. Perhaps they are more like the savage Caribs. Suddenly I feel ashamed for having anything to do with them.

"Thank you," I mumble, and head for the hospital.

As usual, prone men blanket the grounds of the hospital. Many are sick with bowel disease. Others have open sores that ooze. Still others shake with fever. But all wait for a potion or elixir or powder. Once they get it they will return to their huts where many will die.

Perhaps our large cemetery has made me wary of our doctors. Or perhaps it is because they remind me too much of my own physician in Seville, Doctor Hernando Diaz. But I have little faith in them. They are too quick to bleed patients whenever they cannot determine the cause of their disrupted bodily humors. Do they really believe draining men of blood will restore life? After the Lord Himself has told us that "the life of the flesh is in the blood?"

It distresses me that Sebastian has fallen into their hands, but what can I do? Though I have some understanding of herbs, I am not a midwife with a vast knowledge of the healing arts. But at least I can stay by his side, as a wife should.

Though there is a crowd by the door, I push through. This is the first time I have been inside the hospital. It is not the dingy hovel I expected. Rather, it is bright and well-lit by large windows, and separated into two sections. One section is filled with sick men on bedrolls, the other is sparsely furnished with two large tables, a few chairs, and shelving nailed to the wooden posts of one wall—shelving filled mostly with ceramic medicine jars. But they also hold glass vials, a cone of sugar, jars of honey, and several pipes of molasses, as well as herbs.

As I walk to where men lay on bedrolls, my feet cause the dirt from the floor to rise like gritty vapor.

"Señora Villarreal, your husband is not there."

I turn and see Doctor Spinoza. "Where is he?"

Spinoza points to the table where a man, fully clothed, lies on his back. I cannot tell if it is Sebastian, for someone stands by his head. I watch as four men lift him, then place him on the dirt floor in a sitting position. A chair is brought, and one of the doctors, after sitting down, allows the limp body to be propped against the chair's edge. And just as the doctor clamps the man's bloody head between his knees, I see the face, and know it is Sebastian.

Someone hands the doctor a scalpel which he applies to Sebastian's head, and suddenly blood is everywhere. *Why was not the white of an egg applied first to his wound?* Even Doctor Hernando Diaz cleansed wounds in this manner. Next, a metal instrument resembling a sharp pointed borer, is handed to the doctor, and I gasp. I see no dried mandrake soaking in hot water, or sponges drenched with opium for pain.

"You cannot go." Doctor Spinoza clamps my arm when he sees where I head. "They are about to trepan his skull."

"*Trepan his skull?*" Doctor Diaz once talked of this, explaining how the skull is opened to release blood and thereby relieve pressure. He spoke of it as calmly as he spoke of leeching. But I have also heard that many died from trepanning, and those who lived were sometimes left unable to talk or walk. Could Sebastian bear such a life?

"Is this necessary?" I say.

"Necessary? Doña Isabel, your husband's skull has been crushed by a Taino war club. The damaged bone must be removed and the wound dressed with wool soaked in vinegar and oil. Without trepanning, he will surely die."

"How many others were injured in the battle?" I ask, allowing Dr. Spinoza to lead me outside.

"The battle?" Spinoza looks confused, then his face reddens. "No one else, Señora."

He appears eager to leave, and when he moves toward the door, I step in his path. "How is it that only my husband was wounded?"

"Señora, ask the soldiers who were with him."

Again he moves toward the door but I refuse to yield my ground. "Was there a battle or no?"

Reluctantly, Spinoza shakes his head. I dislike the look on his face.

"Then how did my husband receive his injury?"

"Señora, you must ask his commander." There is pleading in his voice.

"I will not leave this hospital until I know the truth!"

Perspiration drips from Spinoza's face, and his bottom lip protrudes as though deciding his course of action. "If I tell you, Doña Isabel, will you give me your word you will leave quietly?"

"I will." My heart thumps.

"Your husband . . . Don Sebastian came upon a pretty young Indian woman and . . . took his pleasure. But while doing so, the woman's husband found them, for it is said she raised a cry loud enough to wake the dead. And instead of allowing Don Sebastian to compensate him for the misunderstanding—for how was he to know the woman had a husband?—the Indian struck him with his club. But be assured the savage was hunted down and executed."

I stand speechless as tears stream my cheeks.

"Do not grieve, Doña Isabel, for whatever happens, your husband's honor has been avenged, and Spanish justice served. Go home now and pray that God will guide the surgeon's hands."

So I go, and all the way home I weep, not out of grief for my husband, but from grief over the hapless Indian woman who has lost both her honor and her husband because of Sebastian's folly.

Chapter 13

S ebastian is dead.

He has lost his head, though it does not hold herbs and swing in some hut. Rather, it is crushed beyond the ability of our doctors to repair. Bone splinters, deeply imbedded in his brain, caused the type of bleeding the doctors could not stop. He never regained consciousness.

I follow behind six men who carry Sebastian's shrouded body to the church. Beneath the shroud, Sebastian wears no clothing, and his arms have been crossed on his chest in the manner of all the burials in Isabela. But he will not be sewn into deerskin as is the custom of Old Christians, for there is none to be had. Nor will he be placed in a wooden box or buried inside the church as is usual for someone of Sebastian's rank. The soil is too shallow, and covers bedrock.

As we make our way along the Plaza, The Mourning Office is prayed, and loud dirges and lamentations fill the air. But I do not weep.

Surely Sebastian's disappointment would be great if he could witness these proceedings. For prudence's sake, it does not follow Jewish law. Nor does it follow the pattern of Old Christians in burying their dead, especially their privileged dead. No public crier has been hired to carry the news of his death, or to tell the time and place of his burial—all customary for someone of Sebastian's rank. Neither have I draped my house in black serge, for I have none. But he was awarded the honor of being washed with scented water by two priests, then anointed with ointment and balsam. It is a small comfort, and I grasp it greedily, for I am full of remorse.

If only I had been a better wife.

165

Why did I not try harder to help Sebastian heal his wounded heart? Oh, how disappointed Beatriz must be! And oh, how flawed is my character!

All through Fray Buil's Mass, my mind whips me with these thoughts. And not even the perfumed vapors coming from Fray Buil's censer, as he waves it over Sebastian's body, can dispel my brooding. It continues as Fray Buil sprinkles Sebastian with holy water and says the *Pater Noster.* Only when he begins the Absolutions—the prayers of forgiveness—do I feel a measure of peace, and not because of the prayers, but because I feel the very hand of the Holy One trying to wrestle this burden from me. But I will not release it.

It was Sebastian's sin that brought about this end, and in some way, Señor Villarreal's, too. For Sebastian was made careless by his father's numerous indulgences. How many times had Señor Villarreal paid Sebastian's gambling debts or soothe an irate innkeeper Sebastian had insulted or cheated?

It is easy to make messes when one does not have to clean them up.

But what of my sin? Did not a wife have an obligation to pray for her husband? And how sorely lacking were my prayers!

I watch Fray Buil, who has already removed his chasuble, pick up a large cross. Then we, the mourners, all carrying lighted candles, follow him to the cemetery that sits alongside the church. There are many of us. Most I do not know. But their clothing tell me they are peasants, peasants who have come for the alms. It is customary for a wealthy man's family to give alms to the poor who follow the procession. The custom will be honored. They will be paid. But I am comforted that Maria and Pasculina carry their candles out of friendship.

We stop at the appointed place. Fray Buil makes the sign of the cross, sprinkles the ground with holy water, then hands the cross to one of the many priests by his side. Next he picks up a shovel and digs the symbolic grave—a shallow trench in the shape of a cross. Rumor says this will be the last burial here. Already, another parcel of land, further from Isabela, has been chosen where the soil is deeper.

For my part I am grateful that Sebastian's grave is here, near enough to tend. And I will do it for Beatriz's sake. Now the two will rest beneath blankets of lavender.

When Fray Buil is finished, two men step forward and dig the actual grave. As they dig, Fray Ramon Pane reads the Psalms. The air is suffocating, and when a breeze does come, it is like a hot breath on our necks and causes one of the diggers to pause, lean on his shovel, and wipe his face with the back of his hand. His actions irritate me for they are so casual, so devoid of emotion, and mirror mine so exactly, that I feel I have been exposed.

When the trench is finished, Sebastian's body is lowered with his head facing west, his feet east, in the manner of all burials in Isabela. And as the diggers cover Sebastian with dirt, I quietly watch with dry eyes.

I stand at the back of the church as gaunt-faced men hurriedly file past. Early Mass has just ended, and plainly the men are anxious to return to their huts and break their fast with the little rations they have. I wait patiently, and when the crowd has thinned, my eyes search for Fray Buil. He stands by the altar talking to Ramon Pane. But though he sees me, he waits for the church to empty before approaching.

"Is there something you need, Doña Isabel?"

"Yes . . . you are papal *nuncio* to the Indies, made so by His Holiness Pope Alexander, himself."

A slow smile curves Fray Buil's lips. "I know who I am, child."

"Of . . . course. What I mean is you have power and influence, and . . . ."

"What is it you want of me?" His voice is kind but strained as though weary of people soliciting him.

"I have been contemplating the life of a *beata*."

Again Fray Buil's lips curl. "Your husband has been in his grave only two days. It is understandable that you would want to withdraw from the world and live the life of a pious woman. But you are young and vibrant. Too vibrant for such a life, I think, Doña Isabel."

"I have given this much thought, and my mind is made up. There are many *beatas* living in small communities alongside the Dominicans and Franciscans. It is to one of these I wish to be sent."

"Any woman who has lost a husband might feel as you do. But during seasons of grief can one know his true mind?"

"I tell you Fray Buil, I *do* know it."

"You must allow the Lord time to heal your wounds."

"It is not going to help."

Fray Buil shakes his head, the look on his face, firm.

"Then you will not assist me?"

"I assist you by not consenting to this rash scheme."

My heart plummets for I know my cause is lost. How can I tell Fray Buil that it is not grief I feel, but weariness? I am weary of this world. And how can I tell him I miss my family, and yearn for them, and still cannot go home because of his fellow clergymen? And how can I explain how terribly terribly alone this makes me feel? "This is your final word?" I say, squaring my shoulders.

"It is."

I turn, and am nearly out the door when his voice stops me.

"I know you did not love him, Doña Isabel, not as a wife should love a husband."

I spin around, stunned by both his frankness and insight. "I . . . I . . . ."

He puts up his hand. "I do not judge you. I only caution you. Grief is a curious thing. It takes many forms, and we grieve for many reasons. And grief is never more acute than when we feel alone. But you are not alone, Doña Isabel. Look to God. And you will see He is there."

I bite back tears, and bow my head in resignation. Right now I see only the black empty hole that is my life.

⌒⊙

I sit at the wooden table in my house. I have sat here for three days, neither venturing outside to cook my meals nor allowing Maria and Pasculina to venture in. *Dear kind ladies.* How worried they looked! But I have slept, and was happy for the respite, though these escapes were often short and fitful. A great melancholia has overtaken me, swallowed me alive like the great fish that swallowed Jonah. And as God was the One to rescue Jonah, He must be the One to rescue me, for I know of no other way.

This state has not been caused by Fray Buil, as one might suppose. Even in my present unhappy condition I see how childish my request was. No, that folly is over. I suffer now because three days ago my ship's boy told me twelve of the seventeen vessels in our fleet will be returning to Cadiz, along with a good number of unhappy settlers. And this pricks my heart, for I will not be returning with them. In addition, I must write a letter to Sebastian's father telling him the sad news concerning his son.

A quill lies by my hand; a stack of rag paper at my elbow. I cannot delay much longer for the ships sail tomorrow. Still . . . how can I write the truth? But can I write a lie? Must I pierce Señor Villarreal's heart with both the news of his son's death and the shame surrounding it? I ask the Merciful One to give me the words, then pick up the quill, dip it into the oxhorn full of ink, and with shaking hand begin:

Dear Señor Villarreal:

What unfortunate news prompts me to write this letter! It grieves me to tell you, sir, that Sebastian is dead. He was given a proper burial and accorded several honors befitting his rank. The size of the funeral procession did him credit as well, especially considering the number of our community who lay sick. I hope you will take comfort in the knowledge that all that could be done was done to assure and convey the proper respect.

I shall now attempt to lay out the circumstances of this tragedy.

The day after the Feast of the Three Kings Admiral Columbus ordered two platoons to explore the interior. Sebastian was one of the first nobles to offer his sword, and so eager, too, in spite of the danger and certain hardships; for the men were ordered to find the Indians responsible for killing the settlers at Navidad, and this on limited rations.

I believe you can be proud of your son's bravery in volunteering, and in his willingness to serve our Sovereigns through their appointed agent, Admiral Columbus.

It was during this time that Sebastian was struck down by an Indian. He never regained consciousness even though the doctors employed all their skill to save him. They assured me Sebastian did not suffer. I was also told the offending Indian has been punished by forfeiting his own life.

Your son leaves behind many friends in Isabela, all from noble families, and to a man, they tell me he will be missed.

I pray the Merciful One quickly heals the wound this letter inflicts. I regret it is my hand that writes it.

I sign it, then blot the page before putting it aside and picking up another. Then I begin my second letter:

Dear Mama and Papa,

I write a message similar to what I have written Señor Villarreal. But at the end I add:

I send this letter and another to Señor Villarreal, along with my appeal to quit this place. There is much sickness here, and with many of the able-bodied men returning to Castile, our ranks are noticeably reduced. Food is rationed, and many of our crops fail to grow. It is a wild country, filled with half clothed heathens and I fear, very dangerous for a woman alone. Only two other Castilian women live in our town of Isabela. Surely the dangers here far out weigh those in Seville. Understanding this, you must allow me to come home.

The fleet's physician, Dr. Chanca, will also return with the ships. He is weary and almost sick himself from attending so many ill in our settlement; further proof that this is no place for a woman alone.

Captain Antonio de Torres will command the fleet during its return voyage and sail on Admiral Columbus's flagship, the Mariagalante. *He is the brother of Prince Juan's governess, a reputed man of honor and highly respected by our Sovereigns. Indeed, he was named town warden by Columbus upon our arrival.*

Captain Torres claims that in several months he will return to Isabella with new supplies, and if you grant me permission, I will sail with him when he returns, yet again, to Cadiz. I am sure I will be safe under his watchful eye. Please grant my request for I do not think I can bear living here much longer.

    Your respectful daughter,

    Isabel

~⊙

I stand on the rocky promontory facing the harbor. It is a beautiful sight. Twelve vessels unfurl their sails as a warm wind blows from the east, catching my bodice and skirt, and causing them to billow like sails themselves. If only the wind could blow me back to Andalusia! I pray the ships will catch the favorable west winds Columbus so often speaks about, and thus ensure a speedy voyage to Cadiz, the faster to carry my letters.

It is the second of February, the month of *Shevat*. Today, I am seventeen. I try not to remember that I am now both divorced and widowed. Rather, I think of the gift I have been given, the gift of a ship carrying my petition. God willing, in a few months, it will carry back a favorable reply.

"Captain Torres will return soon," Maria says, squeezing my elbow reassuringly.

"Yes, and then things will improve," adds Pasculina, whose frame no longer fills out her large skirt and bodice.

I smile at my companions, and feel much gratitude. God has not forsaken me altogether, but has left me two good friends.

"I hear the Admiral has ordered ten thousand bushels of wheat and sixty thousand pounds of biscuit," Maria says. "And bacon and raisins and almonds and sugar—twelve hundred pounds of sugar! Not to mention more seed and livestock." There is giddiness in her voice.

"Have you forgotten we are not salaried? We will not partake of these delights. We must rely on our own crops." I try to keep the worry from my voice. Even using the farming methods learned from the Tainos, our wheat, barley and chickpeas do not grow well.

"Fear not, Doña Isabel," Maria says. "God will help us."

Pasculina shrugs. "How difficult can it be? This planting of crops? You toss a handful of seeds onto the soil and they grow."

"It is not that easy. Each plant has its own secrets; secrets of how much water it requires, or pruning, or mulch, its growing cycle, when and how to harvest." Maria frowns. "It has taken me years to learn these things. If you wish, I can teach you."

Pasculina laughs and shakes her head.

"This food shortage is serious," I say. "It may be the undoing of our Admiral. Every day more and more grumble against him."

"Well, rations are not what they should be." Pasculina frowns. "The Crown promised salted fish, beef, bacon, olive oil, garlic, onions, not to mention wine and cheese and biscuits; and of course, plenty of wheat and beans. Instead, we receive a little rancid bacon and rotten cheese, and only a handful of wheat and beans."

"At least you receive something." Maria's voice is hard. "My family and I must get our food where we can."

"Many claim that while they eat rotten bacon and cheese, Columbus dines on candied citron and dates and rose-colored sugar." I shake my head. "But I do not believe it."

"Oh, it is true! My husband has seen it with his own eyes." Pasculina folds her arms under her ample breasts. "And the nobles, and even the peasants and artisans, are angry. Can you blame them?"

I shrug, for it still puzzles me how men can be angry when they are receiving a share of food, no matter how meager. I wonder if Pasculina understands how great is the uncertainty and fear of not having anything to count on at all.

"And the Admiral has sent a list with Captain Torres requesting new supplies of sweets and dainties for himself." Pasculina's voice drips with indignation. "Not to mention tablecloths and towels and silver cups and copper pitchers."

I ignore her as she prattles on about Columbus's pewter cutlery and brass candlesticks, for I am watching the ships drift toward the horizon and feel an agony of soul.

"I will be happy to see them return," Pasculina says, jutting her chin toward the disappearing ships and finally ending her tirade.

I nod. But while Pasculina yearns for the food and goods the ships will carry here, I yearn for the letter that will grant me permission to be carried away.

"Are you certain you want to do this?" Maria's face is as furrowed as her fields.

"I must. But do not concern yourself. I have prayed for God's protection."

"Are you not afraid?"

Instead of answering, I pull a red and gold silk shawl from my trunk and carry it to the table where I spread it out, then smooth the wrinkles with my hands before refolding it. It is a favorite possession, a gift from Papa; my first silk shawl. It is of the finest quality, and very costly.

"*Doña Isabel?*"

I smile. Maria never calls me Doña when we are alone except when vexed. I do not resent her tone for it is the tone only a good friend would use. "Yes, I am afraid."

"Then why are you going? No gift can undo what has been done."

"I know. But perhaps it can put the matter to rest. Perhaps it can bring healing to two households. Columbus's interpreter told me it is proper to give a gift to an injured party."

"I do not understand this, Isabel. It is foolhardy, even dangerous. And there is no guarantee your gift will be accepted. Why take such a risk?"

"Because *I* need this, to get rid of the sickness I feel in here." I place my hand over my heart.

"Then let Gonzalo accompany you, or my sons."

I pick up the shawl and when I do, I smell the scent of lavender. "This is between women. It is not for a man to fix."

"Then I will come."

"No. You said yourself there may be danger."

"All the more reason I should be with you."

She sounds so much like Mama. I look at her worn, frightened face and nod as I embrace her. "Very well, Maria. Come if you must."

Bata waits up ahead behind a clump of vines. Through a partial opening I see her shiny black hair and the grotesque cotton *zemi* that presses against her glistening forehead. I struggle through the vegetation that snags our hair, clothing, legs and feet. Fortunately, the shawl is safely tucked inside my bodice.

I finally stop at a narrow clearing, allowing Maria to catch her breath. "You can turn back. It is not too late. If anything happens . . . you have a family who needs you."

"Do not speak of this again, Isabel. The matter is settled. I am here, and will remain here by your side." Maria pulls vines from her hair as Bata signals impatiently for us to follow her.

So we follow, winding this way and that along the bank of the Isabela River to where a small unpainted boat, hollowed out by fire judging from its charred interior, sits along the water's edge. Inside are two large gourds of water and two paddles, each resembling a baker's shovel.

Bata gestures for us to get in, and when we do she pushes us off the bank, jumps into the boat as easily as if she were a cat, then hands me one of the paddles while she keeps the other.

It takes some doing but finally my paddle works in unison with hers, and we glide along the river. The beauty of the land steals my breath. The trees are so high they obstruct the sky. And the birds! What songs they sing! Like a choir of angels! It is all so lovely I scarcely mind the hard work of paddling. But presently my arms grow tired and I realize we have been at this for some time.

With each stroke we go deeper into the interior. It is not a comforting thought. Even with Maria sitting nearby I am uneasy. I am about to ask Bata if we are nearly there when she gestures for us to head to shore.

We beach our boat then Bata leads us along a narrow path through tangled vegetation until finally we come upon a large Taino village. Dozens of circular wood-and-thatched houses lay scattered about like tossed dice forming no discernible pattern. But the center is cleared and appears to be a well-graded rectangular plaza. The plaza itself is lined with stone slabs, each a cubit or so high, and painted with figures that remind me of Bata's *zemis*. More than twenty men run from one end of the plaza to the other, tossing about what looks like a small ball made of roots and grass. Though it appears to be a game, the men's fierce whoops and shouts frighten me.

Someone sees us, and points. Then men stop running, stop shouting, stop tossing the ball, and all is quiet. I expect any minute to be attacked, and whisper prayers to the Merciful One. To my surprise only one large man approaches. His face and arms are painted black. Tied around his neck is a stone *zemi*. Another *zemi* is tied around his upper right arm. A golden ornament fills the large hole in each ear lobe. His loins are covered with a colorful cloth, and around his waist is a wide cotton belt of a fine tight weave.

"He *cacique*," Bata says. "*Cacique*."

I have heard this word many times and know Bata is telling me the man is the chief. She talks while Maria and I stand quietly to one side. I do not understand anything she says, but it makes the chief smile. He barks what seem like orders to a man standing nearby, then we follow the chief to a house at the end of the plaza. It is larger than the others, and rectangular instead of round. The roof is high and thatched. Tall thick poles, driven deep into the dirt, make up the frame; while thin branches, tied together by vines, make up the walls.

I enter reluctantly, and only after men holding clubs and bows gather around us. Inside, the floor is covered by pleasant-smelling straw, and some of the walls are decorated with painted bark. Two large balls of cotton sit in one corner. In the other, suspended above the ground, is a bed of cotton netting which Tainos call "*hammock.*" Dozens of grotesque stone carvings, some several cubits high, others as small as my hand, line the opposite wall—the chief's *zemis*. Sitting almost in the shadows is an elaborate wooden chair, the legs of which are carved to look like animal paws, with the front resembling a face with ears and eyes covered in gold.

The chief takes his chair, then Bata gestures for us to sit on the floor. I only hope Columbus's Taino interpreter, who I paid to speak to Bata, has made my message clear, and that now she will relay it accurately. As she and the chief converse, three women enter. One carries a wooden tray of fresh fruit, the other, two gourds of water. They set their offerings on the floor and depart. The third woman, who comes empty-handed, sits down beside us. She is young and pretty, and appears shy, for she gazes only at the ground.

The chief gestures for us to eat, and I do so only out of fear of offending him for my stomach is too uneasy to enjoy food. While I nibble my papaya, the chief says something to the young woman. Then Bata speaks. She talks so long I grow restless. Perhaps she has misunderstood our Taino interpreter, or perhaps she is saying more than she was instructed to say. But I am relieved when at last she is silent.

The shy Taino woman finally lifts her head and looks at me. There is sweetness in her eyes.

Bata stretches her hand toward me, and I pull the shawl from my bodice and give it to her. I know the woman does not understand, but I cannot stop myself from saying, "Please forgive me." And as Bata passes the shawl to the woman, I add, "Please forgive my husband."

The young woman places the folded silk on her lap and studies it intently before allowing her fingers to rub its surface. When she looks up there is a smile on her face and she says something in a sweet, soft voice. I do not understand the words of her mouth, but I understand the words of her heart. I take a deep breath, inhaling the pleasant air of the hut, and feel a lightness I have not felt for some time. The great melancholia that has kept me in its belly these many days has finally spewed me out. And for the first time since Sebastian's death, I feel free of the guilt and shame of his terrible deed.

Chapter 14

W ith a small metal shovel I scoop smoldering ashes from the firebox and sprinkle them into my basin of water. "How many tubers do you have?"

"Enough for a dozen loaves of cassava bread," Maria says, as she sits on a mat by my door shedding *yuccas* with a piece of coral.

"Your family needs ten, and I two. That leaves nothing for the hospital." I dunk my ceramic griddle—the one Bata calls a *buren*— into the basin, and scour it with a handful of straw.

Bata has taught us how to make cassava bread. And when we can, we make extra for the sick men under Doctor Spinoza's care. "I am willing to manage with one loaf. The other can go to the hospital."

Maria tosses the shredded roots into her pot of water. The tubers contain poison which must first be removed by shredding, then by soaking. Later, she will press the shreds through a sieve, then fry the pulp on the griddle, making round unleavened bread.

"Can you manage with less?"

"If you must be a martyr, I suppose so must I." There is a frown on her face. "They will not like it, but my family can do with eight loaves. That will leave you three in all for the sick."

I smile. "It *is* more blessed to give than to receive. God will reward your kindness."

Maria answers with a click of her tongue, but I do not mind. For weeks, something curious has been happening. Since my return from the interior, the Lord has been speaking to me. Not as a voice in my ear, but as an inner knowledge I cannot explain, for suddenly I know a thing when before I did not. And this is what I know: when you are in want, the quickest path to blessing is the path of sharing with others. And though I have not spoken about this to anyone, I have begun tithing my food.

⌒〇

Maria, Bata and I are in Marta, standing on the large tract of land allocated to Sebastian before he died, and which is now allocated to me. All the land is owned by the Crown and distributed by rank. I think this practice foolish, for if the Crown wants Isabela to attract more than adventurers seeking gold, it must issue land grants to peasants willing to work hard.

From where I stand, I cannot even see the end of my vast lands. Only a small portion has been cleared, and this for my earlier crops, many of which have failed. Even planting these troublesome crops on mounds, as Bata taught us, has not yielded a good harvest. So I have decided to change my approach. No longer will I plant that which is ill-suited to this soil.

The ever blowing easterly wind stirs my hair and cools my damp forehead. It is nearly the end of the dry season—the best time, according to Bata, to burn brush. Already, Gonzalo and his sons have dug trenches around the area I wish to cultivate.

Bata stands between Maria and me, wearing the familiar *zemi* tied to her forehead and nothing else. She carries a pot of burning coals in a sling made of soaked roots.

"Ready?" I say, as I reach into the pot with metal tongs. When Maria and Bata nod, I fling coals here and there. Maria does likewise, and we all walk backward until we reach the trench, then hop it.

Presently, the brush ignites. Then flames, like hungry mouths, gobble everything in their path. The mouths snap and pop, and cause embers as delicate as moths to fill the air. And finally, when the mouths can eat no more, they vanish. I sit, then Maria and Bata settle beside me. When the ground cools we will rake the burnt brush, and the soil beneath it, into giant mounds. Bata says these mounds, which she calls *conucos*, can produce crops for more than ten years before having to be destroyed and new ones made. Her knowledge of farming is vast; a collective knowledge passed down by generations of Taino women, for it is the women, and not the men, who do this work.

We sit quietly for some time before Maria breaks the silence. "Your crops will do well. Never have I seen such a wonderful way to farm—root crops at the center and bottom to keep the soil drained and prevent it from washing away; leaf crops on top to provide shade and keep the mounds moist. If I had such knowledge in Seville your father's estate would have been the envy of the countryside."

"It *was* the envy of the countryside. At least your gardens were."

Maria accepts my compliment with a smile. "Still, my husband and sons long for bread made of wheat."

"Like everyone else in Isabela. But we must train our bellies to accept new foods if we wish to survive. It is useless to long for something that will not grow in this soil. These mounds will produce *yucca* for cassava bread. And Bata says if we store the roots in the ground, they can last for three years. Think of it, Maria! Having surplus crops that can be stored means we will never starve. And there are other Taino foods, too, that we will learn to grow. I have already asked Bata to show me how to plant those sweet yellow tubers we both like so much."

"*Batatas*," Bata says, calling the sweet tubers by name.

"Yes, *batatas*." I smile at Bata, wondering if it was from this word that she got her name.

"We will plant other Taino crops, too. Foods we have tried and found pleasing: peppers, squash, peanuts, and . . . ."

"Please, Isabel. You wear me out. Let that be for another day."

I rise, and pick up one of the wooden rakes Gonzalo made. "Yes, let it be for another day. Today we plant *yuccas* and *batatas*. Come. To work."

"Bata is to wed Juan," Maria says, sticking her head into my doorway. "Even now Gonzalo is settling the bride price. And Luis says he is considering one of Bata's cousins as wife, so perhaps there will be yet another bride price to haggle."

I am not surprised, for I have seen Maria's son, Juan, and Bata together. And it is only natural that Luis, observing his brother's happiness, would want this same happiness for himself. "I pray God's blessings on them," I say, standing at my table and bolting the last of my wheat flour through a piece of muslin.

"You have flour!" Maria shrieks when she realizes what I am doing, then heads for the table, her eyes as large as cassava loaves.

"Bata will be a good wife for Juan." I do not mention my concern over Bata's unwillingness to give up her *zemis*, or the fact that she is beautiful and voluptuous, and her constant nudity has created a stir among the nobles.

Maria presses her palms together. "I only pray Gonzalo's leather goods will be acceptable for there are no women to be had other than Tainos. What are my sons to do?" She watches as I continue straining flour through cloth, removing bits of hull. "My sons are all old enough to wed. And they are impatient to make a life of their own. But these Taino women are such heathens! I made Juan swear an oath that once he is married he will not allow Bata to wear those heathen idols, and that he will force her to dress properly."

It is a relief, for aside from *zemis* being offensive to God, the nobles have been burning all the cotton *zemis* they can find, and smashing the ones of stone. It would be dangerous for Bata to wear them when she comes to Isabela to live. And with so many men in want of a woman, it would be dangerous for her to wear only the short skirt of a Taino wife.

"Soon you will have two married sons. A great blessing." I add ground chickpeas to my flour in order to stretch it. "But what of Enrique? Has he not found a woman among the Tainos to please him?"

"Enrique is restless . . . and discontented. I worry. Since coming to the Indies he has grown more sullen." Maria tucks a calloused finger under my chin and forces me to look at her. "But you must marry, Isabel. There are still many high born here. Has not one caught your eye?"

I shake my head. "I will never marry again."

Maria laughs. "Nonsense! You are young and beautiful. And what are women for if not to have children? A simple nod from you would bring many suitors to your door. I have seen the way some look at you. But you refuse to give them the slightest glance. You are too aloof, Isabel. Too aloof."

"I am not aloof. It is just that I . . . lack the necessary disposition to be a proper wife."

Maria dips her finger into the bowl. Her eyes widen when she realizes the great depth of flour in it. "Perhaps you *do* speak your mind too freely, but you have other qualities. You are peerless in the kitchen. See how great your skill is in conserving your stores! Oh, how I envy this ability."

I wipe my hands on my apron and pick up the bowl. "This? Oh, no. It is not mine."

"Well . . . whose then?"

I hand it to her. "I have been saving this for your family's Easter bread. I wish for you to enjoy it after Mass tomorrow."

Maria's cheeks puff like the throat of a Guadalquivir River frog. "Surely not! It is the last of your wheat and beans. I could never accept such a great gift."

"It would be ill-mannered to refuse."

Her eyes linger over the bowl, and I sense her inner struggle. "It *will* please my family. In truth, they will be overjoyed to have wheat bread for Easter. And it will give me pleasure to bake it for them." She cups my chin with one hand. "The only thing that would make my happiness complete is if you honor me by joining us for our Easter meal."

"Then let your happiness be complete."

"You . . . would come?" It is unheard of for someone of my rank to eat at a peasant's house, for it implies equality in a society where rank is closely guarded. "You would come?" she repeats.

"Yes." The look on her face I will never forget. It is one of love and joy and gratitude, for my going will not only reveal to all in Isabela the high regard I have for Maria's family, it will reveal the depth of my friendship with Maria herself. And for the first time in weeks I think of Sebastian, may his memory be for blessing, and all I can do is smile.

It is Easter morning, the month of *Ilay* or April. Last month, in the month of *Nissan*, came the days of Unleavened Bread and Passover, which I did not observe. More and more it is difficult to observe, even in small ways, the Lord's Feasts, since there are so many Christian holidays to honor, and more Saint's days than grains of sand. Also, there are daily Masses and prayers and weekly fasts. It is more than I can manage, and short of becoming a *beata*, which Fray Buil insists I am ill suited for, I must content myself in doing what little I can.

But in honor of today and the One who won my heart by His great sacrifice, I have taken care in my appearance. My hair is arranged in multiple braids coiled at the nape of my neck then studded with pearls and covered by a beautiful veil of shimmering gold silk. I am sure even Sebastian himself would approve. In addition, I wear a beautiful gown of green and gold brocade, adorned with pearls and lace. And around my neck hangs Mama's green stone of Zebulun.

The church bell, a gift from Queen Isabel to our community, chimes Tierce as I head for the plaza. While I walk, I scan the town. It is no secret Admiral Columbus expects Isabela to be the capital of Spain's colony in the Indies. Perhaps one day it will be a grand city, but for now, it is very modest, consisting of a storehouse, a forge, a powder house, and one of the most beautiful spots in all Isabela—*Casa de*

Columbus, the House of Columbus. And I give silent praises to God that we have accomplished even this much with so many sick.

We have even increased our sphere of influence. Our first fort, Santo Tomas, a small outpost really, was built last month in the Vega Real to protect the Cibao goldfields from Caonabo, the Taino ruler believed to have been behind the Navidad massacre. Santo Tomas is less than twenty leagues from Isabela, and manned by fifty-seven men, all under the command of Alonso de Hojeda.

Considering all our privations we have accomplished much. But there are many problems, too. Hojeda has proven harsh. Already he has sent one chief to Isabela in chains and cut the ear off another. And the *Lanzas* are cruel to the Indians, and terrify them with their horses and war dogs. Amid all this is the constant sickness. Many have died. And food is still scarce, partially because the settlers search the riverbanks for gold, like men possessed, rather than planting crops. And everywhere, men whisper of rebellion.

Even my own Fray Buil is at odds with Columbus, for he feels the Admiral is too severe with the men. How is it possible that two men who love the Lord are so incapable of amiability and friend-ship? Everyone knows how sincere Columbus is in his devotion to the Holy One and to Scripture. By Columbus's own admission it was the Prophet Isaiah's words that enabled him to find the Indies. *So why was there no peace between these two?*

To make matters worse, the royal accountant, Bernal de Pisa, is imprisoned on one of the *naos* for talking rebellion and threatening to sail the remaining ships back to Castile with the other malcontents.

Oh, how many malcontents we have in Isabela!

Everyone blames Columbus for the food shortages, and for not finding the quantity of gold they believe they were promised. Many despair of ever becoming rich, and are bitter. All this robs me of sleep when I allow thoughts of it to fester. But today I am determined to push it all from my mind and think only on the One who has sustained me throughout it all.

As I near the church, angry voices fill the air. Surely more discontentment, more complaints. I walk faster, not wishing to hear, not wishing to take my mind from the One we honor today. But it is useless. The talk is too loud, too angry.

"He has no right!"

"His right has been granted by our Sovereigns."

"Flogging two men for insubordination is one thing, but hanging the third is another. I tell you he has gone too far."

"Even Fray Buil feels Columbus has overstepped this time, and threatens to refuse him the sacraments."

I pick up my pace and head for the church. Oh, how greatly La Isabela needs the care and love of the Risen One.

⤙

The first thing I smell, when approaching Maria's hut, is baking bread. The warm, yeasty aroma floats from two greased earthenware bowls stacked lip to lip—Maria's makeshift oven that sits on a bed of coals in her firebox. The smell makes my mouth water, and even while Maria and I hug and extend Easter blessings, I am distracted by it.

"Please go sit at the table." Maria gestures toward the doorway of her house. "It is too hot to be outside. The bread is done and has only to be removed from the oven." Maria shoos me away with her hands

And so I enter her house for the first time. It is smaller than mine, though five grown people live here. All the bedding has been neatly rolled, and leans against one corner. A large wooden table with benches on both sides occupies the center. On the table is the sizeable lead-glazed bowl Maria carried all the way from Seville. Next to it are three knives and five small ridged bowls for individual use. Around the table sit the three Vivar sons while Gonzalo stands nearby.

He braids and unbraids his fingers nervously as he bows. "Come in. Come in, please. You honor us with your presence."

I quickly occupy the empty space beside Juan, who smiles broadly. So does Luis, who sits on the opposite side next to Enrique. Not surprising, Enrique just glares.

I wish everyone a blessed Easter, then turn to Juan. "All is well between you and Bata?" It would be indelicate to ask him directly if Gonzalo found the bride price acceptable.

Juan's face brightens. "Oh, yes. The bride price has been agreed upon, Fray Buil has been consulted, and the date set. Will you come to the wedding, Doña Isabel?"

"He is to be married in a month," Luis blurts, as though unwilling to be left out of the conversation. "And soon Papa will inquire about the bride price of Bata's cousin who I wish to . . . ."

"Enough talk," Maria says, entering the hut carrying a large loaf of bread wrapped in a kitchen cloth. "Gonzalo will pray now." She places the bread on the table. And while Gonzalo prays the blessing, I lift my eyes and see his three sons gaping at the steaming loaf. Before the prayer is even finished, Enrique grabs it.

"Guests go first," Maria says, giving Enrique a sharp look.

He scowls, and I accept both the bread and his ill humor with a polite "Thank you."

"Tomorrow Columbus leaves with the *Niña* and two other ships," Luis says. "He goes north looking for the golden city of Quinsay and the Great Khan."

"I am grieved to hear that. It would be better if he stayed here, having only recently recovered from his illness." I cannot bring myself to utter anything harsh against our Admiral though I find his leaving irresponsible with Isabela facing so many difficulties.

"He leaves his brother, Diego, to govern in his absence, and made Francisco Roldan town warden to assist him," Luis adds.

I nod, and hope my anxiety does not show. Diego is young and inexperienced; Roldan, coarse and ambitious. A dangerous mix.

"Fray Buil looked angry when he announced Columbus's voyage at Mass this morning," Juan adds.

"Everyone is angry, for Columbus leaves Isabela when he is needed most," Luis says.

"No need to share such gossip." Maria ladles fish stew into one of the bowls, and hands it to me. "We should keep our tongues from speaking unkindly. It is not for us to question the Admiral."

"And why not?" Enrique's voice is so sharp that all heads turn in his direction. "Why should we not question him when we are the ones left to do the work? And even if we labor without complaint, what will we gain for our trouble? The Crown controls everything, receiving most of the profits with Columbus gobbling the rest. Even the nobles will be rewarded in lands and titles. I ask again, what do *we* get? I will tell you, we get . . . ."

"Enrique!" Gonzalo's face is white. "Men have been whipped for such talk."

"Diego Columbus can have my flesh to lash if he wishes. Let him enjoy his power while he can. He will not have it long. Already there is talk of . . . ."

"This is treasonous!" Gonzalo barks. "Enough!"

"*Enough?* It is not nearly enough. Change is in the wind. You will see. The nobles will not rule us forever." Enrique's nostrils flair as he looks at me.

All is deathly quiet. Gonzalo, who has been sitting at the head of the table, rises to his feet. For a moment, I think he will strike his son, but then I see the fear in his eyes and know he will not. "You have insulted our guest, and disgraced this house. Get out!" His voice shakes. And for the first time I understand how greatly he fears Enrique. I look around at the others and see the same fear. Obviously, it is only for my sake, and to avoid losing honor, that Gonzalo has dared face his son now.

Maria presses her hands over her mouth as Enrique stands to his feet. Her eyes tear. Does she fear Enrique will disobey his father and that Gonzalo will have to exert his authority by force? Or is she afraid Enrique will strike Gonzalo for daring to speak to him so harshly?

I am not to find out, for Enrique says in a stiff, cold voice, "I beg your pardon, Doña Isabel," and in four strides, exits the hut.

∽૭

My needle moves swiftly, stitching the last bit of open seam on the linen cloth of my new mattress. It is filled with three basketsful of cotton purchased from Bata. I make the final knot, break the thread with my teeth, and lay the bedding across my wooden table. Any minute now Gonzalo will be here with my new bed. He claims it is a gift for coming to his house, but I think it is to make amends for Enrique's outburst, and to soothe any feelings of indignation I might have. But I have none.

Gonzalo says he has also made me a wooden case with four shelves on which to place my dishes, pots and kitchen utensils. And though I have insisted on paying him for his trouble, his refusal was so vehement I dare not pursue it for fear of offending him.

I am filled with joy and anticipation, both, and when I hear a commotion outside I fly to the door where at long last I see Gonzalo and Enrique walking down the street carrying the bed. Behind them, Juan and Luis bring the wooden case. And all are lead by Maria, who holds what looks like a pillow tucked under her arm.

"Gull feathers," she says, handing me the pillow when she gets to the door. "For sleeping and laundry." We both laugh.

Then Gonzalo and Enrique enter with the bed.

"Such a fine bed!" I exclaim when at last they set it in place. It is made of pine, with a head and footboard. On the headboard is carved a large ornate cross. Sturdy hemp, strung through the frame, will hold the cotton mattress. "Surely the finest bed in all Isabela!" I clap my hands in delight.

Next, Juan and Luis carry in the tall wooden case, and after repositioning one of my trunks, they put it near the window. What a delight to finally have a place for my things! I want to hug Gonzalo out of pure gratitude, but such rash behavior would be inappropriate, and embarrass him. So I hug Maria instead.

"Thank you, thank you, thank you."

Laughter and well wishing abound, then I am left alone to arrange my bedding and fill my shelves.

I am kneeling beside the wooden case, filling the last shelf, when a sudden noise makes me turn. The sight of Enrique's large square frame causes me to spring to my feet.

"What . . . do you want?" Enrique remains silent. "Have you forgotten something?" His molten eyes frighten me. There is something terrible and dark in them. I grab a knife from one of the shelves. "You must leave. It is . . . improper, you being here."

His laugh is throaty and coarse as he walks towards me. And before I can stop him, he knocks the knife from my hand, then stands so close I see the thin black hairs that protrude from his nostrils; see the web-like cracks in his lips; see that his bottom front tooth is chipped when he opens his mouth.

"Every woman needs a husband. Even one such as you." When I remain silent he steps closer, forcing me against the wooden case. "Do not think any of these preening nobles can make a life for you here. They are weak. And you have seen enough of that weakness in your last husband."

I push against his chest trying to escape, but he only laughs and shoves me hard against the case. "I will be your husband, Doña Isabel. You will not find better out of this sorry lot. Besides, you married above your station. Why should I not marry above mine?"

"You are too full of pride and arrogance, Enrique. Beware, or it will be your undoing!"

He grabs my arms and pulls them hard behind me. "It is you who are full of pride. You and your race. You call yourselves 'the chosen' as if God only cares for you. And no matter how many of you we try to destroy, still you prosper. You have wealth, houses, lands, livestock. You live like kings while the rest of us . . . . Very well. If you cannot be destroyed, then you can be made to share your wealth. And you will share it, Isabel. As your husband, I will own what you own. Your wealth will be mine."

Suddenly, I understand Enrique's hatred of me, and why he has frightened me all these years. "I will never accept you as my husband."

Enrique releases me and laughs. "We shall see how you feel when the rebellion is over and there is none to protect you from the rabble that fills Isabela. Perhaps I am distasteful to you now, but I believe you will feel differently then. But know this—next time I come, it will be to claim you as my bride."

"Get out before I sound an alarm!" I point to the door with a shaking finger.

His lips curve in a smile, but I see fear in his eyes, too. "I will leave. But for a season, Doña Isabel, only for a season. When things change—and change they will for even now men plot and plan—I will return."

And then he is gone, leaving me to sink to my knees. And in this position of humility and weakness, I implore the Merciful One to take me away from this horrible place.

Chapter 15

"You must stop this!" I say, as I stand by the forge and watch Pasculina's husband, Señor Lopez, crush a pacer nugget. "You must gather the honorable men of Isabela and put a stop to this. Surely you can not approve of what is going on!"

Señor Lopez shrugs as he adds water and quicksilver to the unrefined lump. "The Crown pays me to assay gold." He agitates the mixture, then watches the impurities separate. "I am not the town warden. What can I do?"

"Isabel is right," Pasculina says, her hands on her hips, a fierce expression on her face. "Will you stand idly by while everything around us crumbles?"

"You know how badly things have gone since Admiral Columbus sailed away on the *Niña*," I add. "But instead of assisting Francisco Roldan in keeping order, Pedro Margarite and his soldiers plunder the Tainos—their food, their goods. Some even steal young boys for forced labor. And the women? They are shamelessly taken as concubines. Stories of rape and pillage abound. How can men of conscience allow this?"

Maria stands nearby and I watch her eyes tear. It is mainly at her insistence that I am here. Enrique has joined these worthless men. More than once Maria has told me she fears for his immortal soul. Daily, she lights candles and prays her beads. "Someone must stand against this," I press.

"For two months Diego Columbus has tried to stop the lawlessness by laying fines and punishments upon the men. Even Fray Buil has preached restraint in all his Masses. Am I better than they? Or more powerful? The Governing Council must handle this."

Maria's lip quivers. "Señora Villarreal has already gone to the Council and registered a complaint. They are too frightened to act. You must go to Francisco Roldan and plead with him. It is his job as town warden to right these wrongs."

Señor Lopez pours his mixture into a porous leather bag. "What good will that do? Roldan has turned a blind eye, and worse—he is in league with these scoundrels." Slowly, quicksilver drips from the bag into a pan. When all of it has dripped out, the bag will contain only gold dust, which Señor Lopez will put into a crucible and heat to assay its purity. "If rumor can be trusted, Roldan himself keeps two concubines and eats many a meal from stolen Taino pots."

"Then go to the *Lanzas* at Marta," I say, "and appeal to their honor."

"Appeal to their honor? Embittered men have no honor. Promises were made, promises of riches and glory. Like most here in Isabela the *Lanzas* see these things slipping through their fingers. Many talk of returning to Castile. And if they cannot have gold, they will enrich themselves in other ways, believing it their due."

"Gold! Gold! I am sick of hearing that word. It sweeps our town like a plague. Everyone is mad with it." Pasculina narrows her eyes at her husband as though it was all his fault. "No one is interested in building canals for water. I spend half my days carrying heavy buckets from the river. And where are the roads we were promised? And look how long it took to build the mill! And now that we have it, where is the wheat to grind in it?" She points to the large smelting furnace behind her husband where he refines the gold. A man in coarse homespun and covered in sweat works the bellows, keeping the fire hot. "This will be the downfall of our settlement. You mark my words."

Our pleas are silenced when the church bell rings, and shouts are raised. The forge is outside the storehouse, toward its northern end, and from our position we see nothing amiss. When the shouts grow louder, I dash for the church. Maria and Pasculina follow. And then I see them—three ships on the horizon coming from the west.

A crowd has gathered on the rocky promontory, and I thread my way through it to a suitable vantage point. Columbus's ships would surely come from the north, from the direction of fabled Cipango and Quinsay. My heart pounds like the hoofs of a *Lanzas* horse.

The ships must be from Cadiz.

Someone shouts, "Do they fly the standard?" And I know he thinks my thoughts, for the standard he speaks of is the standard flown only on Admiral Columbus's ships.

"I see none but the flag of Castile and Leon," someone else says, and a murmur ripples through the crowd.

Closer and closer the ships sail until finally someone cries, "No standard flies from their masts. They hail from Cadiz!"

A shout goes up, and men slap each other's backs and praise the Almighty. Joy overwhelms me, and I hug both Maria and Pasculina at once. We stay there, watching the ships throw their anchors. And all the while my heart pounds this secret prayer: *Please God, let there be a letter from Mama.*

Two longboats pull onto the sandbank, and dozens of men climb out. A third boat heads back in the choppy water towards its ship, having discharged passengers only moments before. Two of these passengers are well dressed, wearing velvet jerkins and cloaks. Gold chains hang from their necks. Already, a rumor circulates that they are men of importance. I watch them head to where Diego Columbus and Fray Buil stand waiting. One of them is tall and broad, with grey hair and wearing a red cap. I am struck by how greatly he resembles our Admiral. Next to him walks a young man, bareheaded, and with a neatly trimmed beard. His wavy onyx-colored hair falls below his ears and glistens in the sunlight as though freshly washed. Diego Columbus embraces the man in the cap. And when he says, "Greetings, Don Bartolome," I know it is his brother.

I remain behind, while most of the throng follow Fray Buil to the church to give thanks. And for a long time I watch as men and supplies are rowed to shore. Only after Maria and Pasculina leave do I summon enough courage to approach a nearby sailor. "Have you brought any letters from Castile?"

He looks startled, perhaps because I am a woman in a place where only men are said to dwell. "Now what would I know of any letters, my pretty? Am I the captain?" He leers at me as though I am a tavern maid, but I cannot fault him. My skirt and bodice are coarse home-spun, and my hair is held in cotton netting—the garb of a peasant.

"It is the captain, then, who carries the letters?"

He nods, and points to three men standing together on the sand-bank. Two of the men wear fashionable clothes of velvet. The third wears a leather jerkin.

Carefully, I work my way down to the shore where I come first upon the captain wearing leather. He has separated himself from the others, and stands by one of the longboats issuing orders to a seaman. When he is finished, I approach.

"Pardon, Señor, do you carry letters from Castile?"

"We all carry a pouch of mail," he says, gesturing toward the other captains.

"Then can you tell me if you carry a letter for Señora Villarreal?"

"Your mistress?"

"No. I am Señora Villarreal."

His bushy eyebrows rise like wings. "Pardon, Señora, I meant no disrespect."

"I am not offended, Captain, only anxious to learn if you have mail for me."

"Not in my pouch." He turns to the others. "Perhaps in theirs." Then he quickly makes my request known to the captains.

When both men shake their heads, I thank them and walk away, all the while biting back tears.

❧

I stand by my table, pouring water from the calabash into a large flat-bottomed wash basin which I use for bathing and sometimes for washing clothes. Since learning I have no letter from home I have done nothing but cry.

When the basin is full, I place the calabash on the table. My heart is heavy as I bend and wash my face. *Why did Mama not write?*

And then the thoughts come, like insects nipping at my brain. *Has something happened?* I dry my face then remove the netting and loosen my braid. *Have Mama and Papa fallen into the hands of the Inquisition?* I brush my long auburn hair. *Why did Mama not write?* I pull my hair back, and loosely tie it with a white cotton ribbon. *How much longer can I survive in this horrible place?* Puffy eyes stare back at me in the mirror as I cover my head with a shawl.

I will go to Marta and work my mounds. The feel of earth between my fingers, the kiss of the sun on my cheeks, these will help soothe my troubled mind. And I will not seek Maria's company. I will go alone, and in solitude ask the Merciful One what to do.

Why did Mama not write?

As I fly through the door, I bump into a well-dressed silver-haired man of medium height, a man I have never seen before. "Oh, pardon."

"Are you Señora Villarreal?"

"I am."

"The man bows, then pulls something from his tan velvet jerkin." I have been instructed to deliver this." He extends his hand, and when I see he holds a letter, my heart jumps. *Could it be from Mama?*

"My master will call on you in two hours."

"Your master?" I take the letter from him.

"Yes, for your answer."

"What answer do you speak of?"

"It is all in the letter." He bows and turns to go.

"Wait! Pray tell, who is your master?"

The man looks surprised as though it is obvious. "Why . . . Señor Villarreal of course. Señor Antonio Villarreal."

I am too stunned to speak so I just watch him walk down the street until he turns a corner and disappears. It is then I remember the letter, and rush inside. I sit on the edge of the bed, and with trembling hands break the seal and unfold the pages. Carefully, I spread them across my lap. My heart pounds when I see Mama's familiar handwriting.

My Darling Isabel,

What sad news you send us! Papa and I sat shiva with Señor Villarreal and prayed the Kaddish and mourned for seven days. But nothing can bring Sebastian back, may his memory be for blessing, or ease the pain of losing one's child, a pain I know all too well.

My heart also grieves for you, dear Isabel. It is a terrible thing to be a young widow; for a woman, especially a young woman, should not be alone in this evil world. For that reason, the loss of a husband, even one who has not been husband long, is not easy to bear. Even so, we are all servants of the Most High and must suffer as He wills.

Concerning your request to return home; I must forbid it, Isabel. It is far too dangerous here in Seville. The Inquisition rages like a mad dog, its mouth full of our people's blood. More burn at the stake every day. Fray Alonso is still enraged by your departure, and Sebastian's. But since he has no charge to lay against you or us, he is powerless to order your arrest or ours. It is only God's mercy that makes this so, for, as you feared, Catalina whispered against us. But a sudden illness has taken her life, and silenced her tongue forever—may God forgive her for her treachery. Dr. Hernando Diaz said she died of brain fever. I did not rejoice upon hearing it, but I cannot say I am unhappy that we have one less enemy to worry us.

But it has not gone as well for Señor Villarreal. Isabel, you would not recognize our dear friend! He is thin and pale, and suffers so acutely with gout he seldom stirs from his rooms. Fray Alonso, believing Sebastian to be a potential assassin, tried to implicate Señor Villarreal as a co-conspirator. Our friend has undergone hours of questioning, much to the detriment of his health. But no amount of questioning was able to extract a confession, so Fray Alonso, lacking evidence, could not bring a formal charge against him. Even so, this shows how the high born and well-connected must also fear the Inquisition. But now this news of Sebastian's death! I worry it will weaken Señor Villarreal further.

If you wonder why I write so freely it is because I send this letter by Don Antonio's hand, and know it will be kept safe from the prying eyes of the Inquisition's spies. For your safety and ours, you must burn it after reading. Don Antonio brings it, along with a contract of marriage between you and him. It has been signed by the necessary parties, as well as witnessed, all in accordance with Jewish law. Also, your dowry has been paid.

If you are wondering what has caused this turn of events, let me tell you. Recently, Antonio lost his wife, Doña Maria de Murcia, in childbirth, along with his infant son. Since Sebastian died without an heir, it falls to Antonio to provide his brother one. The proper year of mourning has been waived for you as well as Antonio, due to your special circumstances of living in the Indies with so many men. All agree it is not wise for a young woman to be left so unprotected. As you know, under the law of levirate marriage, Antonio was able, in the halizah—the ceremony of un-shoeing—to release you from your obligation to marry him. This he did not do. Antonio has been so despondent since the death of his wife and child, and has clamored so loudly to be released from his court duties and sent home, that Señor Villarreal urged him to enter into this marriage. He believes the marriage and the move to the Indies are necessary for the wellbeing of his son's mind and heart, both of which are greatly troubled. Señor Villarreal also fears Fray Alonso will try to torment him further by fabricating some charge against Antonio. I believe Señor Villarreal's assumption is based on grief, the grief of a loving father who has lost a son and fears losing another, rather than on any true facts concerning Fray Alonso's intentions. But who can say for sure.

Now you know the events responsible for bringing you your third husband.

I know you have denied your faith. But need I remind you that Maimonides himself said a marriage between a converso and Jew was valid when contracted under Jewish law, and therefore subject to the law of levirate marriage. Since your

*marriage to Sebastian conformed to our law in every respect, this levirate marriage
to Antonio is legal and binding. It is your duty to honor the contract. I only pray
you will do so with the proper attitude.*

*Papa and I miss you terribly. Words cannot express the emptiness we feel, for
with you being so far from our arms it is as if we have lost two daughters.*

*'May the Lord make you like Sarah and Rebecca, like Rachel and Leah.
May you be fruitful, favored by your husband and be blessed with children.'*

You are always in our thoughts. I love you.

Mama

I crumple the letter and throw it to the floor. "No! No, Lord. I
will *not* do it!" I yank off my shawl, and stand as if readying myself for
battle. "I cannot. I will not marry another man who grieves for a dead
wife. Am I stone that You should ask it of me?"

But no voice answers. My mind whirls as I pace the floor like a wild
beast. Surely Mama's reasoning is flawed. Though Sebastian was a crypto-
Jew, a secret Jew, he was a *converso* and so was I. Therefore the marriage was
between two *conversos*, not a *converso* and a Jew as Mama stated. But in my
mind I hear Mama's rebuttal and her quoting Ibn Danan who said that the
laws of levirate marriage should apply to all *conversos*. Still . . . I could quote
Balan's opposition, as well as the fact that most exiled Spanish rabbinical
authorities considered all *conversos*—gentiles, rather than crypto-Jews, and
therefore their marriages not subject to levirate laws. But what is the use?
It is like spitting in the wind.

I pull at my hair, and look up as though expecting to see the Merciful
One peering down. "Do not ask this of me. It is too cruel! I cannot . . .
do it!" Then I drop my head. "Yet . . . how can I refuse? Is not Your first
command to 'be fruitful and multiply' and Your fifth command to obey
our parents? But what of *my* feelings? Do I not matter to You at all?"
Tears stream from my eyes. "Still . . . it is selfish to refuse to marry; sinful
even. But have *I* no rights?" My body sags as I pace. "Yet . . . can I stay in
Isabela without a husband to protect me? No. Not with Enrique as mad
as a bull and determined to ruin me. But wouldn't the *Lanzas* defend
me? Or the town warden? If Juan Ponce de Leon had not sailed back to

Cadiz with Torres, surely I would have found a protector in him. But if not him, then perhaps another. But who?"

Back and forth, back and forth I walk until finally I know what I must do.

With my finger, I absently stir the bowl of ashes—all that is left of Mama's letter—until I hear voices, and stop. From my place at the table I see two men approach the open doorway. One is the servant who delivered Mama's letter. The other is the young man I saw walking alongside Bartolome Columbus earlier. I wipe my hands on a rag, then go to the door.

"Doña Isabel, allow me to introduce Don Antonio Villarreal," the servant says, gesturing towards the young man.

Don Antonio bows, straightens, then draws back his broad shoulders. Grace and elegance mark his movements. And self-assurance, too—certainly from so many years at court. Still, I am surprised by the absence of arrogance, and also surprised that Don Antonio does not resemble his brother in the least. Rather, he is darker of skin, taller, more muscular, and not as handsome.

His apparel is fresh and scented, and of the finest brocade and silk. His short wavy hair glistens like polished onyx. He smiles, revealing one dimpled cheek, while a thin scar arcs across his other.

I, on the other hand, wear the same coarse homespun I wore on the rocky promontory. My hair is tied back, but uncovered, and I am barefoot.

Merriment flickers across Don Antonio's eyes as he observes me. But he shows no disdain for my appearance, nor does he seem offended by my apparent lack of respect for his rank.

"I would never have recognized you, Doña Isabel. When I saw you last you were a skinny little girl only this high." Antonio's hand is waist level.

"Nor I you, for you were not much taller." When he laughs I am reminded of all the stories Sebastian shared aboard the *Tortoise*. I tell myself to be wary, for he has seduced half the highborn ladies of Castile.

I bid him enter, and note that he, with just a slight gesture of his head, indicates for his servant to remain behind. I lead Antonio to the table, and marvel that he shows no disdain for his surroundings. Surely our Sovereigns' horses have better quarters.

"I praise the Holy One for your safe voyage," I say, working my courage like Pasculina's husband worked his porous leather bag, trying to squeeze out the dross of cowardice. "It is no small thing to cross the Ocean Sea, for there are many dangers."

"Like anywhere, Señora, for we live in a time when the concept of safety is as untenable as some of Maimonides's writings."

I bring my hand to my mouth, covering a smile. "And the food on board ship? Was it satisfactory?"

"Yes. I am not a 'gooser' like most nobles at court, and do not crave rich, fatty foods. It was not a hardship to eat salt beef, though I would have preferred chicken."

"Then you have little to worry about. Here in Isabela we have no geese. But then we have no chickens either, except those belonging to our Admiral. I am afraid you will have to content yourself with fish."

Again, Antonio laughs. "Then I am undone. The only fish I have ever caught were the ones in my father's large leather tank which he kept alive only until the cook needed them for the table. But perhaps you can teach me how." He glances again at my clothes, and looks amused. But amusement, and nothing more, etches his face. When he straightens, I notice the large scar below his ear. "You read your mother's letter?" His face becomes somber.

"I have."

"And you are not pleased."

My gaze meets his. Though I am surprised by his insight and honesty, I see God's hand here. I have made a bargain with the Holy One. I will reveal my true feelings, holding nothing back, and if, after my revelation, Antonio still wants me to honor the marriage contract, I will.

"I am not pleased," I finally say, "for I have no desire to marry again." I look, but there is no expression on his face. "However . . . I will honor the contract if it pleases you. Though only after you hear what is on my heart. I am determined that there be no secrets between us."

Antonio fingers the scar on his cheek. "Then let there be no secrets."

"I did not love Sebastian. Nor did he love me. Perhaps for a man that is an unimportant matter. After all, many matches are made to advance a career or forge a new alliance or enterprise. But to a woman, to *me*, it is important. And I have learned it is a bitter thing to be an unloved wife." Antonio's face has become as white as goat's milk. "Also, you must know this . . . I am a sincere Christian; a true follower of the Nazarene. I have broken Mama's heart. Papa's too. And I have made them ashamed. But none of that has deterred me from making a salt covenant with the Nazarene, with Jesus."

I know Antonio understands the significance of this, for salt covenants were permanent, irrevocable covenants going back to the time of Abraham. It was a covenant of loyalty and love. The Holy One made a covenant of salt with King David, also with Aaron the priest. People, too, made covenants of salt with each other—pledging their fidelity by removing a pinch of salt from their salt pouches and depositing it into the other's pouch. Each would then shake his pouch, mixing the two salts and creating an unbreakable covenant, for how could one ever go into the other's pouch and extract his grains to break it?

"If we live as man and wife I will, for your sake, do what I can to observe our Jewish holy days. At least as much as safety permits."

Antonio's hand covers his mouth, and for the first time I notice the many rings he wears. How ill-suited he is to this wild land. So perfumed and jeweled and grandly dressed. He will tell me he cannot abide having an idolater under his roof when he expected a crypto-Jew.

And unlike Doña Maria de Murcia with her vast Old Christian connections, what can I offer as inducement for him to change his mind? Surely, he will issue a bill of divorcement. Then he will sail away. And it will all be for the best.

When Antonio removes his hand I am not prepared for what I see. He is smiling! And his dark eyes sweep over me with kindness and tender pity. "Oh, how great is our God! What a wonder He is!" Antonio says, springing to his feet, and walking the floor. "I have prayed for this, for a wife who is likeminded. But in my heart I scarcely believed it possible, so poor and inadequate was my faith." He thumps his chest. "*I* am a sincere believer, though I have kept it secret from my family. Oh, Isabel, can you not see that God has wrought a miracle by bringing us together?"

I am speechless for I do see it, and the sight overwhelms me.

Antonio returns to the table and sits down, scarcely able to contain his joy.

"It is the greatest possible blessing to find someone like-minded. It delights my heart. But . . . ."

Antonio's jaw tightens. "*But?*"

"But can you ever forget Doña Maria, and make room for another in your heart? Sebastian could not. And had we been married a thousand years I doubt he ever would. It has been said Doña Maria was a woman not easily forgotten. I am not willing to live in another woman's shadow or with a man who pines for his dead love."

Antonio rises and walks to the tall wooden case. "May I?" he asks, pointing to two goblets. I nod, and he removes them from the shelf, brings them to the table, and fills them with water from the calabash. He hands one to me and takes his seat. "What makes you think I loved Doña Maria?"

"Well . . . I . . . that is . . . ." I am at a loss. "Mama's letter," I finally say. "She said your father was concerned over your deep grief caused by the loss of your wife and child."

Antonio sips from his goblet, and again I notice something new. His hands are large with knuckles the size of finch eggs. "I, too, understand what it is like to be in a loveless marriage."

"Impossible," I blurt without thinking, and see amusement in his eyes. "What I mean is, according to Sebastian, your marriage was the envy of the court."

He laughs. It is musical, and soothing like honey coating a raw throat. "You must not believe everything you hear, Isabel, and certainly never when it pertains to court gossip."

"But she was the mother of your child; surely for that alone you loved her?"

A long silence, then finally, "It was not my child. Doña Maria confessed this to me, though I already suspected it since she had many lovers." Antonio fingers the scar on his cheek. "As the marks on my body will attest, for I have fought more duels than I care to remember in defense of my honor. And spilled far too much blood."

"Then why did you marry?"

"Papa believes men should marry before turning twenty, as the Talmud instructs. Also, he convinced me an alliance with the Murcias would secure my future and insulate me, and perhaps my entire family, from the Inquisition. Why Doña Maria married me I can only guess. My wealth? My position at court? Whatever the reason, it was not love, though in the beginning I hoped love would come. I was told it often does. But for Doña Maria and me it never did."

"Then how do you account for your grief?"

"People grieve for different reasons, Isabel. I have long been at court, seen deception, intrigue, the breaking of vows. And my marriage mirrored it all. Doña Maria defiled our bed with men who flattered her vanity. And I killed those men to protect mine. It was impossible for me to remain at court. Even the thought sickened me. I am finished with lies and deceit. Since Doña Maria's death I have prayed for a godly wife. And now the Merciful One has answered."

"But what of your many escapades at court?" I never meant to ask this, but suddenly it seemed important.

"I suppose Sebastian told you that as well?"

I nod.

"I cannot fault him. Before my marriage there were a few indiscretions, yes, but very few. Since then, their number grows yearly among the court gossips."

"Then you are not a womanizer?"

Antonio, who is in the middle of sipping from his goblet, nearly chokes. "Oh, Isabel, you are naïve. But it pleases me."

My cheeks flush as I seek to change the subject. "I often wonder if Mama would have come to love the Nazarene had she never read Profiat Duran's, *Do not be like thy fathers.*"

"She read that?"

"Oh, yes, and what arguments we had! But no matter how persuasive my words, they were unable to erase the absurd image Duran painted of Christians."

"My father read Duran too, but we never argued. Unlike you, I lacked the courage to tell him I was a true convert."

"Perhaps you were wiser. Sometimes I wish I had never spoken. You should have seen Mama's face . . . ." My throat catches when Antonio's fingers touch mine. "Her face . . . was as white as an onion."

"I can picture it," he says, slowly covering my hand with his, "for I remember well the time I incurred her wrath. I was young and oh, how she terrified me! It was at your estate by the groves when she caught me pulling oranges off a tree and . . . ."

◡◠

For the next three Sundays Fray Buil reads the banns announcing my engagement and pending marriage to Don Antonio Villarreal. And since it is not Advent or one of the twelve days of Christmas or Lent or any day between Ascension Sunday and Pentecost, when no weddings are allowed, our marriage will take place next Sunday, and all Isabela is stunned.

❦

My silk gown rustles as I slip it over my linen chemise and whalebone farthingale. It is my best gown; green shimmering silk trimmed in delicate lace. Over that I don a wine-colored cloak of velvet. At my throat hangs the stone of Zebulun. I wear it to ensure "success" today; so that all goes well, and because it helps me feel closer to Mama.

Next, I slip my feet into green velvet shoes, then wooden *pantofles*. The fragrance of lavender swirls around me as I move.

"How lovely you look," Maria says. "Pasculina did a fine job."

I nod. Earlier, Pasculina came and fixed my hair in a style she claimed a great countess once wore. She made it sweep across my ears, then form a single braid—the length of two fingers—at the nape of my neck. At the end of the braid, my hair loosens and cascades down my back. Scattered throughout are pearls and jewels, and over all this I will wear a veil of shimmering green silk.

Now Maria picks up the veil lying across the wooden table and carefully drapes it over my head, then anchors it with a wide gold chain. "Oh, how pleased Don Antonio will be when he sees you!"

She pulls me to the mirror, but before I can glance at my reflection I hear the clomping of horse's hooves, and rush to the door. Antonio approaches on a large grey Andalusian, and leads another by the bridle. The *Lanzas* have loaned us two horses for the occasion, surely a compliment to Antonio since they never allow anyone to use them. I step through the door and hear him gasp.

"You look . . . *beautiful!*" His smiling eyes sweep over me.

My cheeks flame for I think these same thoughts of him. He sits tall and broad, and bareheaded, his hair blowing in the breeze. Though his nose—which is slightly bent where it was broken during a long-ago fight—adds virility to his face, his eyes betray an inner tenderness. He wears a silver-colored silk doublet and breaches that are embroidered with gold thread. His stockings and shoes are silver. Draped across his broad shoulders is a short black-and-gold velvet cape. A thin, black leather belt straps a jewel-encrusted sword to his waist. When he dismounts, I smell the pleasing fragrance of scented soap.

He takes my hand and helps me onto my horse. And then we begin the ride to the church. Men have left their huts and gathered along the streets smiling and waving and greeting us by name. And when we reach the church, we are welcomed by Fray Buil who stands outside. In his hand he holds an open book and wedding ring. Clustered behind him are the dozen members of the clergy. The wedding will take place here, followed by a nuptial Mass inside the church.

We dismount, and someone takes our horses. People crowd behind us, among them Pasculina and her husband, Maria and Gonzalo, and their two sons and their wives.

Fray Buil smiles, then poses the first of five questions asked of all who seek to enter the holy state of matrimony. "Are you of age?" According to Church law a bride many not be younger than twelve; a bridegroom younger than fourteen.

Antonio and I, each in turn, answer, "Yes."

"Do you swear before God you are not violating the Church's law regarding consanguinity?" The Church forbids marriage between blood relatives up to and including third cousins.

Again we answer, "Yes."

He asks the next three questions in rapid order. "Do you have the consent of your parents? Have the banns been read? Are you entering this marriage of your own free will?"

To all three we answer, "Yes."

Following that, we say our vows, then Fray Buil delivers a brief sermon. When he is finished, he blesses the ring and gives it to Antonio.

Antonio's large knuckled fingers lift my left hand. Gently, he slips the ring first on one finger, then the next, saying as he does, "In the

Name of the Father and of the Son, and of the Holy Ghost." Finally, he slips it on my third finger, and ends by uttering, "With this ring I thee wed."

It is done.

⁓◯

We gather at my house or actually around its grounds. There are too many to fit inside. All the nobles and knights in Isabela have been invited. Antonio's servant, Mateo, has made the preparations, with Maria and Pasculina assisting. And this causes me no small discomfort, for normally it is the wife's family who provides the wedding food and entertainment. Still, I am grateful to Antonio for his foresight. Unbeknownst to me, ten barrels of fine wine accompanied him from Castile, and Mateo had them all delivered to my house where they form a triple line outside my northern wall.

The men of Isabela, who, for too long, have been drinking sour rationed wine, cannot believe their good fortune. Today, not only does wine flow freely, it is of the finest quality. And along with an abundance of wine comes an abundance of food. Mateo had my table brought outside and set up near the doorway. It is mounded with wheat bread, made from the fresh wheat Antonio also brought, and baked by Pasculina and Maria. And there are melons from my gardens and platters of other fresh fruit, as well as platters of grilled fish and roasted birds, which were purchased from the Tainos. And most surprising of all is the platter of candied citrons and *confites* of almonds and sugar, and alongside these, jarred peaches covered in honey—all brought by Antonio on the ship.

Men sing and dance in the streets, and shout blessings in slurred voices. Someone plays the fiddle. Someone else entertains with tales of Alexander the Great, David and Goliath, Julius Caesar. I have not seen such merriment in a very long time.

All afternoon we are besieged by well wishers, especially my husband, for all the highborn seek his company. Even Diego and Bartolome Columbus come with congratulations and gifts. Nobles and knights continue to crowd around him, Arias Diaz among them. I notice Arias wears Sebastian's blue velvet jerkin, and it pleases me. After Sebastian's burial I gave one of his three trunks to Arias to share with the rest of the platoon that served under Alonso de Hojeda. To please Sebastian, I think, and to honor his comrades and acknowledge their kindness to him.

Arias smiles and fawns, but I am not concerned. Court life has taught Antonio how to deal with people who seek only their own advantage. My husband is polite, but beyond politeness takes little notice of Arias.

As I watch Antonio woo his fellows with good humor and good conversation, my belly cramps. I have been ignoring these cramps all day but can no longer. I go inside and pull my *sinar* from the trunk, stuff it with folded rags, and lay it aside. From the doorway I signal Maria and Pasculina. When they join me I quickly explain what has happened. And discreetly we go to a darkened corner where they hold up a blanket while I slip on the *sinar*.

I am back outside with my guests when the church bell rings Vespers and Fray Buil arrives to bless our nuptial bed. He greets me with a smile.

"I see happiness in your eyes, Isabel."

I nod.

"Was I not right in discouraging you from entering the cloistered life?"

"You were right."

"Then remember it well. When next trouble comes, stand firm, and do not seek to run from it. Rather, keep in mind how God is able to bring good out of bad if only you love Him and commit your ways to Him."

Without thinking I grab Fray Buil's hand. "Whatever will I do without you?" Tomorrow Fray Buil and most of the clergy will sail back to Cadiz. With him will go many important men of Isabela as well as the deserter, Pedro Margarite, who has been caught and arrested. "What will I do?"

"You have God and a new husband to care for you. I am of no consequence."

"But why must you go?"

Fray Buil chuckles. "It is no secret Admiral Columbus and I are at odds. Isabela will best be served by another cleric. But do not think on these things. Tonight you must think only of your husband. But I will miss you, my child. I will miss you."

I bend and kiss his hand. "And I will miss you," I say, meaning it, though I never thought I would say that to any man of the cloth.

⌒᷅

The bell chimes Martins as Mateo and Gonzalo move the empty wooden table back into the hut. They and Maria are all that remain of our guests.

"I believe everyone had a merry time," I say to Maria who is picking up the last of the oil lamps scattered around the grounds. "If only it would continue. Isabela is in great need of goodwill."

"It is not difficult to create goodwill when bellies are full of food and wine," Antonio says, thumping the wine barrels with his knuckles. "Only four barrels of the ten remain. Enough wine flowed today to make *everyone* happy."

I laugh. "Perhaps my husband's other generosities also helped create the congenial mood? For when has anyone seen a groom give such gifts? A gold piece each to the peasants. Two gold pieces and a fine platter to the tradesmen. Chain mail and shields for the knights. Swords and purple velvet cloaks for the nobles."

"I am happy you are pleased," Antonio says.

Mateo appears in the doorway carrying a platter mounded with food. "As you instructed, Señora, I sent everyone home with a share of the wedding food and distributed your pouch of gold *florins* among the peasants with your good wishes."

Antonio looks at me and smiles. "Your generosity pleases me, too."

"But I held back this little bit for your breakfast tomorrow." Mateo holds up the platter. "I will leave it on the table."

Antonio and I both laugh for there is enough food on the platter for ten breakfasts.

Gonzalo, Maria, Antonio and I, each carrying oil lamps, congregate by the door. And though there is a full moon, we find ourselves standing in shadows.

"I will finish my business inside before Gonzalo and I depart," Maria says disappearing into the hut. Minutes later she appears, carrying a deep saucer-like plate full of food, the portion Mateo had set aside for her. "I will return your platter tomorrow. And . . . I have checked the bed."

Her words prick my heart on two counts. It was a mother's duty to check the nuptial bed for chickpeas or pebbles or any other hindrances to conjugal relations left by a prankster or ill-wisher. And my heart is pricked because I wear a *sinar*.

Tonight of all nights.

Maria shifts the platter to one hand then presses me tightly to her.

"Thank you for your kindness," I say.

"If only I was able to give you grand gifts like those you gave my sons and their brides."

For Juan's and Luis's wedding I gave each a suit of Sebastian's best clothing, which Pasculina, by way of her gift, altered to fit them. For their brides, I hired Pasculina's husband, who is also a silversmith, to melt down four of Sebastian's silver buckles and make them into bracelets, one for each of the Taino women. But they were gifts that cost me little, for what was I going to do with Sebastian's possessions except use them for barter?

"I know how hard you worked," I say, kissing Maria's cheek. "And the many hours you spent preparing the food for the banquet. And I am grateful."

Maria waves my words aside. "It shames me that I gave you so little."

"So little? You have given me that which is most precious. You have given me your friendship."

❧

Antonio and I stand in the doorway of our hut holding our lamps and waving goodnight to Maria, Gonzalo and Mateo, then watch their outlines blend into the shadows. Even so, we linger, I think because we are both a little afraid of going inside.

"Are you weary, Isabel?" Antonio finally says, stepping into the hut.

I follow, and slowly draw the beautiful brocade curtain Pasculina made, and her husband hung for us, as a wedding gift. "A little." I walk to the wooden table where the glass lantern glows, and place my oil lamp beside it. Someone has put a lamp on the stool near the bed; Maria, most likely, when she pulled down the covers. Antonio adds his lamp, and my throat goes dry. Even in the dim light I see the tenderness on his face.

"I am . . . *niddah*—unclean," I say, despising my body for betraying me; despising that I must tell him of my monthly blood flow, for I am telling him he cannot touch me throughout my flow or for a week after it ends. "But if it pleases you, we do not have to follow Jewish law." I hold my breath, for doing the holy deed during a woman's flow is shameful. I have said this because I have no way of knowing if he still honors this practice. After all, he was wed to an Old Christian. But I want him to know I am willing, for it is forbidden for a man to force his wife to lie with him. Everyone knows such a union could produce evil children. At least I will not have that on my conscience.

Without a word, Antonio goes to where Mateo left his trunks, and pulls out a sleeping roll, then spreads it on the floor next to the bed.

"No, Isabel. I will not shame you." His hand goes to remove his jerkin and stops. For a moment his eyes rest on me. Then he picks up the lamps and blows them out, but not before I see the disappointment in his eyes. And as I extinguish the lamps on the table, I wonder if he sees mine.

Chapter 16

"Bartolome Columbus will ask you to sit on the Governing Council," I say, eating cassava bread and watching my husband study the platter of food that sits on the table between us.

"Not without consulting the Admiral." Antonio's large knuckled hand plucks a slice of melon from the plate. "Especially since Diego heads the Council. Bartolome will not usurp Diego's authority; or Christopher's for that matter."

"He *will* ask. Today he loses one of his regents with Fray Buil's sailing. And with him go many leading men of Isabela."

"Including the rogue, Pedro Margarite." Antonio studies me closely.

"Yes, including Margarite." Like everyone in Isabela, I have heard how Margarite deserted his post, leaving over three hundred and fifty soldiers, unrestrained. Every day, stories grow worse of how they brutalize the Indians, steal their food, possessions, and women. "With so many returning to Castile, Bartolome will look for someone of power and influence to help restore order."

"Yes, with Fray Buil goes most of the clergy and many important men of the town, and their influence will be sorely missed. And yes, Bartolome Columbus is too severe with the men, flogging them for minor infractions. And this has caused much resentment toward him and his brother. But you must not worry, Isabel. There are still many nobles who remain loyal to the Columbus brothers." His eyes, full of tenderness, rest on me.

"Perhaps. But there are other concerns, too. Bata tells me ever since Hojeda cut off that chief's ear there has been great anger among her people."

"Isabel, the chief was caught stealing. There must be order, and if necessary, stern discipline, otherwise all will crumble."

"So . . . only Tainos must follow the law while Pedro Margarite's men run lawless with impunity?"

Antonio fingers his beard. We have discussed this before. "Hojeda is a good soldier, and good soldiers follow orders. Admiral Columbus has ordered that a nose or ear be cut off any thieving Taino."

"You see no injustice in a penalty that takes the ear or nose from a Taino who steals three tunics, but takes nothing from a Spaniard who steals all of a Taino's possessions, destroys his hut, rapes his wife and daughter, then disembowels him with a sword, as so many of our men have done?"

"It is rare to see such passion in a woman."

"Do not be deceived, my husband, for more often than not my head rules these passions. And my head tells me the injustices done the Tainos are piling up like rotting sheaves, creating a stench that can no longer be ignored. There is great unrest among the Indians. Already, many have burned their fields and villages, and fled into the forest."

"Yes . . . I have heard. But I have also heard that Caonabo travels the countryside provoking our men, even killing some."

"Have you considered he is just applying *his* form of justice? And avenging our cruelty? Like he did at Navidad?"

Antonio reaches for the goblet in my hand. When I pull away, he smiles. "We will not lie together when you are unclean, but I will not observe it as our parents did. I see no sin in drinking from your cup or touching your hand."

I hesitate, then give him the goblet. My breath catches when our fingers touch, but I feel no shame. To be sure, Mama would be scandalized, for such touching is unthinkable during a women's time of impurity. But Antonio and I must navigate our own waters. And we must trust the Holy One to show us how.

I watch him sip water from my cup. His linen tunic is open at the neck, his hair, disarrayed. Sleep still softens his eyes, and a smile softens his face. He looks so beguiling it requires great control to keep from seeking his arms. I wonder if he feels as I do, for I too am improperly attired, wearing only an undergown with my hair falling loosely over my shoulders. Antonio insisted we not dress for breakfast, our first breakfast together as man and wife, and it pleases me for its simplicity and implied intimacy, though I see danger in it, too.

"So, you believe Bartolome will seek me out?" Antonio pulls another piece of fruit from the platter.

"I am sure of it. He needs to restore order, and he knows that because you are greatly respected at court, the nobles and knights here will also respect you. I think he views you as a means of controlling these men. And there are three sitting on the Council who will back him and approve your appointment: Pedro Coronel, Juan de Lujan, and Alfonso Sanchez de Carvajal. And all three understand that after years at court you know how to manage people, while Bartolome Columbus is a mapmaker who knows little of administering a colony. Perhaps with you at his elbow he will listen to reason. If order is not restored, how will we meet the challenge of a Taino uprising? Carvajal and the rest of the Council will want you. And when they ask, you must be ready with an answer."

Antonio rests his elbows on the table. His tunic is short sleeved, revealing bare muscular arms. "And would that please you? If they did?"

I touch the two scars near the bend of his arm and wonder if the wounds were very painful. "No. God forgive me, but no."

He covers my fingers with his hand. "What are you really afraid of, Isabel?"

"Francisco Roldan."

Antonio nods. "Roldan is a dangerous man; ambitious and base, and one who despises class privilege. Yes . . . he is just the sort who might use our present weakness to advantage. Some say he has already begun to foment rebellion, but I see no proof of that." One eyebrow arcs upward. "But I think you despise class privilege too, and have fought a rebellion of your own. Your friendship with Maria has shattered the time honored separation of the classes."

"You disapprove?"

Antonio's laughter makes my heart flutter. "No, Isabel, for I understand loneliness, and would not deprive you of Maria's companionship. But the high-born in Isabela are displeased. Surely you know that? They tolerate it only because of their affection for you."

"Affection for me?"

"You are an angel in their eyes. Feeding their sick, displaying courage and fortitude. Why, I believe half the men in Isabela are in love with you."

I narrow my eyes as I take another bite of bread. "I am not as naïve as you suppose, for I know you talk nonsense."

"I do not talk nonsense when I say many peasants also disapprove of your friendship with Maria. They see it as condescension on your part. You must remember peasants traditionally hate the privileged class."

"As much as they hate Jews?"

"Only if the privileged one *is* a Jew."

I laugh, but inside I shudder, for I am remembering the expression on Enrique's face the day he delivered my bed. "In a way you shattered class lines too. You are a titled nobleman who married a spice merchant's daughter."

"A very *wealthy* spice merchant's daughter. One of the wealthiest merchants in Seville when you consider that a few peppercorns are worth as much as a cow. And since when is money not able to bridge differences?" He leans over the table. "At least that is what the world thinks. And let it. I have no need of your money. I only have need of *you*."

His face is so earnest and tender I look away. But he pulls me back with his words. "Everyone knows that the Sovereigns' motto, *'Tonto Monta'*, was sewn on their banners. And that it was this motto that unified Castile and Aragon by proclaiming both Queen Isabel and King Fernando equal in dignity and authority. Let that be our motto, too, Isabel, for we are equal in dignity, and we will run our estates and households in joint authority."

Without thinking I brush his lips with my finger tips. How can I explain the love I have for this man who is my husband and not yet fully my husband? It cascades like a raging waterfall, wild and powerful, and waters every part of me, even those parched desert places where I thought no water could ever reach. We lean together over the table, our heads close, our fingers entwined. I am completely undone, and am about to shamelessly tell him how much I love him when I hear Bata's voice, "Isbell! Isbell!"

"Isbell!" she shouts again, pulling aside the curtain over our door. She is sweaty and out of breath. "You must help, Isbell. You must help," she says, entering.

I fill a goblet with water, and bid Bata to sit, which she does. But she waves the water aside. "Help, Isbell. They hurt my . . . ."

Suddenly Juan bursts through the doorway, also panting and sweating. It is obvious they have both been running. "Pardon, Don Antonio." He bows. "Excuse my wife's interruption. I tried to stop her. I ran all the way to stop her, but she was too swift. I told her you were not to be disturbed. Pardon, please pardon us." His face, and Bata's, tells me something is wrong.

Antonio gestures for Juan to sit, then points to Bata's water goblet. "Refresh yourself, then tell us what has happened."

Juan guzzles the water, leaving it unchecked to dribble down his chin and onto his rough tunic. "They are dragging Bata's uncle and five other men to the Plaza," he finally says, without bothering to wipe his chin. "They are dragging Bata's uncle by the hair, a *cacique*—a chief.

They show no respect for his rank. They say they are going to kill him. They threaten to kill them all."

"Who is going to kill them?" Antonio asks.

"The nobles. They say they are going to cut off their heads, or hang them, or maybe burn them at the stake."

"Why? What did they do?"

"It is all a mistake. A terrible mistake."

"*What did they do?*"

"They buried a rosary and medal of the Virgin in one of the plowed fields, and pissed on them."

Antonio's face grows white. "That is *sacrilege*."

"You do not understand, Don Antonio. It is their custom to bury their gods in the fields and piss on them, in order to bless the fields, in order to insure the land will be fertile and yield a good crop. They were only trying to honor us by burying what they believed were our *zemis* in the ground."

Antonio shakes his head. "You expect me to condone such heathen practices?"

"They meant no disrespect. I swear it! Please, Señor, they will kill them." Juan clasps his hands together, pleading.

Antonio glances at me. I know my eyes plead too, but I cannot help it. Too many Tainos have already died by our hands. "Surely, mercy can be shown to these misguided six?" I say softly as I watch Bata weep.

The bell rings Tierce as Antonio rises from the bench and pulls on hose, breaches, a doublet and finally a pair of leather shoes. When he is finished, he runs his large-knuckled fingers through his hair trying to put it in order but it does little good. With a final glance at me, and instructions to "stay here," he leaves with Juan at his heels. When Bata rises to follow, I stop her. "We must wait."

Women must always wait.

༒

The bell rings Sext before Antonito returns. When he does, there is a sag to his shoulders, but his mouth is as rigid as bark. Juan enters quietly behind him. "I could not save them," Antonio says, lowering himself onto the bench.

Bata, who has been sitting at the table nibbling from the fruit platter, drops her slice of melon, and wails. In an instant, Juan is by the bench pulling her to her feet. "Thank you, Don Antonio," Juan says, towing Bata to the door. "You have been most kind." And then they are gone, leaving us with only the fading sound of Bata's cries.

Slowly, I draw the curtain, then return to Antonio and sit beside him. He is resting his chin on folded hands, looking greatly fatigued. "What happened?"

"Bartolome put the Tainos on trial, if you can call it that. Then had them burned at the stake."

I quietly run my hands over Antonio's shoulders. It is as I feared, for while Bata and I were waiting, smoke drifted across Isabela, the kind one smells at an *auto de fe*.

"I told them what Juan said. The Council listened, but by their faces I knew they wanted blood. It was no surprise when they found the six Tainos guilty of sacrilege."

My hands gently knead the muscles of Antonio's neck and back. They are sinewy and well-formed but tight, too, carrying in them all the tensions of the morning.

"When it was over, Bartolome asked me to join the Council." Antonio turns to me. "And I accepted. It is plain that cooler heads are needed."

I press my cheek against his shoulder. "Then God help us both."

∾⊙

I stand next to Maria and watch the new chief follow the prescribed ceremony. The Tainos have many chiefs, each ruling a family or group of families, some numbering only a few dozen, others numbering hundreds. The new chief places a gourd of water and loaf of cassava on the freshly dug mound where Bata's uncle lies buried. The water and bread have been placed near the head. Bata, who stands beside her husband, wails loudly. She is surrounded by relatives all covered in *zemis*. But surprisingly, she wears no *zemis* herself.

Bata has told me this burial is not in keeping with her uncle's high rank. Normally, a chief is buried only after he has been cut open and slowly dried over a fire. But her uncle's body was too charred to afford him this customary honor. While I think their practice barbaric, I cannot judge them, for I belong to a people who have proven themselves far more barbaric in their treatment of these gentle Tainos. And for this I feel great shame.

Behind me stand Luis and his wife, and Gonzalo. Antonio has not come, though he offered, and for that I bless his name. Since returning from the trial of Bata's uncle and the five Tainos, he has not been well. I have suspected that even before our marriage Antonio's bodily humors were out of balance. The voyage across the Ocean Sea affects many that way. But this morning he was so fatigued he could barely get out of bed. And as I watch yet another burial of someone who has died in this strange land, I remember the look of weariness on Antonio's face. If I had rose petals I would have made him a blood tonic. But none was to be found in my spice box. So instead, I made an infusion of five dried bay leaves in hot water. The brew will help clear Antonio's head and promote better health in his bowels. His bodily humors seem to become more unbalanced every day, and my growing fear is that I will be unable to balance them again.

I fold the clean red-and-gold silk skirt and bodice, then place it atop the towel that is spread across my wooden tabletop. To that, I add clean undergarments, a fresh bar of scented soap, a hairbrush, red velvet shoes and a golden silk veil. Then I carefully fold the towel, forming a neat bundle which I tuck under my arm.

I glance at the bed as I pass, remembering the linens must be changed for ritual purity's sake. In one of my trucks are stored fresh cotton sheets, folded among sprigs of dried lavender. I only hope Antonio loves the scent of lavender as much as I.

My husband left earlier to meet with Bartolome Columbus and the Governing Council. He still looks pale. But the bay leaf tea I have been giving him for two weeks must be working, for he is not as lethargic, and his bowels do not seem as troublesome. At least that is what he tells me, and I pray it is so. One thing I have learned about Antonio, he dislikes worrying me.

I am happy my husband is not here, for this morning I go to Marta to the Isabela River where I will immerse in a *mikveh* and ritually bathe to purify myself for him. I did not tell Antonio that today marks the end of my time of impurity, for I wish to surprise him. It makes me blush to say it, but I have dreamed of nothing else for the past two weeks. Every time his hand touches mine, or his lips brush my cheek I think of us doing the holy deed. And I know it is the same for Antonio, for I have seen the hunger in his eyes.

I try not to think that such an experienced man is bound to be disappointed by someone as novice as I. Instead, I think only how tonight I will finally show Antonio how much I love him.

Even before my little boat—made for me by one of Bata's cousins—rounds the corner and I see Isabela, I smell the smoke. It is not the smell of an *auto de fe*, but of burning wood and grass. And when my boat approaches the sandbank below the rocky promontory, I see large billowing clouds. It is as if black serge drapes the whole of Isabela.

My silk skirt rustles as I jump from the boat. "What has happened?" I shout to someone standing overhead.

"It burns," he answers, turning towards me and revealing a soot-streaked face. "Best you stay away."

"What burns?" I shout.

"The Poblado."

My heart jumps. The Poblado is the section of Isabela that houses the peasants and tradesmen. "What sector?" I yell, for it is divided into central, south and east.

"Central."

Again my heart jumps. *Maria's sector.* I grip my bundle of dirty clothes and run up the dune. Smoke fills my nostrils and burns my eyes. It swirls around me in dark angry waves. I slow to a walk and flail one arm hoping to create a path through which I can see. It is useless. The smoke invades everything with its choking smell, its sting, its thick black soot. When I reach the Plaza, it is empty. So is my street. Every available man must be in the Poblado trying to stop the fire from spreading to the church or armory or powder house or the elite section where the nobles live.

I race past my house, and without slowing, toss my bundle inside the open doorway, then head east. The smoke is even thicker here and I cover my nose and mouth with my hand. As I walk, I try not to stumble against trees or huts, or over scattered fireboxes and stools.

The closer to the Poblado, the less visibility. My ears guide me now to the voices ahead. I stop when I feel heat. Through the smoke I see red flames devour a roof before jumping to the one beside it.

"What can I do?" I shout when a man bumps into me.

"Throw this on the flames, then hand it back." He shoves a heavy bucket of water into my hands. I discern, rather than see, that men have formed several lines all the way to the Isabela River and are passing buckets back and forth. I go as close as I dare before throwing my water. Then I pass the empty bucket to hands I barely see. Behind me, men are pulling down the huts that have yet to be touched by the flames, then clearing away the debris in an effort to deprive the fire of new fuel. We work like this for hours, and when the flames are finally subdued, Poblado Central is nothing but a charred field.

❦

"Are you injured?" I say to Maria when at last I find her. Her clothes are singed, and black soot covers her face.

"We have lost everything but our lives."

I embrace her, and marvel that she does not weep. "You must stay with Antonio and me until you rebuild."

"No. It would be unseemly. But do not concern yourself, Isabel. Pasculina has already offered her home."

I nod. Pasculina lives in Poblado South which was not touched by the fire. "And your sons? What will they do?"

"They will each live with their wife's family. We will be scattered, but only for a short time. Then God willing we will start all over."

We kiss goodbye, and with a heavy heart I go in search of Antonio.

❦

The first thing I do when I reach my house is remove my clothes that reek of smoke. Quickly, I fill the washbasin with water and wash my face, my hair, then my body. I am just slipping into a fresh silk skirt and bodice when I hear Mateo's voice through the drawn curtain.

"Doña Isabel? Doña Isabel!"

I pull back the drape and see Mateo's strained face. "Don Antonio has collapsed. They have carried him to the hospital."

Without waiting for more information, I bolt past Mateo, not caring that I am barefooted. I ignore the small pebbles that grind my soles as I run; ignore my heart that pounds like a shipwright's hammer; ignore the air that is pungent with smoke, making it difficult to breathe.

I think only of Antonio. I never found my husband after leaving Maria. But I never imagined he was in danger.

Be merciful, Lord.

I reach the hospital, and burst through the door in time to see Doctor Spinoza about to bleed my husband.

"Stop!"

The doctor turns, startled. "Doña Isabel, your husband is very ill. You must not interfere."

Mateo, who has been running behind me, finally enters, breathing heavily. "Doña Isabel . . . you must allow the doctor to do his work." I feel his hand on my arm. "Please come outside with me."

I break from Mateo's grasp and lunge for the doctor. "You will not bleed him," I say, knocking Spinoza's hand away from Antonio's arm. "You will *not* bleed him."

Spinoza looks at me as though I am mad. "Your husband has great influence at court. I must bleed him. If I do not and he dies, our Sovereigns will have my head."

My hand locks around the doctor's wrist, and I squeeze until he drops the knife. "Do not fear for your head," I say in a low, flat voice. "If anything happens to him, the Sovereigns can have mine."

I turn to Mateo whose mouth has dropped. "Please carry Don Antonio back to the house."

Mateo shakes his head. "Doña Isabel, think of what you are doing. Your husband must stay here. He is sick with fever."

"I will care for him at home."

"Impossible! He is vomiting and has . . . lost control of his bowels. He must stay here."

I glance at Antonio who lies on the table and is covered with soot. His eyes are closed, and his breathing is shallow and uneven. I touch his forehead. It burns with fever. Forcing my arm under his neck, I bring him to a sitting position. With my other arm, I lift his legs.

"Doña Isabel!" Mateo says in alarm. "He is much too heavy for you."

"Either you bring him or I will."

Mateo signals to a nearby man who comes and stands over Antonio. Then slowly, gently, Mateo removes my arms, and the two men pick up my husband and carry him out the door.

And as I step into the doorway to follow, Doctor Spinoza shouts after me, "You are wrong to do this, Doña Isabel! May God have mercy on you, for if anything happens, I will not."

$$\backsim \! \! \circ$$

Mateo removes Antonio's clothes while I fill the wash basin with fresh water. Then he helps me carry the basin to the bed—where Antonio lies, unconscious—and places it on the mat flooring.

"He has not felt well since the voyage. But the teas you made helped him keep the sickness at bay." Mateo takes one of the cloths from my hand to wash Antonio's body. "But he has not wanted to worry you. Many who sailed here with Antonio are sick. It is the hardship of the voyage and this infernal heat and strange Taíno food that brings on the bowel disease."

I listen as I wash the soot from Antonio's face, taking care with the scar on his cheek even though it is completely healed and needs no such care.

"When the fire broke, he was the first highborn at Poblado Central hauling water, pulling down huts. I tried to make him stop but he only laughed and said you would be angry if anything happened to Maria's house and he did nothing to prevent it. I tried to discourage him, Señora, I tried to . . . ."

"Peace, Mateo. I do not blame you."

And so we wash Antonio in silence. I, his hair, face and shoulders; Mateo the rest. And when we finish, Mateo puts a wide leather sheet beneath Antonio's buttock. "It will prevent him from soiling the bed. There are more sheets in his trunk. Whenever he needs to be bathed, send for me, and I will come."

I shake my head. "I will tend him now."

"*Doña Isabel* . . . surely you do not mean that? It is . . . it is unseemly!"

"I am determined, Mateo. I will not be moved."

"Is there nothing I can say to make you change your mind?"

"No, nothing."

Mateo sighs. "If you will not let me or the doctor help, then at least allow me to supply you with fresh water. I can have someone carry it from the river every day."

"That would be kind. Thank you."

Mateo picks up the washbasin. "I do not approve of what you are doing, Doña Isabel, but it is I who should thank you. You have made Don Antonio happier than I have seen him in years."

༄ᜆ

I hold Antonio's head over a large bowl as he retches for the third time. When he has finished, he drops back onto his pillow and moans. His eyes are closed, and by lamp light I see beads of perspiration dot his forehead. I wash his face with a wet cloth, then begin washing his body, which burns with fever. The cold rag makes him shiver. In addition to throwing up the contents of his stomach, he has lost control of his bowels, the fourth time tonight. His bodily humors are greatly disrupted.

If only I can bring down the fever.

When the bathing is done and I have put a clean leather sheet beneath him and washed the soiled one, I prepare yet another brew of fennel and chamomile—to calm the spasms in his stomach. To this brew I add a spoon of dried basil to subdue the fever.

Aunt Leonora, may her memory be for blessing, shared her knowledge of herbs with me. But I was a poor student, preferring, instead, to learn about commerce and Papa's ledgers. Now I am sorry, for how can knowledge of buying and selling and adding columns help Antonio?

I massage my forehead as though trying to shake loose all the knowledge Aunt Leonora imparted. *Think, Isabel! Think!* I concentrate until I hear Aunt Leonora's voice in my head.

"To maintain balanced bodily humors, the last portion of every meal must create harmony between dry and wet, cold and hot."

I strain the tea and pour it into a lead-glazed goblet.

"Radishes and apples close up the stomach and prevent the vapors from rising."

Steam curls around the lip of the goblet, and after I take a sip to make certain it is not too hot, I carry it to the bed and sit beside Antonio.

"Tea made from flowers of hollyhock help firm the bowels. As does tea from the bark of the rose bush."

I cradle Antonio's head in the hollow of my shoulder and bring the tea to his lips. He moans and pulls away. I try again, but it is no use, so I carefully return Antonio's head to the pillow.

"Lemon balm cools the brow."

I place the goblet of hot tea on the stool beside the bed and cradle my head. *Useless. Useless. Useless.* What good is knowing Aunt Leonora's remedies if I lack the ingredients? Tears puddle my hands.

When Antonio moans, I lift my head and see his handsome face grimace in pain. *This will not do.* What good is crying over what I do not have? I must ask the Merciful One to bless what I do.

I wipe my tears with the back of my hand, and rise to my feet. My mouth forms prayers to the Merciful One as I walk to the tall wooden case and retrieve a small spoon. At the bedside, I slip the spoon into the goblet. Thankfully, the tea still steams. Perhaps the heat will force the fever out. Carefully, I lift Antonio's head and put two more pillows behind him. Then I sit on the bed, curling my legs beneath me. I wedge the goblet between my knees to secure it, then ladle a small spoonful of tea and bring it to Antonio's lips. With two fingers, I pinch his cheeks and force the spoon and liquid into his mouth. I do this over and over until the goblet is empty.

Sweat runs down Antonio's temples like miniature rivulets. He moans through chattering teeth as I place the empty goblet and spoon on the stool. The rustle of silk mingles with the sound of his irregular breathing as I stretch out on top of the covers. I tuck the sheet and blanket beneath his chin, then spread the folds of my skirt over his shaking body. Lastly, I enfold him in my arms.

I can do no more.

Now the tea must have its time to work. In a few hours I will make another brew. And a few hours after that, yet another. And tomorrow, I will send Mateo to buy one of Admiral Columbus's chickens to make chicken soup like Mama used to make when I was sick.

I must use what I have. And if God is merciful, He will bless it.

"Doña Isabel, no chicken is worth this much." Mateo looks down at the gold *florin* I have placed in his hand.

"It is if it helps Antonio get well."

Mateo stands at the doorway and glances over my shoulder to where Antonio lays sleeping. "He looks peaceful. And his body does not shake. You say his fever has broken?"

I smile. "God was gracious. But now Antonio needs more than tea to regain his strength. He needs something his bowels are accustomed to. It must be chicken with its broth. And I will cook some of the barley you brought from Castile, and add a little to the soup."

Mateo runs his fingers through his silver hair and glances one last time at Antonio, surprise and awe etching his face. "Then I will get your chicken. But not for a *florin* if I can help it!"

As I stir the pot, which hangs from the spit in my firebox, a potpourri of smells—chicken, bay leaves, basil, cloves and cinnamon—swirls

around me. It is Mama's recipe, and except for the dried rose petals for
making rose water, I had all the needed spices to follow it exactly. Next
to the soup hangs a small pot of cooked barley.

I have been cooking for hours, ever since Mateo returned with
the hen which Don Bartolome sent with his compliments and sincere
wishes for Antonio's recovery. The sight of the squawking chicken so
delighted me that when Mateo handed me the gold *florin* I refused to
accept it, and made him keep it, instead.

Now, I hum and stir and watch the soup bubble. The pots and
firebox are hot. So is the air, making me damp with my own sweat, and
no breeze to bring relief. But nothing can dampen my joy. All morning
Antonio has slept soundly, so soundly, in fact, that I felt the need to
check him more than once to make certain all was well. And all *was*
well, for he neither shook nor moaned nor breathed uneasily, nor was
his skin any hotter than mine.

I place the spoon on the stool, then cover the pot. With a small
shovel, I begin banking the coals. The soup is finished, and the banked
coals will keep it warm until Antonio awakes. As I move the last coal, a
voice calls my name, making me drop the shovel and rush inside. And
there is Antonio sitting up in bed! How wonderful he looks with hair
tangled over his ears and a crooked smile on his face.

"Well, at last you are awake," I say, folding my arms across my
chest, pretending to be vexed.

"Have I been sleeping long?"

"Long enough to develop an appetite."

Antonio looks puzzled. "Yes, I *am* hungry. Famished, actually."

I laugh with joy, and watch his puzzlement deepen. "I will bring
you soup." I rush to the tall wooden case and grab a small bowl, then
disappear outside where I fill it, mostly with broth, but with a little
chicken and a spoonful of barley, too. I must not tax his bowels too
severely.

Back inside, I hand him the bowl, then go to the table where I sit
on the bench and watch him eat.

"This is delicious," he says between spoonfuls. "I have had none better." He pauses for a moment, the spoon near his lips. "But I thought you said there were no chickens in Isabela."

His words, the way he says them, the very sound of his voice thrills me beyond measure because there were times during the night that I wondered if I would ever hear him speak again. "No, dear one. What I said was 'we have no chickens except those belonging to our Admiral.'"

He plunges his spoon into his mouth and barely swallows before adding, "Well, then, how did you manage to get your hands on one? Did you have to steal it?" His face tells me he is teasing. "You have more, I hope?" He holds out his bowl. "I feel like a hollow reed."

I grin and take his bowl, go outside and refill it, the same way as last time, making it mostly broth. When I return and hand it to Antonio he says, "Truly, how did you get the chicken?"

"Don Bartolome gave it to me, with his best wishes for your recovery."

"Recovery? Have I been sick?"

"Yes . . . very."

Antonio frowns. "I remember the fire, and trying to put it out." He looks around the room. "Praise be to God it never reached here. How much of the town was destroyed?"

"All of Poblado Central."

"Then Maria and her family have lost everything."

"Yes."

"A pity. But if it pleases you, we will help them rebuild." A strange look suddenly comes over his face. "Have I been burned? Is that why I am here in bed?" With one hand he pulls up the covers and looks, then slowly replaces them. "What was the nature of my illness?"

"You had fever, and could not hold down your food."

He brings the bowl closer to his mouth, and eats without saying a word. When he is finished, he places it and the spoon on the nearby stool. "Mateo insisted he pack the leather shields. He said many who sail on long voyages sicken and lose control of their bowels. I must thank Mateo for tending me." He frowns. "It *was* Mateo who ministered to me, was it not?"

When I fail to answer, his frown deepens. I cannot bear the look on his face so I turn away, and when I do I hear him laugh.

"After a husband has been bathed from head to toe by his wife can he have any secrets left? Though it is hardly fair since I have not had the similar pleasure and since you promised there would be no secrets between us." His gaze is one of tenderness and love, and something else, too, which I can only describe as admiration.

Without a word, I slip off my skirt, then bodice, then undergarments until at last I stand naked before him. "Now . . . there are no secrets between us."

For several minutes he stares silently at me. And strangely enough, I feel no awkwardness.

"Unloose your hair," he finally says in a low, throaty voice as he extends his hand. "For you know a bride should have nothing bound when on her nuptial bed."

I shake my head. "You are weak. You must rest and regain your strength and then..."

"Unloose your hair," he says again, his voice a near whisper, his hand still outstretched.

And so I loosen my hair, and walk to the bed where I take his hand and allow him to pull me onto the mattress. And when we are in each others arms, I feel his lips on my neck then hear his voice tenderly whisper, "I love you, Isabel. I love you."

Chapter 17

"Don Bartolome has declared this a day of abstinence," Antonio says, nibbling the roasted fish I bought from Bata's cousin this morning. "In honor of Saint Michael, the Archangel, he has banned the eating of meat and eggs and dairy; and of course all grease and fat in order to keep the bodily humors cool and our minds on spiritual matters." He licks one finger, then sips wine from his goblet. He no longer wears the jewel encrusted rings he wore the first time he came to my door. "I have cautioned him to exercise moderation in his declaration of fasts and penances, but he is bent on forcing all Isabela to observe the three Christian vows of poverty, chastity and obedience."

I sit across the table, sharing our noon meal. "We have no meat or eggs or dairy, anyway. And little grease or fat to tempt us. But this privation has not increased my devotion. In fact, I am ashamed to say, it has done nothing to help me remember any of the saint's days or even our holy day of *Rosh Hashanah* which has come and gone without a nod from me. Now, I ask you, why is that?"

"Nothing provokes carnal desires more than being told you may not have something. That is why I worry over Don Bartolome's severity. If only he was acquainted with the *Baghdad Cookery-Book* that affirms two of life's six pleasures are food and scents." Antonio's voice is playful.

"Both overrated pleasures when compared to the pleasure of a wife lying with her husband."

Antonio chokes on his fish, then wipes his mouth and grins.

I blush when I see the merriment in his eyes, for it is apparent that once again I have spoken rashly. "Pity there are no monasteries here in Isabela with all the excellent fish available." I flake off a piece of codfish with my knife. "It would provide the monks a good livelihood in salting and drying."

"Not to mention endless fighting. Each monastery would surely squabble over these rights, for such a valuable income would hardly be relinquished without a struggle."

I laugh and picture a squadron of monks running the banks of the Isabela River while another runs the seashore claiming every foot their own. "With so much money to be had in fish, it is fortunate we have laws forbidding fishmongers to price gouge, at least during Lent."

"True . . . for as you know, greed, like lust—which you seem to understand well enough—is one of the seven deadly sins."

When Antonio leans over, covering my hand with his, I again notice the scar below his ear, and without thinking, I touch it. "How did you get that?"

He shrugs, and since I suspect it is from one of his many duels over Doña Maria's indiscretions, I drop the matter.

"No, Isabel, it is not from a duel." His mouth forms a crooked smile. "I received it defending King Fernando. I dislike speaking of it for people always want to make more of the matter than it deserves."

"Now you really must tell me for certainly a wife should be allowed the privilege of being proud of her husband."

Antonio's smile widens. "Pride? Another deadly sin, Isabel?"

I shrug. "What can be done with a character as flawed as mine?"

"You are not completely flawed. You do have one virtue"

"And that is?"

"Your love for me."

"My *great* love for you."

"Yes, your *great* love for me." Antonio releases my hand, and sips wine from his goblet. "I suppose I must tell for how can I withhold anything from one who loves me so greatly?" He rests his muscular arms on the table. "Do you remember almost two years ago, when King Fernando was attacked by that assassin, Juan de Canamas?"

"Yes, the news was everywhere."

"I was there in Barcelona, and saw it all: the attack, Fernando's fall, his blood pooling the marble steps of the Palace of Justice. He would have died had he not been wearing the heavy chains of his office. It kept the assassin's sword from severing his head."

"That still does not explain your scar."

"I drew the assassin away before he could finish his work."

"You fought him?"

"No. Only distracted him until one of Fernando's guards came. I was unarmed."

Again I touch the large scar below his ear. "Distracted him? By offering him your own neck to sever?" Antonio blushes. It is the first time I have seen him blush, and by it I understand he is uncomfortable with praise, but still I cannot resist bestowing it. "You are a champion. No doubt King Fernando owes you his life."

Antonio removes my fingers from his scar and kisses them. "I assure you it was not heroic at all. I did what any man loyal to the Crown would do. And my wound was nothing compared to the king's. When I was partially healed, the Queen sent me to her castle in Sequovia to complete my recovery. It was a great honor, for Sequovia is where she lived as a girl, and remains her favorite fortress."

"We were told you were sent because of overwork, and needed rest."

"It was as I wished, for I did not want to cause my family concern. Sequovia was lovely, and all the bridges I travel enroute, were new. Did you know that our Sovereigns are constructing bridges everywhere?" Antonio absently fingers his neck.

How skillfully he has turned the conversation from his heroic deed. I am about to veer it back when I hear shouts outside our door.

"The *Niña*! It is the *Niña*."

Antonio and I rush outside and follow the throng of nobles to the rocky promontory where I see three ships with full sails coming from the north.

"Look," someone shouts, as the ships enter the harbor and lower sail. "The middle one flies the Admiral's ensign and arms."

"It is the *Niña*, all right, for she has no hawseholes in her hull," says another.

We all stand quietly, and, I think, are grateful that at long last our Admiral has returned. I send up silent prayers that with his return life in Isabela will finally improve.

Our silence continues as men are lowered in boats. More silence as the boats cut through foaming waves on their way to shore. Then, as one boat beaches, silence gives way to shouts of alarm. There is our Admiral, in plain view for all to see, lying prone in the boat; still and pale as death.

And when four men get out and carry him over the dunes toward his house, people in the crowd begin asking "What is wrong? What has happened?" And soon others whisper that Christopher Columbus is gravely ill and even blind. And as the rumors float around our heads, Antonio quietly slips his hand over mine and leads me back to our hut.

"The Admiral has named Don Bartolome, Governor, in his place," Antonio says, stepping through the doorway of our house.

For two days we have listened to gossip swirl across Isabela like locust, devouring our town's peace. Claims that the Admiral was on his death bed flew alongside other claims that what kept him low was not impending death at all, but a drunken stupor.

"He has not made Bartolome Governor of the Indies for nothing. He must be gravely ill," I say, standing at the table cutting hog plums.

"The Admiral is neither dying nor drunk. The doctor says he has gout." Antonio walks to the table and standing behind me, slips his arms around my waist. "But it is true that Admiral Columbus cannot see, for his eyes bleed. The doctor has covered them with salve and bandages." Antonio reaches for a plum. "Even in ill health he shows concern for what is happening in Isabela. He has officially commissioned Fray Pane to study the religious practices of the Tainos, to more easily convert them, and also, I believe, to discover the means of establishing a better friendship between our people.

"He has also addressed the food shortage. With our crops failing and Tainos burning their fields, Columbus has ordered some of the livestock butchered and distributed among those salaried by the Crown."

Antonio pulls me closer. "God knows I want to have children with you, Isabel. But with all the problems plaguing our settlement, is it wise? Am I selfish in wanting to put you through all that childbirth entails?"

I put down my knife and wipe my hands. "I do not fear childbirth. I only fear that once you have satisfied your obligation by providing Sebastian an heir, you will grow weary of this harsh and terrible place, and want to return to the gaiety and opulence of court life, and . . . leave me behind."

Antonio throws back his head and laughs.

"What is so amusing?" I push him away. "Can you not understand that a mind is an instrument of torment? And that my mind torments me daily with this very thought?"

"Then let your mind be at rest," he says, in a teasing whisper. "You are my heart. Can a man leave his heart behind, and live?"

Antonio opens his pouch of salt and places it on the table. He is silent while I open mine. We sit across from each other. Mateo stands nearby, serving as witness. I have told Antonio this is unnecessary. Even so, he insists there be a salt covenant between us. I know it is only because of my confession yesterday.

Antonio removes a pinch of salt from his sheepskin pouch, and I remove a pinch from mine. Then, with a nod of his head, my husband places his pinch in my sack, and I place mine in his. That done, we tie our pouches and shake them. It takes but a minute to seal the covenant by which we promise each other a lifetime of love and fidelity. And though I believe Antonio has only done this to ease my doubts, in some inexplicable way I know my heart and his have been permanently fused together.

⌒◯

"Gonzolo has finished our hut," Maria says, pulling me out of my house. "Come see his handiwork. Oh, what furniture he made!"

I ask no questions—not wanting to spoil what she clearly means to be a surprise—and allow her to tow me through the streets in silence. Poblado Central bustles with activity. New dwellings are everywhere. But among them are some charred remains of former dwellings that have been abandoned by the disenchanted. Still, life has taken root once again as evidenced by the potpourri of voices, the smell of food cooking over fireboxes, the freshly washed clothes hanging on poles to dry.

"And your sons?" I say, almost panting, for Maria is moving at a fast pace. "Are their huts finished, too?"

"Yes, Juan and Luis have worked day and night. Their huts are large, and look more like Taino dwellings than ours, and decorated inside with all manner of weavings by their wives. But at my insistence—for I still fear these women will turn my sons into savages and make them sleep on those strange *hammocks*—they have built proper beds, and shelves and tables, too. Now all is in readiness. And high time, for both wives are with child." Maria has finally slowed and turns toward me, I think to see my pleasure when telling me the good news.

I smile, and squeeze her hand. "God has been good to you and your family. I pray He will continue to bless you all."

"Yes, God has been good. Only . . . I wish Enrique would separate himself from those rogues he has befriended. Whenever we see him, he talks of nothing but seizing land for himself. He says, 'Why should only the wealthy be landowners? Why not peasants also? Cannot peasants better themselves here in the Indies?'

"He has brought himself low with talk against the Admiral, and threats to overthrow him. This is *treason*, Isabel. *Treason!* And if that were not enough, it is rumored he illegally searches for gold in the Vega Real, forcing Tainos to dig and pan the placer fields, then keeping what is found. So now he is a thief as well! Stealing what belongs to the Crown and to our Admiral. How brazen he has become. And cruel. Oh, what stories Bata tells! If only half are true Enrique will surely burn in hell. I am so worried, Isabel, I hardly sleep nights."

I know not what to say, for I, too, have heard these stories, and know it is only a matter of time before the Holy One brings down judgment upon Enrique's head, for such cruelty and thievery cannot go long unanswered.

Maria meets my gaze, and as if knowing my thoughts, drops my hand, then gestures toward her door. "I think the bed will please you. Gonzalo has decorated the headboard with beautiful rose carvings."

I am about to enter when I hear an awful wailing coming from the Plaza behind us. I stop and glance back. The cries and shouts are so terrible it would be unthinkable to continue with Maria. "We must see what is wrong," I say, heading for the Plaza, with Maria close behind.

In the Plaza, two Taino men, their faces bloody, their bodies battered and bruised, stand before a group of nobles. Nooses drape their necks, the ends of which dangle down their bloody chests.

"I tell you these are the ones who surprised our patrol yesterday and strangled three of our men," says a noble with raised fist. Even from where I stand I can see the blood on his knuckles.

"Beat them again! Make them confess," someone shouts.

Then all becomes quiet as the Governing Council approaches, Don Bartolome and Antonio among them.

"Caonabo, the ruling chief of Maguana, is a king who also rules over eighty other chiefs," Antonio says, stepping forward, "chiefs who are obliged to align themselves with him in time of war. Already he is forming an alliance against us." The wind catches Antonio's hair, making it fall across his eyes. Absently he brushes it aside, revealing an earnestness of expression. "What better way to show Caonabo we wish peace than by displaying mercy? Let these Tainos live and return to Caonabo as proof of our generosity and goodwill."

"And show ourselves cowards?" Don Bartolome says.

Then everyone begins shouting at once.

"And allow spilled Castilian blood to go unavenged?"

"We must show these devils who is master."

"Hang them!"

"Burn them at the stake!"

When Antonio looks up and sees me, he gestures with a slight movement of his head for me to leave. It is apparent he expects the outcome to be bad. And sure enough, sometime later, after I have returned from seeing Maria's new home and carved bed, and am kindling the firebox for the noon meal, I detect the familiar smell of burning flesh coming from the direction of the Plaza.

Bata, Maria and I sit outside my door weaving mats for their new huts when the church bell rings. Since it rang None only a short while ago, this new ringing was surely an alert. We leave our weaving, and as we head for the church I see four ships approaching from the west. In the distance they look more like gulls skimming the water than *naos* or *caravels*. Surely they come from Castile since Columbus's ships are all anchored in the harbor.

Shouts and cheers go up, and pebbles skitter as men run to the edge of the large rocky promontory. We run with them, and stop only when we reach land's end. More than one man shouts, "It is Antonio de Torres."

"Can it really be Torres, with so few ships?" Maria says.

I shrug. It is hard to see any identifying flags for the vessels are still far off.

"Torres was to return with thirteen ships filled with a year's worth of food and goods for a thousand people. Surely this *cannot* be Torres," Maria persists.

But who else? I wonder.

Diego and Bartolome Columbus suddenly appear on the rocky ledge. Antonio is with them, and when he sees me, he leaves the others.

"Much needed supplies," Antonio says, coming alongside me and gesturing with his chin toward the ships entering the harbor.

"Some say it is Torres. But how can that be? He was to return with more than a dozen ships."

"It *is* Torres." Antonio leans closer as though not wanting anyone to hear. "When the Admiral learned only four ships were seen on the horizon, he flew into a rage. He is certain Fray Buil and others have blackened his name by whispering falsehoods in our Queen's ear. He sees no other explanation for the Sovereigns cutting our provisions by sending this small fleet."

My stomach knots. What is to become of a colony the Sovereigns no longer support with a full heart? But I hold my peace, and watch the ships throw anchor. Then watch as longboats load up with people and supplies. When they are filled, the boats are lowered and slowly rowed to shore. And suddenly I am overcome with joy, for first to arrive is a boatload of *women*! Ten at least, and as many children. And yes, in the next boat too. Another fifteen, and more children. The men have seen them too, and shouts and woops go up as husbands recognize their families. I break from Antonio, and run toward where the women and children are now making their way up the promontory.

Maria and Bata have joined me, and we all stand waving and shouting our greetings as one by one the women, with their children, pass us on their way to join their husbands. When I glance at Antonio, our eyes meet. And I know what he is thinking, for my thoughts are the same.

Perhaps this will be a civilized enough place, after all, to raise children.

⌒◦

I am preparing for Twelfth Night or the eve of the Epiphany. Tomorrow, on the Epiphany or Three Kings Day, we will celebrate the baptism of Jesus as well as remember how the Magi visited the King of Kings in that humble stable and lavished Him with presents. It is a time for ending a twenty-one day fast. It is also a time for giving gifts. And I have two gifts for Antonio. One is a chicken I purchased from Admiral Columbus to make soup. It is cooking in a pot hanging on the spit of our firebox. And while I cut fresh fruit and stack it on a platter, I try to visualize the look on Antonio's face when I share my second gift.

Considering all our colony's hardship and that more than half of those who recently arrived with Antonio de Torres are sick, it has been a wonderful twelve days of Christmas. It began with Christmas Eve, or "Adam and Eve Day" when Antonio and I, and the Vivars, and many of the new women with their children, decorated one of the trees in the Plaza. Having no apples, which is the customary fruit used, we used hog plums.

Since coming to Isabela I have not seen such contentment. There has been little complaining, and though everyone is concerned about the Tainos, the usual rumor that they will massacre us in our beds has not circulated. Antonio de Torres and his fresh supply of livestock and medicines and wine and food and the thirty odd women and their children have greatly raised our spirits.

And there is even more good news, for our Admiral has regained his eyesight. Though he is still bedridden, it is rumored he will soon leave it and mount an expedition against Guatiguara, the subchief who recently attacked the newly built fort of Magdalena, killing fifty Christians.

More bloodshed.

I suppose the Admiral is obliged to restore order, even if the Indian attacks are only reprisals for our own cruelty. For my peace of mind I must leave these matters to the men, and not stew endlessly over them. I am learning to turn all these burdens over to the Savior. And, oh, how willingly He takes them! It is only because He has, that I am able to take this much pleasure in Twelfth Night. Even now I sing the *Pater Noster* as I work.

"What a pleasing voice you have, my love."

I turn toward Antonio and see his face shine with excitement. He holds one hand behind his back.

"What are you are hiding?" I say, pretending only modest interest as I place the fruit on a platter. I am certain he is holding my gift, which I suspect—from the many times he has met with Pasculina's husband—is a piece of jewelry.

"It is your gift," he blurts. "And I must give it to you now."

"But we agreed to exchange our gifts after the noon meal."

"I cannot wait." He thrusts out his hand. In it is a folded red silk ribbon that plainly holds something, for it bulges.

"But we agreed . . . ." Antonio's face is so earnest and full of excitement I have not the heart to put him off, so I take the ribbon and carefully unwrap it. I gasp when I see a beautiful gold chain holding a gold medallion on which is engraved Antonio's coat of arms.

"Turn it over." Antonio is grinning, hardly able to contain himself.

When I do, I see engraved initials, side by side; his and mine, and beneath them the words, *Tonto Monta.* "It is beautiful," I say, falling into his arms. "So perfectly beautiful."

"For my perfectly beautiful wife."

We embrace, and I smell lavender and rosemary, the oils of which he now uses on his hair. "But it is hardly fair you give your gift early, and I do not." Now it is my turn to quiver with excitement as I place his hands on my belly. Antonio smiles, but looks puzzled. "I am with child," I finally blurt when I see he has not guessed my secret nor is likely to even if I waited until next Twelfth Night.

And when my words sink in, Antonio laughs and dances around the room like a boy. And then he comes to me and cups my face in his hands. "No gift could make me happier."

⁓◎

The heat from the furnace forces me to step backward. I am with Pasculina and two of the women who came on Torres's ships with their husbands—men knowledgeable in metal. I have accompanied the women to the smelting furnace, for each has brought her husband a flask of wine to wet his parched throat. "Will they finish in time?" I say to Pasculina.

"My husband has not been home for nearly a week. He promised today all will be done."

It is good to be in the company of these simple women whose society is filled with talk of domestic life. They are earthy and honest, and make me feel part of a culture that is alive and real, and that will endure. Now more than ever, with my child growing inside me, I feel the need to be part of something enduring.

"He promised all will be done today," Pasculina repeats.

"As if there is a choice," says one of the other women. "For Torres sails tomorrow."

We watch as the men take long drinks from their leather flagons before returning to work. They have been melting lead for days. Some for shot—replacing the dwindling supply due to all the Indian trouble—but mostly for sheathing to protect Torres's ships on the return voyage, sheathing that will keep both the torredo worms and the salt of the Ocean Sea from damaging the hulls.

The fumes from the furnace sting my eyes and burn my throat. That, mingled with my morning sickness, which has plagued me for weeks now, drives me further from the furnace. When I can tolerate it no longer, I bid the women 'goodbye' and walk around the storehouse toward my hut.

I am almost home when I hear the most awful wailing I have ever heard, more terrible even than the cries of the two Tainos who were beaten in the Plaza. And these cries come not from one throat or two, but from many.

I rush toward the sound, and when I reach the Plaza, I stop in disbelief. The square is packed with sweating, exhausted Tainos; men and women, both. The women wail in each other's arms, and the babies they hold wail, too. The men stand together looking dazed. Some try to bolster the courage of their companions, but most look as though it is the end of the world. Surrounding this sea of bodies are Columbus's soldiers, and at their head, Admiral Columbus himself.

A platoon of soldiers penetrates the crowd, causing more confusion as women cling to each other in fear, and men look alternately threatening and defeated. But oddly, no one attacks the soldiers, though they are badly outnumbered.

One by one, the soldiers separate—as though culling a herd—the most desirable males and females, pulling them by the hair or arm, and roughly shoving them into the space they have cleared. I watch in horror as more than five hundred are culled, then shackled with chains, and forced into longboats. Cries and wails of both those on the boats and those left behind rise to a deafening pitch as the captives are rowed to Torres's four anchored ships. It is clear husbands have been separated from wives, and wives from husbands.

I run up and down the sides of the Plaza, frantically looking for Antonio. Surely Admiral Columbus has not sanctioned this! Then I see Columbus by the clearing, talking to his commanders as he calmly watches the longboats row away.

Unthinkable. Our Admiral would never order this. Surely it is a mistake.

But the horror continues when a commander loudly issues an invitation to all the populace of Isabela to take from the remaining Tainos—who number nearly a thousand—anyone they desire as slaves or concubines. Nobles and peasants alike sift through men and women, inspecting their bodies for blemishes or signs of disease, then bind their choices with ropes and lead them away. Some of the more raucous men sling Taino women over their shoulders and carry them off with no more troubled conscience than if carting away a sack of flour. And when this orgy of flesh peddling is over, nearly six hundred Tainos have been taken. The four hundred remaining in the Plaza look utterly bewildered.

I see Bata crying and waving her hands as she heads for the edge of the promontory. "They take my sister," she screams, pointing to the harbor where the ships are anchored. "They take my sister!"

I go to her out of fear she will throw herself off the cliff. With great effort I lead her back to the Plaza. "Stay here," I order when I see Antonio talking to Don Bartolome by the church. Then I dash to my husband's side.

When Antonio sees the look on my face he grabs my arm and pulls me far away from Don Bartolome.

"Do something," I say. All around us the remaining captives weep. Many have collapsed on the ground. Some stand looking up at the sky as if waiting for their deliverance. "You must do something," I repeat.

"You know Queen Isabel believes pagan lands are hers by right of conquest."

"But you said she ordered Admiral Columbus to treat the Indians kindly, and to convert them to Christ."

"These Tainos were taken in battle. They are hostiles. They have raised their hand against us. And Columbus was given permission to enslave all hostile Indians. In war, the conquerors have the right to make slaves of the conquered. There is no pity in this world, Isabel. You of all people should understand that. How many Jews, your relatives even, were expelled from Castile, then sold as slaves by the very people they hired to transport them to safety?" His lips form a tight line. His face is the color of ash. "If they were capable of doing that to us, their own fellow Castilians, what are they able to do in time of war and to hostile heathens? After the fall of Malaga were not Moors taken as slaves? Were not a hundred of them sent to Pope Innocent as a gift? And did not our own Queen send her cousin thirty as well?"

I am about to answer when I hear the commander tell the remaining Tainos—the ones none of the settlers wanted—that they are free to return to their homes. And I watch in horror as many of the women, who carry babies in their arms, place them on the ground and run away, leaving the Plaza a littered field of squirming, crying infants. I turn to Antonio. "*Do* something."

"I cannot . . . I *will* not," he says between clenched teeth. "Do not ask it of me."

And so I back away, tears flowing down my cheeks, and feeling, for the first time, angry with my husband, and disappointed, too. And I see by his eyes, which are hard as flint, that he is angry with me, also, for expecting something he is incapable of doing—namely, defying Spain's time honored tradition of dividing the spoils of war.

I shade my eyes from the bright sun as I watch the little fleet of four ships sail away. The spot where I stand on the promontory is deserted; a circumstance that fuels my feeling of loneliness. A wave of nausea sweeps over me—the customary morning sickness, which, according to Aunt Leonora, should pass in another month. But it adds to my feeling of misery.

I squint at the horizon. One of the ships carries my letter to Mama. In it I have written the news that she is to be a grandmamma. I did not tell her that along with my letter the ship carries a cargo of slaves. Nor did I share any details of the difficulties of life in Isabela, or of the imminent danger of a Taino uprising. Nor did I tell her that every day more and more of our men grumble against the Columbus brothers.

As I watch the ships become specks, I think of yesterday's terrible scene when men and women were shackled and loaded onto longboats.

And worse, I see the Plaza littered with crying babies and their mothers sprinting to freedom. Now that my own child grows within me it is hard to imagine a mother leaving her child. *Surely the Tainos are no different? Surely bond between parent and offspring knows no country or race?* After only a moment's reflection I decide there is no difference. For fear and love guide us all. When Bata and I and some Taino women carried the abandoned infants to a nearby village, I saw the love that inspired the women there to take to their breasts infants who were not their own. In this same manner *conversos* took in children who converted and were left by parents who were expelled from Seville because they had not.

I feel sorry for all those who have been ripped from their homes and are being carried off to an alien land. And my sorrow is more acute since I have not been able to share these feelings with Antonio. I have not seen him since yesterday for he never came home, not even to sleep. But I know him well enough to know it was not anger that kept him away.

When I feel a hand slip over mine, I turn. There is my husband beside me. He is rumpled and tired, and his hair wind-tossed, but to my eyes he is a delight.

"We live in a cruel world, Isabel," he says, without looking at me. "I am only a man, and will not always measure up to your expectations. And to me, that is a painful reality. But we must never be cruel to one another. Let there be peace between us."

"And I am a woman of flawed character," I whisper, "with a rash and impetuous nature. Please forgive me."

"There is nothing to forgive. But just so you know why I did not come home it is because I spent most of the night arguing with the Admiral, trying to convince him that our Queen would prefer the Tainos as converts and loyal subjects rather than slaves."

"And what did he say?"

Antonio's arm encircles my shoulder. "He said he believed that too."

"Then why did he make slaves of them?"

"Because he felt compelled to defuse Fray Buil's bad report, and to justify the Sovereigns' faith in him as well as to compensate the Crown for their investment in his expeditions. And he could only do that by sending something of value. And since he had little gold to send, or pearls—for he has yet to find the fabled pearl beds—he sent slaves. Perhaps next time Columbus will remember our conversation." His words work through my hair as he kisses my forehead. "Perhaps it will save the lives of other Tainos."

"No," I say, as the last ship disappears over the horizon. "I fear the gentle Tainos will not survive our harsh Castilian ways."

And as if to prove me right, within a month Alonzo de Hojeda captures Caonabo, the great Taino king, and brings him back to Isabela in chains. The Tainos, outraged by Caonabo's capture and treatment—for he was chained and kept imprisoned in one of the ships—plan revenge. Their hostility is met with brute force as Admiral Columbus and his infantry slaughter hundreds and hundreds of Tainos with firearms, swords, pikes and war dogs.

And all Antonio and I can do is stand idly by.

Chapter 18

" Can you feel that?" I move Antonio's hand over my belly to a pulsating knot that is our child's kicking foot.

"He is strong."

"It could be a girl." We are both lying in bed; I, flat on my back, Antonio beside me, propped on one elbow. His free hand roams over the wide expanse of my protruding belly. "I pricked my finger yesterday and forced a drop of blood into a goblet of water. The blood floated. Aunt Leonora, may her memory be for blessing, always said if the blood floats it is a girl. Would you mind a girl?"

Antonio's large hand lingers over the moving bulge as though in a caress.

"A boy would be better for Sebastian, to carry his name. But to me, boy or girl, what difference? I will love it just the same."

I run my fingers along the neckline of Antonio's fine cotton tunic. It is well past Tierce and still we linger in bed, I suppose because outside it is pouring, and neither of us wants to begin the day.

"Aunt Leonora said a woman must guard her eyes before lying with her husband in case she conceives, for it will affect the child. But for the life of me I cannot remember seeing anything but your handsome face."

"And if you had seen, say, a lamb?"

"According to Aunt Leonora, I would conceive a weak child."

"And a pig?"

"A disagreeable child, very disagreeable." I snuggle closer to my husband, for the wind has picked up, and now it, along with the heavy rain, beats loudly against our hut. "But I do not believe it because I do not believe the Creator would fashion a child in this manner, for it is too careless."

Antonio laughs. "You are a strange mix of passion and logic."

"And Doña Maria? Did she believe such things?" I know not why I ask; perhaps because being here like this with Antonio and talking about our child has suddenly made me jealous thinking he might have done this with her.

Antonio props two pillows against the headboard and sits up. "I once heard Doña Maria tell a maidservant she feared she would have a crippled child because she saw an old cripple begging alms at the gate just before she believed she conceived. But hers was a mind full of fears. Even her dreams were troubled, for often, from my room, I would hear her scream in the night. At such times, I would go to her and offer to pray Psalm Ninety-One, but she always refused."

I nod. Everyone prayed Psalm Ninety-One when trying to rid themselves of demons.

Antonio fingers my cascading hair, and when he says, "You have no reason to be jealous," shame overwhelms me. How ungracious to want Antonio to speak ill of a woman who is dead. Can I grow in my husband's estimation by diminishing another?

"I hope Aunt Leonora has taught you well, for no midwife came with the other women on Torres's ships, only the new physician, Doctor Martinez."

I hear the worry in Antonio's voice, and pull up my bulky frame until I am sitting erect. "She was a good teacher, I a bad pupil. But I believe my knowledge is greater than the average woman's." My hand touches his. "Women have been birthing babies since the beginning of time. Do not fear."

Before Antonio can respond, a sudden blast of wind flutters my hair, making me glance at the doorway. There, Maria stands holding the curtain to one side. Behind her, the pouring rain looks as solid and grey as the sheathing Pasculina's husband forged for Torres's ships.

"Pardon, Doña Isabel," Maria says, dripping water that puddles at her feet. "But you must come at once. It is Bata. She is laboring hard. The baby should have come hours ago. I fear something is wrong."

I try to rise but Antonio stops me. "You expect my wife to go out in this howling wind and rain?" His voice is uncharacteristically sharp. "It is as if the devil himself has descended upon us. Just listen!" Antonio points to the opening as though Maria has no prior knowledge of what is happening outside. "Would you have my wife risk herself when she is so near the end of her own confinement? Get Pasculina or one of the other women!"

"Doña Isabel's aunt was a midwife. Bata knows this and will not be comforted by anyone else." Maria's voice is pleading.

"Is Doña Isabel responsible for Bata's comfort?" Antonio shakes his head. "No, I will not allow it! Find another to comfort her."

"Since the time Bata's Taino midwife was taken away on Torres's ship, Bata has scoured other villages for a new one, but all have fled to the mountains. Even so, Bata is brave and was willing to have the baby alone. But now this . . . this . . . terrible pain." Maria's eyes meet mine. "In God's name please help her, Doña Isabel."

Slowly, Antonio releases my arm. "Dress," he says, without emotion. "I will go with you." But I know what this is costing him. And while I put on my skirt and bodice I pray to the Holy One to give us strength. Then I ask Him to bless my hands and help me remember everything Aunt Leonora taught me.

I stand by Bata's bed, trying to ignore her groans and the howling wind outside. Her pain is so great she cannot sit on the birthing stool but lies writhing in bed and pulling at her hair. Quickly, I brush aside her hands then spread her hair across the pillow, for nothing must be tied or constricted when one gives birth. Maria has already removed the pins and untied all the knots in the hut. And since the weather is so bad, we bypass custom by not removing the coverings on the door and windows, for Old Christians follow these customs as well as Jews.

Next, I open my box of spices, take out a pouch of dried fennel and sprinkle a handful around the bed to ward off demons. I pray it works, for Aunt Leonora always used fresh.

Since the hut is only one room, and the men cannot go outside due to the fierce storm, Juan and Gonzalo have strung a blanket for Bata's privacy. I open the jar of massaging ointment just as Bata cries out in a loud voice. I cringe, for I know Antonio listens on the other side, and that her screams only enhance his worry for me and my own birthing to come.

Maria has already arranged Bata's clothing, exposing her large belly. I am wet to the bone from walking to Poblado Central, and drip water everywhere, including on Bata, but this cannot be helped. After a brief hesitation, I lean over and apply the ointment, massaging it gently in circular motions. Bata shrieks and digs her nails into my arm. Without a word, Maria tears rags and binds Bata's wrists to the frame of the bed.

I feel Bata's belly to determine the position of the baby's arms and legs, but stop when I feel the head. "Let me see your hands," I say to Maria. When she holds them out, I am disappointed to see they are larger than mine.

"Bring me a goblet of wine." I tremble inside for the work I must now do. While Maria pours the wine I pick through my herbs until I find the wormwood. I take a few leaves, crush them between my palms, then drop them into the liquid. Aunt Leonora mixed this with another herb but I cannot remember what.

"To help ease her anxiety," I say, hoping I am right.

I sit on the bed creating a wet ring on the covers. Maria holds Bata's head while I hold the goblet and force Bata to drink. When she is finished, I ask Maria to bring a bowl of olive oil. Then I pull off all of Bata's covers, exposing her legs.

"The baby lies sideways in your belly, and must be turned." I dip my hand into the bowl Maria holds. There is fear in Maria's eyes, and rightly so, for many women have died from being unable to deliver a baby thus situated.

I climb on the bed, feeling like a cow with my heavy wet clothes and great belly. With difficulty, I position myself between Bata's legs; then ask the Merciful One to guide my hand as I slip first two oiled fingers inside Bata, then a third. My fingers are long, enabling me to feel the opening of her womb which is wide and soft and ready for delivery, but unless I get all four fingers into the birth canal I will not be able to reach the baby. I pray, then gently push my fingers upward. Bata screams and cries and gnashes her teeth, and if Maria had not taken it into her head to hold Bata down, I doubt the rags would have held.

I am on my knees now, trying to turn the baby with my fingers inside and with my hand outside; pushing and prodding between contractions.

"Quickly, grind five peppercorns," I shout. "For the baby is nearly turned."

And minutes later when Maria brings the ground pepper, I slip out my fingers and know the baby is not far behind. It is pointless to take Bata to the birthing stool. She is much too weak, and in great pain. She must deliver in bed.

"Blow the pepper into her nose," I say, "but not all of it." And when Maria does, Bata sneezes, and I see the crown of the baby's head. "Again!" I shout. And again Maria blows pepper. This time when Bata sneezes the head pops out. One more contraction and I am able to pull the baby free.

"A beautiful girl," I say, when it is all over.

On the other side of the blanket the men shout praises to God. Then Juan leads them in the *Pater Noster*.

Maria hands me a knife, and I cut the umbilical cord and tie it off. Then I give the baby to Maria who washes her with salted water, then rubs her gums with honey to stimulate appetite. Next, Maria dries her, swaddles her bottom in a wool cloth, and finally wraps her tightly in a small linen blanket. And while Maria shows the baby to the men, I pour another goblet of wine for Bata, who is exhausted and weak and having difficulty expelling the afterbirth. To the wine I add a pinch of savin which will help her with this. "Drink," I whisper, "then I will massage your belly. Just a few more contractions and you will be able to rest."

⁓౧

When we leave Bata's hut the sky is so dark it looks like the bell should be ringing Compline rather than Sext. Almond-size drops of rain pelt us relentlessly as we move slowly across Poblado Central. Not a soul is stirring, and I wonder if we should return to the Vivars. Bata was frantic when we left, begging us to stay and shouting, "*Guabancex! Guabancex!*" over and over, which Juan said means "Lady of the Winds" and is the goddess of what Bata calls, "*hurricane.*"

But their hut is too small for so many, and being exhausted I wanted to return home, and Antonio felt the same way. Now, I fear we have made a mistake.

"Do you think we should turn back?" I shout, trying to be heard above the wind that howls and tears at our hair and clothing like a beast. And though I cling tightly to Antonio's arm, it has knocked me down more than once. "Should we turn back?" I repeat.

"We are half way home. It would be pointless. Either way, the distance is the same."

I wipe the water from my eyes and am alarmed to see the side of someone's hut blow over our heads. I am reminded of the time Fray Buil saved my life by lashing me to the mast of the *Tortoise*, and suddenly, as trees sway and bow to the wind, I am greatly afraid.

"We must hurry, Isabel," Antonio shouts, "for the wind is getting stronger!"

And so I run, holding Antonio's arm with one hand and my great belly with the other, feeling grateful I left my spice box with Maria. A thatched roof flies by, then another. Lightning and thunder fill the sky. And the incessant wind flogs us unmercifully. Something hits Antonio in the head. He falls, and I with him. And as I try to rise I hear the sound of cracking timber, and see a nearby tree list, then hear it creak and groan as it plunges down on top of us.

♻

I hear a voice, but it is far away. I know that voice. It is Antonio's. But I cannot answer. I try. Oh, how I try, but my tongue cleaves to the roof of my mouth. It is dry, my mouth, like a wad of Bata's spun cotton. I try moving my lips but they remain like lazy slugs and will not obey. I am cold and wet. But I am not afraid, for suddenly I smell the fragrance of lavender and rosemary, then feel Antonio's strong arms lift me into the air. But why does he weep and call my name? Do not weep, Antonio, I am here. I am here! Only . . . I do not know where that is, exactly.

♻

I look up and see sky—beautiful blue sky with rolling clouds that look like giant foaming waves. I close my eyes, and my fingers crawl over the space by my side. Surely I must be mistaken, for I feel mattress beneath me. Can I be lying on my bed and outside at the same time? Surely no one has moved the bed. I look again and see the same blue sky, but something else, too. A thatched roof. And after staring for some time, I realize I am seeing sky through a large hole in the thatch. I have hardly gotten my mind around this oddity when I hear a faint sound and notice Antonio kneeling on the floor beside the bed. His eyes are closed, his head bowed in an attitude of prayer. The *Pater Noster* streams softly from his lips. But his face, the way it is pinched,

259

and his entire body, which is doubled over, reminds me of one travailing in . . . childbirth.

Childbirth.

Suddenly, I remember Bata and her baby, the storm, the tree. "Antonio!" I shout, and am surprised to hear my voice dribble out in a whisper. "Antonio!" I say again, this time sounding louder. And when he lifts his head, I see the terrible fear in his eyes.

"You are . . . awake."

I raise my hand to touch his tears, but my arm is too heavy and drops back onto the bed. Then I see the deep gash along his right cheek, and the wounds around his neck. "What happened?"

"Do you remember returning from Bata's house, and the storm?"

"Yes, I remember. And the falling tree, too. Is that where you got those?" Since I cannot lift my arm to point I gesture with my chin and am surprised to find even that requires great effort.

"These are nothing. A few scratches." Antonio rises from his knees and sits on the bed. "But you . . . the full weight of the tree fell on you, while I was protected by your body. I wish to God it was the other way around."

His eyes tell me something terrible has happened. I try to sit up but my muscles refuse to obey. With great effort, I slide my hands over my hips until they rest on my belly. And instead of feeling the large familiar mound, I feel a soft, empty pouch.

"You lost the child, Isabel," Antonio says, lying down next to me. "The tree crushed him."

"It was a *boy?*" I try not to cry, for Antonio's sake. He looks so sad I can hardly bare it. But still the tears come.

"Doctor Martinez says you are strong." Antonio scoops me in his arms. "But you have lost more blood than ten bleedings would have drawn, and it will take time for you to recover."

"And children? Did he say I can have more children?"

"Yes," Antonio answers, but there is something odd in his voice. "No need to think of that now. You must rest, Isabel. Rest."

And after a long while, when Antonio thinks I am sleeping, I hear him weep.

~⊙

It is two weeks after the *hurricane,* and all Isabela is still cleaning up the debris and making repairs. Many huts are destroyed. Many more damaged. Only the stone buildings were spared, though the church roof was torn off because it was thatch.

Though I am still weak, and though Antonio disapproves, I am participating in the baptism of Bata's baby. Normally, a baby is baptized the same day it is born, but the church's roof has only now been repaired. I walk behind Luis's wife who follows Maria. Both are godmothers. Maria carries the child, a child you can barely see for the long flowing robe of silk she wears. The silk is my christening gift to Bata; the robe was made by Pasculina as her gift.

Luis's wife holds the baby's silk train. Since I served as midwife, I have the honor of carrying the christening bonnet, and am the third in the processional heading for the church. Behind me walk the rest of the Vivar family. Antonio has been included in this group, a dubious honor since many of the nobles appear resentful.

Since the baby is a girl, two godmothers, but only one godfather, may be chosen. Thankfully, the Vivars used good judgment and did not ask Antonio. Certainly this would have infuriated the nobles even more.

I think of Antonio now as I walk. Though he has been most caring throughout my convalescence, something has changed. I have asked, but he will not say what is wrong. Perhaps it is anger or resentment, for our own child's birth and baptism would be but two months away had he lived. It would be understandable if Antonio harbored these feelings for I, too, feel both anger and resentment, though I fight it.

How could the Merciful One so cruelly take my son from me?

261

I scold myself for being so sullen. Today, I am determined to be happy for Maria. Bata is not here since the Church considers her unclean until her period of confinement is over. The similarity between this and my old tradition is striking, for after a Jewish woman gives birth she too is *niddah*.

As we near the church, the smell of fresh pine cuttings fill the air, for they decorate the door. The smell is strangely comforting and draws my heart back to the Savior. What sorrows can I have that the Savior does not feel them too? What sorrows can I have that He is not able to heal?

I take these thoughts with me as I enter the church. Already, Maria has laid the baby on a silk-cushioned table, and is undressing her. When she is finished, the priest dips his finger into holy oil and makes the sign of the cross on the baby's forehead. Then Luis, the godfather, hands the baby to the priest who immerses the infant into a baptismal font, a font decorated with linen and velvet. Luis's wife dries and bundles the child, and I place the christening cap on the baby's head to protect the holy oil.

When this is done, Luis carries her outside so that all can greet Teresa Maria Vivar, the new member of Holy Mother Church.

I am among the last to exit the church, and when I do, I find Antonio staring out at the Ocean Sea with such longing that I understand, for the first time, how much he desires to leave this place.

Of the four ships in the harbor prior to the *hurricane*, only the *Niña* survived. The others were destroyed. For several months, shipwrights at the shipyard by the lagoon have been building two new vessels from the wreckage. I stand there now and watch. One ship, which seamen have nicknamed *India*, is nearly ready. A small crew seals her hull. Others work on the second vessel, scurrying about with spikes and bolts, and a gudgeon for the rudder.

Many Tainos, imprisoned on the three lost ships, have died, but the great chief, Caonabo, is not among them. He still languishes in the bowels of the *Niña*. It is difficult to imagine how anyone can survive in the hold of a ship so long. I fill my mind with these thoughts because I do not want to think of Antonio. He has become distant. And no matter the coaxing, he will not reveal what troubles him. Nor will he touch me. Every month I immerse in the *mikvah*, and every Sabbath I remind him of our sages' instructions that tell us a man and wife should do the holy deed on this day, but he will not heed.

Have I become repugnant to him?

He spends more time at the shipyard watching the men work than he does at home. And I do not know if it is to pass the time or to see how quickly the ships will be ready to sail to Castile. And my growing fear is that when they are, Antonio will want to sail with them.

"Queen Isabela told me that at Prince Juan's marriage, his wedding fleet will be one hundred and fifty ships strong, and carry thousands of soldiers. And here . . . here her Indies colony has but one small *caravel*."

I turn at the sound of Antonio's voice. "But soon to be three." I smile, determined not to be dreary.

"Do you know how long it takes for a letter sent from Rome to reach Venice?"

I shake my head.

"Three days." The muscles of Antonio's face tighten. "Would that it took only three days to get from Isabela to . . . to . . . a place of civility and safety."

"You must miss Castile very much. Or is it the court you miss?"

"The *court*?" Antonio's voice is incredulous. "Where lies and intrigue rule? And where poets mock *conversos*, making rhymes, to everyone's delight, of the food we eat, saying how the Host becomes twisted into eggplant casseroles and other such nonsense? Oh, how they delight in writing about how we eat chickpeas and fat and stuffed chicken necks! And you should hear what they say about our supposed sacks of money! Miss court? Hardly."

"Then, what is it? What is wrong? Is it your father you worry about? I know he has suffered greatly at the hands of the Inquisition, but . . . ."

"Yes, I worry about Papa. He is old, and in ill-health, and I do not know how much longer he has to live."

"Then perhaps you should return to Castile." I gulp air, for I feel as though I am drowning. "A father should not be deprived of his son's company during his time of illness." When there is no reply I turn and see surprise on Antonio's face.

"I could never leave you," he says, as though my statement was utterly foolish. "And you cannot return to Seville as long as Fray Alonso is alive." There is a long pause. "But I must confess the thought of living here has become detestable, for how can I keep you safe, Isabel? It drives me mad that I know of no place in this world where I can protect you."

"Life is hard in Isabela, but I think we are safe enough, and I am content."

"How can you be content in a place where you must work like a peasant?" Antonio's mouth forms a bitter line. "How can you be content in a place where I cannot provide for you as I should? A place where you have nothing when I can afford to give you *everything*?"

"I am content because I have *you*." I stretch out my hand but he shakes his head and backs away. I move closer, but still he will not take my hand. "You once said though the world is cruel we must never be cruel to one another. Why, then, are you cruel now?"

"Cruel? I am a man devoured by love. I almost lost you, Isabel. I cannot . . . I will not go through that again."

"But I lived," I say, understanding for the first time my husband's torment. "God was merciful. Let us rejoice in that. Come home with me and take comfort in my arms." Again, I hold out my hand.

Antonio shakes his head. "I will not give you another child, Isabel. I will never risk losing you again."

There is famine in the land. Tainos and Christians alike are starving. And everyone in Isabela repeats the old proverb regarding dearth, "If the lark flies overhead, she must take her grain of barley with her."

But this famine has come by our hands, and perhaps by the hands of the Just Judge Who sees all, and acts accordingly. Since the capture of the great king, Caonabo, Admiral Columbus has forced every Taino over the age of fourteen to pay tribute. The tribute is in the form of a large hawk's bell full of gold, panned from the streams of the Vega Real or dug from the Cibao mountainsides. If the Tainos are unable to pay this, then they must give twenty-five pounds of spun cotton in its place, and this every three months.

When a Taino pays his tribute, he is issued a copper or brass token to wear around his neck. Tainos caught without the token are punished by having their hands cut off, leaving them maimed for life, but more often, to bleed to death. Some soldiers have altered the punishment, out of boredom or cruelty I know not which. So instead of cutting off hands, they make wagers on how many strokes of the sword it will take to cut off a head or split a man in two.

Can the Merciful One witness this and not pass judgment? Already we are losing His favor as evidenced by the poor harvests. Even Tainos have little food to steal, for the work needed to satisfy the tribute keeps them from planting their own crops or tending their mounds. It is a cruel irony that Tainos now steal food from our poor fields. The tribute system, along with our new Castilian diseases, and the harsh life of forced labor, are killing the Tainos at an alarming rate.

But my mounds flourish. And I have gutted and removed the heads of so many fish, and dried them in the sun, that I have enough stockfish for Antonio and me to last well into the feast of the Three Kings.

Maria and I have agreed not to sell our surplus crops. Instead, we give them away, first to those Castilians sick in the hospital, then to the maimed Tainos who cannot care for themselves. And whatever remains, we give to any in need.

Many nobles and even peasants scour the land for food, but there is so little to be had you can scarcely find a fallen hog plum, even a rotten one, and many is the time I hear a soldier or peasant quote another old proverb, "Fruit by the roadside never gets ripe."

Juan and Luis, and sometimes Gonzalo, take turns protecting our mounds, sleeping at Marta by night and patrolling them by day. But since so much of the produce goes to the sick and needy, few attempts are made to pilfer them. Indeed, it is rumored many nobles have ordered that my mounds are not to be touched.

"Praise be to God for His mercy," I say, working alongside Maria. We have been at Marta all day, pulling weeds. "It is the dry season and still our mounds grow well."

"Yes, well enough that you need not work so hard. Certainly the bell has chimed None. Time to return to Isabela and prepare the evening meal."

"Just another mound or two, then we will go." How can I tell Maria I do not want to return? That I come to Marta more than I need to in order to be away from Antonio? Antonio, who is always polite, always gentle, always distant. It breaks my heart, this wall between us, this wall that Antonio has erected and that I keep trying to tear down. Antonio and I—we who have been great friends and lovers—are becoming strangers. And though I have prayed for the Merciful One to intervene, I wonder if Antonio and I will ever be as we once were.

Mateo's voice floats through the doorway of my hut as I approach. "I saw it once, the necklace King Fernando gave the Queen as a wedding gift. They say it is worth forty-thousand *ducats*."

"Perhaps when the king purchased it, but I think it far more valuable now." It is Antonio's voice.

I wonder at their frivolous conversation, for while I have been tending the mounds at Marta, four new ships have anchored in Isabela's harbor, all flying the flag of Castile and Leon.

I step through the door, brimming with curiosity. "More ships, I see."

Antonio, who sits at the table, looks up and smiles. But I see the hurt in his eyes when he notices the dirt on my hands and face and clothing, dirt from working the mounds.

"It is good to see you, Doña Isabel," Mateo says, ladling some sort of fish stew into a bowl and placing it before Antonio.

"I have asked Mateo to cook for us," Antonio says. "But I fear it is another fish stew. Tomorrow, though, there will be beans and beef and rice and wheat and other good things to eat, for new supplies have come from Castile."

Mateo fills the washbasin for me, then bows and quietly leaves the hut.

"The stew smells wonderful," I say, stripping off my clothes and washing. "But I must confess I would rather fill my mouth with beans and beef, even if the dried beef always tastes like one of Gonzalo's old leather jerkins."

"Oh? How long have you been nibbling on Gonzalo's jerkins?"

I laugh, and slip on a clean chemise and unloosen my hair. I care not that I am improperly dressed. I do not even bother tying the strings of my chemise. I so want Antonio and I to be casual and intimate, as we used to be.

I take a seat opposite him, then quickly fill my mouth with stew, feeling perverse delight in finding it is not as good as the one I make.

"It is not as tasty as yours," Antonio says, as though reading my thoughts. For the first time in months I see merriment in his eyes. "But you should not have to cook after . . . ." He reaches and takes my free hand, turns it over, then runs his fingers across the calluses on my palm. "You work hard enough."

"Tell me about the ships," I say, trying to change the subject. "Who has come? Torres?"

"Would that it were. But no, it is Juan de Aguado."

"Someone you know?"

"Yes, from court; an arrogant and ambitious man. He brings fresh supplies and livestock and many new settlers, and dozens of skilled craftsmen, including the master miner, Maestro Paolo."

"So what troubles you?"

"Christopher Columbus was right. The complaints of Fray Buil and others have reached the ears of our Sovereigns. Queen Isabel has commissioned Aguado to find out why there is such discontentment here. And he has new orders from the Crown. But before reading them to the Governing Council, Aguado roundly denounced Christopher Columbus's current absence from Isabela as well as his continuous exploration and quest for Quinsay while neglecting the trouble here. Don Bartolome was furious. And when Aguado began talking about the colony's rations, and how precisely they must be allocated, as though the Crown suspected the Columbus brothers of stealing everyone's food, Don Bartolome grew as white as one of your linens. Then when Aguado added to this insult by itemizing each man's monthly ration, saying how they should include eight pounds of bacon, two pounds of cheese, four gallons of wine, wheat—about one and a half pounds, in addition to biscuits, beans, oil and vinegar, and of course, dried fish for the days of abstinence, I feared Don Bartolome would draw his sword. But no, he just sat there clutching the arms of his chair."

"Is Aguado's coming so terrible? Perhaps he will bring sanity to Isabela, for he has what you do not: orders from our Sovereigns. Everyone is weary of Don Bartolome's severity. He whips men for insubordination, and hangs others for stealing a small bowl of wheat. But soldiers can chop off Taino hands and heads without even a word of reproach from him."

"Isabel, we have been over this. There is nothing to be gained by doing it now. Yes, Don Bartolome is severe. But I fear Aguado will only foment more trouble, and make matters worse." Antonio presses his palms against the table. "If only I could take you to safety. But where in this mad world is there such a place, where we can live in peace?" He rises to his feet. "I fear everything may fall apart now, and I must get you away before it does."

"You are not God, Antonio."

My husband is silent for a long time. And when he finally speaks, his voice is so strained, I tremble. "Once . . . I saw a man gored by a bull. It split him open from side to side. But he did not die right away, as he should have. Instead, his was a slow, painful death. That is how I felt, Isabel, after the storm when I thought you were going to die. I was like that man, split from side to side. That is how I feel even now. And the only remedy is to take you away from all this."

"Do not ask the impossible, Antonio. No one can give you a guarantee that sadness and heartbreak will never touch our lives." I put out my hand. "Do not waste time anguishing over what you cannot control, and what might never be."

Antonio clenches his fist. "I will get you to safety, Isabel. I *will* do this." Then he walks out the door.

I spoon a ladle of hot stew, full of beans and rice and chunks of bacon, into the small ridged bowl Rodrigo holds in his trembling hands. He sits erect on his bedroll, propped against one of the hard poles of the hospital wall.

"God bless you, Doña Isabel," Rodrigo says. He is a noble, brought low by sickness; the only noble in the hospital who has told me he knows he is going to die. So, in addition to bringing him food, I occasionally read to him from my Book of Psalms which he claims is a great comfort. "God bless you, Doña Isabel," he repeats. "God bless all the Señoras." He makes a feeble effort to jut his chin in the direction of the five women who are busy feeding others in the hospital. "I pray a rosary for you daily."

I smile and thank him, and walk to the next bedroll where a man, another noble, sits holding an empty bowl. Mateo walks behind me, carrying the heavy kettle of stew. I fill the man's bowl, then watch him forsake his spoon and bring the bowl to his lips. His arms, like Rodrigo's, are covered with sores and "coppery" spots. He is feverish and listless. Like many of the men in the hospital, his body bears sores not unlike the sores I once saw on Catalina's legs. It is whispered this disease comes from lying with the Taino women. Though the women themselves seem to suffer little from it, among our men it is a killer, as if it were a form of revenge.

"You are a saint, Doña Isabel," says the noble, sipping from his bowl. "I swear by the bones of St. Paul I will make a pilgrimage to Chartres after I return to Castile, and there I will crawl the labyrinth of the nave on my knees in your honor. For many of us would die if not for you organizing these other good women, and daily bringing us food."

I smile, and move on to the next, then the next and the next . . . . There are so many, not only with skin lesions but with bowel disease and fever. Some are wasting away and no one knows why. Every day, new graves are dug in the cemetery on the outskirts of Isabela. And every day, Antonio becomes more frantic.

"You will come back tomorrow?" asks the last man I feed.

"Yes," I answer. I have been coming every day. Even on those days when I go to Marta to work the mounds, Mateo goes to the hospital and collects a small portion of each man's rations in order to cook their stew. It is hard to stay away, for the need is so great, and our numbers dwindle daily.

There are times when I wonder if any of us will ever leave this island alive.

౿౿

I am washing my hair in the basin when Bata bursts through the door carrying her baby. At first I think something is wrong with the child for Bata babbles so fast, and mostly in her native tongue, that I only understand a few words.

"You must speak slower," I say, wrapping my hair in a towel and coming over to check the infant.

"No, no, no. Not baby. It *Guabancex*. *Guabancex*, Lady of Winds." With her free hand she clutches her chest. It takes me a second to see that hidden beneath her coarse tunic is a *zemi*. "*Hurricane*," she says. "Soon here. You come to cave with Bata."

I am doubtful. I hear no wind or rain. But when I go to the door I see the sky has darkened, and that the wind is beginning to pick up. Even so, I do not know how Bata can possibly know a *hurricane* is coming, though I refrain from questioning her. Instead, I pull a skirt and bodice over my chemise. "First, I must find Don Antonio," I say, tying back my hair.

"I go home now." Bata heads for the door. "You meet me there. You hurry. I no wait long."

I rush along the street heading for *Casa de Columbus* where Antonio said he would be, and as I do, I remember the sick in the hospital. If Bata is right, what will happen to them? So instead of continuing to Columbus's house, I head for the church and tell Fray Pane of Bata's visit. I know not if it is because he has studied the Tainos and believes Bata's *zemi* can actually tell her of a pending *hurricane*, or if he believes the Tainos have seen enough *hurricanes* to know how to read the signs, but whatever the reason, he rings the bell in alarm. And as people come running from every direction, I head for the hospital and Doctor Spinoza.

"You expect me to move all the sick because one native girl believes a storm is coming?" He looks at me in disbelief. "I will not do it." There is resentment in his voice. Since refusing to let him bleed Antonio, Doctor Spinoza has held me in contempt. He tolerates me because I am a Villarreal, and because I feed his patients. Even when I lost my son, it was Doctor Martinez who treated me, for Spinoza sent him instead of coming himself.

"You must go to the church. If the winds are as bad as last time, you will be safer in a stone dwelling."

"Do you presume to tell me what I must do?"

"I do not mean to offend. I hope Bata is wrong. But did you not hear the bell? Fray Pane believes her. And if she is right, can you leave your patients so exposed? Once the storm comes, it will be too late to move them."

Some of the stronger patients have gathered around. Even Doctor Martinez, who is generally timid, comes over. I see by the way he pinches his lips then throws back his shoulders that he is working up his courage.

"Perhaps it would not be unreasonable to let all those who can walk, go to the church," Martinez finally says. "Then if the weather turns, we have only the others to worry about."

Many of the nearby patients nod in agreement.

"Señora Villarreal, look outside," Doctor Spinoza says, ignoring Martinez and the others. "The sky is grey, yes, and the wind rustles the branches, but I see nothing amiss. I see no storm on the horizon. If I thought there was danger I would be the first to order an evacuation."

"Then do so at once," says a voice I do not recognize, but when I turn, I see Juan de Aguado standing behind me, perfumed and dressed in silk and brocade. "Are lives so cheap here in Isabela we can afford to squander them needlessly?"

Doctor Spinoza's face is ashen. "Yes, Señor Aguado. I mean, no, Señor Aguado. I mean . . . I will vacate at once."

And as I rush out the door to find Antonio, I see the look on Spinoza's face and know that today I have made an enemy.

❧

We—the Vivars, Antonio and I—wait out the *hurricane* in the cave Bata has brought us to, and listen to the wind howl for hours, and the rain beat, and palms whoosh, and trees and structures creak and collapse.

And when it is over, half of Isabela is destroyed along with Juan de Aguado's four ships. And many lives are lost, among them the great king, Caonabo, who had been transferred to one of Aguado's vessels. But not one patient from the hospital is lost, though the hospital itself lies in ruins, for all were safely moved to the church. Nor is one cubit of our hut—Antonio's and mine—damaged. I tell Antonio it is the Lord's way of showing us we can trust Him, and he nods and says, "Yes," but his eyes tell me he is not persuaded.

∽◌

Antonio and I stand overlooking the shipyard at the lagoon. The *India* is finished and the second vessel, not yet named, nearly so. It has been two months since the last *hurricane* devastated our colony.

"I still marvel that neither ship was destroyed during the storm," I say, feeling uneasy for I know Antonio has brought me here for a purpose.

"Yes, it is fortunate, for the *hurricane* destroyed much."

There were still signs of devastation everywhere. Many damaged huts, rather than being repaired, have been abandoned by owners despairing of Isabela all together. And everyone knows these men have left for the interior to live off the Tainos and illegally search for gold.

"When will they leave? Columbus and Aguado?" I ask, the noise of hammers filling the air.

"By week's end. Admiral Columbus will command the *Niña*. Aguado is to take the *India*. I am certain the Admiral will use all his skill to get to Castile first in order to plead his case to the Queen before Aguado arrives. Columbus knows Aguado will not bring back a good report."

"Will the Admiral not wait until Don Bartolome returns from the Rio Haina with the news of his exploration there?"

"The only news the Admiral wishes to hear is if Maestro Paolo and his miners have found the ancient gold mines believed to be located in the south."

My stomach lurches. "Gold. Always gold. And if they find it we shall see more trouble; more fighting with the Tainos. And the taking of more Taino slaves to work the mines."

"Evil resides in the hearts of all men, Isabel. Including mine."

I am startled when Antonio gathers me under his arm. I watch the breeze play with his hair, slapping it against his cheeks as though in a gentle rebuke. Sweat dots his forehead like flecks of glass. But there is a look of peace about him I have not seen for some time. I do not press, for in time he will tell me what is on his mind. Rather, I turn my gaze to the shipyard, and watch the men work. Before long, I hear my husband sigh.

"I have acted the fool—forgetting I am a servant of the Most High, and seeking to be master instead. In this world there will always be tribulation. Who can say what will happen? To Isabela or us. Surely, our life will be difficult. But as I look at these ships, and think of Columbus and Aguado sailing to Castile, I know the only life I want is with you. And if that life can only be lived here, in this place, then God will give us the strength to endure it." He turns to face me. "Forgive me for squandering these past many months. For allowing my fears and worries to devour them like locust. Forgive me for wanting to be in control of our lives, and our futures, instead of allowing God."

I smile into his kind eyes, then kiss his lips. What need was there for words?

"Gold! They have found gold in the Rio Haina!"

The shouts penetrate the curtain hanging over our door, then fade as the man brings his news further down the street. But the announcement has shattered the peace in our hut, where I lie in Antonio's arms.

"We must dress," Antonio says, but by his eyes I know this news is as unwelcome to him as it is to me.

I rise and fill the wash basin with water. Antonio washes first, and while he dresses, I wash. But I am as slow as a slug, for I have no heart to go to the Plaza and hear more of this. My hair still hangs wildly about my shoulders, and I am just putting on my chemise when Antonio finishes dressing.

"If you wish, you can remain here," he says when he sees my face. "I will go to the Plaza and learn of this news."

I blow him a kiss, and watch him disappear through the door. I am weighed down by thoughts of what this new discovery of gold will do to our men; what it will do to Isabela. I have barely finished dressing and fixing my hair when Antonio enters the hut, breathless.

"Don Bartolome has indeed found gold. And Pasculina's husband claims the large nuggets Don Bartolome sent back to Isabela are of exceptional purity. The new site has been named San Christopher, in honor of the Admiral. They say it will far surpass the gold of Cibao and Vega Real. But that is not all. The Admiral sent orders instructing Don Bartolome to find a site for a new settlement. Isabela is to be abandoned!"

Chapter 19

Antonio and I are in Marta, lounging on the south bank of the Isabela River not far from the large oval kiln that is capable of firing a thousand pots at once. Nearby is a much smaller one which now fires several dozen including our two large earthenware pots with handles. The pots were made months ago for Antonio and me by the *ollero*, the potter who specializes in them. But only today has he pronounced ready for firing and removed from the drying shed. I watch as the *ollero* makes another round handled pot on his pit wheel. Nearby, another potter kneads wet clay with his feet.

It seems odd to see them work, for Isabela is partially abandoned. Most of the other potters have already left for the new settlement since there is little need for clay goods of any kind, here.

"I leave for Santo Domingo tomorrow," Antonio says, breaking the silence.

I look down at my husband who lies prone on the matted vegetation with his head on my lap. "Why all of a sudden?"

Antonio laughs. "It is hardly sudden, my love. It has been months since Columbus sailed for Castile. I have stayed this long only because I was loath to be parted from you. But since Captain Niño brought the news of the Admiral's safe arrival in Spain, and the official orders sanctioning the abandonment of La Isabela by the Crown, Don Bartolome grows impatient. He wants the Governing Council to go to Santo Domingo at once, and establish order."

"You mean to better secure the gold mines at San Christopher."

"Do not think poorly of him, Isabel. He follows the Admiral's orders. And though it is barely a patch of cleared land now, perhaps one day we can make Santo Domingo a great city."

"Can you not make it great with your wife along?"

"I must build our house, a house of stone, with a proper tile roof and a lime-mortar floor, and with many rooms. At least I can do that much for you."

"But why can I not come with you? I can help and . . . ."

"That is precisely what I do not want. You work too hard, and God knows you would be tempted to mix plaster or whitewash walls. I have already hired an army of peasants for that."

"An *army* of peasants? There are hardly a dozen who are willing to hire themselves out. Most are busy laboring in the mines of San Christopher."

Antonio laughs. "All right. I have found only five. But they will work swiftly. I have promised them a generous bonus if they finish before the Feast of Saint Luke the Evangelist."

"October! I am not to come to you until October?"

"Only two months, my love. And it will greatly ease my mind if you remain here, where you have a roof over your head, and food; for your mounds grow well, and Captain Niño's three ships have brought fresh supplies of wine and wheat and dried beef and pork."

Antonio sits up and gazes out over the area of the kiln with its numerous pit wheels, drying tables, and sheds. "Here, at least, is some civilization. And you will not starve. Nothing but a fort has been constructed at Santo Domingo. Men refuse to build the town, preferring to search for gold instead. The Council has much work to do before it is a fit place to live."

I sigh in resignation. "I suppose it is best I stay, for who will feed the sick?" I lean against Antonio, taking in the pleasing fragrance of lavender and rosemary. "But I will miss you so."

"You will have Maria for company, and some of the other women, too."

I am about to say Pasculina has already followed her husband to Santo Domingo, where he is busy assaying the San Christopher gold and where they most likely have only a miserable hut for shelter, and still he allowed his wife to come; but I think better of it. What is the point? Antonio would never be swayed by this. Still, Roldan worries me greatly. Rumors abound how he is agitated by the Admiral's orders to abandon Isabela and relocate to a place where he might not be town warden.

"Is Don Diego capable of commanding Isabela while Don Bartolome is away, do you think?"

"Do not worry, Isabel, Roldan will not dare raise his hand against him," "But Roldan *is* the town warden and has great influence."

"Only among the baser elements."

"Precisely why he is so dangerous. He surrounds himself with men of little honor and little allegiance to the Columbus brothers. Only yesterday, I overhead him say the Council of Santo Domingo will not command his loyalty. When he speaks of the Council of Santo Domingo—he speaks of *you*, my love."

"I doubt he was thinking of me when he said it. And he still swears loyalty to our Sovereigns."

"But not to the Columbus brothers. According to Roldan, they are *conversos*, and by the law of blood purity, it means they are 'offspring of perversion' and unfit to have authority over any Old Christian of pure blood like himself. And certainly unfit to own land, which, Roldan claims, Columbus and his brothers will take the best of for themselves."

Antonio frowns. "Ah, yes, land. And there is the heart of the matter. Roldan wants land and an allotment of Indian labor like the nobles. As a common soldier, he resents the privileges of class; perhaps even wishes to abolish them. But I do not believe he cares one bit about the purity of anyone's blood. I have seen this before, Isabel."

I think of Enrique, and his hatred of me and my race, of his jealousy and resentment. I have not told Antonio about Enrique, and cannot do so now for fear of worrying him. But a sudden thought springs to mind. *What if Enrique returns to Isabela while Antonio is away?*

"It will be another month before Niño and his three ships sail back to Castile. No trouble will arise as long as he is here. Also, I am leaving Mateo behind. And I have hired the sword of Arias Diaz for your protection. I cannot name a better swordsman in all Isabela."

"Everyone knows *you* are the best swordsman in Isabela." I force a smile then kiss my husband lightly on the lips. Soon, Antonio will leave, and it will not do to have him worry. He has done his best to secure my comfort and safety. And two months is not such a long time. Surely I can manage that long without him.

But in my heart there is a terrible dread.

The letter in my bodice crinkles when I bend to pull on my old leather ox-mouths. Since receiving Antonio's letter, I have carried it around so I can read it whenever I feel the need. I have read it so often the edges are frayed. But it is the only letter I have received in three weeks, and it is what keeps me from missing Antonio to distraction.

The bell chimes Sext. Soon Mateo will be here to carry the kettle of stew to the partially rebuilt hospital. There are fewer than a dozen men to feed now, and they eat less every day. The other patients have been moved, at Bartolome Columbus's orders, to outposts scattered across the island. But the sick remaining in Isabela remain because, according to Doctor Spinoza, they are dying. And it is true. I think only a handful will last past week's end. And Doctor Spinoza tends them all since Doctor Martinez has gone with the others, dividing his time between the posts.

While I wait for Mateo, I pull the well-worn letter from my bodice, and though I have memorized the contents, begin reading:

My Darling Isabel,

I believe Santo Domingo will be a good settlement, for it is perched on a hill overlooking a beautiful river the Tainos call Hocama. It also overlooks a fine harbor so large I believe it could hold even Prince Juan's entire wedding armada.

Fine progress is being made on our house. The stone foundation has been laid and the walls are going up at a rapid rate. In addition, our large kiln, which has only recently been completed, is even now firing the tejas that will be used on our roof. Each day the house is nearer completion, meaning each day you are nearer, too.

I have not allowed anyone to cut down the trees that surround our house for they provide a cooling shade, a shade especially pleasant over a section of the courtyard where I, even now, picture you sitting. But fear not, there is ample sun in other portions, sun enough for your pots of lavender as well as for a small herb and vegetable garden.

It is an extraordinary thing, but a bird of brilliant color—all shades of yellows, greens and blues—comes every day and perches on one of the trees. And then he sings the most melodious song! The first time he came I could hardly believe it, but now, after so many days, he is like an old friend, a friend I believe the Merciful One sends to dispel my loneliness.

I hope you are well. Write when you can. I know couriers are scarce and it is difficult for any mail to travel across this strange, overgrown land.

Being away from you is more difficult than I imagined. I can endure it only because I know that by the Feast of Saint Luke you will be by my side.

I send you all my love,

Antonio

"Try to eat, Rodrigo," I say, cupping his gaunt face in my hand, and offering him a spoonful of stew.

His dark, sunken eyes roll as he shakes his head. His body reeks of death.

"At least drink the broth." I hold the bowl closer to his lips but he turns away. All around, it is the same. Men languishing, smelling of death, unable to eat. Already three have died this morning. Less than half a dozen remain.

Nearby, Maria tends another man. Only she and I have come. Many of the other women, like Pasculina, have already left Isabela with their husbands. Those who remain say they cannot bear seeing any more death.

I am about to take the bowl away when suddenly Rodrigo's dry, bony fingers curl around my arm. "He . . . has it. I saw."

I feel the heat of Rodrigo's hand. When I touch his forehead it burns, too. Surely a feverish delirium has set in. I place Rodrigo's bowl on the floor, then send Mateo for a goblet of water.

"I saw it yesterday." After a futile attempt to sit up, Rodrigo slumps backward on his pillow. "It fell out of his jerkin."

"You must not distress yourself." I take the water from Mateo and bringing it to Rodrigo's mouth. He takes a sip then runs his badly coated tongue over cracked lips.

"He hides it from you."

I lean closer. "Who? What does he hide?"

"Your . . . letter . . . from Captain Niño's ship."

"*My letter?*" I put down the goblet. "I have a letter?"

Rodrigo closes his eyes. He is so pale and still, and his breathing so indiscernible I am certain he is dead. "Doctor Spinoza has it," his raspy voice finally sputters.

Mateo, who has heard all, leaves the stew pot and crosses the room to where Doctor Spinoza stands by a table grinding herbs. Mateo says something to him as he points to Rodrigo, and soon they are both standing over me.

"Rodrigo says you have a letter for me." My voice is barely under control.

"The man is mad with fever."

"It is not . . . right . . . what you do." Rodrigo's head lolls backward like the head of a bird whose neck is broken. There is a rattle in his throat. Death is not far off. "Give Doña . . . Isabel her letter."

Doctor Spinoza bends toward the reclining Rodrigo, and when he does, Rodrigo's skeleton-like fingers claw the front of his jerkin. When Rodrigo's hands drop to his side, I know he has died.

I wonder at his valiant effort on my behalf. To me, a letter from home would mean so much. But what could it mean to Rodrigo that he spent his last ounce of strength trying to secure it? Was it gratitude for the meals and my reading of the Psalms these many months? Or did he want to right a wrong, albeit small, as if in doing so he could right all the larger wrongs he had perpetuated on the Tainos since coming to Isabela? I cannot answer for only God knows, but I ponder it while I rise to my feet.

"I hope you are satisfied. Agitating a dying man over some fictitious letter." Smugness coats Doctor Spinoza's face like ointment. "It has only hastened his death, for surely if it had not been for you perhaps he would have lived a few more days. Add that to your conscience."

"I meant no harm. It was Rodrigo who brought up the matter of the letter. Not I."

"Yes, but oh, how quick you were to believe me capable of some maliciousness conduct. A woman of better breeding would apologize at once."

"There is nothing lacking in her breeding, nor does she have any reason to apologize." Mateo comes alongside us, holding a letter. He glances at me. "It was behind the ointment jars. Perhaps we should ask Captain Niño how it got there."

Spinoza's face turns the color of a pomegranate. "The captain gave me the mail to dispense since I know all the inhabitants. And I discharged that duty. Perhaps . . . well it appears . . . that your letter was mislaid. Accept my apology, Doña Isabel." He bows slightly. "Even so, I do not believe this small matter worthy of mention. To Captain Niño or . . . Don Diego."

I tuck the letter into my bodice, then step around him to the next man lying on a bedroll. And while I prepare his bowl, I am only partially aware that Doctor Spinoza hovers nearby, handing me a clean

towel, then the ladle, then holding the man's head while I bring spoonfuls of stew to his lips, for my thoughts are full of Mama and Papa and
Seville, and all the possible news from home.

⌒〜〇

I sit on my bed holding Mama's letter. Her familiar handwriting com-
forts me as I read.

Darling Isabel:

*There is so much news I hardly know where to begin. We have heard of
Admiral Columbus's return from the Indies, and of his many enemies at court. It
is rumored he dresses in the coarse garb of a Franciscan monk, and some mockingly
say it is in order to do penance, but for what I know not. I only hope he has not
gone mad, as some suppose. But he is, even now, trying to garner support for yet
another voyage to the Indies. Señor Villarreal supplies us with such details, still
having many friends at court.*

*And sad news. Prince Juan has died in Salamanca of a mysterious illness,
and so soon after taking a bride. The royal physicians were unable to determine
the cause, but as you can imagine, speculation runs as rampant as harbor rats. All
the cities were strewn with banners and white serge. He was only nineteen, and
leaves behind his beautiful bride who, it is rumored, is with child. Queen Isabel is
devastated as any mother would be. They say she dresses only in black, and always
has Prince Juan's dog, Bruto, by her side. As a mother, I cannot help but feel her
pain. The death of one's child is a grievous loss.*

*And more sad news. Seville, too, has sustained a loss, for her great Inquisitor, Fray
Alonso, has died. A man of low birth, a water carrier by trade, stabbed the friar in the
neck with a dagger. He tried to justify this villainy by saying Alonso had violated his
daughter. You can be sure the water carrier received his due punishment at the stake.*

*The last bit of news is also cheerless. Señor Villarreal has taken a turn for the
worse. Surely, it is best that his son, Antonio, and you with him, return home at the
first opportunity, for you are both needed to tend his father and manage the estates.*

I pray for your swift and safe return.

Your loving Mother

I cannot believe my eyes. Mama has carefully cloaked the details in her letter in case it fell into the wrong hands, that much is clear. But she has also told me I may return home, then provided a reason to do so. I read the letter again to make certain I have not misunderstood. No. There is no misunderstanding.

I am to go home.

I dance wildly around the hut, for my joy is boundless. Home. With Antonio. To see Mama and Papa and Señor Villarreal. To live, once again, in my beloved Seville. Oh, the joy of it!

Then I stop. Captain Niño sails to Castile at week's end—only two more days. Not enough time to get word to Antonio and have him return to Isabela. And if we miss the sailing who knows how long it will be before another ship comes to the Indies?

My heart pounds with indignation. Just what has Doctor Spinoza's malfeasance cost me?

"You must sail around the island, to Santo Domingo," I say, after explaining my situation and relaying the news of Señor Villarreal's ill health. "It is too late to send for Don Antonio, and we *must* return home."

I am seated in the great-room of *Casa de Columbus,* a sparse area containing only a long wooden table and several cushioned chairs. Beside me sits Don Diego Columbus and Captain Peralonso Niño. I am dressed in silk and brocade, and my hair is neatly braided and studded with pearls for I have learned that men, too often, judge worth by outer appearances, and nothing must impede my mission.

Captain Niño leans forward in his richly carved chair. His face is lined with concern. "Doña Isabel, I understand your plight, but I cannot lead my small fleet on an adventure that will add days, perhaps weeks, to my voyage unless I am ordered to do so by the Governor."

My stomach tightens, and I draw in a long, slow breath to keep myself from speaking rashly. "Sir," I finally say, "as you well know, our Governor, Don Bartolome, is away seeing to the construction of Santo Domingo. But our host, Don Diego, has been given authority in his absence." I turn to Don Diego. "Surely, you can grant this concession for one as esteemed as Don Antonio?"

Don Diego folds his hands neatly on his lap as though they are a pair of elegant gloves. "Doctor Spinoza's error is indeed a grievous one. But as he explained to me earlier, it was only that, an error." He pauses as if expecting me to raise an objection. But I do not. It is useless to accuse Spinoza of misconduct I cannot prove. Rodrigo is dead, and who is left to say my letter did not fall behind the ointment jars on its own?

"The good doctor violently regrets your letter was mislaid," Diego continues, "and that this mishap will cost you and your husband the opportunity to sail with Captain Niño. I am grieved as well. But the Crown's interest must take precedence over the interest of a single individual."

"Meaning?" I stare boldly at Don Diego.

"Meaning there will be other ships, and that Captain Niño must depart as planned."

"Meaning it is best Don Antonio stay and assist Don Bartolome in the building of Santo Domingo." Since Niño's arrival, rumors have been abundant concerning Admiral Columbus's difficulties in persuading the Sovereigns to finance another Indies voyage due to their grave concerns over the situation in Isabela. Viewed in that light, Christopher Columbus, in particular, and his brothers, in general, cannot afford to have Santo Domingo fail, for all their future wealth and titles depend upon it. "Am I to assume you consider your family's interest equal in importance to the Crown's?" Throughout our discourse Diego has held my gaze, but now he turns away.

"I will not deceive you. It is best for Don Bartolome and for Santo Domingo, both, if Antonio stays. But that is not my only consideration. Due to our own food shortages here in Isabela, Captain Niño has left all the stores he dared, and carries only enough rations for a quick return voyage to Castile. I am told Santo Domingo has no food reserves at all, so it will be impossible to resupply the Captain's ships if they sail to her port. Therefore, delay is not advisable and could put his vessels and men in jeopardy."

I do not know if Columbus speaks truth or lies. Antonio did not mention food shortages, but then again he would not for fear of worrying me. And it is well known that food *is* scarce all over the island. So what can I say? To press the matter will only suggest I am unconcerned for the lives of others. I have lost, and Columbus knows it. Doctor Spinoza's malfeasance has cost me much. But what I have no way of knowing is just how much more it will cost.

⌒๏

"I do not want to leave you, Doña Isabel," Mateo says, as we stand in front of Bata's house.

"You must take this to Antonio." I thrust my letter into Mateo's hands.

"He will not be happy I have left you." Mateo's brow knots. "And why hurry? Niño leaves tomorrow, and nothing can be done."

"I know. I know. But couriers are scarce, and those I trust, scarcer still. We may not come across such able guides for some time." I glance at the two men that linger nearby. Both are Bata's relatives, tall men past their prime but still evidencing vigor by their bright faces and agile bodies. Bata has sworn me to secrecy, telling me the men plan to flee into the mountains to escape the tribute system. But she has made them promise to first lead Mateo safely to the other side of the island.

"Don Antonio will send for you by the Feast of Saint Luke. It is only one month more. I believe, given a choice, he would wish me to stay here even if that means being deprived of this news a little longer."

"I would agree, but only yesterday I learned that Don Diego does not intend to send his *caravel* back to Santo Domingo for many months. His house here is large and comfortable. Plainly, he is loath to leave until he is certain to find sufficient comfort at Santo Domingo. In light of this pending delay, how will I get to Antonio? Few Tainos still live around Isabela. Who will guide me? Must Antonio wait for months, perhaps a half dozen months before he hears Mama's news? And Captain Niño indicated he expects to return to Isabela in just a few short months. If he comes and Antonio is not here, we could miss yet another opportunity to sail back to Castile." I glance again at Bata's relatives. "You will be in good hands."

"But who will care for you? Whose good hands have I to leave you in?"

"Arias Diaz is here. I will be safe enough."

"That popinjay? He cares only for gambling, for taking the wealth of others with his dice. I fear Don Antonio has made a bad bargain in hiring him."

"You must not fret so, Mateo. There is still Maria and the Vivars. Now, go with God. I shall pray for your safety." With that I kiss his cheek, then watch him gather his bundle of food and clothing, and head for the interior with his guides.

"I am greatly worried, Isabel," Maria says, entering my hut in a sweat, and coming to where I stand at the table washing clothes in my basin. "Ever since Don Bartolome left, Roldan has not ceased grumbling. He says Don Bartolome cares nothing for the sick. That he has sprinkled them throughout the interior like unwanted chaff. And he complains the storehouse is full, while he and his men starve. And if that were not enough, it is whispered Roldan is outraged over Don Bartolome having flogged his friend, the one who violated the chief's wife."

"Yes, I too was surprised to hear about that. Such punishment has rarely been administered. But if the chief had not been Guarionex, ruler of Vega Real and the Cibao gold fields, I doubt such punishment would have been applied. Plainly, Don Bartolome wants nothing to hinder Guarionex's cooperation in collecting tribute from his people, nor any obstacles standing between him and the gold fields. I think Roldan knows this, too, and that accounts for his anger."

Maria clamps my arm and looks so fearful I pull my hands from the water and dry them. "What is it? What is it you have come to tell me?"

"Bata's relatives say Roldan is on his way back to Isabela."

I am puzzled for I see no reason for alarm. Recently, Diego Columbus sent Roldan and his men to Cibao to deal with those Tainos refusing to pay their tribute. It is only natural that once the work was done, Roldan would return. "Why should that be a concern?"

"Roldan has openly declared rebellion against the Columbus brothers. Some of the men deserted him, not wanting to become rebels against the Crown, but Bata's cousin says at least seventy remain loyal to Roldan, and now all are headed here to *capture* Isabela."

My head reels. Are Don Diego's forces strong enough to overcome Roldan's? Many of them appear sickly and weak, and few profess any love for Diego. Without a word I go to Sebastian's last remaining trunk. The others were given away or used for barter long ago. I rummage until I find Sebastian's gilded sword, then pull it out. It feels clumsy in my hands. Two wild slashes in the air convince me it is much too heavy. So I return it to the trunk and rummage again until I find a small sheathed dagger, then place it on the table. "I do not think we have anything to fear. But wisdom demands we be prepared." I see Maria wringing her hands. "What else? What other news do you have for me?"

"It is Enrique. Bata's cousin says . . . he says Enrique has joined Roldan."

Suddenly, I understand that what I see in Maria's eyes in not fear for herself, but for *me*. And after reassuring her that all will be well, she leaves, and I go to the table, pick up the dagger, and slip it into my bodice.

~⊙

Shouts and gunfire wake me from a fitful sleep. Surely, I am dreaming. But the noise continues, making me jump from bed and race to the door of my hut. It is early. Outside, I see nothing but the rising sun. Then suddenly, more shouts and gunfire, all coming from the south, the direction of the church or . . . perhaps *Casa de Columbus*. Soon I hear these same sounds coming from the north, in the direction of the storehouse. I am trying to determine what all this means when, to my surprise, I see Arias Diaz running towards my hut, sword in hand.

"Dress yourself, Doña Isabel, for we are under attack. It is Roldan and his men; low cast devils, all. They have seized the storehouse and are stealing food and weapons. Some of Don Diego's forces tried to stop them but are now pinned down. Others barricade themselves behind the walls of *Casa de Columbus*. Even now Roldan's thugs surround them. Many lives have been lost. Ours more than theirs. I fear Don Diego's forces are no match for Roldan."

"But why must I worry? Certainly I am of no importance to Roldan and his men?" Though I try to sound brave, my voice breaks. If Enrique is with Roldan then I have much to fear.

"You are a Villarreal, and could garner a great ransom. These men are beasts; the lowest of the low, and lack honor."

And so I understand. It is not surprising, after all, that Arias is here, for the rebels are all lowborn. It is obvious my protector has decided to cast his lot with the nobility, much like he casts his dice. But this time he gambles for his future, a future that either lies with the Crown and aristocracy, and will reap great rewards if he succeeds, or . . . possibly death if he does not.

"Dress quickly," he says, pushing me inside the hut while he himself remains outside. "You must go to the mountains and hide."

I hastily gather my clothes and pull them over my chemise. Then I feel under my pillow for the dagger placed there last night. Finding it, I tuck it inside my bodice all the while thinking of Antonio. It has been over a month since Mateo left for Santo Domingo and I have not heard a word. But I am happy Antonio is not here now, for he would be compelled to fight Roldan and his rebels. At least I can take comfort in knowing he is out of harm's way.

I pray to the Merciful One for strength and courage as I wrap three loaves of cassava bread in cloth and tuck them into a sheepskin pouch. To this, I add papayas and stockfish. Who knows how long I must hide.

But where? Where am I to go?

⤺⥁

Arias and I stay close to the huts as we make our way to Poblado Central. There is chaos all around, with men grabbing whatever they can find to steal and carrying it away to some secret place. The air is heavy with the smell of gunpowder and raucous male voices. While pressed against the wall of a hut, I watch Roldan's men cart away pikes, swords, armor. Others carry flagons of wine which they must have filled from the many barrels in the storehouse. Already men are drunk and lounge by the roadside, while others sit eating stolen food.

Shouts still come from the south, by Columbus's house, and occasionally, gunfire, but it is clear Isabela is firmly in the hands of the rebels.

As we creep deeper into Poblado Central I smell smoking fireboxes, hear the lowing of cattle, and the chatter of men. We duck into an empty hut where I peek through the shaded window and watch soldiers lead three cows to an empty lot; cows belonging to the Crown and meant for breeding. There they butcher them, then pass the meat among the gathering crowd.

Arias is already sitting on the ground, and when I turn, he indicates for me to do likewise. The hut is empty except for a bedroll leaning against the wall. I unfurl it and spread it across the dirt floor, all the while trying to persuade myself I am safe here in Poblado Central where Enrique will not think to look.

I know not how long we sit, for the church bell no longer chimes. It has been taken to Concepcion de la Vega, near the Cibao gold fields. But I know by the silence outside, and by the position of the sun and by the smell of beef roasting over fireboxes, that several hours have passed.

Finally, Arias signals for us to leave, and we rise and go to the door. Laughter and shouting still fill the air but they are far away. We move carefully, staying close to huts and clumps of vegetation as we creep along the most northerly street of Poblado Central, the one edging the lagoon and the refuse dump. We advance one hut at a time, one tree at a time, until we reach Poblado East. Then suddenly, out of nowhere, there appears a roaming band of rebels.

"Halt!" one shouts, running towards us. Clearly, Arias's drawn sword has alarmed him. The others, at least six more, follow behind, some carrying crossbows, others, firearms or swords. And Arias, seeing himself so outmatched, surrenders without a fight.

We are surrounded now. And after a soldier takes Arias's sword, he studies him as if deciding what to do. I believe he would have killed him on the spot if a voice had not shouted, "Stop!" I know that voice, and turn to see Enrique Vivar sauntering towards us, a crossbow cocked in one arm.

"These are valuable prisoners," Enrique says, boldly entering the circle as though in command. "Put this one with the other nobles." He points to Arias. "And this one, to house arrest." He does not even point to me but simply juts his chin in my direction.

"You have no authority to arrest me," I say, my anger rising.

Enrique bellows with laughter. "Do you see any *other* authority in Isabela? No, Doña Isabel. We are masters here. And we will do what we want, take what we want."

"And what can you want with me?

"You are a Villarreal."

At the mention of my name the others appear fearful. One man lowers his weapon, another steps backward, several stare at me with open mouths. But Enrique raises his crossbow and points it at my heart. "You are worth a king's ransom." He thumps his chest with his free hand. "And I will be the one to collect it." Then he leans closer. "Though I do not know why anyone would pay good money for one such as you."

For three days I remain a prisoner in my own hut, with two armed soldiers continually guarding my door. Aside from the guards, I see no one, not even Enrique. And not even Maria or the other Vivars, though many times I expected Maria to come bounding in and tell me it was all a mistake; that she had spoken to Enrique and made him see reason. And the fact that she did not has broken my heart.

On the fourth day, Enrique enters, looking weary and disheveled. His eyes are red from too much wine, and he possesses an air of one who has satiated all his appetites.

"Come!" he barks.

"Where are we going?" I finger my linen bodice where the dagger lies hidden.

"Roldan is finished here. We have taken all we desire. Now we go to the interior."

Quickly, I pick up my small sack of cassava bread and papayas and stockfish which I have kept packed all this while, and follow. And before I am out the door I already know that at the first opportunity I must make my escape.

Chapter 20

La Isabela to Santo Domingo, Española

I follow two soldiers to the Plaza. Enrique walks behind, carrying his crossbow and a bundle, which I suppose contains food and clothing and whatever else he has found to steal. Though I keep pace with those in front, every few steps Enrique places his hand on my back and shoves me forward. This is, no doubt, meant to show his contempt, as well as to humiliate. It is all I can do to keep my balance. More than once I have stumbled against one of the men in front of me.

By the blazing sun I know it is well past Sext. I find this late start curious. We will hardly travel ten leagues before dark. And that suggests Roldan is not worried about being followed.

Have Diego Columbus and all his men been killed?

The Plaza swarms with rebels, who, I suppose, are meeting here before leaving Isabela in force. But otherwise, the town appears deserted. The smell of wine mingles with the smell of unwashed bodies. And as I pass these soiled, worn men they appear surprised to see a Castilian woman among their number. Some smile politely. Others look away, especially when Enrique shoves me so roughly.

Suddenly, Roldan appears at my elbow, and by the look on his face I think perhaps I am saved.

"What is the meaning of this outrage!" Roldan glares at Enrique. "Do you not know this is Señora Villarreal? How dare you treat her with such contempt? Unhand her at once."

"She is my prisoner. A spoil of war. She will fetch a generous ransom."

"You dare hold her for ransom? And insult our Sovereigns? Would you make us the contempt of Castile? A byword for rogues and cut-throats?" Roldan's hand moves toward the hilt of his sword. "Release her!"

Enrique responds by raising his crossbow, and several soldiers press in as though making ready to defend Roldan. The air is brittle with tension, and Enrique would surely have been killed had he not dropped his arm.

"She is a *converso*, an 'offspring of perversion' and the wife of a *converso*," Enrique says, smiling sheepishly. "Have you not told us *conversos* are to be held in contempt? Not deserving of loyalty? And that only by deceit and treachery have they gained their wealth and titles?"

Streaks of red claw Roldan's neck. Enrique not only dares to defy him, but dares to use his own words against him. My heart sinks, for after speaking ill of *conversos* for so long, indeed, after using imaginary deficiencies and malfeasances of *conversos* as an excuse for rebellion, how can Roldan come to my aid now? His men watch with interest.

"*Converso* or not, Don Antonio is highly favored by the Crown. I have no wish to make an enemy of our Sovereigns in order to satisfy your greed."

"Then let it be known this is my doing, not yours. And let it be on my head."

Roldan pulls on his sword, revealing blood-smeared steel. For a second my hope revives, but when Roldan jams the blade back into its sheath I know I am lost. "Then it *shall* be on your head. If they come for you, I will not lift a finger in your defense."

Enrique laughs, and for the first time it occurs to me he might be mad. "So be it," he says with such arrogance I am certain its offensive nature will once again arouse Roldan's wrath. But Roldan merely turns on his heels, then barks orders to his commanders to vacate Isabela. And when one of them asks if the men surrounding *Casa de Columbus* should not hang back, I know Diego Columbus and many of his men have survived.

We form a ragged line, with Enrique and me somewhere in the middle, and begin our trek. I keep pace with the men in front, holding tightly to my sack of food. Inside my bodice, I feel the bulky sheath of the dagger rub against my skin. It is one of two consolations. The other is that Enrique no longer feels compelled to humiliate me, and allows me to walk unmolested. His victory over Roldan seems, for the present, to satisfy his need to prove himself superior.

As we walk, I see no signs of life. Where is everyone? Do they all cower inside their huts? Or behind the walls of *Casa de Columbus*?

Is there none to rescue me?

We pass the church, heading toward Poblado South, where I spot Doctor Spinoza with two men carrying a shrouded body, obviously on their way to the cemetery. His jaw drops when he sees me, and as the realization that I am a prisoner slowly dawns, his face takes on a forlorn expression. It is as if he has placed upon himself the full responsibility for my plight, and I feel pity.

"*Please.* You cannot do this," he says, leaving the shrouded body and coming alongside us.

The grief in his voice pricks my heart. Can I be so stingy in love that I leave him conscience stricken? I must forgive him his misdeed. Surely he never intended for his action to have such dire consequence. "Be at peace, Doctor Spinoza," I shout, trying to convey forgiveness in my voice. "All will be well."

And then I feel the familiar prodding of Enrique's hand. "Quiet!"

And quiet I remain until we near the edge of the settlement and I see Bata. Her glistening arms and forehead tell me she has been running. "Isbell! Isbell!" she shouts, coming so close I could touch her. She slows, and paces Enrique. "No take Isbell! No take Isbell!"

"Get out of here," Enrique growls. "Go home."

"No take Isbell," she repeats, reaching for me but Enrique knocks her hand away. Around us, soldiers snicker. Some utter obscenities, others proposition her as if she were a whore. One tries to grope her, and suddenly I am afraid.

"Go home, Bata. *Please.* Go home now!" And I think she understands my fear, for she suddenly stops and nods, and stands quietly by the road before dropping her head and walking away.

As we continue our march, my eyes dart here and there, looking for Maria. Surely she will come. If Bata knows my plight, Maria knows too. And up until the very moment we step into the tangled fringe of the interior I expect to see Maria come racing to my rescue. And when at last I understand she is not, I feel as forlorn as the day I sailed from Cadiz.

Sweat drips down my face, and my wet bodice clings so tightly I fear Enrique will see the dagger I have hidden there. This fear causes me to walk with hunched shoulders and head tilted towards the ground. And after walking this way so long, my body aches. But that is nothing compared to my thirst. My lips feel like dried twigs, my tongue like leather. Over and over, I have chided myself for failing to bring a calabash of water. How could I have been so careless?

When I first hear the gurgle of water, I think thirst has impaired my senses. But then, between the trees, I see a large, glistening stream! It takes all my willpower to keep from breaking rank and racing toward it. Someone shouts, "Halt," and I think that some of the men have done what I wish to do, but no, I quickly realize the order means we will be allowed to stop and refresh ourselves. We have been marching for hours.

Another order is given, and men scurry to the stream. It is a mass of noise and confusion as some leap into the water, while others drop to the ground and plunge in faces, heads, hands. I see an empty spot along the bank, and am about to run towards it when a large hand jerks me backward.

"Not so fast. Where do *you* think you are going?"

I turn, and see Enrique's scowling face. "To the stream."

"You will not contaminate this water, *converso*. You will drink when all our men have had their fill."

So I am forced to stand near the bank and listen to the water lap the shore, and watch men splash about and drink. Finally, when the throng of soldiers thins, Enrique orders two men to guard me while he takes his turn. In slow motion, he dips his hands, pours water over his head, splashes some on his face, then drinks and drinks and drinks.

Tears fill my eyes. I brush them away with the back of my hand, feeling angry for displaying such weakness. Plainly, Enrique delights in exposing my helplessness and his power over me.

He scrambles to his feet when the order to march is given, then gestures for me to come and drink.

"Be quick about it," he barks.

And I only swallow two mouthfuls of water before he yanks me away.

"Enough! We go now."

And then I am on my feet, stumbling forward as he shoves me along, my mouth so dry it feels like a sand dune, my thirst greater than ever. But I have learned a valuable lesson. Never again will I show Enrique any weakness.

It is the second day of our journey. We have been marching since sunrise, heading for Concepcion, which Roldan plans to attack. My body aches from sleeping on the hard ground, and my tongue is still like leather. Last night I ate an entire papaya, just for the juice, before I took my first bite of cassava bread.

But I force myself to look at the blessings, too. Oh, how I praise the Holy One for the sturdy pair of leather boots I wear! Any other shoes would be shredded by now. The terrain is so dense and inhospitable that soldiers must hack pathways for us with their swords. But such overgrowth will make it easier for me to hide when I make my escape, another blessing for which to give thanks. In addition to my praising God for these blessings, I have begun watching Enrique; studying his habits, looking for signs of carelessness. Sooner or later, an opportunity will present itself, and I must be ready.

⌒⊙

We have been following the same river since yesterday. And when the order is given to stop and refresh ourselves, I refrain from running toward the bank like the others. Instead, I stand in place, showing little interest.

"You do not wish to drink?" Enrique says, surprise in his voice.

"I believe our Andalusian summers have conditioned me. I find I lack the need or desire to drink often. Perhaps when we stop again I will take some refreshment."

Enrique's eyebrows knot. "Are you mad, woman? Surely the bowels of hell can be no hotter. Would you cheat me of my ransom? Can I expect my full price if you are shriveled to half your size, or stand near the edge of death? Go at once and drink!" Enrique's hand shakes with rage as he points to the stream.

"If you wish," I say, walking to the bank.

I just finish drinking my fill, and am about to cool myself by wetting my neck and hair when I hear Enrique's angry voice. I turn, expecting to see him shouting at me. Instead, he is off to one side shouting at someone I cannot see. I quickly splash myself, then rise and go to where Enrique stands. He has discovered a young Taino boy—about eight or nine by the look of him—crouching behind the large leaves of a stubby palm. Beside him lies a woman, unconscious, and who, I assume, is his mother.

"Come boy, you will carry my bundle and crossbow."

The boy does not move.

"I said, come!" Enrique's voice rises, causing soldiers to gather. "Come!" Enrique shouts again, and when the boy neither moves nor answers, Enrique tries pulling him to his feet but the boy clings to the lifeless looking woman and will not let go. Finally, Enrique pries the boy's fingers loose and drags him to the clearing, but as soon as he lets go, the boy scrambles back behind the palms.

Enrique follows, leaving his crossbow and bundle on the ground. And what transpires next happens so quickly I can scarcely believe it. Without saying another word, Enrique pulls the knife from his belt, grabs the boy by one shoulder, tosses him to the ground, plunges in his blade, and runs it down the entire length of the boy's abdomen.

I cry out in dismay, and rush to where the boy lies on his back. His eyes are wide in disbelief as he cradles his spilling bowels.

Oh, merciful God.

Enrique wipes the blade on his jerkin, then calmly returns it to his belt.

"Finish the job," a soldier says, stepping around me. "You have cut him deep enough to kill, but not deep enough to make death swift. You cannot leave him like that. He could linger for hours."

Enrique laughs and pushes past the soldier, and when he sees me, he grabs my arm and roughly pulls me away, but not before I see the soldier raise his firearm and shoot the boy in the head.

⌒◯

The rope bites into my wrists as Enrique gives it one final pull before knotting the ends. All the while he taunts me about how he will kill me if I try to escape. Willpower alone keeps me from crying out from pain as the rope digs deeper into my wrists. I keep my lips tightly compressed for even the slightest utterance will encourage his cruelty.

It is the morning of the third day, and we have finally reached the outskirts of Concepcion. Even now, Roldan is planning the attack with his commanders, while his soldiers prepare for battle, checking their crossbows, pikes, and other weaponry.

"Keep your eyes on her," Enrique says, talking to three soldiers too sick with bowel disease to fight today, and who will remain behind. "For if she escapes, I will gut you like I did that boy."

For five days Enrique ties me with ropes in the morning, gives the same instructions to the sick men—who now only number two, for one has died—then goes off with Roldan and the others to conquer Concepcion. But when Concepcion shows no signs of falling, Roldan finally orders his men to pull out.

We head southwest to the Province of Xaragua. We have been walking for days. It is at Xaragua that Roldan plans to make his camp, living off the Indians and gaining strength. Already, other renegade soldiers have joined our party, and from seventy our ranks have increased to over a hundred. Also, the further south we go, the more Tainos join us, for Roldan has promised they can take revenge against the Columbuses for all the hardships imposed on them.

The soldiers have grown used to me, and talk openly as if I am not here. This serves me well, for from their conversations I am able to glean what lies ahead. For instance, I have learned that Roldan, after he gathers enough men, plans to return to Concepcion and again try to capture it. If he is successful, he will move against Santo Domingo, where, it is rumored, he plans to kill Don Bartolome.

I have also learned that when we reach Xaragua, Enrique intends to send his ransom demand to Antonio at Santo Domingo. But is Antonio still there, or has he returned to Isabela? Does he even know about the attack and my abduction?

‿ଓ

I trudge wearily behind a company of soldiers. Nearby, walk two Tainos, new to our group. Neither wears the customary token, indicating they have not paid their tribute, and are renegades. One of the Tainos, in particular, catches my eye. He is slight of build, with a large red scar running the length of his forehead, the kind made by a sword. Had he come across a soldier who noticed he lacked the proper token, and been forced to fight for his life? The wound, by its color and size, looks only months old. His gait is unsteady, and I wonder if the injury to his head is not the cause. In addition to the scar, he looks drawn, as though suffering from some malady.

He seems curious about us too, Enrique and I, for he often glances backward as though checking to see where we are. He carries a war club bigger than his arm, and I shudder to think of how many heads he has broken with it. There is a fierceness about him that is disquieting, and something else, too . . . he looks familiar. But I am certain I do not know him. And yet I am just as certain I have seen him before. It is very strange.

As I walk I try not to think about how hungry I am. The food I brought has been consumed long ago, and my current ration—which Enrique doles out every morning—consists of half a loaf of cassava bread "to keep me vigorous enough to walk the distance to Xaragua," he says, "but not too vigorous to be any trouble." I fear I grow weaker by the day. Soon I must make my escape or I will lack the strength to do so.

Suddenly, there is a commotion ahead, and the column stops. Men shuffle their feet, they whisper, they swear under their breath until finally the news of what is happening trickles down the line. A group of soldiers seeking to join Roldan has brought news that Christopher Columbus has returned from Castile with six ships; three anchored in the harbor of Isabela laden with supplies, another three circling the island. Furthermore, Bartolome Columbus and his soldiers are searching for Roldan in the interior.

At once, men swear by the saints, others grow pale; still others vow to fight to the death. But no one is happy except me; for I know my deliverance is near. And though I try to stifle it, my joy finally bubbles to my mouth creating a smile, and Enrique sees it.

"Pray Columbus does not find us," he whispers, "for if there is a fight, you will be the first to die."

Roldan has pushed us hard all day, trying to reach Xaragua before Bartolome Columbus's men find us, for he believes more Tainos will join his forces there. But it is doubtful their number will be enough to ensure victory over Columbus. And the rebels know this. They also know that with the Admiral's ships come enough reinforcements to crush the rebellion and send them all to the gallows or back to Castile in chains. The men march as though carrying a millstone around their necks. Only the Taino with the club seems unaffected. He walks in his customary uneven gait, and continues to glance back at us.

At last, the order is given to stop and make camp. Everywhere, soldiers mill about. Some open flagons of water and drink, for there is no more wine to be had. Others find a soft spot among the vegetation and lie down. Still others pull cassava from pouches and eat. The Taino with the club, and his companion, settle near me. He takes what looks like a root from the cotton pouch he keeps slung over his shoulder, then eats it before beginning his meal of cassava and dried fish.

I, too, remove cassava bread from my bag. I have become accustomed to eating my ration in small portions throughout the day. But today, though it was difficult, I have saved it all for now. I plan to make my escape tonight, and will need the strength it gives me. If Columbus's men get any closer, I fear Enrique will make good his threat to kill me.

~⌒∂

My lids feel as heavy as rocks, and I close them despite efforts not to. It takes all my willpower to open them again. In the darkness, men snore or turn this way and that. Someone coughs. Another mumbles under his breath. I have been laying here for hours, waiting for all to fall asleep. But in the distance, voices still whisper. I must wait a little longer. And then I will creep into the night. But now I will close my eyes. For just a little while. For just a little . . . ."

~⌒∂

An owl's hooting awakens me with a jerk. It is still dark. And all is quiet except for an occasional snore. I do not know how long I have been sleeping, but I cannot afford to tarry for who knows how soon the sun will rise?

I roll onto my left side, facing Enrique, who sleeps beside me. I listen for any sound telling me he is awake, but all I hear is the sound of my own breathing. As usual, Enrique has looped a rope, like a noose, around my ankle, tightened it, then tied the other end around his own leg—this to keep me from escaping.

I pull the dagger from my bodice, carefully unsheathe it, then curl into a U and begin cutting the rope. Enrique groans and rolls on his back, causing me to stop. From the many nights I have spent at his side, I know he is a sound sleeper and that it takes much to wake him. Still, I wait for his breathing to slow before resuming. The dagger is sharp, and after making a quick end to the work, I rise, sheath the blade, then tuck it away.

It will be easy to slip past the sentries. Roldan always posts them the same way, mirroring the four compass points: north, south, east and west. Not a league east of here is the cave I spotted earlier. My plan is to break from camp, go a goodly distance, then hide in the underbrush. At first light, I will make my way to the cave, and stay there until Roldan's men leave for Xaragua. I doubt Roldan will waste time pursuing me since he opposed my abduction from the onset.

As I carefully step over Enrique, the heavy dagger in my bodice presses against my chest. What if Enrique follows? Will I be able to use my weapon? *Will I be able to kill him?*

The darkness compels me to inch my way toward the dense thicket, carefully stepping over sleeping bodies until at last, at the edge of camp, I am swallowed by vegetation. My progress is even slower now, and the brush so thick I need to protect my face. Even so, branches scrape my cheeks and forehead while vines entangle my arms and legs. More than once I stumble and fall. I am cut and bruised and tired, but still I move in the direction of the cave.

Deeper and deeper into the brush I go, until at last I stop, and sit. Here I will stay until sunrise, then search for the cave. And though I am bone weary I have no fear of falling asleep, for my eyes are as wide as Mama's prized platters. I pant like a beast as I grope the ground. It is rough and thorny, but I remain sitting, barely aware of my discomfort. My body tingles as though on fire. My senses are sharp. I hear every sound: the wind in the trees, the scurrying of an animal, the flutter of a bird overhead, even my own heart as it beats wildly. The Prophet Jeremiah said, "the heart is deceitful above all things and desperately wicked: who can know it?" But at this moment I do know it. I know I *am* capable of killing Enrique Vivar.

As the sun creeps over the horizon, I leave my hiding place and walk toward where I believe the cave to be. And when I have walked nearly three leagues I know with crushing certainty I have missed it. *Have I been walking in circles?* The vegetation is too dense; my sense of direction, gone. It is useless to search for the cave any longer.

But what should I do? Where shall I go? I pray to the Merciful One for guidance, and no sooner is the prayer finished that I come upon a clearing and see a small Taino village. Only five huts. I remember the fierce Taino with the club, and hesitate. Surely no Castilian would be welcome here. I look back into the dense forest. Though I have tried following the direction of the rising sun, eastward toward Isabela, I am hopelessly lost. And hungry, too. My face and arms and legs are scratched and bleeding; my body stiff and racked with pain. How much longer can I wander these woods, and live?

"Oh Merciful One," I whisper, "give me one ally here, just one friend to help me." And then I step into the clearing. Since it is early, I am not surprised there are no signs of life. I creep to the first hut, and when I see the doorway barred by two crossed spears, and that it is empty inside, my heart sinks. I go from one hut to the next but it is the same with them all.

The village is deserted.

I must not panic. *Think, Isabel. Think.* Normally, Tainos bury roots for planting future crops. I look around for a small mound, and finally finding one, begin digging with my hands until I feel tubers and pull them out. *Yuccas.* Poison when raw. I discard them. But among the *yuccas* are *batatas*, too. I brush the dirt off one and devour it. It revives me, and quickly I gather a dozen more before recovering the mound. I abandoned my empty food pouch long ago, so I use my outer skirt, gather it to my waist, then tie it before placing my *batatas* inside.

Since it is unsafe for me to wander in the woods with Roldan's army so near, I have decided to wait, perhaps a day maybe two, before venturing out, and when I do, I will travel northeast, keeping the rising sun slightly to my right, and head for Isabela. But for now, I will hide in one of the huts.

Choosing the smallest—for it is tucked among three large palms and not easily seen—I remove the spears and enter. It is neat and clean, with matted straw on the floor. To my delight, I see a large wooden bowl filled with fruit, and find two papayas not rotted. I slip one into my skirt pouch, and with my dagger I peel the other, then eat it. When

I am finished, I put my knife away and lean against the wall facing the door. Presently, I drift into a restless sleep.

⁓❍

"Did you think I would not find you?"

My eyes open, and there is Enrique filling the doorway, his crossbow pointed at me. Gulping air, I scramble to my feet.

"You left a trail a child could follow."

"If you let me go I swear I will not bring any charges against you. I will even plead your case to Don Bartolome."

Enrique tilts his head back and laughs. Then he lowers his crossbow. "No Doña Isabel, promises will not save you now."

By the fierce look in his eyes, I know it is useless to plead further, so I pull the dagger from my bodice.

"Ah, then you plan to kill me?" He laughs again, and tosses the crossbow onto the straw, then pulls open his leather jerkin revealing his chest. "Go ahead. I give you your target."

He still blocks the doorway. If only I could squeeze past him! Then lose him in the brush. I move to my right, hugging the wall, hoping to force him to move as well, but he remains firmly planted. I notice a window nearby. It is covered with a heavy thatched shade. I try to calculate if I can open it and climb out before Enrique reaches me, then decide I must try. It is my only hope. I lunge for the window, and before I can maneuver the shade I find myself thrown to the floor. The dagger flies from my hand and lands several cubits away.

Enrique laughs like a madman, tearing my clothes and grabbing my thighs. And I know what he plans to do before killing me. I push hard against him still hoping to make a lunge for the door. And just when my strength is about to fail, and I feel unable to fight him any longer, I hear a loud thud, and Enrique slumps against me as one dead. It takes a second to see the Taino standing over me. And another second to recognize the scarred forehead. His club is raised in the air, and

I close my eyes for surely he will strike me next. When I feel Enrique's body move, I open my eyes and see the Taino pulling him away. Then he extends his hand and helps me to my feet.

The Taino and I, using two wooden shovels we found in another hut, dig a grave for Enrique. I have insisted we bury him. I do not know if this insistence springs from a belief that even Enrique deserves a proper burial or because I fear he will be found, and I will be hunted all over again.

We work quickly, then place Enrique into the deep pit and cover him with dirt. Over the dirt we throw pebbles and bark and vines and anything else that will disguise this spot as a grave.

When we finish, I pray a portion of the burial *Kaddish*, and think of the irony that Enrique's final prayer is a Jewish one. And then I think of Maria.

How will I ever be able to tell her about this?

My rescuer's name is Savique, and this is his village. He calls me The Kind One, for he has heard of me and how I have fed the maimed Tainos. I learned this through gestures, and a mix of Taino and Castilian. We sit in his hut now, sipping fresh water from his gourd. It is a hut of generous size— much larger than the hut I hid in earlier, and contains three *hammocks*. Everywhere there is evidence of a woman's caring hand. Numerous wooden bowls, suspended in rope slings, are filled with fruit—now rotten—and even loaves of cassava bread which are still good, for I have already, at Savique's insistence, eaten one whole loaf myself. Two clean cooking stones lie on the floor in the corner.

I sit quietly against the wall waiting for Savique to tell me his story. He pulls the familiar root from his pouch, then talks while he eats.

I do not understand all his words, for he uses both my language and his. But I understand enough to know that this was a village of renegades escaping the harsh tribute system, and many, like him, barely escaping with their lives. But all have died from a strange disease Savique has never seen before. His wife, too, fell ill, so he took her and his young son north where he knows certain curative roots grow. He points to his pouch, and I know he is talking about the roots he carries, and that he, too, is ill.

He goes on to tell me that he hid his wife and son near a river bank while gathering the roots. When he returned, both were dead. I have trouble understanding how his wife died. His explanation is too garbled to follow. But it is easy to understand Savique when he speaks of his son's death. His eyes grow hard as he describes his son being slit open and left with intestines spilling onto the ground and a steel ball embedded in his forehead. I finally understand why Savique looks so familiar, for now I see the son's face in his.

Sevique tells me from the lead shot he knew it was the work of soldiers, and so he followed their trail. Once he joined our ranks it was easy to learn who killed his son, for bored men tend to retell their stories, and the story of "mad Enrique" still circulated. So he stayed close to us, and when I escaped and Enrique followed, he saw his opportunity for revenge.

I see the odious glint of satisfaction on his face as he finishes. But who am I to judge? I, too, am happy that Enrique is dead, though I know how much this displeases the Savior who forgave all His tormentors. But try as I might, I am still unable to forgive Enrique. Or Maria, for that matter—Maria, who so cruelly deserted me. My heart feels heavy as I think of her now. Just how am I going to tell her about her son?

And will she ever be able to forgive *me?*

⁓◯

"I go now." Savique slaps his chest with the flat of his hand and I know he is telling me he doesn't wear the necessary token.

I nod, and look down from our perch on the mountainside, and see Isabela. "Yes, *please* go quickly." If Savique is caught, he will surely meet the same fate as his son. I urged him to leave me long ago, but he insisted on guiding me to a place where it was impossible for me to get lost, and so he has led me all the way from his village, graciously sharing his food and allowing me to keep the *batatas* which I stole. I return them now, what is left, for his trip. He plans to go back to Xaragua and join Roldan once again, for Roldan promises to end the tribute system. I have tried to tell him Roldan and his men have no authority to abolish the tribute. In addition, they have committed more atrocities against the Tainos than even the nobles, but Savique will not listen. I suppose because, having lost his family and those in his small village, he has nowhere else to go. And I suppose because a roguish life is preferable to slavery.

I wave goodbye as Savique disappears into the thicket, then turn once again towards Isabela, and for the first time in weeks I feel joy thinking perhaps Antonio will be there waiting for me.

Antonio is not in Isabela. He is with Don Bartolome's men searching for me and Roldan. But ten days later, after a courier finally finds him and gives him the news of my safe arrival, he returns to my arms. And my heart, which is murderous as well as deceitful and wicked, melts in his tender embrace.

Antonio and I stand in the courtyard of our new stone house in Santo Domingo listening to the trill of a bird perched on a nearby tree. The sound is a lovely opus to my ears. Every day for the past three months, we have gone to the courtyard and stood under this tree listening to

Antonio's "friend" sing. When the song is finished, the bird flies away, leaving the courtyard silent.

"Admiral Columbus and Roldan have finally come to terms," Antonio whispers as he bends and kisses my neck. "The nobles grumble that the terms favor only Roldan, for Columbus has given all the rebels grants of land, and Roldan even retains the title of town warden."

I breathe in the familiar scent of Antonio's lavender and rosemary. My heart is so full I have no wish to leave this place of love for thoughts of the hateful world of Española.

"These grants of land," I say, reluctantly allowing Antonio to draw me back into the larger world, "which Columbus has been authorized to distribute to the soldiers and peasantry is a great concession for the Crown. But a good thing, I believe." I am thinking of Maria and her family who have stayed behind in Isabela, not wishing to move to Santo Domingo for they have purchased my land with its mounds.

"It is good only if the settlers honor their agreement and work the land for four years, otherwise they will lose it. But Columbus has brought such rabble with him on his last voyage I doubt they will do any work. I believe, in the end, they will be of little benefit to our colony here."

I remain silent since I fear my husband is right. Columbus has brought all manner of rogues with him, including pardoned convicts, for no one else would sail with him to the Indies.

"Nor do I believe this is the end of Columbus's trouble with Roldan or his men," Antonio continues. "Already they are buying and selling Taino women, some as young as nine. Getting one hundred *castellanos* a piece, the same price the Crown is charging for a farm in Santo Domingo. What can you do with such men?"

Again, I remain silent, for I am thinking of Enrique. What, indeed, could be done with such a man?

Antonio encircles me with his arms. "But we need not concern ourselves, my love. For as soon as a ship leaves for Castile, we will leave with it."

"It cannot be soon enough."

"Will you miss nothing of Isabela or Santo Domingo?"

"Nothing." I think of the seven men now swinging on the gallows in the Plaza, men executed by Bartolome Columbus as rebels. I think of the many others so hungry for gold they would rather dig in the San Christopher gold fields to feed their greed than dig mounds to feed their stomachs. I think of the young Taino girls sold to lecherous men; of the tribute system, of the enslavement of an entire race. How can I miss such a place?

"Will you not miss Maria?"

I tense at the mention of her name.

"What is it you have not told me, my love?" Antonio pulls away so he can see my face.

"I have told you everything about Enrique. I have held nothing back."

"Yes, everything about Enrique, but not Maria, I think."

I turn from his gaze. "No. not Maria." With tear filled eyes I tell him how neither Maria nor any of her family, except Bata, came to my aid. And of how deeply wounded I feel over Maria's betrayal.

"Is that why you did not tell her of Enrique? That he is dead?"

"I could not . . . face her with it. But she knows. I saw it in her eyes. She knows everything."

"Because she knows her son, Isabel. But it is too painful for her to tell you so."

I push away, not wanting to understand Maria's pain or her great fear of Enrique. I can think only of my pain; the terror of those days and nights in the interior; not knowing if I was going to live or die.

Suddenly the church bell rings, and someone outside shouts, "Ships sighted! Vessels from Castile!"

I am about to venture outside to see them for myself, when Antonio stops me. "You have a great capacity for love, Isabel. Do not be stingy with it now. Remember, we all have the ability to do what is easy rather than what is right. Have compassion. Do not leave this island without making peace with Maria, for I fear you will regret it all your days."

⌒◯

Tomorrow we sail for Cadiz. A few weeks ago, when Antonio and I were discussing Maria in our shaded courtyard, Francisco de Bobadilla arrived from Castile with two ships and the Crown's authority to serve as the new Governor of the Indies, replacing Bartolome Columbus. He quickly brought the three Columbus men before a hearing board. After vile accusations were leveled against them, Bobadilla felt his only recourse was to clamp the Admiral and his two brothers in irons, sequester them in one of his ships, and order their return to Castile where they will stand trial.

It is strange to think that once again I will be sailing with Christopher Columbus but under, oh, such different circumstances. And it is hard to believe that instead of commanding the ship, the Admiral will be confined to its hold in chains like a common criminal.

I sit at the table in the beautiful stone house Antonio built me, hardly sorry that I will soon leave it. In front of me is a blank sheet of paper. I have been sitting here since before the bell chimed None, and now it chimes Vespers and still I have not put pen to page. I had in mind to write Maria a letter. Instead, I have employed my time thinking on my life in the Indies.

I leave here different than when I first came. I am no longer a girl, but a woman, a woman greatly loved by the man I greatly love, and that is no small thing in a world full of hatred and cruelty. And I am a woman with child. I have not told Antonio. Nor will I tell him until we reach Cadiz, for he will worry so all during the voyage home. But these are not the only changes. In this dangerous and uncertain place, I have come to terms with who I am: a Jewess who has found her Messiah and Savior. And though I will forever walk between these two worlds I am at peace.

Now I return to Castile with a husband who helped save King Fernando. Perhaps that in itself will not be enough to ensure us a happy and serene life; or enough to keep us safe from the malice of the Inquisition. But even if it does not, I am content, for I have learned from Antonio that though we live in a cruel world, we need not be cruel.

With a sigh, I pull the stone of Zebulun from my pocket and place it on the table. It will go with the letter that I am finally ready to compose. After all, a woman must have some security. I finger the stone for a moment and smile. Then slowly, I pick up the quill, dip it into the ink pot, and begin the last letter I will ever write on these shores.

Dear Sister,

I call you that, Maria, for that is what you have been to me. No sister could have been kinder. What would I have done without you in this strange, harsh land? What would I have done the first day on board the Tortoise when you . . . .

THE END

Useful Information:

Glossary
Bells
Jewish Months and Feasts

Glossary

arquebuse: a type of gun fired by a matchlock and trigger, and supported on a forked-shaped rest while firing

Ashkenazi: Jews from Central and Eastern Europe

auto-de-fe: public execution of heretics

Avignon cloth: cloth from France

Aylsham cloth: English cloth, highly prized and found in the royal palaces of England

batatas: sweet potatoes

beata: a pious woman who lived withdrawn from the world, either alone or in a small community attached to a Franciscan or Dominican order

berakhots: Jewish benedictions

binnaclelamp: a lamp attached to the ship's compass box

brigandine: a flexible coat of armor comprised of metal rings or scales

buren: flat stone griddle for cooking cassava bread

caballero: gentleman, knight

cacique:	a Taino chief
camlet:	Oriental cloth made of silk and camel hair
carvel:	a small, fast moving sailing ship used by the Spaniards and Portuguese
catheads:	wood or iron beam to which the anchor is hoisted and fastened
cedula:	royal decree
chasuble:	a sleeveless outer vestment worn by a priest at Mass
Cipango:	Japan
codpiece:	a bag or flap placed in the front of a man's tight stocking-like pants during the 15th and 16th centuries
confites:	sweets made of almonds, pine nuts, hazelnuts or other fruits and seeds and covered with sugar
consulta:	conference toward end of trial held by the Inquisition
conucos:	Taino mounds
converso:	convert from Judaism to Christianity; usually implies a forced conversion
courtier:	aristocrat, noble
cowl:	the hood of a monk's cloak
crypto Jew:	a convert from Judaism to Christianity but one who continued to secretly practice his/her Jewish faith
cubit:	18-22 inches; the length from a man's middle finger to his elbow
cuirasse:	leather breastplate
dagged sleeves:	irregularly shaped
deadeyes:	a round, flat block of wood used to fasten a ship's shrouds or ropes
doublet:	a man's close fitting jacket
ducats:	gold or silver coins valued from 83 cents to $2.32
empanadas:	pastry filled with various types of food
Española/	

Hispañola:	present day Haiti and the Dominican Republic
farthingale:	a hoop frame made of whalebone or other material and worn under a woman's shirt to fill it out
fenugreek:	a clove-like plant whose bitter seeds are used to season food
forecastle:	the upper deck of a ship
forenoon watch:	from 8:00 a.m. to 12:00 p.m.
fortnight:	2 weeks, 14 days
galingale:	an aromatic root of the ginger family
gold florin:	a gold coin probably worth about $200 in current US dollars
grains of paradise:	peppery seeds from West Africa
graylag:	a wild gray goose
guayas:	dirges of sorrow and affliction
gudgeon:	a shaft or metal pin at the end of an axle on which a wheel turns
gunwale:	the upper edge of the side of a ship
halakah:	Jewish oral or traditional law
hawseholes:	holes in a ship's bow through which a cable or large rope is passed
hidalgos:	minor nobles
jerkins:	a short, close-fitting jacket, usually sleeveless
Kaddish:	prayer, usually of mourning
La Isabela:	Columbus's settlement in Haiti
Lanzas:	fierce fighting men who formed part of cavalry during the reconquest of Spain from the Moors, and who later formed part of the King's national police force, often called the *Santa Hermandades* or Holy Brotherhood
las buas:	scabs or sores resulting from venereal disease

league: the distance of two crossbow shots

mail: body armor made of small metal rings or scales

Maimonides: famous Spanish rabbi, philosopher and theologian who lived from 1135 to 1204, still revered and studied even today

marrano: term often used for Jews who converted to Christianity, and means pig or swine

menorah: a 7-branch or 9-branch candelabrum used in Jewish celebrations

mikvah: ritual bath

nao: large 3 or 4 masted ship—stable and big enough to carry provisions for long sea voyages

Neilah: the concluding service of Yom Kippur

niddah: a state of defilement when a wife cannot have relations with her husband due to her menstrual cycle or childbirth

nuncio: person who issued announcements to the general populace on behalf of the Inquisition. The Inquisition's spokesman.

ollero: pottery maker of cooking and table goods

pantofles: wooden platforms worn under shoes to keep them from getting ruined in the dirty streets

Pater Noster: the Lord's prayer, the Our Father

pogroms: persecution of Jews, usually of a violent nature

posada: an inn

quarterdeck: the after-part of the upper deck of a ship, usually reserved for officers

Quinsay: the city of the great Khan

Rashi: famous medieval French rabbi whose works are still studied by Jews

ratlines: any of the thin pieces of rope that serve as a ladder for climbing the rigging

reales:	the standard silver coin of Spain during time of novel
redan:	a fortification of walls or parapets
Responsas:	scholarly responses to issues and questions facing Jews of that day
rood screen:	an ornamental screen separating the nave and church choir
Sephardic:	Jews from the Iberian Peninsula
Shema:	a prayer, "Hear, O Israel, the Lord our God, the Lord is One."
sinar:	an apron-like cloth used to hold rags and worn during a woman's menstrual flow.
slickstone:	something heavy and easy to slide over cloth and clothing to remove wrinkles
spars:	any pole, as a mast yard, boom, or gaff supporting a ship'ssails
stomacher:	an ornamental triangular piece of cloth on a woman's garment that covers the chest and abdomen
surcoat:	a loose, short cloak often worn over armor
surplice:	a loose, white, wide-sleeved cloak worn over a priest's cassock
tally sail:	to attach two corresponding sails together
Talmud:	Jewish civil and religious laws consisting of the Mishnah (text) and Gemara (commentary)
Tanakh:	canon of the Hebrew Bible
tefillin:	small leather boxes containing Torah scriptures that Jewish men wear while praying in the morning
tejas:	curved clay roof tiles
Torah:	the Pentateuch or first five books of the Old Testament
trencher:	stale slice of bread used as a plate
trepan:	to open the skull with a boring tool

tuyere:	the pipe or nozzle through which air is forced into a blast furnace or forge
venera:	an image of the Virgin, usually on a silver medal
waist hatch:	the main hatchway leading to the bowels of a ship and though which cargo can be lowered
zemis:	idols, both large and small, of Taino gods

Bells:

Martine—midnight

Lauds—3 a.m.

Prime—6 a.m.

Tierce—9 a.m.

Sext—midday

None—3 p.m.

Vespers—6 p.m.

Compline—9 p.m.

Jewish Months:

Nissan—March/April/ The first month in Jewish calendar. Passover is in this month.

Lyar—April/May

Sivan—May/June. Shavout is in this month

Tammuz—June/July

Ave—July/August. Tisha B'Av is in this month

Elul—August/September

Tishrei—September/October. Rosh Hashanah, Yom Kippur, Sukkot are in this month

Mar Cheshvan—October/November

Kislev—November/December. Hanukah is in this month.

Tevet—December-January

Shevat—January/February

Adar—February/March. Purim is in this month.

Epilogue

When Christopher Columbus returned to Spain in chains, Queen Isabela was outraged. He never faced trial, and on May 9, 1502, embarked on his fourth and final voyage to the Indies. Though this voyage was of little value, the realization he had discovered an entirely new continent rather than a quick route to the Indies was finally dawning. He died May 20, 1506 at age fifty-five. Queen Isabela herself died three weeks after his return from his third voyage.

In 1509 the title of Viceroy was finally returned to the Columbus family and, Christopher's son was appointed Viceroy of the Indies. He served until 1524.

In just fifteen years, from 1493 to 1508, the Taino population in Española/Hispaniola (modern day Haiti and Dominican Republic) went from over one million to just sixty thousand. To compensate for the dwindling workforce, the Spaniards, in 1502, brought five *caravels* of African slaves to Santo Domingo, thus beginning the importation of black slaves that lasted for years. By 1524, Tainos ceased to exist as a people group.

After La Isabela—located in what is now Haiti—was abandoned, Santo Domingo became the capital of Española/Hispaniola and is currently the national district capital of the Dominican Republic.

The Inquisition raged on in Castile and Aragon, and spread to Portugal. To escape, many *conversos* fled to the New World. By 1509, King Ferdinand was charging *conversos* 20,000 ducats to emigrate for a two-year period where many of them returned to their former faith. Word quickly spread that the New World was a safe haven for *conversos*.

They came and settled in outposts scattered across Jamaica, Barbados, Cuba, Mexico, Brazil, Peru, and the American Southwest. But by 1515 the Inquisition was arresting *conversos* in Santo Domingo, and by 1524 it made its way to Mexico where it was not abolished until 1834.

By the beginning of the 16th century, the Spaniards' cruelty in both the Inquisition and their colonization policies caused them to be called *La Leyenda Negra*, the Black Legend.

Author's Note

What a debt we Christians owe the Jews! From them come the Old Testament and the springboard to the New. But more importantly, from them comes our Jewish Savior, Yahshua, Jesus.

Even a superficial study of history reveals the suffering and persecution of the Jews after the Diaspora, the scattering. Nation after nation treated them with contempt, forced them to live in isolation or forced them to convert under penalty of death. And if that were not enough, they often confiscated their property and wealth, all making possible the atrocities seen during the World War II Holocaust. Sad to say, this was done more often than not by "Christians." Yet throughout the ages, the Jews survived, and in many cases prospered. Is there any doubt that God's hand is on them? Or that they are truly God's chosen?

Now, anti-Semitism is rearing its head yet again as anti-Jewish sentiment begins to sweep across Europe. Like in days of old, Jews are named the cause of all problems. Even in their own land of Israel, Jews are vilified as the stumbling block to peace. Nothing can be further from the truth. And Arab nations vow to "wipe them off the map," while Christian denominational churches propose "boycotts" of Israeli products. Even the United States government, once a strong ally of Israel, has made unreasonable demands of giving up "more land" and refuses to stand firmly with our best friend in the Middle East.

I believe the time is fast coming when Christians will be faced with a choice: to either stand with Israel and God's chosen, or to do what so many Christians did during Hitler's Holocaust—turn a blind eye and deaf ear.

We need to remember that Jesus was a JEW and that His apostles were all JEWS, and that there would be no Christianity without them.

May we learn the lessons of the past and stand strong for our wonderful Lord and Savior, and His people.

Blessings to all,

Sylvia Bambola

Website: http://www.sylviabambola.com

Email: sylviabambola45@gmail.com

FYI

For Readers

When researching for this novel I came across many contradicting facts. One small example relates to the number of Indians Christopher Columbus brought back with him from his first voyage. One source puts this figure at six, another seven, and still another claims ten. Therefore, I have tried to take my information from the most valid or scholarly sources, using, for example, information from Columbus's own logs and letters, and the information from Kathleen Deagan and Jose Maria Cruxent who spent ten years excavating the site at La Isabela. Many other respected resources were used as well (see below). Even so, while the historical figures and events are accurate, the main characters are fictitious, and I have employed poetic license when needed, some of which I detail below:

1) Although Fray Alonso is a fictitious character, he is a reasonable composite of the 15th century clergy, in general, and those involved in the Inquisition, in particular.

2) Most historians claim no women came on Christopher Columbus's second voyage. However, Consuelo Varela, the Spanish historian, believes at least one woman did. Her name, Maria Fernandez. The remains of a female European substantiates the fact that a Spanish woman did live in La Isabela. It is also possible that women were among those who came with Antonio de Torres in the winter

of 1494 since Ferdinand Columbus, referring to the spring of 1495, wrote that the Christians "numbered only six hundred and thirty, most of them sick, with many children and women among them," indicating the presence of Christian women. Since few Tainos converted it is safe to assume these Christian women were European.

3) The name of Isabel's ship, the *Tortoise*, is fictitious as well as the characters of Doctor Spinoza, Doctor Martinez and Arias Diaz

4) Fray Buil is a historical figure and depicted accurately except for his sermon on the Feast of the Epiphany dedicating La Isabela and his interaction with Isabel. The sermon is purely a fabrication but reflects his position on the matters mentioned. His many disputes with Christopher Columbus caused him to threaten to withhold the sacraments from him, and Buil finally left La Isabela in disgust to become one of Columbus's most outspoken critics at court.

5) Though there was a hospital in La Isabela I was unable to find a description of it, and so my depiction is pure invention

6) Though the sequence of events is accurate, I have, beginning with the first hurricane, compressed the timeline for the sake of the story. While the story suggests the passing of perhaps a year from the time of the hurricane to the time when Christopher Columbus was sent back to Spain in chains, in reality more than four and a half years passed, depending on whose dates you use, as different scholars claim different dates for the hurricanes.

7) I have not used the standard measurements of that day (arrobas, quintales, and cahices) but converted it to present day measurements to avoid confusion.

8) Christopher Columbus went by several names throughout the years, Cristobal Colon being the one most used and the one by which he was most likely known in Spain. However, since

he is best known in modern times as Christopher Columbus, I have used that name in my novel. Also, I have used the more familiar spelling of Seville rather than the correct one of Sevilla, but chose to use the correct spelling of Espanola, Queen Isabel and King Fernando rather than the more familiar versions of Hispaniola, Queen Isabela and King Ferdinand.

Below are some of my research sources but by no means all, nor does it include some of the excellent sources I found on the internet.

- *Christopher Columbus*, The Four Voyages; translated by J. M. Cohen
- *Columbus's Outpost among the Tainos*, Kathleen Deagan and Jose Maria Cruxent
- *Christopher Columbus and the Conquest of Paradise;* Kirkpatrick Sale
- *The Ships of Christopher Columbus*; Xavier Pastor
- *Life in a Medieval City*; Joseph and Frances Gies
- *Fast and Feast*, Food in Medieval Society; Bridget Ann Henisch
- *A Drizzle of Honey*, The Lives and Recipes of Spain's Secret Jews; David M. Gitlitz & Linda Kay Davidson
- *The Tainos*, Rise and Decline of the People Who greeted Columbus; Irving Rouse
- *A Brief History of the Caribbean*; Jan Rogozinski
- *The Origins of the Inquisition in Fifteenth Century Spain*; B. Netanyahu
- *The Spanish Inquisition*; Joseph Perez
- *Sephardi Jewry*; Esther Benbassa & Aron Rodrigue
- *Heretics or Daughters of Israel*, The Crypto-Jewish Women of Castile; Renee Levine Melammed
- *Hidden Heritage*, The Legacy of the Crypto-Jews; Janet Liebman Jacobs
- *The Marranos of Spain*; B. Netanyahu

Questions for Reading Groups/Clubs

1) The old admonition to avoid discussions of religion and politics hints at the explosive nature of these subjects. Yet, the opening chapter of *The Salt Covenants* broaches them both. One of them (religion) has divided a family; the other (politics) threatens to endanger their lives. Can you think of any other topics capable of doing this? How in times past has religion and politics changed your personal world? Or the larger world of your generation?

2) Is Isabel's mother justified in her anger and hurt feelings regarding her daughter's conversion? And is she right to blame herself? Just how much responsibility should parents take in shaping their children's spirituality? As much responsibility as their education and character? More? Less? And can one's character and one's spirituality be truly separated, one from the other? Have you ever known anyone totally void of a moral compass? If so, what was he/she like?

3) Early on we learn that Beatriz is much loved and possesses a gentle and submissive nature. But later we see she is unprepared to cope with the realities of the world as evidenced by her inability to keep tabs of wages due; her naivety, even childishness, in the face of danger. Can't people be both "wise as serpents, and harmless as doves" (Matthew 10:16)? Have you ever known such a person? How did he/she balance out their personalities?

4) Isabel's deep love for her sister is obvious. But when Beatriz is ordered to the Holy House doesn't Isabel display her own shortcomings by feeling left out of the loop and thinking like a child instead of trying to understand the danger and the strain under which her parents labor? What kind of emotions and behavior does stress generally bring out?

5) Beatriz's confession that she is pregnant rocks the household. Given Beatriz's gentle personality was it a shock when you learned she took her own life? It was, after all, an act of extreme violence. If yes, why? If no, why? Is her action reasonable when she had such a loving, supportive family? Women have faced this issue for centuries. Why can some women, with marginal support or no support at all, survive what Beatriz went through, and others cannot?

6) Isabel, due to her sincere conversion, is forced to perform a balancing act between the world of Judaism and Christianity, feeling like she fully belongs to neither. Yet the cruelty of her sister's imprisonment in the Holy House and the cruelty of the many *auto de fes* she was forced to witness aren't able to change her course. Would you say she was a woman of deep conviction? Or foolish? Why?

7) Were you shocked by the seemingly insignificant charges leveled against the Judaizers at the *auto de fes*? What kind of society permits such a gross miscarriage of justice? What collective mindset is necessary? Where there other factors besides religion that permitted this type of mind set?

8) In chapter 4 Isabel is scandalized when her parents don't observe *Shavuot* and *Tisha B'Av* even though she has repeatedly warned them about doing so. Is her distress a sign of immaturity? Or just the strain of seeing so much upheaval and changes in her life? Have you ever persisted in trying to change a situation and when it finally changed, you resented the change?

9) Were Isabel's parents right in forcing Isabel to marry Sebastian and move to the Indies? What lengths would you, as a parent, go to protect your child from danger and injustice?

10) Isabel and Sebastian's marriage was a marriage of necessity and convenience. Though "arranged" marriages are a thing of the past, at least in our culture, some men and women still marry for necessity and convenience. What of the woman who marries a wealthy man to secure her financial future? What of the ordinary-looking man who marries a beautiful woman to secure his ego? Have you known of such marriages? Did they work out? Was some mutual ground of respect achieved? Did love take root?

11) Beginning from Isabel's marriage to Sebastian and throughout the long trip on foot to Cadiz and the voyage to the Indies afterward, we see Isabel change from a girl into a woman. It is said hardship can make you "bitter or better." What hardships have made you better? Were you able to be grateful for your hardship after you saw how you had grown as a person? Can people really grow without some hardship, stress, or difficulties? If yes, explain.

12) One of Isabel's loneliest moments was when she sailed from Cadiz. She was leaving everything and everyone she loved. Was there ever a time in your life when you felt stripped of everything you held dear? How did you react? What helped you cope?

13) During the storm on board the *Tortoise*, Fray Buil saves Isabel's life. And later she comes to value him to the point of not wanting him to leave their settlement and return to Spain, and this in spite of the fact he represented everything she detested and feared. How many times have we misjudged? Or made sweeping pronouncements only to find we were wrong? Is it ever right to be biased if that bias is based on generalizations

and not facts? Have you ever had a preconceived opinion of someone only to have it change after getting to know him/her better?

14) Sebastian neglected and ignored Isabel. Was it his own pain that made him do this? Or was it his selfishness and childishness? Or both? How would a more grounded and mature individual handle this? Can emotions be controlled or subdued by maturity?

15) Isabel crossed a time-honored line when she befriended Maria, that of social class. In the time period and culture of the story, class distinction was paramount. Does class distinction exist today? If "yes" how can it be overcome?

16) Isabel had a strong work ethic in a culture where work was considered abhorrent. In what other ways was she out of step with her time?

17) After Antonio arrives at La Isabela with a marriage contract, Isabel decides to be honest with him, half hoping, half expecting him to back out of the marriage. If he had, what other options, if any, were available to her?

18) Though Isabel loves Antonio deeply, she is bitterly disappointed in him when he refuses to stop hundreds of Taino captives from being chained and taken to Torres's ships. Do we expect too much from those we love? Do we sometimes hurt them by our unrealistic expectations? Is it really possible to always be kind to each other in an otherwise cruel world?

19) When Isabel loses her baby, is Antonio's reaction a valid one? If so, why? If not, why? Can such things really come between a husband and wife and alter their relationship? Even if that relationship was a solid one?

20) Enrique feels compelled to destroy that which he fears and hates as evidenced in his treatment of Isabel. Are there similarities between him and someone in an organization like the KKK? What about the Nazis? Can you think of other groups

or persons who behave like this today? People or groups that allow their fears and hatred to drive them?

21) In the end, Isabel opts to forgive Maria. But throughout the book there are many opportunities to extend forgiveness or ask for it, such as when Isabel brings her silk shawl to the young Taino woman Sebastian raped. What are some of the others? Where did Isabel fail? How important is forgiving those who hurt us? Can one truly overcome adversity without it? Can there be healing without it?

CPSIA information can be obtained at www.ICGtesting.com
Printed in the USA
LVOW11s1612140115

422812LV00002B/398/P